A DETECTIVE INSPECTO

A RITUAL
FOR THE DYING

NEW YORK TIMES #1 BESTSELLER **TONY LEE** WRITING AS

JACK GATLAND

Hooded Man
MEDIA
INSPIRATION • PRODUCTION • PUBLICATION

Published by Hooded Man Media.

First Edition: August 2021

PRAISE FOR JACK GATLAND

'This is one of those books that will keep you up past your bedtime, as each chapter lures you into reading just one more.'

'This book was excellent! A great plot which kept you guessing until the end.'

'Couldn't put it down, fast paced with twists and turns.'

'The story was captivating, good plot, twists you never saw and really likeable characters. Can't wait for the next one!'

'I got sucked into this book from the very first page, thoroughly enjoyed it, can't wait for the next one.'

'Totally addictive. Thoroughly recommend.'

'Moves at a fast pace and carries you along with it.'

'Just couldn't put this book down, from the first page to the last one it kept you wondering what would happen next.'

Before LETTER FROM THE DEAD...
There was

LIQUIDATE THE PROFITS

Learn the story of what *really* happened to DI Declan Walsh, while at Mile End!

An EXCLUSIVE PREQUEL, completely free to anyone who joins the Declan Walsh Reader's Club!

Join at www.subscribepage.com/jackgatland

Also by Jack Gatland

COUNTER ATTACK

For Mum, who inspired me to write.

For Tracy, who inspires me to write.

CONTENTS

PROLOGUE

SIMON WASN'T SURE IF THIS HAD BEEN ONE OF HIS BETTER ideas, and he was very vocal in explaining it to Alfie. However, the words were simply swept away, flying off like notes on the wind as Alfie chose, as per usual, to ignore them.

They were currently standing at the Southern entrance to Greenwich Park in South East London; giant, wrought-iron gates held between six tall, pale brick pillars, each adorned with an enormous lamp and with the gates themselves spiked, the black painted vertical tines of the wrought-iron resembling spears, as if warning all who enter to play by the rules... or be punished.

Simon had seen photos of Blackheath Gate, as it had been called from around ten years earlier; they used to be far more ornate, with large, flowing gold motifs along the top but sometime in the last decade it had been decided by the council to remove these and renovate them into the stark, cold gates that the park now had in order to widen the roadway entrances, allowing larger vehicles to enter.

Alfie didn't care about the gates; for him, they were too

modern, too normal. Alfie was there for the mysteries and the histories. Simon envied Alfie for that. He'd been like this ever since school, and university hadn't exactly pulled him away from his passion, allowing him to join organisations like the university paranormal society, which had led him down the path towards other, non-university based esoteric organisations.

Simon hadn't gone to university. Simon had left school after his GSCEs and had joined the post office. But he'd still kept in touch with his best mate, even in their late twenties.

Alfie was now examining the railings, checking his watch. It was close to eight pm now, and the sign on the gate stated that in April, the park closed then. Simon knew that for the plan to work, they needed to get into the park and hide in the undergrowth before the rangers and park police did their last sweep of the area, which didn't exactly give them much time.

'Dude, we need to leave,' he hissed. Alfie turned, smiling. He was dressed in a black bomber jacket over a similarly black hoodie, black jeans and black boots completing his all-black ensemble. He had a charcoal grey backpack over his shoulder; this carried the tools of his trade, and the items that they'd be needing tonight, as well as a cheese ploughman's sandwich, some *Quavers* crisps and two bottles of Wild Cherry *Lucozade*.

'I think we should do the intro here,' he said. 'It'll only take a moment.'

Simon looked around. They were a little exposed but at the same time there were about a dozen other people nearby, all talking into cameras, either on their phone or on gorilla-grip hand-held mounts, likely recording for their own *YouTube* channels.

Which was exactly why Simon and Alfie were also there.

'Sure,' Simon said, dropping his own backpack to the pavement and pulling out a Canon EOS SLR camera with a slim, fur covered directional mic sticking out the top and facing forward. Simon loved this camera; it was his pride and joy, and he knew that part of the reason that Alfie had let him join the channel was partly because he was an expert cameraman and amateur editor in his spare time but more importantly he was the owner of this beauty, which had cost him over a grand when he bought it new. Sighting through the digital screen on the back, he nodded to Alfie, now finding a suitable spot on the pavement to stand.

'Ready whenever you are,' he said.

Alfie nodded, counted to five and then made a circular motion with his arms; he did this so that they could tell on a continual clip when a new take had started. It made it easier to skim through the footage when working on *Final Cut Pro*.

'Hi there, and welcome to another episode of *Ghost Bros*,' he grinned. 'Tonight, in a last-minute change of plan, Simon and I are examining the mystical and horrifying tales of Greenwich Park, here behind me.'

Simon forced himself not to laugh at the name of the channel; he'd done so the last time, and they had a nightmare removing it from the edit. It had been Alfie's idea, to follow on from some of those American paranormal shows like *Ghost Adventures, Ghost Hunters* or *Haunted Towns,* as they had been more grounded than the UK options such as *Most Haunted,* which mainly revolved around scared people wandering around dark rooms with a Spiritualist medium, which meant that a lot of the 'evidence' found was often through the mouth of a man or woman who honestly could have read the wiki page of the location before they arrived. Although they'd used a medium themselves a few months ago, Alfie had wanted a fresh start recently, mimicking the US shows that were more grounded in technology; EVP, or *electronic voice phenomena* sessions, where questions were asked into a digital recorder and then listened back to see if spirits had manifested answers, specialised devices that recorded EMF, otherwise known as *electromagnetic fields*, which gave scientific proof that something was or wasn't around them and other items, such as handheld and static digital video cameras, including thermographic and night-vision options, although a lot of this was for show.

Simon and Alfie had all of these, although one of the static night vision cameras had gone missing a couple of months ago, probably borrowed by Alfie to do god knows what at night in his bedroom. They'd also emulated the style of the US shows more than the UK ones, two friends actively antagonising spirits, almost daring them to show themselves, aiming to get the ghosts angry and provoke a reaction, as this gave them more chance of reaching a US based audience, which gave them the opportunity to be seen by US television networks. Alfie believed implicitly that this was possible, and that even though they only had a couple of thousand subscribers, soon they'd hit the big time with something.

All they needed was a killer show, he'd continually told Simon. With Greenwich being barred to tourists at night, the idea of being able to record an overnight lockdown there was something that nobody else had really done. And, with it soon coming up to the end of April, the weather was now clement enough for it.

Simon returned to Alfie, still working on his introduction.

'Although this has been a royal park since the fourteen hundreds, this area has been a place of ritual worship, sacrifice and bloody battles for centuries before that,' Alfie said to the camera now, revelling in his role as presenter. 'Just behind me are dozens of Anglo-Saxon burial mounds, one of the largest collections in the world. But did they die peacefully or in battle, buried with the weapons they *killed* with? Come with us as we're locked down overnight in the park.'

'And cut,' Simon said, although he didn't really need to say anything, grabbing his backpack and hurrying Alfie along. 'We've got seven minutes.'

Even though the park was due to close soon it wasn't empty of people, as many tourists came to catch the sunset over London from the vantage point beside the Royal Observatory. Alfie and Simon used this to their own advantage, hurrying along Blackheath Avenue, the wide, tarmac road that had parking spaces on either side, turning right at the Pavillion Cafe, heading down the red-gravelled Great Cross Avenue before cutting across the grass, making their way to the ancient fallen tree known as *Queen Elizabeth's Oak*, and the wild undergrowth that was just past it. Simon knew that if they could hunker down there, they could wait out the police and the wardens as they did their last patrol of the night. All they had to do then was wait until it was fully dark, and emerge out from hiding, recording their pieces *guerilla-style* while alone in the park. They wouldn't even be visible as they did this, as they'd be using night vision cameras, meaning no torchlight.

They found a place to hide and, making themselves comfortable, they waited for night to fall; Simon constantly alert, watching for any last-minute park ranger checks as he listened to a podcast, and Alfie snoring beside him, headphones on, already asleep.

It was close to eleven when they finally dared to move from their hiding place, emerging back onto the path that led to the crossroads of Temple Walk and Lover's Walk. Simon started his night vision camera, aiming at Alfie who, in the night seemed to wear grey clothing, thanks to how the camera saw things through the filter.

'This is a place of great spiritual and ethereal power, and you can definitely feel it here at night,' Alfie said as he started walking backwards towards the junction. 'Queen Anne's House, at the north end of the park is the right-hand junction of two known *Ley Lines*, from which a straight line travels all the way down Blackheath Avenue, across Blackheath Common, where many died during the Cornish Rebellion, passing through All Saints Church in Blackheath, which was built with *six hundred and sixty-six pews.*'

He let the number hang in the air for a moment before continuing.

'Is this a message to the Devil? Is it a coincidence that Elizabethan Occultist John Dee would travel to the park at night, hunting a hidden occult library? And what of the folk-tales that talk of a mighty Celtic battle occurring here, at the base of this valley, which leads to One Tree Hill on one side, and an ancient, Megalithic stone, turned into a fountain on the other, a stone that has no reason to be here, and has possible links to another sacred stone, *Kit's Koty* in Kent?'

He'd reached the crossroads now, where a small path led to the aforementioned megalithic stone, once adapted by Victorian engineers into a drinking fountain, now nothing more than a curiosity.

'And what of the long-lost tunnels under Greenwich?' he asked the camera. 'What horrific acts occurred under this very path we walk down? Let's find out.'

He pulled out a digital recorder, holding it up to the air, pressing record.

'Is there anyone here?' he asked, pausing for a moment to allow a reply.

'What's your name?'

Another pause, and then

'How did you die?'

Alfie stopped the digital recorder, rewinding it to the start. With Simon moving closer, still filming, he held it up to the ear.

'*Is there anyone here?*' Alfie's voice could be heard, and then a slight hiss of static followed.

'Yes!' Alfie exclaimed. 'That was a definite *yes!*'

Simon wasn't sure about that, but kept quiet as they listened to the next two answers. The second had nothing but the third had a kind of stutter sound, which sounded like *stuh* to Simon.

'Stone!' Alfie almost shouted, lowering his voice as he remembered they were technically trespassing. 'Do you mean the ancient stone? Were you killed by it? Beside it?'

He'd started moving towards the stone fountain, gingerly making his way in the dark, unable to see through a camera like Simon.

'We need to grab a Mel-meter,' he said excitedly. 'Check the readings—'

'Dude, stop,' Simon spoke suddenly, his tone urgent. 'Don't move.'

'What is it?' Alfie asked as he complied with the command. Simon aimed his camera at the fountain behind his friend.

'There's something by the fountain,' he said. 'On the floor.'

Through the camera, Simon could see a figure, lying on the ground, stretched out in front of the stone itself.

'I think it's a person,' he said.

'Might be a homeless person trying to sleep,' Alfie whispered back. 'Some of them come here because it's safer than the streets.'

'No offence, mate but you would have woken them up by now,' Simon replied cautiously, moving closer, 'and we'd have seen them arrive. I think it's someone whose had a heart attack or something.'

He turned the camera away, clicking on a pen torch.

'I just want to check they're alright—'

His words died in his throat as he now stared at the body on the ground beside the megalithic stone fountain.

It was a man, lying face upwards, and placed so that his head was at the furthest point on the path. Simon knew someone had placed him, because the position was too unnatural, too straight, as if he was lying to attention, his arms to his side. He was obviously dead, his eyes open and staring through his horn-rimmed glasses, his wispy greying hair combed and positioned. He wore a tweed suit, with a white shirt, green cravat and what seemed to be a burgundy coloured waistcoat, with tan brogues completing the ensemble. The cravat was loose at the throat, and Simon thought he could see a redness around it.

'Christ,' Alfie muttered, moving closer, kneeling down to examine the body. 'He's definitely—'

'*Don't touch him!*' Simon hissed. 'Don't get your DNA or fingerprints on him!'

Alfie jumped back as if scalded, but it wasn't from the warning.

'Oh my God,' he said, staggering back to the edge of the

path, turning and vomiting up his hastily eaten sandwich from earlier in the evening. 'He's had his hand cut off.'

Simon leaned in and saw what Alfie had noticed, that the body's right hand, hidden from sight by the angle had been cut off and removed, with only a stump remaining, a tiny amount of dark blood having pooled around it.

'Why take a hand?' he asked, leaning closer to the throat. 'And was it taken before or after they hanged him?'

Alfie looked up. 'Hanged?'

'Yeah, look,' Simon, seemingly far more comfortable with the body than Alfie was, shone the torch beam at the body's throat. 'That's rope marks. He's been hanged.'

Alfie rose. 'This isn't just a murder,' he whispered, now backing away. 'This was a ritual. We need to get out of here.'

'What do you mean, a ritual?' Simon asked, as Alfie grabbed his backpack and hurriedly pulled it onto his shoulders.

'Taking the hand of a hanged man, it's what you do when you create a *hand of glory*,' Alfie replied. 'It's an incredibly powerful occult item. There's one in the museum in Whitby.'

Alfie was already moving quickly up Temple Walk, away from the body. 'Either way, I want nothing to do with it!'

Simon glanced back at the strange, tweed suited body that was missing a hand, and started after Alfie.

'At least you were right about one thing,' he said as they made their way towards the closest and most easily climbable gates at Maze Hill. 'All we needed was a *killer show*.'

1

MOVING DAY

To be brutally honest, Declan had expected Anjli Kapoor to have more *stuff*.

He'd agreed to Anjli's suggestion of becoming a housemate a few weeks back but it had been on the condition he sorted out the house first. It was technically a four-bedroom property, however one bedroom was small, one bedroom was once his parents and now his room, one was reserved for Jess when visiting (if, of course, Liz ever allowed Jess to return to Hurley) and the final room was the ex-study of Patrick Walsh, complete with fake plasterboard wall and secret room. Declan had destroyed a chunk of the wall with a sledge-hammer as a way of gaining some kind of closure but it had still left the remains of a room, one that was simply not suitable for a new housemate, especially one paying towards the cost of the house to live in.

And so for the last few weeks, Declan had been allowing a local contractor named Ryan, the same guy who'd fixed his broken window a few months earlier, to remodel the upstairs a little; it had also been pointed out to him that although the house itself was in quite good nick, with a small en-suite with shower in Declan's bedroom and a bath in the main toilet, there was a good opportunity here to add to the sale value by installing a *second* en-suite in the ex-study, using the space that had once been a secret room complete with filing cabinets and a crime board across one wall, to do so.

The cabinets and the paperwork for the moment lived in the smallest of the four rooms, currently a small storeroom of boxes.

Now, a month after Anjli had first suggested moving in, the room was ready. It was medium-sized and completely unfurnished, as per Anjli's request; she'd brought her own double bed, wardrobe and desk from her old place, and had sorted out a side deal with Ryan to have the walls painted an off-white colour, and to have a couple of walnut wood floating shelves secured onto one wall.

With the furniture, new uplighter and the paint job, Anjli's room looked better than Declan's, which was effectively exactly the same as it had been when his father lived in it. He almost considered changing the rooms before she arrived, and taking this for himself.

Almost.

He didn't have a *death wish*, after all.

It was a warm Sunday afternoon near the end of April when Anjli finally moved in. She'd given her notice at the place she currently lived at a month earlier, and although she technically had the room there until May, she'd eventually reached the end of her tether, deciding that if she didn't get out as soon as she could, she'd end up killing someone. Besides, the deal she had with Declan was a far better one than she had there; for a start, she wasn't paying rent in Hurley.

The decision had been made early on by Declan that as he owned the house outright, didn't have a mortgage to pay on it and was only paying the bills, that if Anjli covered half the expenses and bills, he'd allow her to live there rent free; after all, she was doing him a favour, he'd save on costs and she'd be able to save up a small deposit for her own place down the line. Also, Declan felt a little bad about making Anjli pay rent on a place that she'd barely see, as the last few months had shown them both that long hours at the *Last Chance Saloon* were par for the course.

Declan didn't even have to drive her into work every day, as Anjli had been sharing rides with PC Morten De'Geer, constantly guilting him to pick her up on his Triumph Bonneville motorcycle as he made his way to the office in Temple Inn. And, as he lived just outside of Maidenhead, and Hurley had been his old stomping ground, Morten had said that he was happy to take Anjli in whenever she needed. That said, Bullman, on hearing this and deciding that Anjli probably needed her own car for travelling around now that she was out of the 'London Belt' and her usual chauffeur, DC Billy Fitzwarren, was office based had started the paperwork to requisition another car for the Unit, one that Anjli could use personally.

Declan just hoped that it wouldn't be better than the battered Audi he currently owned. That would have *really* pissed him off.

So, with a minor case involving an extortion racket between solicitors on the Grays Inn Road being closed up the previous week, and with no fresh case yet on their books, Declan and Anjli had decided this would be the day that she moved into Hurley.

Anjli had arrived just after noon, with a small moving van

driven by two men who both seemed to be called Dave, and as they started taking items of furniture into the house, carrying these awkward and heavy items with an ease that made Declan feel insecure in new and interesting ways, Anjli punched him on the shoulder in greeting.

'You sure you want me to have the room?' she asked seriously. 'I mean, it's slightly bigger than the one you're in, even with the en suite. I'd understand if you wanted to move.'

'It's fine,' Declan replied with a faint smile to show that he was indeed okay with it. He'd also been in the room the previous day with a tape measure, and although it might have looked bigger, the room was marginally smaller.

'You sure?' Anjli insisted. 'You could hide in the bathroom and pretend it was a secret study. I could make sliding *whoosh* noises when you closed the door if it helped.'

'You've been working on your jokes. I like it,' Declan nodded as he spoke. 'Keep going. One day you might actually be funny.'

'So, when do we start the redecoration?' Anjli was looking around the living room, and Declan groaned inwardly. Another reason he'd agreed to let Anjli live in the house was because it would actually kick-start him into sorting out the interior design. He'd lived there roughly six months, and he hadn't even replaced his father's iMac, which had been stolen a few weeks after he'd moved in.

'Can we just get used to being in the house first?' he muttered as Dave Two walked past with some drawers from the wardrobe. Anjli shrugged.

'Sure,' she said, as if realising that this was a sore subject. 'Oh, and I had a question about parking.'

'Yeah, you should be able to get both cars out the front,'

Declan replied, knowing that Bullman had spoken to Anjli about this. Anjli, however, shook her head.

'I meant for the bike.'

'What bike?'

'Morten's helping me buy a bike,' Anjli explained. 'A Triumph.'

'You're in your what, mid-thirties now?' Declan walked into the kitchen to place the kettle on. Anjli, suspicious, followed.

'And what's that got to do with things?' she asked. Declan grinned.

'Just that it's a little young to be getting your mid-life crisis,' he replied casually. 'Tea or coffee?'

The two Daves had already finished moving the minuscule amount of items that they had into Anjli's room and so, passing them a small wad of notes, Anjli bid the removal men farewell, gratefully taking a coffee from Declan, grimacing as she tasted it.

'Christ, that's foul,' she hissed as she poured it into the sink. 'Looks like we'll be teaching you how to make good coffee. Where's the machine?'

Declan pointed at a jar on the counter. It was a supermarket's own brand.

'I only buy it for the caffeine,' he explained. Anjli sighed.

'Day one and already I'm in hell,' she muttered. 'I'll buy us a proper one. You'll thank me, I promise. No wonder Jess doesn't come here.'

'She likes green tea,' Declan explained with a hint of mock superiority. 'With oat milk. And her coffee is *bulletproof*, whatever that means.'

'It means she has better taste in coffee than her dad,' Anjli laughed, before getting serious for a moment. 'Any movement there?'

Declan shrugged. Anjli knew the full story about Declan and his estranged family; a couple of months earlier Declan's daughter Jess stayed with him during an investigation into a local serial killer, and in the process had almost been murdered by the killer's insane German daughter. In fact, it'd been Anjli and Billy who'd arrived to save her. From that point onward, Lizzie, Declan's ex-wife and Jessica Walsh's mum had wisely banned Declan from his daughter's life, something that had lightened a few weeks earlier when DI Theresa Martinez had spoken to her on the phone; Theresa had been a teenage detective and had almost died frequently because of this, and so had a unique angle on what Jess was going through.

Of course, Theresa then turned out to be a murderer and part of a plot to steal four million pounds while killing five different people, so as a character witness, she was a bit rubbish.

It didn't stop Declan missing her, though.

But since then, even though his suggested mediator turned out to be the worst potential choice, Liz had actually relaxed a little; Declan was given Jess' new number and allowed to text, and Liz had actually applauded Anjli moving in, as it meant *someone grown up would be in the house if Jess visited again.*

Declan ignored the veiled insult, happy that Liz was even considering the option.

'We'll see,' he replied. 'We're hitting GCSE time for her, she's sixteen soon, and she's on revision break in a week or two, so with luck I might get to say hi.'

'Well, if there's anything I can do to help, just let me

know.' Anjli stopped as a familiar mechanical *brrrr* could be heard approaching. Declan groaned. He knew that engine sound.

'Sounds like De'Geer,' Anjli smiled. 'Still not talking?'

'We're talking,' Declan muttered, walking to the door and watching as PC Morten De'Geer, in full bike leathers and helmet roared up to the front of the house on his black and chrome Triumph Bonneville. 'Just not about bikes.'

'You're overreacting,' Anjli smiled, opening the door and waving at the visitor as he pulled off his helmet. 'He's not any different from before he learned about the bike.'

Declan groaned again. A couple of weeks earlier, while talking about motorbikes in the office, Declan had let slip that, when he left the Military Police and started working in London with DI Derek Salmon, he'd ridden a *Suzuki Marauder,* a rather beautifully designed, in his opinion, cruiser. De'Geer was impressed with this until Monroe, who'd seen the bike back in the day, pointed out that because Declan had only passed his *Compulsory Basic Training* test, not his *Direct Access* training, the Marauder wasn't the popular 800cc model but had been the smaller, 125cc bike. Which, in the grand scheme of things, was about as powerful as a scooter, was only allowed on A-Roads, and couldn't go far above forty miles an hour. Declan was sure that ever since then, PC De'Geer had treated him differently, as if realising somehow that Declan was weaker than the others and needed to be protected.

'Guv, Sarge,' De'Geer said, stopping at the doorstep, even though Anjli had stepped back to allow him entry.

'I've said before,' Declan interrupted. 'It's Declan and Anjli when we're not talking business.'

'Actually, I'm here about that.' De'Geer looked uncomfortable as he spoke. 'I'm here on a bit of a professional favour-asking request.'

Declan watched De'Geer as he spoke. He was usually the calmest in the room, and his immense, almost seven-foot tall, blond and bearded, muscular frame made people think of *Vikings*, who were far from nervous. But here, De'Geer seemed reluctant to speak.

'What is it?' Declan asked now, moving to the door. 'Has something happened?'

De'Geer nodded. 'I've been doing a night course at Queen Mary University,' he replied. 'Nothing too taxing, just the political and religious history of the British Isles, between 1560 and 1700.'

'Oh, so a light course,' Declan mocked, and was horrified to see De'Geer nod, as if accepting this.

'The lecturer on the course is Professor Rupert Wilson,' De'Geer continued. 'He's often on TV as one of the go-to historians—'

'Oh, him!' Anjli exclaimed. 'His Scottish accent is to kill for. I'd happily let him read me bedtime stories.'

'I think you mean Neil Oliver,' Declan suggested. 'The one who wears the scarf.'

'Yes, him,' Anjli nodded. 'I meant him. Sorry.'

'I could ask Monroe to read you bedtime stories, if you're into that accent,' Declan offered.

'No, I'm fine.'

'You sure?' Declan was smiling now. 'I could get him to say *lassie* to you more.'

'I think De'Geer had something important to say?' Anjli desperately attempted to change the subject, and Declan looked back at De'Geer, patiently waiting in the doorway.

'Sorry,' Declan finished. 'Carry on, please.'

'Anyway,' De'Geer carried on valiantly. 'He was a good professor, and I wondered—'

'You said *was*,' Anjli interrupted. 'Fired or dead?'

'Dead,' De'Geer replied. 'They found him in Greenwich Park early yesterday morning.'

'Suspicious?'

'Rope marks around the neck and his hand cut off.'

'I'd call that suspicious,' Declan nodded. 'But Greenwich Park, that's likely to be Deptford police, or—'

'I—I know, sir,' De'Geer was nervous as he stammered an interruption. 'And I contacted a friend there, Sergeant Byrne, and he said they're all tied up in some organised crime thing and they've put aside the Wilson case for the moment due to lack of human resources.'

'And you thought we could take it on?' Anjli looked to Declan. 'Well, we have just cleared our decks.'

'And Professor Wilson had a flat on Chancery Lane,' De'Geer eagerly explained. 'So technically he was covered by City Police.'

'You've spoken to Monroe already about this, haven't you?' Declan enquired innocently. De'Geer flushed but shook his head.

'No, sir,' he replied. 'Just Doctor Marcos, purely for her opinion on the medical side. And Jo—I mean DC Davey.'

'And they said?' Anjli grinned now. The sight of such an imposing man blushing like a schoolboy was amusing to her. 'I mean, *professionally* said. We don't need Joanne Davey's sweet nothings.'

'They said it was interesting,' De'Geer nodded.

Declan sighed. *For Doctor Marcos to find something interesting meant that it was likely to be a nightmare of a case.*

Luckily, that was what the *Last Chance Saloon* excelled in.

'So then,' he forced a smile. 'Looks like we have a fresh case for tomorrow morning.'

And, before De'Geer could reply, Declan returned to the kitchen, pouring his now luke-warm, terrible coffee out into the sink and reaching for a whisky, now in a cabinet above the counter.

He had a feeling that this was going to be a *very long week*.

2

HAND OF GLORY

IN THE END, DE'GEER STAYED THROUGH THE AFTERNOON AND into the evening, splitting an Indian takeaway with Declan and Anjli as they discussed what they knew about Rupert Wilson, while using the detective powers of *Google* to learn more about the man. And, after calling both Monroe and Bullman on a Sunday evening, phone calls that could have been problematic but were actually easy to make because Declan knew they were just as eager for a new case as he was, he went to bed that night already aware that not only was the murder of Rupert Wilson likely to be their next case but that Doctor Rosanna Marcos had already been subtly sent to the Deptford Command Unit to have a quick examination of the body.

De'Geer had disappeared shortly after Declan had received this news, and both he and Anjli agreed this was because De'Geer was now riding his motorcycle down to Deptford to join in. It was no secret he found forensics fascinating. Well, it was that or DC Joanne Davey he found fascinating, anyway.

The following morning, Declan drove Anjli into London; De'Geer had offered before leaving but the weather report for the Monday had been rain, and Anjli didn't have any wet-weather gear yet. And therefore, it was around eight-thirty in the morning when Declan and Anjli arrived at the Temple Inn Command Unit, known in both the City and Metropolitan Police as the *Last Chance Saloon*. Even though she hadn't yet unpacked, Anjli still looked more organised than Declan was; while his suit and shirt were crumpled and unironed, Anjli was in a spotless and obviously dry-cleaned grey suit with pastel pink blouse, her hair now grown out and around her shoulders and pulled back into a neat ponytail.

Declan's hair, even though he'd combed and styled it, looked like he'd run through a hedge on the way there. Feeling a little self-conscious, he audibly groaned as he saw DC Billy Fitzwarren waiting for him by his own car in the carpark, a top-of-the-line Mini Cooper. The groan wasn't because of Billy, though; Declan enjoyed Billy's company and found him to be an outstanding police officer. It was the fact that of everyone in the *Last Chance Saloon,* Billy was the most stylish, always dressed in three-piece Savile Row suits, and always with expensive bespoke shirts underneath. On a day when Declan already felt like the drunk uncle at a wedding, seeing Billy's sartorial elegance didn't really help matters.

'I hear we have a new case,' Billy said, falling into step with them as Anjli and Declan walked to the main entrance. 'Davey wouldn't say much about it though, just that she couldn't tell me anything because I was too innocent.'

Declan looked at Billy, at his fresh face under styled blond hair. He looked too young to be in the force, let alone be a Detective Constable.

'She's right,' he replied as they passed through the reception area, nodding to the desk sergeant as she buzzed them through. 'But you make up for that with gumption.'

'And that I'm the only one who knows how to use the network properly,' Billy replied with a smile and, as they entered the upper floor office, he peeled off to his bank of monitors while Declan and Anjli continued to their desks. However, Declan only had time to place his jacket on the back of his chair before DCI Alexander Monroe and Doctor Marcos entered the office behind them.

'Briefing, two minutes,' Monroe said as he passed the detectives, entering his office and pulling the blinds closed.

Anjli sniggered.

'What?' Declan asked. Anjli pointed at the windows with her thumb.

'Bet you a tenner that when he comes back out, he's wearing a fresh shirt and tie,' she said. 'Nothing like a good walk of shame.'

Declan looked at Doctor Marcos, now in the briefing room, talking with DC Davey. 'You think that—'

'I know that,' Anjli nodded conspiratorially. 'Monroe's usually so well dressed. And today he's wearing the same suit that he was on Friday and arriving at the same time as Marcos.'

'I'm wearing the same suit,' Declan contested. 'And we arrived together.'

'Yeah, but that's because we live in Gorgeous-upon-Thames and car share until I'm allowed my own,' Anjli leaned in. 'Monroe left with Marcos on Friday. When you called him yesterday, he was irritated, but Marcos was on her way to Deptford before you could call her. As if she was in the room when the call happened.'

'You think they spent the weekend together?' Declan

looked back at Monroe's office, where the DCI was now opening the blinds.

With a different coloured shirt and tie on.

'I do,' Anjli grinned again. 'It's no secret they've had a thing for each other. Just look at how she cared for him when he was attacked. And, she almost killed Bullman when she heard he'd been taken in Birmingham.'

Declan nodded. The attraction between Monroe and Doctor Marcos was one of the worst-kept secrets in the Unit.

'As long as they're happy,' he smiled. 'I mean, it must be so lonely when you're that old...'

Even though he'd spoken softly, Declan noted Doctor Marcos look up at him from the briefing room, and for a split-second he wondered if she'd used her bat-like hearing to overhear what he'd said. But she simply waved for Declan and Anjli to join her and, with Billy following, they gathered their things and entered the briefing room.

A few moments later, De'Geer entered, followed by both Bullman and Monroe, who stood at the front, beside the plasma screen.

'I'll be honest,' Monroe started the briefing. 'I didn't know we'd gotten so desperate for a crime that we've started actively poaching from other Units. However, thanks to PC De'Geer, we've got an interesting one.'

'Were Deptford okay with passing this on?' Anjli asked. Bullman nodded.

'They've got their hands full with a couple of small organised crime cases,' she replied. 'Hadn't even examined the body yet. I think they were actually relieved to get rid of this one, as it's a little strange.'

'How strange?' Billy, probably the only person in the room that didn't know the full case history, looked around.

'Open up the file and throw the images on the screen and you'll see just how strange,' Monroe said as, on the screen, an image of Rupert Wilson, screen-shotted from a TV show appeared on the plasma screen behind him. It was only a couple of years old and although his hair was visibly thinning, it was still brown here, over Rupert's trademark style of tweed jacket, velvet waistcoat and green cravat.

'Rupert Wilson,' Monroe started. 'Or, rather, Professor Rupert Septimus Wilson. Professor at Queen Mary University, London and Fellow of Corpus Christi College, Cambridge. Also, the main go-to guy for any history-based show on *Sky Arts* or *BBC Four*. Sixty-eight years old, found dead in Greenwich Park late on Friday night, or to be more accurate, early Saturday morning.'

He tapped the screen, switching to the next image, now showing Professor Wilson in his final resting place, laid out beside a megalithic stone fountain.

'Doctor Marcos?' Monroe gave way to the *Last Chance Saloon's* Divisional Surgeon, who rose to give her own notes.

'I didn't attend the scene but Deptford's photographer was very thorough,' she explained. 'On examination in the Deptford morgue, however, I could confirm that cause of death was strangulation; the ligatures on the neck are deep and around half an inch wide, and I agreed with their own forensics that this was most likely caused by a rope.'

'So he was hanged?' De'Geer asked. Doctor Marcos shrugged.

'That's a tough one,' she replied. 'Usually a hanging also breaks the neck in some way, with the sudden snap of gravity. There was no damage here, so if he did hang himself, or was hanged by someone else, it was slow and deliberate. He didn't die of a broken neck but by slow asphyxiation.'

There was a moment of silence in the briefing room as everyone took in what had been said here.

'Was it at the park?' Declan asked.

'Doubtful, as the body's time of death seemed to be earlier on the Friday,' Doctor Marcos explained. 'Most likely he died elsewhere, and was then brought to the park.'

'And the hand?' Declan continued. Doctor Marcos tapped the screen and the next image appeared, showing the severed stump of Rupert Wilson's right hand.

'As you can see there was no blood at the scene, apart from a small spattering,' Doctor Marcos was using a pencil as a pointer. 'Score marks on the ground seem to imply that they cut the hand off with a serrated device at the location. Most likely a bone saw, judging from the markings on the edges of the wrist.'

'So someone hanged Rupert Wilson, cut him down, took him to Greenwich Park to lay him out and then cut his hand off?' Monroe mused. 'Why?'

'We have a theory,' Doctor Marcos nodded now to DC Davey, who rose.

'They found the body after two men called the police,' Davey read from her notes. 'Alfie Wasley and Simon Tolley. They claimed they'd snuck in that night to film some kind of paranormal *YouTube* show and found the body by chance.'

She looked up from the notes.

'In fact, the footage of them finding it gives us our best video of how the body had been left.'

'Have we checked their channel?' Bullman asked. Davey nodded.

'Yes, Ma'am. It's called *Ghost Bros,* and it's, well, it's not very good.'

'Could they have killed Wilson to add some pop to their

show?' Anjli asked. 'I mean, I'm sure people have done worse for less. Andy Mac comes to mind.'

'We've asked Deptford to transfer them over to us when they send across the body,' Davey was writing in her notepad. 'They've held them since Saturday on charges of trespass, but we'll have to let them out today if we can't find anything.'

'You said that you had a theory?' Declan asked.

'Well, actually, it was one of the ghost hunters,' Davey admitted. 'Alfie Wasley. He claimed he knew a lot of occult history, and he believed they had cut the hand off to make—'

'A hand of glory,' Billy interrupted, almost without realising that he'd spoken.

Davey, stopping as he spoke, nodded.

'That's it exactly.'

'And how would you know about such a thing, DC Fitzwarren?' Bullman asked, half amused and yet half surprised. Billy, realising now that he'd brought attention to himself, shrugged.

'You pick up things,' he replied cautiously.

'Spill, laddie,' Monroe sternly commanded. Reluctantly, Billy sighed.

'My family has an interest in the occult,' he explained. 'My great-uncle's really into it. I remember hearing about things like this from when I was a kid.'

'Maybe we should chat to your great-uncle then,' Bullman suggested, but Billy shook his head.

'I don't think he'd speak to me,' he replied. 'It was his son, my *uncle,* that I sent to prison for the Ponzi scheme.'

Anjli looked confused at this.

'No offence, Billy, and I'm not sure if you *landed gentry* types have other rules here, but surely your uncle is the brother of one of your parents, which makes his father your *grandfather*, not your great-uncle?'

Billy nodded.

'Yeah, sorry, I didn't mean by blood,' he explained. 'My great-uncle is my grandfather's brother, which makes Bryan, his son technically my father's cousin, and my second cousin. But my father never had brothers or sisters, and they were real close, only a year or so apart in age, so therefore all my life he was known as *uncle* Bryan, hence my uncle.'

'Oh,' Anjli smiled. 'I just assumed this was an inbreeding upper class thing.'

'Either way, *you're* our new expert,' Monroe said to Billy as he pointed at the severed stump on the screen. 'What's a hand of glory, and why could this be one?'

Billy thought for a moment.

'A hand of glory is a powerful occult item,' he started. 'And, before you start with the jokes, it's all about the belief. Voodoo might be real, or it might not but if you *believe* that it's real and someone uses it to curse you, you'll be utterly convinced you've been cursed, right up to the moment your heart gives out.'

Declan noted De'Geer was nodding at this. 'You believe in Voodoo?' he asked.

'I believe in all magic, Guv,' De'Geer replied. 'I find it's best to hedge my bets. And my family are agnostic heathens, pretty much part-time followers of the Norse gods, so it'd be a bit hypocritical to say no.'

'As interesting as this is, can we get back to the hand?' Monroe sighed. Billy was typing on his laptop, as if searching for something. Finally, with a tap of the return key, he sent a new image to the plasma screen; a line drawing of a severed hand, runes and symbols on it, and with flames emerging from the fingers and thumbs as if they were now candles.

'The act of cutting off a thief's hand isn't new,' he started. 'The Code of Hammurabi is a Babylonian code of laws from ancient Mesopotamia, now Iraq, and was enacted by Hammurabi, the sixth Babylonian king in around 1772 BC, giving us the famous quote an *eye for an eye*. Which basically meant that if you caused the death of someone, you'd be put to death; if a poor man knocked out the eye of an aristocrat, his eye would also be knocked out, and if a son struck his father, they'd cut his hand off.'

'So Rupert hit someone?' Declan shuddered. 'That's a little harsh.'

'It's probably more than that,' Billy replied. 'According to an old European belief, a candle made from the dried and pickled severed hand of a criminal who was hanged has supernatural powers.'

'Hand of glory.'

'Exactly. Traditionally, it was the pickled hand of a criminal, used by burglars to send the sleeping victims in a house into a coma from which they couldn't wake.'

He pointed at the image on the plasma screen.

'There are a couple of versions in the history books; in one, they used a clenched hand as a candleholder, with the candle held between the bent fingers. In another, all five fingers of an outstretched hand were lit. The magical properties vary from story to story but they always relate to things that would help a burglar enter a house at night.'

'Like what?'

'Giving light only to the holder whilst others are in darkness, making the owner of the hand invisible or being able to burn forever, things like that.' Billy was ticking these off on his own hand as he spoke. 'Having the power to open any lock, putting to sleep occupants of a house, or rendering still anyone who sees it alight... If one of the fingers didn't catch light, the burglars knew that someone in the house was still awake.'

'How do you make one?' Declan knew he was being ghoulish as he asked.

'Well, usually the hand is taken from a criminal while hanging on the gallows, but it's not a hard and fast rule. It had to be taken at the dead of night, preferably during a lunar eclipse.'

'That's not for another month,' De'Geer interjected. Nodding, as if also aware of this, Billy continued reading from whatever site he'd found on his laptop.

'Once you have the hand, there's an entire process involved in creating the item, accompanied by certain rituals including a poem or incantation chanted when the hand is used.'

'So it's a magic burglar's hand,' Anjli commented.

'It makes the owner invisible,' Billy replied. 'From anyone and anything, so if someone thinks they're cursed, they can use this for protection.'

'So straight away, we have a line of enquiry,' Monroe spoke up.

'You believe this?' Declan asked, surprised.

'I believe that there's a chance that *someone* believed this,' Monroe replied. 'I'd like to know what Professor Wilson did that would be classed as a worthy deed to have a hand removed. I'd also like to know where he died, and whether there was any other reason they cut his hand off. Billy? Look for photos—'

'He hid the hand,' De'Geer mused. 'When he gave

lectures, he kept it out of the way. But as he was left-handed, I didn't really pick up on it.'

'Check into that,' Monroe ordered. 'I want to know who had issues with Wilson, how his body was brought into the park, why he died and where he died. Anything I'm missing?'

'Why he was placed in the park beside the stone,' Billy muttered. 'It seems almost ceremonial.'

'You need to have a chat with your great-uncle,' Monroe scratched at his ear. 'DI Walsh, take DC Fitzwarren and chat to these ghost hunters at Deptford. If they're no use to us, cut them loose, as there's no point tying up a squad vehicle to bring them over here. Then go join DS Kapoor having a look around Greenwich. There won't be much forensically around there by now, but you might find some locals with a bit of knowledge. De'Geer? You're with me and Doctor Marcos, we'll go have a look at Wilson's Chancery Lane flat.'

He nodded to himself.

'Okay then. Let's go fight the great unknown.'

3

THE BEAST'S LAIR

To say that Rupert Wilson lived within the City of London's boundaries was bordering on the fanciful; there was a sharp point at the top left of the boundary map, and this was where 67-69 Chancery Lane could be found, slightly south-east of the city junction of Chancery Lane and High Holborn, which ran along the north of the buildings. The entrance to the apartments, built over the top of several shopfronts could be found neatly hidden between a Unisex Hair Salon and a Lebanese Delicatessen, with a pair of narrow, glass-fronted double doors, no wider than a standard door as the way in. They didn't need to buzz for entry; the body of Rupert Wilson had conveniently left the keys to both the external door and his own apartment in his jacket pocket and, with these in hand, Monroe opened the main entrance-way, nodding to an elderly lady who walked out.

'Excuse me,' he asked, pulling out his warrant card and quickly showing it to her. 'Rupert Wilson?'

'Up the stairs and to the left,' the lady pointed with a long, spindly finger. 'But you won't find him there. He's dead.'

She thought about what she'd said for a moment.

'I'm guessing that's why you're here.'

Monroe smiled. 'What sort of man was he?' he asked politely. The woman sniffed with disdain.

'He was all right in himself,' she muttered. 'It was his visitors that were the problem.'

'Visitors?' De'Geer asked at this.

'Oh yes,' the woman, now finding an eager audience, continued. 'Not in the apartment, oh no, that was only for the *prettiest* of them. So he talked to the rest in the lobby.'

'Can you describe them?' De'Geer asked. The woman shrugged.

'Load of dodgy Goth types. Always lurking around like *shit vampires*.'

If Monroe was surprised by the coarse insult from the woman's mouth, he didn't show it. In fact, it was Doctor Marcos who stepped in.

'Did he have kids?' she asked. 'Maybe they were related?'

'The only relations he had with them were the carnal type,' the woman checked her watch. 'I'm late for brunch. You should speak to the doorman. He saw Wilson with his groomed little dolly birds all the time.' Nodding curtly, she turned and walked off towards High Holborn.

'Grooming?' Monroe mused, as they walked up the stairs. 'That doesn't sound very *old man*.' He looked at De'Geer. 'You had him as a teacher. What did he seem like to you?'

'What she just said matches, sir. He was always flirting with the students,' De'Geer replied.

'And he was sixty-eight?' Monroe sighed. 'I must be doing something wrong.'

He caught himself before he continued, smiling at Doctor Marcos.

'Not that I'm looking, of course.'

De'Geer noted the comment and smiled. He'd been told by Joanne Davey that Rosanna Marcos and Alex Monroe were finally dating, although secretly, and that this was likely to be Monroe's way of letting Doctor Marcos know he was quite happy with the arrangement.

As they walked up to the front of the apartment, Monroe working through the ring of keys to find the one that opened it, De'Geer looked around, frowning, as if trying to pinpoint something just out of reach.

'For God's sake, laddie, stop your glowering and tell us what it is,' Monroe opened the front door, letting it swing inwards as he pulled a pair of blue latex gloves out of his jacket pocket, indicating for De'Geer to do likewise. 'The sight of you frowning will terrorise the neighbours.'

'There's something about this place, the address,' De'Geer had already pulled out his phone and was typing on it. 'I can't shake the feeling I've heard of it before.'

'Your lecturer lived here,' Monroe suggested as they entered the apartment. 'Maybe he talked about it?'

'Gloves on,' Doctor Marcos muttered, almost as a habit, not really noticing that the others were doing so.

The room they entered was a high-ceilinged space, with bookshelves along three of the walls, a variety of first edition leather books and ornaments on many of them. The green carpeted floor had an oval, burgundy and gold patterned rug under a black and glass topped coffee table, which sat in front of a large black leather sofa. On the wall facing it, the only wall that didn't have doors and bookshelves was a television cabinet with a large, fifty-inch screen on top of it. The wall behind was a different, darker shade of green and on it were a series of A4 sized frames, with what looked to be black and white artwork within, all based around the same strange, squiggly shapes. On the table were several books, strewn about as if used currently; books on Pagan Religions, Aleister Crowley, John Dee and even Siberian Shamanism were visible. Glancing at them, De'Geer looked up, visibly paling. It surprised Monroe that a seven foot tall Viking could look scared, but here he was.

'Now what?' he hissed. De'Geer pointed at the books.

'Crowley,' he half-mumbled, obviously nervous. 'I knew this was familiar. Number 67 to 69 Chancery Lane. It's where he lived.'

'Aleister Crowley lived here?' Doctor Marcos was examining what looked to be a metal chin-up bar, bolted into the wooden struts behind the wall, using her hands, now within her own grey latex gloves, to pull herself up to have a closer look at it. 'Cool.'

'And Aleister Crowley is who?' Monroe asked.

'He was a black magician around the turn of the century, sir,' De'Geer replied.

'I'm guessing you don't mean *doves out of sleeves and rabbits out of hats* kind of magician?' Monroe smiled, making a joke here. However, De'Geer took it as a serious comment.

'No, sir,' he replied stiffly, nervously looking around the room as he spoke. 'He was what was called a *Magus*, a practitioner in the dark-arts until he died after World War Two—'

'I get what you're saying,' Monroe raised a hand to interrupt. 'However laddie, they built this building after the millennium. You can rest assured if he lived here, it was in a building long gone.'

He scratched at his chin.

'Gotta say though, for Rupert Wilson to buy an apartment

at the same address that some infamous dark magician once lived at shows dedication to the cause.'

With his pen in hand, Monroe moved the books on the coffee table. He stopped as a selection of A4 sheets became visible.

'What do you make of these?' he asked. De'Geer leaned closer, gently separating the pages so that they spread out on the table surface.

'Map printouts,' he said. 'The line drawn on them goes up from Chislehurst, through Blackheath and Greenwich Park —' he checked the next sheet, which seemed to be a continuation of the line, '—and then continues up into Mile End. The other one looks like locations of underground caves and tunnels under Greenwich but it looks ancient. They probably don't even exist now.'

De'Geer looked at a series of handwritten phrases along the side of one of the map sheets.

IT'S ON THE CLIFF IT'S ON THE CLIFF IT'S ON THE CLIFF

'The Observatory is on a kind of cliff,' he noted. 'And there are a few chalk cliffs around, maybe Chislehurst Caves?'

Finishing his analysis, De'Geer looked back at the prints on the wall, taking a photo of them with his phone.

'There's something familiar about those images,' he muttered to himself as he placed it back into his police jacket.

'Could this be some sort of boundary line?' Monroe asked, still staring down at the maps.

'Probably a Ley line,' Doctor Marcos replied from across the room.

'And you'd know this how?' Monroe was impressed until Doctor Marcos pointed at one of the bookshelves.

'He has an entire row of books on it. That and books on south east London tunnels in between what looks like archaeological finds.'

'Sounds about right,' Monroe said, as he turned from the table. 'What else have you found?'

'There's a chin-up bar here, bolted into the wall itself, easily able to take a man's weight,' Doctor Marcos was checking the skirting board beneath it. 'I think he hanged from it, the rope tied off on the door over there.'

She pointed at a door to the kitchen, where a length of frayed rope was still attached to the handle.

'He stood on that stool, probably kicked it away. He struggled, kicked around but strangely didn't leave any scuff marks on the wall, and then stopped.'

'And how did he get to Greenwich?' Monroe was already at the door, examining the rope. 'This was cut.'

'Yes,' Doctor Marcos pointed across the room to a desk by the window. Under it was a second coiled length of rope. 'I'd bet the noose itself is under there.'

She frowned.

'If he kicked and dropped, then there should have been neck damage, where the jolt snapped at it but there wasn't,' she walked to the rope under the desk, pulling it out to reveal a noose. 'Second hypothesis? Someone held him under the chin-up bar, a noose was placed around his neck and then someone or some *people* pulled on the rope, raising him up so that he was above the ground, tying the rope off at the door. But then he would have *definitely* scuffed the wall.'

'So one option is suicide, the other is murder,' Monroe looked around the small apartment. 'The question is still how did he get to Greenwich Park?'

THE DEPTFORD COMMAND UNIT WAS A SMALLER BUILDING than Declan had expected but the interview rooms were to the same size and design as almost every other one he'd been to, with stark grey walls, a table in the middle and chairs either side. There was a recording device at one end of the table and on the facing side, sitting in the chairs, were two scared looking men in their late twenties.

'We didn't do anything,' the first of the men said, nervously pulling at the strings of his black hoodie. Declan smiled and sat facing them, Billy reluctantly joining him. Declan knew Billy would be annoyed at being dragged out to a police station; one reason he'd left the *Last Chance Saloon* a few months earlier was because of the field work. Billy had been a cyber-crime detective, and the dangers he'd encountered in the recent cases had weighed heavily on him. He'd only agreed to return when Bullman offered him a pretty unlimited budget for a new cyber-crime system. That said, Declan knew Billy was doomed to field work the moment he opened his mouth about the *hand of glory,* as he was now the resident occultism expert.

'I know,' Declan said, relaxing in the chair. 'That's why you're both here. It's a chat, not an interview.'

He pointed to Billy.

'That's Detective Constable Fitzwarren, and I'm Detective Inspector Walsh.'

'Hello,' Billy gave a nod, opening his notebook. 'Big fan of your show. Nice production values.'

The second man, a more nervous looking, slightly taller one, smiled at this.

'Thanks,' he said. 'I spend all night editing them.'

The man in the hoodie glowered at his companion. 'And I write the scripts as well as presenting.'

Good god, Declan thought to himself. *They're actually arguing about a bloody compliment.*

'Well, I hated it,' he added, determined to spoil the mood in the room. 'And we're not here to talk about your failed art school project, we're here to talk about the serious trouble you're in. Which one of you is Simon, and which one is Alfie?'

'I'm Alfie,' the hoodie man said sullenly. 'And all we did was film in the park at night. For that we've been here for two days.'

'No, what you did was break into one of the Queen's Royal Parks,' Declan replied, emphasising the *Royal* in the title. 'Breaking and entering and then trespassing inside a Royal premises is classed as *treason*, and can come with a *twenty-year sentence.*'

He felt Billy stiffen as he spoke. Billy was likely to be the only other person in the room that knew that there was no such sentence and that trespassing would most likely entail a fine. But he wanted to keep these two off balance, and keep them grateful for any opportunity to get out of this room.

'You utter *prick*,' Alfie snapped at the now stunned Simon. Declan stayed silent, allowing them to explain.

'Simon organises the venues,' Alfie muttered in explanation. 'We had a night planned for Pluckton in Kent on Friday, as it's one of the most haunted towns in England.'

'I told you, they cancelled on us,' Simon snapped back. 'They'd been given five times what we offered for a paranormal event thing. You'd been on about Greenwich for ages, and as we had everything booked out anyway, I said we should do it. You could have said no.'

'Maybe I would have, if I knew we were *committing treason?*'

Declan gave it a moment before continuing.

'However, I've spoken to the wardens and they're happy to waive the charges, especially as you alerted them to the body, even if it was after the park police caught you climbing up a gate to escape. And that you've cooperated with our own enquiries, which I'm sure you're willing to do...?'

Two eager nods agreed to this question. Declan smiled to himself as he opened his own notebook.

'Good,' he said. 'So, why Greenwich?'

'I'd wanted to do it for a while but as he just said, we only did it because of a cancellation in our actual location,' Alfie replied. 'I mean, we knew we could guerrilla-film there with no permits and I knew we could hide out until it was truly dark.'

'Not that it's ever truly dark,' Simon added. 'The light pollution is shit and really plays havoc with night vision filters.'

Declan wrote this down. 'And why were you in that particular part of the park?' he asked. 'I mean, for ghost hunters, surely there's a ton of ghosts around the burial mounds on the other side of the park?'

'There's ghosts everywhere,' Alfie retorted irritably. 'Just because you're dead, doesn't mean you have to hang around the graveyard.'

'Fair point,' Declan nodded. 'So this area was picked because...?'

'The *Motherstone*,' Simon added. 'There's history, so we thought it was a nice place to start. And there's a bunch of old trees on the ridge behind it, with bushes and branches that reach the ground, making a small hollow within that we could hide in until the wardens and the police left.'

'The police?' Billy was surprised at this. Alfie nodded.

'Park police. They have a car drive around with a powerful torch,' he explained.

'So you camp out in this hollow, at the back of the stone fountain,' Declan was writing as he spoke. 'And you saw nothing?'

'First off, the fountain's in a dip,' Simon replied. 'You follow a small path down, and there's a gully next to it. Behind the fountain there's a rise, and then the trees. Even if we looked directly at the fountain from where we were, we'd only see the top of it at best, and that's a good six, seven feet above the path.'

'Which you never went down.'

'Not until later.'

'So you settle in. And you see nothing? *Hear* nothing?'

Simon shook his head. 'Alfie sparked right out,' he explained. 'He has this ability to sleep anywhere and puts headphones on, listening to white noise. You know, raindrops, waves, all that shit.'

'I was not!' Alfie exclaimed indignantly. 'I was working out the presentation in my head.'

He looked at Billy.

'It's part of my preparation.'

'Is part of your preparation snoring?' Simon snapped. 'Anyway, Alfie wasn't paying attention and I was mainly watching the path beside the tree. Nobody walked past.'

'And again, you heard nothing?' Billy enquired. 'Say, like a sawing noise?'

Simon shook his head again. 'I had my AirPods in too,' he admitted. 'Was listening to a podcast.'

'Okay, so let's jump ahead,' Declan continued. 'You hide out until close to midnight and then emerge.'

'We were pretty much filming from the start,' Simon said now, more eager to help than he had been. 'You can see everything.'

'What we saw was Mister Wasley here talking about a *Hand of Glory* without even examining the body.'

'So I know some stuff,' Alfie muttered. 'Doesn't make me a killer.'

'Did either of you know the victim?'

Simon nodded. 'I saw him give a talk on *Hereward the Wake* a year or so back in London, if that helps?'

Declan leaned back in the chair, watching the two men.

'So neither of you knew the victim personally, voices drew you to the stone on a recorder and it's coincidence that you fell upon the body.'

'The energies led us there,' Alfie replied almost defensively. 'There's a sixteen metre wide band of energy that runs through the park.'

'And that links to this stone because it's on the line?' Declan pursed his lips as he waited for an answer.

'Well, no,' Alfie admitted reluctantly. 'Lover's Walk was once called Pauls Walk because it pointed directly at St Pauls, before it burned down. A lot of the paths lead to churches. And the stone is rumoured in folklore to have been moved to his house from Kent by Duke Humphrey and if that's true, then it *would* have been on the line at one point.'

Declan looked over to Billy, currently closing his notebook. 'I think we can let these men go,' he said. 'I don't think they can help.'

'Wait,' Alfie suddenly blurted out. 'I don't know if it helps, but there was one thing that struck me as odd. As we were finding a hiding place, I looked down to the junction of Lovers Walk and Temple Walk, where the *Motherstone* is. There were two women walking to the right, up Temple, pushing a wheelchair.'

'And what was weird about that?' Declan leaned closer now.

'There was nobody in it,' Alfie replied with what sounded like a hint of *mystery* in his voice. 'Why would you walk around with an empty wheelchair?'

'Did you see this too?' Declan asked Simon, who shook his head.

'Sorry, I was examining the hiding place.'

Declan looked at Billy.

'I can check CCTV, when I get back to the office,' he said. 'That should be easy enough to find.'

'Look, I know it probably means nothing but I think he *wanted* us to find him,' Alfie added. 'He left us a message on the EVP.'

'Shame he didn't leave a better one,' Declan said as he rose. 'Maybe something like the name of who did this to him.'

Opening the door, he nodded to the officer outside.

'Turf them out,' he said as he nodded to Billy to follow.

'Hey! What about our footage?' Simon asked. 'What about my camera?'

'You can pick up your camera when you leave,' Billy chimed in, 'but the SD card is currently evidence in a murder enquiry.'

'So we can't use any of it in our show?' Alfie looked crestfallen.

Declan didn't reply. There was no point.

Some people just couldn't be reasoned with.

4

MOTHERSTONES

ANJLI HAD CALLED AHEAD BEFORE TURNING UP AT GREENWICH, hoping that a local expert could be there to meet them when they arrived, but apparently detectives hunting murderers wasn't that high an interest because by the time she arrived outside the Greenwich Observatory to meet with Declan, flushed and out of breath from his riverside walk from Deptford, she'd had no replies. Nevertheless, the two of them, after Declan had grabbed water from the drinks stand at the side of the road, made their way down to Lovers Walk and the Motherstone.

'How did you get here so quickly?' he asked. Anjli smiled and tossed him a set of keys.

'Your Audi,' she said, nodding across the road to where the car was neatly parked. 'Billy said you were taking the scenic route, so I thought I'd be helpful.'

'First it's the house, then it's the car. What else will we be sharing?' Declan mock-complained as they walked along the narrow tarmac path that wound its way through the park; there was green grass on either side, the left of the path dropping downwards towards the valley within the two rises, while the other side was a field of trees, bootcamp instructors and dog walkers.

'I'm just getting started,' Anjli replied as they walked past Queen Elizabeth's Oak, a fallen piece of ancient tree, which local legend had as the tree that Queen Elizabeth herself had sat under as a child. Which, considering the location and the age, was quite possible. 'I've always wanted a daughter. I reckon Liz will let me be Jessica's new father instead of you.'

'You're welcome to try,' Declan laughed. 'But fair warning, it involves talking to Liz.'

There was a Roman temple buried somewhere nearby, as Declan remembered seeing it on *Time Team* around twenty years earlier but he didn't have time right now to play tourist and so he stopped at a tree at the back of the *Motherstone*, the branches falling to the ground.

'This is where they claimed to stay the night,' he said, peeking into the canopy and looking around. 'There's definitely some disturbance on the ground, and you can see where someone's brushed away the twigs.'

Anjli looked through the leaves. 'Well hidden, nobody's going to find you here, unrestricted view of the path outside.'

She leaned out of the branches, following the path to the crossroads.

'Limited view of Lover's Walk, no view of the stone and only a partial view of the continued path up the hill, and the walk to the right.'

Declan was already walking down to the crossroads, nodding to a dark-haired lady walking a black spaniel in the opposite direction. The megalithic fountain still had some crime scene tape around it but it had been torn and trampled on. After the police had left on the Saturday, the tourists would have entered to see what had happened and any evidence that had remained would have been contaminated. Declan understood why Doctor Marcos hadn't wanted to come here now. She would have probably started killing people if she'd seen this.

He stared down the short path to the stone, looking back along the other roads.

'If they came with a wheelchair, there's three options,' he said. 'West down Lovers Walk, which means they could have entered through the main entrance at St Mary's Gate'—'

'Which would be good, as that's the route from Greenwich and there's loads of CCTV,' Anjli commented as she knelt by the stone, not touching but looking closely at it. Declan nodded.

'True,' he replied. 'Or you go straight ahead, towards Maze Hill Gate, or continue southeast to Vanbrugh Park Gate. Both could have CCTV we could use.'

'Or, they didn't use any of them,' Anjli rose, walking back to Declan. 'Maybe they walked around the park, did a *Weekend at Bernies* with the dead professor.'

Declan shuddered at the thought. 'Let's hope they didn't,' he eventually replied, pausing as a woman on a bike slowed down as she reached them. The bike seemed odd to Declan; the wheels were almost too small for it but the woman seemed okay with this. She was young, maybe mid-twenties, with jet black, shoulder length hair, straightened and with red streaks in revealed as she pulled off her cycle helmet. Her makeup was minimal, her clothing stylish but functional; a tweed jacket over a long dress. She smiled as she got off the bike, using a small kickstand to keep it steady as she approached the detectives, holding out her hand.

'You must be DS Kapoor,' she said, warmly shaking

Anjli's hand before turning to Declan. 'The park called me. Said you needed to speak to a local historian? I'm Lucy Shrimpton. I live just down the road.'

Declan shook the hand, noting a small, crescent moon-shaped scar on the back of it, between the thumb and index finger. 'That looks painful.'

'Yeah,' Lucy replied, staring down at it absently. 'My mum had one. Thought I'd be cool and follow her, so I deserved whatever pain it gave.'

Anjli nodded to Declan. 'I told you the park would help.' She looked back at Lucy.

'To be honest, we were hoping to find someone who could give us some insight into the park, help us understand why someone like Professor Wilson would be left beside this stone with his hand cut off. You know, whether it was a satanic ritual or something.'

Lucy laughed but it seemed nervous. 'Well, it won't be satanic, but it's likely a ritual,' she said as she looked at the stone at the end of the path. 'You wouldn't bring him here unless you wanted something.'

'Did you know Professor Wilson at all?' Declan asked.

'Only in passing, not to talk to,' Lucy shook her head, pulling out a packet of cigarettes and lighting one up. 'Mum did, though. Everyone *knew* Rupert. Well, anyone who knew the park's history. He was a rock star.'

'Why?' Declan frowned at this. Lucy shrugged.

'Back in the mid-nineties there was this great hoo-hah about some giant steps in front of the Observatory, bloody great concrete things which would have destroyed tons of natural habitat, disrupting all the healing energies of the park, in particular the energy lines running through it,' she explained. 'Every ten years it's brought back up, as if someone has a hard-on for having their name on a plaque somewhere. And every time it's mentioned, the locals knock it back. One of the most famous people against this? Rupert Wilson.'

'So he made some enemies there then?' Anjli raised an eyebrow. Lucy shook her head.

'Sure, he pissed people off, but not enough to *ccrrrkkk*—' she ran a finger across her neck. 'So, what else do you want to know?'

Declan glanced at Anjli. 'We were wondering about this line?' he asked, almost nervously, as if expecting to be mocked.

'You mean the Greenwich Line?'

'Not the meridian—the one GMT starts on, but the *other* one.'

Lucy grinned. 'I know, it's also called the Greenwich Line. Or sometimes the Dee Line, after Doctor John Dee.'

She pointed up the path, back towards the observatory.

'Runs along the main road, and keeps going south and north. Hits lots of amazing things on the way. To the south, it passes through All Saints Church, which has six hundred and sixty-six pews, Blackheath Common where Jack Cade's rebellion was stopped in blood and the super-haunted Chislehurst Caves, while northwards it carries on through the park, site of some major Celtic battles, St Anne's Limehouse, where Hawksmoor deliberately placed the church and its strange pyramid to line up with it—'

'No offence but you could throw a stone in London and land on somewhere historical, mysterious, or where some battle was once fought,' Declan interrupted.

Lucy nodded at this.

'Disbelievers,' she muttered, reaching into a tweed

messenger bag and pulling out an iPad. 'I thought you'd be that way.'

Unlocking it with a fingerprint, she looked up at Declan.

'Throw a stone in London and hit a nuclear reactor. No, better still, hit two.'

'I wouldn't, because there aren't any,' Declan replied.

'Wrong,' Lucy smiled, her half-finished cigarette hanging loose in her mouth as she showed Declan a map of London. 'There were two in the sixties. One was at the Royal Naval College, where Lovers Walk leads, and they built the other at the same time, housed at Queen Mary University in Mile End. There're rumours that the first might still be there.'

If she saw the twitch that Declan made at the University's name, she didn't comment on it, instead zooming in on the map.

'Both places? On the Dee Line,' she said, as if this made everything understandable.

Declan, however, wasn't looking at that.

The Dee Line went through Essian Street in Mile End; in fact, it went through the very house that Bernard Lau had lived in, as well as the same University he'd studied at. And, when Declan looked a little closer, he saw that the line nudged gently beside a certain boxing club in Globe Town that he was very familiar with. Bernard Lau's death had led him to the Mile End Unit, the same Unit where, weeks earlier Anjli had been removed for going against DCI Ford's orders and smacking the living shit out of a wife beating enforcer that worked for the *Twins*, the local crime lords.

Both actions had led them to the Last Chance Saloon.

Looking to Anjli, he saw that she, too, was staring in surprise at the map.

'I can see the Dee Line's connected to you two,' Lucy said mysteriously. 'It's not an accident that both of you are here.'

'But the stone isn't on it,' Declan replied. Lucy shrugged.

'Well, it's not on it *now*,' she agreed. 'Nobody actually knows where it came from. People claim it was from Kent but there's nothing on any of the designs. The Victorians wouldn't have dragged a stone here to make a fountain in the middle of nowhere now, would they? No, it was here, in the park somewhere until someone in the 1800s attacked it with chisels and turned it into a fountain.'

She nodded to the bowl in the stone's front.

'There used to be tin cups that people could drink the water from, until they remembered they created it with lead pipes and turned it off,' she explained. 'People believe the stone being cut that way altered the energies, so on the festivals, people cleanse it with water brought from the Glastonbury Chalice Well.'

Anjli, on hearing this, walked back to the fountain, examining it. Lucy, however, stopped talking, observing Declan silently as she dropped her finished cigarette to the ground, stubbing it out with the heel of her boot.

'What?' he asked.

'She's with you,' Lucy said, leaning in, talking softly so that Anjli couldn't hear. 'The dark-haired woman.' At no response, Lucy continued. 'She was taken from you too soon. I get... I get an adolescent love, maybe an *unrequited* love?'

'I think we're done now,' Declan turned away, but with an intensity not seen so far Lucy grabbed his arm, the physical and sudden act bringing his attention fully to her.

'She says that she forgives you,' Lucy carried on, her voice soft and calm, emotionless. 'That she misses you, that you don't visit her anymore. She says that you should, that he's moved on now and they won't tell him. Do you understand?'

Lucy moved in even closer now, whispering more words but Declan wasn't listening, forcing the tears that threatened to well up back into his soul. Kendis Taylor had been his childhood love, one that stayed even when they split up in their teens. They'd reconnected a few months back but she was murdered by Malcolm Gladwell, and this had forced Declan on the run until he proved Gladwell's guilt. However, at the funeral, Pete, the widowed husband, most likely aware of the one-night stand between Kendis and Declan the day before she died had knocked Declan to the floor with a hard punch, telling Declan that if he ever returned to the grave, Pete would know. The threat was left unspoken.

Nobody knew that. Nobody had been close enough to see that.

And Declan had never spoken of it.

Lucy was still speaking to Declan as he stared into her eyes; deep eyes that pierced his soul.

'Let her go,' she breathed. 'Listen to what your heart —*Declan?*'

Declan turned, confused to stare at Anjli, the speaker of his name, as she watched in concern at him.

'Are you okay?' she asked. Declan looked back to Lucy, finding that she was no longer there. In fact, he could see her riding away on her strange bike, a good two hundred yards away.

But she'd only just been here, he thought to himself as, unable to explain what happened, Declan shifted his stance, as if shaking his body back into movement.

'I was talking to Lucy,' he said uncertainly.

'Yes and then she looked at her watch, said she was late

for work and rode off on her bike, while you stared off at the trees like some kind of love sick spaniel.'

Anjli moved closer now, obviously worried.

'She's been gone a good minute. That's why I called out to you.'

She stared off down Lovers Walk, back towards the Naval College and the tiny figure on the black bike.

'I almost bought one of those,' she said. 'A Brompton. Brilliant for commuting. Ride the bike, fold it up, carry it on a train. Perfect.'

Declan was only half listening, still trying to work out how he'd lost a minute. *Had he been so focused on Kendis and the memories he had of her that he'd simply gone into a trance?*

'I think we should go back to the office,' Anjli said, already rummaging through his jacket pocket. 'And if it's alright with you, I think I'll be driving.'

Declan nodded, taking one last look at the *Motherstone*. He really had told no one about the confrontation with Pete. Lucy could have learned of his connection to Kendis through the news but there was no way she could have known that.

Are you really there? he thought to himself. *Are you here with me, Kendis?*

There was a rustle of wind through the trees and, shuddering, Declan followed Anjli back to the Observatory building, and the car.

MONROE HAD FOUND MARGARET DONALDSON, THE administrator at Queen Mary University, to be frustratingly obstructive; A tall, thin, stern woman, she knew little about Professor Wilson and his work, she didn't know anyone there who *knew* about Professor Wilson and his work, and the only person who she could even consider allowing them to speak to would be Professor Wilson's research assistant, who wasn't in the office right now, and therefore, no matter how many times they suggested it, they couldn't wait *in his office* without a warrant. It was almost as if something was going on with Rupert Wilson that the University didn't want to talk about, and this was annoying Monroe.

In fact, he'd been one step away from actually calling up a warrant to search the office, if only to silence this annoying jobsworth when Margaret glanced across the reception floor towards the main doors, a relieved expression appearing on her face.

'Ah, good,' she sighed. 'You're no longer my problem.'

'Whose problem are we, then?' Monroe looked back to the entranceway, but all he could see was a young woman, currently folding up a black *Brompton* bike, removing her helmet and freeing her black hair, picking the folded bike up with one hand as she entered the building. She'd noticed Monroe as she walked across the floor, and so she crossed over, placing the bike down and offering her hand.

'I'm Marie Wilson,' she said with a nod. 'I'm guessing you're here about Rupert?'

'Aye I am but I don't really know what—' Monroe went to continue but Marie held up a hand to wave him silent, a crescent-shaped scar visible on it.

'No need to explain,' she said sombrely as she glanced around the lobby, as if looking to see who was watching. 'My late father has been all over the news, and we've been expecting you.' There was a slight quiver to her voice, as if she was holding her emotions in check.

'And after all, I've been his research assistant for about a year now, and probably knew him better than anyone else,' she finished, taking a deep breath and nodding to the administrator who, glad for the help, left quickly as, with a faint, welcoming smile, Marie Wilson looked back to Monroe.

'So, what do you want to know?' she asked.

———

5

GATHERING THREADS

Monroe was still out when Anjli and Declan, now back to his normal self, returned to the Temple Inn Command Unit. Doctor Marcos was with DC Davey in the morgue; the body of Rupert Wilson had finally arrived, giving them more time to work on a second autopsy, while De'Geer was talking to the uniforms at Deptford and Billy was utilising every monitor at his disposal as he scanned through CCTV footage of London.

'Find anything?' Declan asked as he took his jacket off. Billy nodded, his eyes still glued to the screens.

'The one thing I love about working here is that it's never dull,' he replied as he pulled up some images on the left-hand screen. 'Most places it's simple stuff, like follow a car, or search for the last known location of a missing man, but here it's hunt female assassins with wheelchairs, examine the myth of a long forgotten Ley Line, hunt down the history of long-lost occult objects and try to find photos of a victim's hand.'

He looked back at Declan and Anjli.

'It's like *Where's Wally* but with *Goths*,' he grinned.

'So what *do* you have?' Declan walked over to Billy's bank of monitors as Anjli started typing up notes on her own computer. Billy pointed at an image, blurry and black and white, of two women walking what seemed to be a man with sunglasses and a cap on, in a wheelchair, in a park.

'Vanbrugh Gate, seven-forty pm, twenty minutes before closing. Two ladies and a gentleman in a wheelchair enter the park, walking westwards,' he tapped on his keyboard, and a second image appeared, one that was the same location so likely the same camera, but with the two women leaving, the wheelchair now folded and wheeled beside them, empty of any inhabitant.

'Eight-oh-three, as the park closes the same women leave, but now the gentleman with the glasses is gone.'

'Can you get a better image?' Declan asked. Billy shrugged.

'I'm trying, but the camera wasn't at the gate, so this is pretty zoomed in. What it shows though is that our *Mostly Ghostly* hunters weren't lying.'

'*Ghost Bros*,' Declan corrected.

'Yeah, that's a stupid name,' Billy replied calmly as he scrolled through other images on the CCTV feed. 'I prefer mine.'

'Are we sure they're women?'

'As much as I can be from grainy footage,' Billy admitted. 'I'd honestly say that we're looking at two middle-aged ladies, one blonde, one possibly red haired, the former around a size sixteen dress size, the latter maybe a twelve?'

'That's specific,' Anjli, listening while working commented.

'I used to work in Debenhams as a teenager,' Billy replied. 'I have an *eye*.'

'Well, don't use your eye on me, or you'll get a smack in the mouth,' Anjli smiled.

'Anyway, thanks to the witness, we know they walk to the *Motherstone* and then back,' Billy continued. ' From distance and speed of walking here, I'd say they had a good fifteen minutes there.'

'Why so long?'

'Probably needed to wait until everyone had left,' Billy suggested. 'Also, the police would have driven down Lovers Walk, as it's one of the wider roads. They probably wanted to ensure they had some alone time.'

'So then these two ladies lay the body down, cut off the hand and then leave?' Anjli rose from her desk, walking over. 'Why do it there? Surely there's every chance of being seen?'

'Might not have been them,' Declan said, watching the screen. 'Someone could have come along later. With one of our witnesses listening to podcasts while the other slept with headphones on, there's a chance that anyone in the park could have sawn off the wrist after lockdown, any time between eight and eleven pm.'

'Which gives us the possibility that someone followed the two women,' Billy nodded. 'I'll start checking the cameras for anyone entering who isn't seen leaving... but that could take a while.'

'Do that,' Declan rubbed at his chin as he thought. 'Any more on the victim?'

'Actually, yes,' Billy started pulling up newspaper and blog articles. 'He's been connected to Greenwich for years.'

'Because of his efforts in trying to save parts of it,' Anjli pulled out her notebook, reading from it. 'We were told about his mid-nineties activities.'

'That might be *something* he did, but that wasn't all they knew him for,' Billy smiled. 'Our Professor Wilson was a treasure hunter.'

'What sort of treasure?' Declan looked at Billy in mild surprise. 'I mean, are we talking *Indiana Jones* here?'

'In a way, yes,' Billy brought up an image of Greenwich Park. 'The land that Greenwich Park was built on is riddled with secret caves, underground streams, and caverns. There was a famous one found on Blackheath Hill in 1790 called *Jack Cade's Caverns*, old chalk mines which extend hundreds of feet underground. And there are old tunnels, some used as water conduits in the sixteenth century, that lead to the Naval College.'

'So what, there *are* hidden caverns down there?' Anjli laughed. 'I'll get my metal detector and shovel.'

'Seriously,' Billy nodded. 'See here at the north of the park? Park Vista? Turn of the century they built a new house there and found a tunnel that led to some underground caves.'

He tapped on the screen and an old newspaper cutting appeared.

DISCOVERIES AT GREENWICH - UNDERGROUND CHAMBERS

'This was a piece on the chambers when it happened,' Billy said. 'The experts reckoned a seventeenth-century house had been built on a monastery, and these were the crypts.'

"Nice, but also creepy,' Anjli replied. 'And how do you know that?'

'Guy I went to school with,' Billy admitted. 'Told us all the time about it. His family owns the house. He still lives there and I play squash with him every Thursday.'

'My friends at school were lucky to have a house,' Anjli said as she pointed at Declan. 'And *his* friend at school was a serial killing mechanic.'

Declan went to reply, but Monroe and De'Geer entered the room, Monroe already waving towards the briefing room.

'Come on, let's see where we are on this,' he said, already entering through the door. 'This bloody case is giving me the willies, and I want it sorted quickly.'

With Anjli and Billy behind him, Declan entered the briefing room, sitting at his usual spot beside the full-length glass window. At the back, De'Geer nodded to DC Davey and Doctor Marcos as they entered. Finally, Bullman stood by the door, motioning to Monroe to continue; not actively part of the case, but still overseeing it.

'We'll start,' Monroe nodded to Doctor Marcos to join him at the front. 'We attended Professor Wilson's apartment on Chancery Lane, which PC De'Geer informs us was once the address of Aleister Crowley, an apparently well-known and infamous magician, although not the *Paul Daniels* kind.'

Declan glanced at De'Geer at this to see him visibly shudder as Monroe continued. 'Anyway, the room was clean, no signs of a fight, some weird bloody paintings on the wall and what looks like some '*borrowed*' Middle Eastern antiquities on the shelf but you can't account for taste, some maps and lines on pieces of paper, and the remnants of a noose on the floor.'

'So he hanged himself there?' Anjli looked up from her notes.

'Either hanged or *was* hanged,' Doctor Marcos corrected. 'As of yet, we have no proof either way. No signs of defensive marks on his remaining hand, but then he might have used the one that was removed. That might even be the reason it was cut off. The noose was looped over a high chin-up bar and tied to the door, and the rope matches the ligature marks on the victim's neck. However, it was cut with a knife at some point, probably when someone came to cut him down, although it was a straight edge blade and they're ten-a-penny to buy.'

'So he died in Chancery Lane, and then was taken to Greenwich,' Declan mused.

'Aye,' Monroe nodded. 'So you have anything on that?'

'Alfie Wasley said that he saw two women wheeling an empty wheelchair,' Declan replied. 'Billy found them on the CCTV, and it looks like they arrived with a body in the wheelchair about twenty minutes beforehand, but then left as the park closed without it. However, as he was wearing headphones and had no line of sight, he couldn't confirm if anyone else was there to cut the hand off between eight and eleven pm.'

'Any reason why Wilson was dumped by the stone?' Bullman asked.

'We spoke to a local expert who reckoned that the fountain's a bit of a favourite with the local pagans,' Anjli read from the notes. 'Rupert Wilson was very fond of it. Maybe it was like when you scatter ashes at a beloved location?'

'Apart from the fact that they glossed over the 'creating the ashes' part,' Davey replied. 'Grim little gift to leave.'

'I was just telling DI Walsh that Wilson was known for

being a bit of a treasure hunter,' Billy chimed in. 'He'd been a part of the park for ages, but there was a belief in the nineties that there was a hidden, occult library under the park, and people spent years looking for secret tunnels and suchlike.'

'Why would you hide a library under the park?' Declan shook his head. 'What am I missing?'

'The time of the hiding,' De'Geer suggested. 'Duke Humphrey had powerful enemies back in the day.'

'And Duke Humphrey is?' Bullman asked.

'Humphrey of Lancaster, Duke of Gloucester until 1447,' Billy said, pulling up a wikipedia page onto the plasma screen. 'He created Greenwich Park, back in 1428, when he built a palace called *Bella Court* by the Thames.'

'But he was also a collector of occult books and items,' De'Geer added. 'In fact, people believed that his occult library was the best in the world.'

'So what happened to it?' Monroe asked. De'Geer shrugged.

'Nobody knows, sir. And the folklore is that somewhere under Greenwich in a blocked off cavern is an Aladdin's cave of magical items and power.'

'Or, he burned them,' Declan folded his arms.

'All we know is that Wilson claimed that he'd *found* it,' Billy grinned now. 'Around the mid-nineties, there was a fever pitch of amateur treasure hunters out there, thanks to a ton of books about *Templars* and *secret bloodlines,* all the things that Dan Brown *DaVinci-Coded* a few years later. There were hundreds of people hunting the lost library.'

He pulled up a series of photos of Rupert Wilson, all taken at various times over the years.

'Wilson stated at a press conference aimed at stopping the renovations that he and some friends had found it,' he explained. 'Now De'Geer mentioned earlier that the missing hand was one he never really saw. And in these photos, we see here that Wilson has no issues with the hand, yet a few years later he makes an effort to hide it, while *not* doing so. A bit like Jeremy Beadle.'

'The TV presenter?' Monroe looked baffled. 'How does he fit into this?'

'He had *Poland Syndrome*,' Doctor Marcos added from the back of the room. 'It meant that one hand was smaller than the other. But unless you were looking for it, you'd never know. He was a master of hiding it.'

'Exactly,' Billy nodded. 'If you knew what you were looking for, you'd see it. Otherwise your brain bypasses it.'

At this, he opened another photo of Rupert Wilson on the screen; it was recent, about twelve months old and was a posed, magazine article shot of Wilson, his hands in front of him making the two-handed 'illuminati' triangle sign with his thumbs and index fingers. The palms of his hands, visible here, were covered in black pen, a variety of symbols and words that had been written all over them.

'This was a photoshoot for the *Pagan Dawn* Spring news-letter last year,' Billy took a laser pointer and made the dot on the screen spin around the right hand. 'In the other photos, after 1998, he hides this hand. At best, I could see that some-thing was on it, something dark, but it was impossible to make out. But here, twenty years later, he's hiding it in plain sight.'

'The letters on the palm are different,' Anjli leaned closer. 'They're thinner.'

'Bingo,' Billy zoomed in. 'They covered the hands in pen and ink, but on his right palm? That's a tattoo.'

He cropped the image so that the tattooed symbols were more visible.

'As you can see here, there are three interlinking circles, each with symbols in, around a fourth magical design,' he explained.

'What the hell does that mean?' Monroe peered closer.

'I don't rightly know, but it's probably some kind of magical warding, and it's faded. It's been on his hand for a good couple of decades.'

'Like *Dr Strange*?' Bullman asked. 'If we're bringing Benedict Cumberbatch in, I'd better get my hair done.'

'Kind of,' Billy replied. 'Wardings are symbols often used because you think you're being attacked. It's where the term *warding off* comes from, as if you're warding off a blow, or to ward off evil.'

'Evil eyes and horseshoes, that sort of thing?' Anjli nodded. 'If he believed someone was attacking him, it could explain why he died.'

'Yes but this was maybe twenty years ago,' Declan considered. 'Whoever was against him then might not even be alive now.'

'They're not all old,' Doctor Marcos pointed at tattoos on the four fingers of the hand. 'Those are recent for the photo. There are still small scabs from where they're healing.'

Everyone looked at the four fingers, where sets of strange symbols could be seen.

'Hold on,' Billy said, rotating the image around on his laptop and zooming in. 'Here's the image in more detail.'

'I think it's Enochian,' De'Geer was leaning closer now. 'I watched a show about it on *BBC Four* a year back. It's the language of the Angels, as described to John Dee and Edward Kelley in the fifteen hundreds, when they tried to communicate with them.'

'So it's Angel emojis,' Bullman stated matter-of-factly, as if this was the most obvious answer. 'Any other tattoos?'

'Actually, yes,' Doctor Marcos nodded. 'He has tattoos all over his body. Some seem handmade, others more professional. But they all look like magical spells and wardings, lots of circles. Weird little letters and pentagrams.'

'Nothing wrong with tattoos,' Declan mused.

Billy pulled up a photo; it was an archaeological dig in Israel. In it, a younger Rupert Wilson was shirtless, laughing, a Panama hat on his head.

'This was early 1998 in En Esur, in Israel. He was at the archaeological site many times over the next twenty years and, as you can see, he's a clean canvas here, including the hand,' Billy replied. 'As the first photo I've found where he hides the tattoo on his palm was three years after this was taken, I reckon it's somewhere around the turn of the millennium where he started this obsession.'

'I'll send you photos of the tattoos on his body,' Doctor Marcos was already working on her iPad. Maybe you can translate them while you work on the hand one.'

Billy shook his head.

'As I've said a dozen times, I won't be able to, as this wasn't my thing, Ma'am,' he replied. 'Maybe we can ask about, see if we can find some other experts?'

'I'd like to keep this close to our chests right now,' Monroe mused. 'We don't know yet who we can trust out there. These so-called experts might be the ones who killed him.'

He scratched at his chin as he stared at Billy, now flustering under the gaze.

'No secret contacts who can help? Either with you or De'Geer?'

De'Geer shook his head at the back of the room but Billy sighed, nodding.

'Unfortunately, I think I know a man who could,' he muttered.

'Your great-uncle?'

Billy nodded.

'Yup,' he said morosely. 'My great-uncle, whose son I had arrested for fraud.'

'Right then,' Monroe nodded. 'We'll carry on looking for these mysterious women, and you go have a heart-to-heart with your family, see why Wilson would have such a thing tattooed on his hand.'

He looked to Declan, now rising.

'Go with him,' he suggested. 'We might need a referee on this one.'

'And if you get to talk to the great-uncle, see if you can get any gossip about Billy,' Anjli grinned. 'Baby photos are preferred.'

Billy made a pained, groaning noise and left the briefing room. Declan felt sorry for him but his woes meant Anjli wasn't concentrating on Declan and the whiteout that he had in the park. That he'd lost over a minute disturbed him.

It wasn't something he wanted to repeat.

6

DUSTY BOOKS

BILLY HAD BEEN QUITE SURPRISED TO HEAR ALMOST immediately from his great-uncle; he was currently in town, staying in a hideously expensive suite at the St Pancras Hotel on the Euston Road and had suggested that Billy (and Declan by default) meet him on Museum Street, just south of the British Museum. Apparently there was an old bookshop there that he had a standing order with for antiquated books, and as he was likely to be there all afternoon, that was the best place to meet. Considering that this was only a ten or fifteen-minute walk from the Command Unit, Declan and Billy left almost immediately.

Billy's great-uncle was, in a way, exactly as Declan had expected him to look, while at the same time completely different. He was in his sixties, or a well looked after early seventies, with brown curly hair peppered with white that showed more in the bushy beard that sprouted from his chin, a tweed jacket, waistcoat and deep blue corduroy trousers. The jacket was a standard grey, while the waistcoat seemed to be a khaki colour, the white shirt underneath collarless, in the 'grandad' style that seemed so fashionable a few years earlier. Declan assumed also that the jacket and waistcoat were bespoke, likely from Savile Row, just like Billy's suits.

They probably had accounts with the same tailors.

He was standing outside the *Atlantis Bookshop* when Declan, Billy and De'Geer arrived, the last of the trio having changed out of his uniform and now in just a pair of police-issue black trousers and white shirt under his biker jacket, and allowed to attend because, apart from Billy, he was the best qualified field officer in the unit to discuss the case with an occult expert.

Declan meanwhile didn't really have a clue what was going on.

Declan had however expected a cold confrontation here; he'd known about Billy's problem with his family since he'd arrived at Temple Inn; while in cyber-crime, Billy had found himself in the unenviable position of either siding with the force and arresting his uncle (or whatever he truly was to Billy by blood) for an online Ponzi scheme, or siding with his family, and likely losing his job. As it was, Billy had chosen the former, to arrest his own uncle, in the process becoming disowned by his family for the temerity to go against them. And, ironically, because the Fitzwarrens had very good ties with the higher ups in the Metropolitan Police, the fallout following this actually ended with Billy being removed from his position and suspended, effectively unemployable.

Until Alexander Monroe appeared with an offer of a new career in the *Last Chance Saloon,* that was.

However, the cold confrontation was not to be, as the moment that he saw Billy approach, his great-uncle's face brightened as he bellowed out, 'there you are, you lazy bugger! I've been waiting hours for you!'

Billy squirmed as he was reluctantly brought into a giant bear hug with his great-uncle.

'It's been half an hour,' he complained. 'DI Walsh, PC De'Geer, this is my great-uncle.'

Declan noted Billy hadn't given a name, so held his hand out to shake.

'We weren't told your name,' he explained. 'Billy never seemed to get around to it, Mister Fitzwarren.'

'That's because he's a good boy,' the genial great-uncle boomed through his bushy beard. 'He knows that names have power. In my game it's better to ask what you'd prefer to be called, rather than what your name is.'

'And your game is?' Declan asked.

'Why, the occult, of course!' came the booming reply as Declan's hand was finally shaken. 'Call me Chivalry.'

Declan glanced at Billy to see what his reaction to this name was and, seeing none, he assumed that this must have been an often used *nom de plume*.

'I'm guessing that this is to do with Wilson?' Chivalry asked conspiratorially. 'I heard he was dead. Also heard that his hand was missing.'

He grinned through the beard at Billy.

'You think someone wanted an eye for an eye there? Maybe that's something our *family* could go back to?'

Billy didn't reply to this but Declan did.

'Mister Fitzwarren, I know we arrested your son Bryan because of Billy's actions,' he said. 'But if you have any issue with him, you can take them up with me, his superior. I read the case report, and your son deserved everything he got.'

There was a long moment of silence as 'Chivalry' Fitzwarren stared at Declan. Then, with a smile and a nod, he guffawed, a loud, bellowing laugh.

'Don't worry yourself,' Chivalry continued. 'I'm probably the only one in the family who doesn't blame William there for what happened. Bryan was an arrogant cretin and deserved a humbling. But then I'm more of a *live by the sword* kind of man, *Declan.*'

Declan went to reply, to ask how his name was known but then stopped himself. Of course this man would know his name. He'd probably swotted up on everything the moment he put the phone down.

Well, two could play that game.

'It's *Detective Inspector Walsh*, while we're on duty,' he replied. 'As you said, names have power, and I'd hate to accidentally call you *Steven.*'

'Oh, he's good,' Chivalry smiled at his great-nephew. 'I see now why you turned down Harrington's job offer.'

He looked back at the others.

'Right then,' he said, his voice still turned up to max. 'Let's have a spot of luncheon in *The Plough*, eh? And as I'm effectively consulting for you, I think you can pay.'

THE PLOUGH WAS A SMALL PUB ON MUSEUM STREET; CLOSE enough to walk to, but not close enough to avoid at least one anecdote from Chivalry, something about the Earth being hollow and a wager involving the Channel Tunnel drill, but by the time they arrived in the pub the story seemed to be over and Chivalry was already checking the bar's range of expensive whiskies.

'So go on then, ask me your questions,' he eventually said as they sat down around a table in the bar's corner, sipping at his neat scotch, no ice. 'Did I know him? Yes. Was he a pretentious prick? Yes.'

'We're more interested in his hand,' Declan said, watching Chivalry's expression for any changes as he spoke. The man was either an expert at keeping his emotions in check or he had no clue what Declan was talking about, as he gave no look of surprise or recognition at this. Declan assumed it was the former though, as already he could see that Mister Fitzwarren was a player of games.

'You mean the tattoos,' Chivalry breathed. 'The secret ones that nobody knows about, that he never shows, on the palm and fingers of his hand.'

'You know about them?' Billy spoke, obviously irritated at this, most likely hoping for an excuse to end the meal. Chivalry smiled, nodding.

'Of course I do. Worst kept bloody secret in the occult, that was. He got the first one a year or so after the boy died.'

'Boy died?'

Chivalry nodded. 'Some idiot student got caught in a cave-in a few years after the five of them claimed they'd found the *Lost Ark of the Covenant,* or whatever it was.'

Declan leaned back.

'Assume we're not the people you usually chat to,' he said. 'Assume we haven't got a bloody clue what you're talking about and are completely without context or frame of reference here.'

'Oh, yes, of course,' Chivalry was relaxing into his role as narrator. 'Speak to you like children. Rupert Wilson, John Gale, Miriam Shrimpton and Julie-Anna Watson. The *Four Musketeers,* always buggering around in that park, looking for lost libraries and hidden treasures.'

Declan noted the name *Shrimpton* down, assuming this was Lucy's mother.

'You said five.'

'There was someone who helped, Marcus something but he wasn't a staunch member of the gang. Wasn't even mentioned in the news pieces. Probably more *the guy in the van*, if you get my drift. Hardly worth a footnote.'

'Did they find it?' Billy asked. 'The library?'

'They claimed to,' Chivalry shrugged. 'But then Wilson also claimed he was a tantric sex expert, and between us? I've heard he's more of a *quick study*, if you know what I mean.'

He stopped.

'*Was* more, I suppose,' he corrected himself. 'Shame though, it must have been truly soul crushing for them all when they had to retract everything.'

'Why?' Now it was De'Geer asking.

'Well, when the Royal Park came for them, throwing *cease and desist* notices, especially after they showed their exciting items and everything. Four items, one for each. I don't remember what they all had, I think Miriam had a scrying mirror, Rupert an old blade, like some kind of Templar sword, Julie-Anna a book... I just remember John and his bloody dagger. Made of obsidian, it was, and he slashed it around like he was a sodding *Musketeer* in more than just name.'

Declan went to reply to this, to ask what Chivalry meant, but before he could, Billy pulled up the *Pagan Dawn* image of Rupert with the tattooed hands on his phone, showing it to Chivalry.

'You've seen this?' he asked.

Chivalry nodded.

'And, like you, I worked out what was the actual tattoo, and what was sharpie.'

He rose a little in his chair in realisation.

'You're here for a translation!' he exclaimed delightedly. 'You don't know what it means!'

'Not everyone is an expert in Enochian, Mister Fitzwarren,' Declan muttered.

'True, but surely you could have chatted to more specialised departments,' Chivalry continued. 'I mean, there's Specialist Crime Directorate whatever number it is on Russell Square, they probably know...'

He sighed.

'Fine,' he continued. 'I'll tell you, but it means nothing.'

'What's the image on the palm?' Declan asked. Taking the phone, Chivalry zoomed in on the tattoo.

'The symbol in the middle of the three circles is the *Monas Hieroglyphica*, or rather the *Hieroglyphic Monad*. It's a kind of composite of varying esoteric and astrological symbols.'

'And the circles?'

'Borromean rings,' Chivalry continued. 'Named after the Italian House of Borromeo who put them in their coat of arms in the 15th Century, although they were used well before that.'

He looked at De'Geer.

'You descended from Vikings, lad? *They* used them, too. And Romans, and Buddhists. Even Christians claim it represents the Holy Trinity. They're linked, so that if you take away one ring, the other two would fall apart. Because of this, people used Borromean Rings as symbols for strength in unity.'

He smiled.

'They also represent the karmic laws of the universe and the interconnectedness of life. You do something good or bad? Expect it to come back onto you, thrice-fold, in a brutal cause-and-effect.'

'The three-fold-law,' De'Geer whispered.

'The symbols in the circles are wardings,' Chivalry continued. 'Aimed at changing perceptions.'

Declan looked confused at this, so Chivalry smiled.

'Harry Potter's invisibility cloak,' he explained. 'This is a tattoo that stops the owner from being seen. Not by people, but by the *elements*.'

He looked at Billy.

'Rupert Wilson was hiding from the curse.'

'What curse?' Declan asked.

'Oh, there's always a curse or two,' Chivalry kept smiling, and it was annoying Declan. 'He was scared, something was after him and he was hiding.'

'Something was, or he *believed* that something was?' Declan asked. Chivalry grinned.

'Same thing to some people,' he replied enigmatically. 'I'd heard that Marcus wasn't talked about because he'd died, and then there was the cave-in on the student...'

He smiled.

'One death? Accident. Two deaths? *Curse*.'

Declan nodded as he wrote this down. 'And the Enochian on the fingers?'

'Four lines, from left to right,' Chivalry replied. 'You see, we can link the letters to the English alphabet, but it creates gibberish. This was the language of Angels, and letters could mean entire words, or beliefs. The first four glyphs spell *Oali*. It means 'I have placed'. The next six spell *Salman*. It means 'in the house'. Next line down? The six glyphs spell *Soboln*, 'in the west', while the last five spell *Laiad*, which means 'the secrets of truth."

'*I have placed, in the house, in the west, the secrets of truth,*' Billy intoned. 'What does that mean?'

Chivalry laughed. It was light at first, but then rose in sound as he couldn't stop.

'No bloody idea, my boy!' he guffawed. 'Nobody's had a sodding clue for years! Annoys the hell out of collectors like me!'

Declan looked at De'Geer, to ask why the Viking had been so quiet, but found him staring at Chivalry in a mixture of horror and excitement.

'Something the matter, PC De'Geer?' he asked carefully. De'Geer, still staring at Chivalry, nodded.

'I know what it means,' he said. 'Mister Fitzwarren, did you ever visit Rupert at his apartment?'

'You mean the Aleister Crowley address?' Chivalry shook his head. 'Nobody did. Only pretty Goth girls were allowed there, and he led them straight into the bedroom. Why?'

'You walk north up Chancery Lane,' De'Geer was thinking as he spoke, his fingers moving as he mentioned directions, as if mentally drawing a map. 'The entrance is on the right side, so you turn east. Up the stairs, and the door is on the left. North. You enter, turn left into the main living room...'

He nodded to himself.

'Rupert filled the room with books, three walls of them. But the fourth wall, the west-facing wall, has prints on them,' he pulled out his phone, opening the photos app. 'I took a photo of them.'

He showed it around the table, and Chivalry immediately

grabbed it from him, zooming in with his fingers, his face paling.

'The art,' he whispered. 'It's terrible but there's Enochian in it. The bastard was playing with us all along. The secrets were in his house and in the west!'

'So what does it mean?' Declan asked, but stopped as Billy grabbed the phone, taking it from Chivalry.

'You've hunted for this for years,' he said quietly to his great-uncle, his tone emotionless. 'This is a clue that only a few have, that we know of. And in translating it, you're learning it. It's priceless.'

Declan was confused where Billy was going here, but Chivalry wasn't.

'Your family would be proud of you,' he replied. 'And I'd personally vouch for you. Point out that my son was a bloody fool and deserved what he got.'

He grinned.

'An eye for an eye, indeed.'

Billy thought for a moment and then passed the phone back, and now Declan realised what had just happened.

By getting Chivalry to translate this, he was allowing Chivalry to see a clue that only a few had seen before. And he was using this to buy his way back into his family.

'It's beautiful,' Chivalry said. 'I mean, the art itself is terrible but the text is simplistic. It leads to a second clue, which likely leads to a third, as such is the way of quests. That said, I think I can read this.'

He leaned back, staring at the ceiling as if working out the phrasing in his head.

'I inscribed the secrets on the tribute tomb,' he said carefully, working through each word. 'To the west of the Devil's Temple.'

He frowned.

'There's not really a translation of this last word, but it effectively means to look at someone in history, and consider what they're known for.'

'And do you understand this?' Declan asked. Chivalry shook his head.

'There are a lot of pagan temples in London,' he replied. 'Romans loved the bloody things. Give me a day or two though, and I'll come back to you.'

'Do you believe in the lost library of Duke Humphrey?' De'Geer asked, as if hoping that by saying yes, Chivalry would answer all his questions.

'I do,' Chivalry replied. 'And I know that if it exists, it's already been found and ransacked. There's a black market for occult items out there, and the prices are high enough to kill for.'

'Kill and cut off a hand?'

'Oh, that and more,' Chivalry pondered for a moment. 'And with Rupert playing silly buggers with all of this, he was being smug and goading people to notice, to work it out as if he was leading the way rather than just being a smug bastard. We all know that over the years someone would have seen it, or more likely found out the location from the others connected to this.'

He looked up at Declan.

'Who are now probably walking around with targets on their back, if there's a fortune to be made.'

Declan looked down at the notes he'd made in his notepad.

John Gale, Miriam Shrimpton and Julie-Anna Watson were also involved in this, somehow. And Declan needed to find them before *someone else* did.

Declan's phone buzzed, and he pulled it out, checking the text that had just arrived from Monroe. Looking up at Chivalry, he forced a smile.

'Lunch is on us but we need to leave,' he said, already rising. 'Thank you for your help in the investigation.'

'Thank *you*,' Chivalry waggled the tumbler of scotch. 'Pay for it as you leave, there's a good man.'

Billy walked to the bar to pay the tab as Declan, after shaking hands with Chivalry one last time, exited the pub onto Museum Street.

'What was on the message, sir?' De'Geer asked. Declan felt the wind on his face and took a deep breath.

'Nothing, Monroe just wanted to know what was going on,' he replied as Billy emerged out into the air behind them. 'I just needed to end that meeting before Chivalry Fitzwarren took over the case, and Billy's soul.'

And with nothing more said, Declan started south down Museum Street, looking for a cab to hail.

7

COFFEE TIME

Lilith Babylon sat in Costa and sipped at her coffee, rocking gently back and forth as she hummed a childhood song to herself, even though she was now in her late thirties. She was nervous, and probably shouldn't have been drinking caffeine too but it was warm and soothing. It was something familiar for her to drink.

They'd taken the body.

She shuddered as she put the image out of her head; it was what he wanted.

Damn what he wanted. That's not why you joined.

Lilith almost spoke out aloud at this opinion but she knew her thoughts were correct. She hadn't joined the *Ladies of Avalon* to help Rupert Wilson. She'd joined a year ago to gain revenge on him, to help her niece in her fight with him.

No, it was more *avenge* than revenge. The two words were quite different. *Revenge* was the action of hurting someone in return for some kind of injury or wrong that had been suffered at their hands.

She hadn't expected him to die.

Meanwhile, *avenge* was a verb, meaning to punish a wrongdoing with the intent of seeing justice done. Not just harming for harm's sake. And Lilith needed to *avenge*, if only to clear up her debts with Alés, dead these last twenty-three years.

Dead at his hands.

There was a motion at the door to the coffee shop, and Lilith looked up to see Cindy, her fellow *Lady of Avalon,* enter. It was raining outside, and as per usual she hadn't worn a coat, her peroxide blonde hair now plastered to her head by the rain. However, rather than call out, Lilith slid further back into the alcove, allowing Cindy to walk by as she looked for her own seat in the coffee shop. Lilith was wearing an olive *Barbour* coat and had a beanie over her red hair, a colour usually held for girls half her age; it wasn't anything like her usual attire, and she had hoped this would help her blend into the surroundings, but now she was worried that she'd still stand out.

That Cindy would see her and know why she was there.

Even if Lilith didn't.

It had started on Saturday evening; Lilith had called Cindy, mainly to check up on her. The events of the night before had been stressful, especially the waiting with the body, crouched down in the small dell beside the *Motherstone,* ensuring the police were long past but still able to escape before the park closed with an empty wheelchair, but she needn't have worried, as there'd been nothing announced on the news about people wheeling in bodies and dumping them that night. Just that Rupert Wilson was dead, and it was a tragedy.

He wasn't supposed to be dead. He was supposed to have been cancelled, his reputation in ruins.

Lilith didn't know how Rupert had really died, all she had was Cindy explaining that she had to cut the rope off his throat, but she knew something was wrong with the picture. After he'd contacted them both, Cindy was too quick in replying. It felt *off*, somehow. And the journey had been stilted, awkward. It was like Cindy knew what to expect.

And Lilith was suspicious of this. Of *her*.

Cindy ordered at the counter and found a small table at the corner of the coffee shop, a round wooden table that was big enough for two. She was facing the door, so at a ninety-degree angle to Lilith, across the room.

'If you keep staring at her, of *course* she'll notice you,' a woman sat down opposite Lilith now, having emerged from the bathrooms. She was slim, in her late fifties, and with her own spiky, peroxide-blonde hair, at least two decades out of style and age bracket. She wore a long green coat, pulled tight around her. 'Has she said anything?'

'She's watching the door and drinking a green tea,' Lilith replied as, through it, a man entered. 'Shit. It's *John*.'

Slim, tall and in his late sixties, his grey hair slicked back into a ponytail and his wire-rim glasses reminiscent of John Lennon spectacles, John Gale looked around the coffee shop, seeing Cindy wave at him, the familiar wave of someone he knew well. Adjusting his brown leather bomber jacket, covering what looked like a pink lipstick kiss on his neck he walked to the counter, bought a bottle of sparkling water and with it now in his hand walked over, sitting down with Cindy, huddling together in some sort of conspiratorial conversation.

'He'll recognise you,' Lilith whispered. The spiky-haired woman shook her head.

'Doubtful,' she replied casually, watching the couple

intently. 'I didn't look like this the last time we argued. I hadn't been touched by the *Gods* back then.'

'But Cindy will!' Lilith was nervous, but the spiky-haired woman placed a hand on Lilith's own.

'Cindy might know *of* me,' she whispered. 'But she's never spoken *to* me. I'm just a footnote in his pillow stories.'

She thought for a moment.

'You think they did it?' she asked. 'Killed him and took his hand?'

'I didn't know she knew him,' Lilith muttered nervously. 'He was in the room. With Rupert. They were...' the sentence trailed off as Lilith shuddered.

'The video would have affected him too,' she said. 'He wasn't supposed to be there.'

'But he was,' the spiky-haired woman shrugged. 'He was trying to find his way out. Maybe she sent him.'

Lilith glanced back at the woman. 'I didn't send it to his wife,' she said. 'Did you?'

The woman snorted. 'I should have sent it everywhere,' she replied. 'But honestly, I didn't send it directly to her.'

Lilith looked at the table, noting the use of the word *directly*. 'If they're going against the pact, if they're looking at breaking the curse.'

'If that's the case, they picked the wrong piece to cut off,' the woman almost laughed. 'Because the hand sure as hell doesn't save them from me.'

'You?'

'Of course. *I'm* the curse.' The woman looked away. 'Does Lucy know the hand is gone?'

Lilith nodded.

'The news mentioned it. But they just focused on the juicier stuff, like how he'd just been suspended and all that.'

'Are you happy about that?' The woman asked. Lilith shrugged.

'I thought I would be,' she replied. 'Until he died.'

'That's not down to you though.'

'What if it is? Christ, Jules, we destroyed his academic career! Maybe he decided there was no way out?'

She paused.

'What if Lucy *did something* to him?'

'Like what?'

'I don't know! You've seen she can get in your head, make you second guess yourself. You should know, you taught her! Maybe she told him to hang himself!'

Lilith sipped at her coffee, the cup shaking now.

'I don't think she'd do that, and it doesn't really work that way,' the spiky-haired woman pursed her lips as she thought. 'But now he's gone, what's Lucy's plan now?'

'She keeps changing her mind,' Lilith admitted. 'Originally it was all about revenge, but then he died and now she's convinced she's going to be blamed for it. If what she planned led him to hang himself, she could be up for manslaughter. That's not just a custodial fine.'

The two women sat in silence for a moment. Across the coffee shop, John and Cindy spoke in hushed, nervous tones.

'There's something wrong with Rupert's hand, and it's not magical,' the spiky-haired woman pondered. 'Lucy knows this, and I can't see her cutting it off for a keepsake. So, we need to stop whatever *those two* over there are planning.'

'So go over and confront them,' Lilith leaned back, getting angry now. 'You know if you turn up, he'll back down. I've heard the stories, how he always did.'

'Because there were four of us back then, four people who would be affected by each other's actions,' the woman replied. 'Now, with Rupert dead and Miriam gone, there's only two. And we know that prick would happily see others suffer with the curse. He's got nobody left to worry about.'

'His wife's definitely divorcing him?'

'Wouldn't you? After what you saw on that footage?'

Lilith paled. 'We didn't know she was connected,' she whispered.

Across the coffee shop John leaned in, kissing Cindy, before rising and leaving. Cindy waited a minute before pulling out her phone and texting, climbing out of her seat, finishing her drink as she stood beside the table, and then walking out without a backward glance at the two women watching her.

Lilith's phone beeped.

Without the spiky-haired woman noticing, Lilith glanced down at the new text from Cindy.

You know my secret now. But I also know yours. 10pm, the usual spot.

'Problem?' The spiky-haired woman asked. Lilith forced a smile.

'Arranging a date,' she smiled.

'With that man again? He's too young for you.'

Lilith smiled.

'I really like this one, and there's only a few years' difference,' she said. 'You've seen him, what do you think?'

The spiky-haired woman shrugged.

'I think seeing him is terrible for you,' she replied.

LUCY SHRIMPTON, ALSO KNOWN AS MARIE WILSON, STOOD ON the Westbound platform of the Mile End Central Line, surrounded by other commuters, the folded up Brompton bike in her hand. It was raining, and she hated cycling in the rain. Besides, she'd only brought the bike today because she had to go to Greenwich Park—and that had been a blowout. The police were staying quiet, and she could only fit in the tiniest of escape plans into the day. Still, the Underground might be cramped but at rush hour it was far easier to catch a tube to Holborn than cycle in the rain right now.

The reason for her melancholy wasn't because of Rupert's death; she didn't care about that. Whatever happened, he deserved everything he got, *eye for an eye* style. It was because she knew that when they worked out who she truly was and what he'd truly been doing, they'd not only take her in for *murder* but most likely *treason,* too.

The old detective at the University, when she'd played the loyal daughter, had explained they were still looking for the hand, but it was Monday now, so God only knew where the damn thing was now.

But Lucy knew someone had deliberately taken it and left with it that night, which meant that they knew exactly what it held. Rubbing at her own hand, unconsciously stroking the crescent-shaped scar on it, she nodded to herself.

She didn't need the hand. She had her own.

Lost in thoughts, she wasn't ready for the voice that spoke from behind her.

'Don't turn around,' the voice, a man's, said.

Lucy nodded. She knew the voice. It was the slightly accented voice of the *Consortium.*

'Hello Yossi,' she said, staring straight ahead, hoping that when the train arrived, she wasn't going to be pushed in front of it.

'You don't have it, do you?' Yossi, otherwise known as the *Consortium* said, still close to her ear. Lucy shook her head.

'I assumed you had it,' she guessed. There was a shifting of weight behind her, and the lack of an answer showed she was correct.

Only two of you knew where you went that night, she thought to herself. *Which one of you gave it up, and for what?*

'I don't mean *that*,' the voice was harsh, spoken quickly. 'I want the *location*.'

Lucy stared straight ahead, now convinced she was about to be thrown in front of the train.

'I don't know what he promised you,' she replied honestly. 'I was never part of the meetings.'

'He promised me riches,' Yossi said, his tone sounding more angry than regretful. 'And your father promised me salvation.'

So 'he' was someone else, Lucy almost nodded at this. *Yossi's been talking to John.*

'Which of those do you want?' she asked carefully.

'I don't know what I want anymore,' the voice was soft, confused for a moment. 'Maybe I should just jump off the cliff, let the sea take me...' Before Lucy could comment on this, the strength and anger returned to it. 'There is no discussion. The deal needs to be completed by the end of the month.'

'What deal!' Lucy was confused now. 'Rupert never told me—' she stopped, realising what he'd said.

Maybe I should just jump off the cliff, let the sea take me.

Lucy didn't want to think what this meant. But she had to know.

'Where's the watchtower?' she asked casually.

'On—on the cliff,' the *Consortium* replied, almost automatically.

Lucy felt a trickle of fear slide down her back.

Oh, you stupid bloody witch.

'I'll see what I can do but you have to give me time,' she said, continuing the conversation. 'The police are looking for answers, and I'm the obvious target.'

She strained to glimpse Yossi out of the corner of her eye as she looked down the platform, trying to get an idea of his temperament, but all she saw was his bald head with a scar on his temple in a blur of motion.

'Look, do what you want with the hand. That was his business,' she muttered.

'It was family business. And are you not family?'

'No,' Lucy replied firmly. 'And you bloody well know that.'

'He left everything to you, including his debts. Including the *curse.*' The *Consortium's* voice shifted, as if he was adjusting position. To the right, Lucy could see her train approaching.

He's preparing to push me.

'My mum worried about the curse,' she said firmly. 'The curse should worry about *me.*' And, with that, she spun around to face her mystery companion, only to find the tiled wall of the platform facing her. Ten yards further on down the platform, she saw a bald-headed man in a camel coat duck out through the exit to the Hammersmith and City Line. Yossi Shavit had obviously decided chat time was over.

By now the tube had arrived and, grabbing her bike in one hand, she stepped into the carriage, on her way into central London, already tapping on her phone.

Someone had got to the *Consortium*. And Lucy knew it was a bad idea to play with them.

She needed help, and *fast.*

JOHN GALE STARED AT THE *MOTHERSTONE*. IT WAS EVENING now, three whole days since they had found Rupert here. In a way, it felt like he was still around.

'Are you?' John spoke aloud, looking around him as he did so. 'Did you find your peace at the end?'

Walking up to the megalithic rock fountain, John placed a hand on it, feeling the cold stone under his fingers. Miriam always claimed that it was a hot stone, that the energy was strong and deep within, but even though John had believed this fully back then, he now believed he'd just been caught up in the moment.

Magic was for children's shows and kids' movies.

John glanced around again as the thought popped into his mind, almost as if he was guilty for thinking such a thing.

'If you are here, I'm sorry you're dead,' he muttered to the stone. 'Now it leaves me and Julie-Anna, and since the zap she's become mental.'

He felt a rustling of wind past his cheek, as if it was caressing him.

'I don't believe,' John whispered. And then, louder and more determined, '*I don't believe.*'

He took a deep breath.

'I don't believe in this anymore. I don't believe in the curse anymore.'

He looked at his hand, where, across the palm, was a very faint scar.

'I've left the Library alone for a quarter of a century. I spent years looking for it, and when I found it, I agreed to let it stay hidden. I took a crappy stone blade and my reputation being destroyed as payment. And then this month, with the footage coming out, showing what we did...'

He looked around, ensuring he was still alone.

'No more,' he hissed loudly, walking from the stone and standing in the path crossroads. 'This Beltaine, I'll return and gain my treasures. Damn the curse and *damn Julie-Anna.*'

He stood, as if expecting to be struck by lightning, his eyes shut tight just in case. And then, slowly, he opened one eye, looking around.

A lone raven stared at him from the branch of a tree.

'Tell Odin I still believe in him,' John chuckled as the raven flew off.

Breathing in the evening air, John looked back to the *Motherstone*, his anger and frustration now passed.

'I'm sorry that you died,' he whispered. 'I didn't mean things to go that far, but you should have just *told* me.'

This last apology stated out into the evening, John Gale brushed some leaves off the *Motherstone* as if thinking by tidying it, he could stave off some retribution and then walked off, back towards Blackheath.

8

ESOTERIC LECTURES

DECLAN HADN'T MEANT TO STAY IN LONDON AFTER THE Monday shift ended, but De'Geer had mentioned that he was going to a lecture that evening that could help possibly with the case itself, and as Anjli was still moving in and hadn't yet spent time on her own in the house, Declan thought she could do with a night alone so he passed her the keys to the Audi and explained he'd either catch a train home, or share a bike ride with De'Geer.

That said, Anjli was working with Billy on CCTV footage, and Declan expected her to still be in the office when he returned later that evening.

De'Geer had changed into normal clothing, claiming that the last thing he wanted to do was show up in police uniform and fail somehow to merge into the background, but then the clothes he'd chosen; biker trousers, jacket and boots, topped off with a band tee-shirt of someone called *'Five-Finger Death Punch'* still made the seven foot blond Viking stand out a little. Declan, meanwhile, made the singular effort of blending in by removing his tie. And, planning to grab a deli sandwich on the way, Declan and De'Geer walked out of Temple Inn, taking a gentle walk to Holborn Station and a pub a few doors down called the *Princess Louise*, where the talk was taking place in an upstairs room.

'Rupert was supposed to be talking there tonight,' De'Geer explained as they walked up the Kingsway, Declan munching on a peri-peri chicken sandwich. 'I saw an advert for it in the window of the *Atlantis Bookshop* earlier today.'

'Surely they'd have cancelled it?' Declan was surprised at this, but De'Geer shook his head.

'I checked the Facebook Group, and they've turned it into some kind of memorial,' he explained. 'Which means people telling stories about Rupert. Friends turning up to pay respects.'

Declan nodded, seeing where De'Geer was going with this. 'We might find our killer here, or at least someone who might know them,' he said, finishing his sandwich and throwing the wrapping into a bin. 'Good catch. What was the talk supposed to be about?'

'Something about lost treasure in Greenwich,' De'Geer checked his phone, where the details of the event were saved. 'The blurb for the event said he was going to break open the conspiracy that Greenwich Park had sat on for years.'

'PR talk,' Declan muttered. 'They wanted bums on seats.'

'I'm not sure,' De'Geer replied as they turned onto High Holborn. 'He spoke about it a few times at the end of lectures. He was angry, frustrated, and I think he'd decided to tell the world something he'd been holding back.'

'Interesting that he died three days before this,' Declan raised an eyebrow. 'Maybe someone didn't want him telling the world, breaking open the conspiracy.'

They found the room where the event was being held via

a staircase at the back of the bar, one that brought Declan and De'Geer up into a large open function room, a bar running along most of the left side and windows covering the far wall. The theme was cream and mahogany, with a burgundy carpet softening the steps of the people in the room and filled with tables and chairs. A small space beside the bar had been cleared, most likely for the speaker. Declan and De'Geer paid the five-pound entry fee, informed that this was mainly to cover the room hire, and found a table to sit at in the room's corner, De'Geer then going to the bar to grab a Guinness for Declan and a lime and soda for himself, as he was still riding home later. Returning to the table and placing the drink in front of his boss, De'Geer smiled.

'It's about five minutes before the talk starts,' he said. 'What shall we talk about?'

This was what Declan had been dreading, talking to De'Geer. It always ended on bikes, and he couldn't take the patronising looks from the Viking motorcycle fanatic anymore.

'Anything but bikes,' he said, sipping at his pint. 'I've already apologised for my rubbish Suzuki.'

De'Geer laughed. 'Guv, the Suzuki Marauder isn't a rubbish bike,' he replied. 'And the 125cc one still looks good, gets you from A to B and, more importantly, doesn't look like a scooter.'

He shuddered, as if the thought of scooters scared him, as he finished.

'If you ever want to try my bike—'

'I think my bike days are over,' Declan smiled. 'It was a means to an end, and I enjoy being dry in the rain.'

De'Geer nodded.

'I get that,' he admitted, looking around the room,

deciding to change the subject. 'I see a couple of people from my course here, but nobody else I recognise.'

'I do,' Declan nodded at the bar, where a woman with black and red hair stood. 'That's Lucy Shrimpton. I think she's Miriam's daughter.'

He rose from his chair.

'I'm just going to have a chat with her.'

'Please don't arrest her before the talk starts,' De'Geer almost pleaded. 'I really want to see what people say.'

Declan smiled, and Guinness in hand, walked to the bar, and the now nervous Lucy Shrimpton.

'Miss Shrimpton,' he said cordially. Lucy nodded warily.

'Detective,' she replied.

'Declan, please,' Declan placed his pint on the bar counter. 'I'm off work right now.'

'I thought you CID types were never off the clock?' she asked. Declan shrugged.

'Depends on the case.'

'And that the victim of the case is being talked about here, tonight, at a talk venue that I've never seen you at?'

Declan smiled sheepishly. 'Okay then, I am working. A little.' He nodded to De'Geer. 'Although one of my men is a little nervous as he *is* off duty.'

'Yeah, I've seen Thor over there before,' Lucy smiled back. 'So, did you need more about Greenwich?'

'I might do,' Declan nodded, watching the organisers as they glanced in his direction. 'More on his friends. Was Miriam your mother?'

Lucy nodded. 'She knew Rupert well,' she admitted. 'But she won't be answering questions. She died just over a year ago.'

'Sorry to hear that,' Declan replied. 'Can I ask how? Professional habit.'

'Believe it or not, lightning hit her but at the time she had terminal bone cancer anyway, so it was a matter of time and a coin toss. Probably a better outcome, really,'

Lucy sipped at a drink that looked like coke but had a distinct coconut smell to it.

'Cancer came with her job, unfortunately.'

'Which was?' Declan was surprised at the answer. Most cancers didn't have employment related issues.

'Classified,' Lucy said. 'Sorry.'

Declan took a sip of his Guinness, allowing the awkward moment to pass.

'Well, I'm sorry for your loss,' he said. 'I'll leave you to it.'

He turned to leave, but stopped.

'One thing,' he said. 'When we spoke earlier, you were talking about seeing someone with me, and I kinda zoned out. I wanted to apologise.'

'No need,' Lucy smiled but, like before, it felt forced. As if she was enduring this conversation. 'People find grief in many forms. I hope you get past yours.'

'Did you get past yours?' Declan asked, adding when Lucy stared confused at him, 'your mother?'

'She wasn't a great mother,' Lucy tried to smile, as if making a joke. 'But the grieving is a work in process.'

Declan paused again before continuing.

'How did you know?' he asked. 'About Kendis?'

'Was she the love?' Lucy shrugged. 'I received the message.'

'No, really,' Declan moved closer again. 'You spoke of things that nobody should know.'

'That's par for the course,' Lucy nodded. 'I know you want

me to go 'ta-dahh' and show you how the sausage is made but there's no answer to that question. Not every case can be solved, detective.'

'So you never read about me in the paper?'

Lucy shook her head. 'No, I've definitely seen you in the paper but never to the extent of learning about your love life.'

She thought for a moment.

'You should see a medium,' she said. 'See if anything else—'

'I'll pass on that,' Declan nodded, leaving Lucy Shrimpton alone now as he walked back to the table, De'Geer watching him.

'That didn't seem like a fun conversation,' he said.

'A bit too close for comfort,' Declan replied. And it was— in the last few months Declan had lost his father and his first love in quick succession. Luckily for him, though, he'd found the bastards responsible for both and punished them.

Was that what Lucy Shrimpton was doing? Punishing the person who caused her mother's death?

Declan scratched at his chin as he watched Lucy, now talking to a bald, bearded Asian man at the bar.

'Just a gut feeling that there's more going on here,' he replied, shaking it off. 'Anyone else here you recognise? Wilson's assistant, perhaps, the one that spoke to Monroe?'

'Never saw her,' De'Geer admitted. 'He had me go to Deptford while he went to Mile End. I think he's still scared of people being with him when he's there.'

Declan agreed with this; Monroe had history in Mile End, especially with Johnny and Jackie Lucas, the 'Twins' of the East End. It was a history that Tom Marlowe, Monroe's almost-nephew had alluded to when he gave Declan a USB stick with data about Monroe's past on, a USB stick that

Declan had ordered Billy to destroy. The last thing he needed to know was Monroe's past in Globe Town, or even what Monroe was worried about people seeing there.

Globe Town. Which was on the Dee Line.

Declan almost laughed. He was getting spooked by bloody map coordinates now.

At the bar, the Asian man with the beard was waving for silence. The crowd, gathered mainly at tables drinking, quietened down.

'Thanks for coming, everyone,' the man said. 'I know this is a talk we'd all looked forward to and that Rupert's death is something that has affected us all.'

There was a mumbling at this and Declan thought he sensed a slight discomfort from a couple by the window, a man and woman, the man sitting with his arms folded.

'Tonight we've decided that rather than cancelling, we should instead turn it into an opportunity for healing, a memorial to Professor Wilson's work.'

'Nonce,' the man by the window finally muttered, his accent sounding European. It was a single word, possibly intended for his companion, but it cut through the room like a knife.

Realising he was now the centre of attention, the man continued.

'He was a nonce,' he insisted. 'Rupert groomed students. Did things with them. At his age.'

'He was no such thing,' another man, long-haired, with giant grommets in his earlobes, extending them out rose angrily. 'He did nothing wrong.'

'Oh yes?' the European skeptic asked. 'Then why did the University suspend him?'

'That wasn't because of his liking for younger women!'

Grommet man argued. 'Rupert taught university students. Many of them were post grads or mature. He didn't have a single girl in his class under twenty. And that's not illegal.'

'It's disgusting,' the European rose, his anger now visible. 'What he *did* was disgusting. I have a child that age and I have a father his age. How is that acceptable?'

The Asian man waved a hand.

'What consenting adults do together is their own business,' he said. 'I think you've said enough, you've shown you don't want to help heal tonight and so I think you should leave.'

'Oh yeah?' The European stumbled a little as he looked around, and Declan realised for the first time that he was drunk. 'Come on then, show me out.'

'If you do not leave quietly, it will force me to ask the police to restrain and arrest you,' the Asian man replied as he looked directly at Declan and De'Geer. 'They're sitting right there, so they've seen everything.'

As Declan looked at the others in the room, now staring at him, he wondered how the hell the organiser had guessed that he was police; *did he really give off 'police vibes'?* De'Geer's rock god disguise wouldn't have given it away, so it had to be Declan. *Maybe it was when Lucy had spoken to him?*

However, he was surprised to see De'Geer nod at this and rise.

'It's not like it's the first time I've had to tell you to leave, Sven,' he said, to a smattering of nervous laughter. 'And again I see you have had too many before the talk even starts.'

The European, mortified, nodded at this, grabbing his jacket and meekly walking out.

'Sorry, Morten,' he mumbled. 'Sorry everyone.'

De'Geer nodded back to the Asian as he sat back down.

'Sorry,' he whispered to Declan. 'I should have mentioned that they know I'm City Police. Michael's asked for my help a couple of times.'

'Yeah, that would have been nice to know,' Declan replied as the Asian, now apparently named Michael, smiled at the group.

'Now, with that unfortunate interaction aside, I ask that, as you tell your stories, you remember that Marie Wilson is here, so let's keep it to pleasant ones, right?'

The audience murmured agreement to this as Declan looked around the room. Monroe had spoken to Marie Wilson earlier that day; it seemed incredulous that both she and Lucy Shrimpton would both be at this event. But, as he tried to work out which of the women in the room was most likely to be the candidate, Lucy stepped forward.

'Thanks, Michael,' she breathed. 'I know Rupert would have appreciated this. Even Sven being his usual dickhead self.'

She glanced at Declan as she spoke.

'Tonight we talk about my father,' she continued. 'Tonight we tell stories. Will they be true? Unlikely. But they will be epic.'

She raised her glass.

'Skol!'

As the gathering in the room grabbed their glasses, shouting back the toast in force, rising to their feet and blocking Declan's view, he rose also, trying to spy Marie Wilson, or rather Lucy Shrimpton, by the bar. But she wasn't there anymore; in fact, she was nowhere to be seen, having left the room through the entrance to the stairs.

'Back in a moment,' he said as he ran out of the function

room, knocking over several glasses of half-filled drinks as he did so. 'Stay here and listen.'

Running down the stairs into the main bar, he couldn't see Marie anywhere; a part of his mind wondered if she'd simply needed a call of nature, and he was making too much out of this but the door to the pub opened, and a familiar figure entered the bar, looking over his shoulder as he did so.

'What man?' he was saying as, turning to the bar, he faced Declan.

'Oh, hello,' he said. 'DI Walsh, right?'

Declan smiled at Simon Tolley.

'I think you're late for the talk,' he said. 'Was that Marie Wilson leaving?'

Simon opened and shut his mouth a few times.

'I think so,' he eventually replied. 'I don't know her that well. Is she in trouble?'

But Declan wasn't listening, already running out of the pub. As he exited, he saw, across the road, Lucy running East towards Southampton Place, some kind of folded device in her hand, most likely the bike that she had in Greenwich.

'Lucy!' Declan shouted. 'Stop!'

He went to run after her but a group of beefy looking men in their twenties, men who'd been drinking and smoking outside, blocked his way.

'She said she was being stalked,' the lead man said. 'Said that she was scared.'

'You should stop scaring girls,' the second beefy drink continued. 'Or we'll call the police.'

'*I am the bloody police!*' Declan snapped as he pulled out his warrant card, waving it at them all. 'Now get out of my bloody way!'

Admonished and confused, the wall of muscled men

melted away as Declan ran across High Holborn, entering Southampton Place and the three storey Georgian Town-houses that lined the sides of the row, continuing up to the end, where the street joined with the A40, with Bloomsbury Gardens on the other side.

Where Lucy now stood.

'I'm sorry,' she shouted. 'I should have told you, but I need to fix everything before you take me in.'

'Fix what?' Declan couldn't cross; the cars were still pass-ing. Lucy, meanwhile, was turning her folded device into a bike.

'He wasn't my dad,' Lucy replied. 'I pushed him too far and what he truly was came out.'

'What?' Declan raised a hand, taking a gamble and step-ping into the road, the cars finally stopping. But by now Lucy was already on the bike, foot on the pedal.

'The Great Beast,' she said, kicking off and riding it off into the park at full speed.

Furious, Declan hissed to himself as he chased after her, realising halfway through Bloomsbury Park that she was long gone. She could have gone any number of directions by now, and Holborn was a rat-run of streets and mews.

He'd known there was something wrong.

She'd faced him, calm as anything before leaving. She'd deliberately barred his way with drinkers giving toasts and burly men with pints.

She knew exactly what she was doing.

What Declan had to do now was work out *what it was* before she did it.

9

SECRETS AND LIES

With his quarry gone, the burly men at the entrance suitably admonished and Monroe calling him an *unfit bampot,* or something that sounded like that but was probably ruder when he called it in, Declan made his way back up to the talk, trying his best to sneak in through the back of the crowd but finding that the entire room stopped as he entered through the double glass doors.

As he faced the room of silent watchers, he felt a little flush.

Great. They all saw me chase the guest of honour out of the room.

He looked at Michael, watching him with interest from his perch beside the bar.

'Um, sorry,' Declan said. 'And sorry for the drinks I knocked over.'

He nodded to a couple of unimpressed women at another table.

'Instincts took over, you know?'

There was still a silence in the room, as if they expected

him to explain his actions. They obviously *didn't* know. Neither did Declan, scrabbling quickly for an answer to explain his actions just then.

De'Geer, catching his eye, glanced at the recently emptied chair by the window, and back.

'The Nonce guy,' Declan started awkwardly, understanding the clue and grabbing onto it like a lifeboat. 'Sven? Yes, Sven, he seemed angry about Rupert before he left, and during the toast I saw Marie Wilson leave, and I was worried he might confront her outside as it was only a minute later.'

'And you ran to protect her,' Michael smiled. 'Looks like the police are good guys after all.'

'Hey,' De'Geer shouted back, hurt. The room laughed, the tension of the moment now passed and Declan could return to the chair and his half-finished Guinness, as the next speaker started with a tale about Rupert Wilson at Wayland's Forge, whatever that was.

Still feeling eyes on him, Declan nodded a silent *thanks* at De'Geer before glancing across the room, staring at Simon Tolley, locking gazes with him.

Oh, we're having a chat after this finishes, mate, he thought as he took a sip. *You know way more than you're saying, don't you?*

LILITH BABYLON STOOD BESIDE THE HAWKSMOOR PYRAMID AND checked her watch for the fifteenth time that minute. It was five past the hour and the night was dark. Lilith shuddered, as if someone was walking over her grave; she hated being in Limehouse even at the best of times, but alone, in a churchyard? That was just asking for trouble.

Cindy was late.

Honestly? Cindy was always late. It was her 'thing'. But it didn't stop it being irritating. If she hadn't been on task, she'd have never made friends with the bloody woman.

There was a rustling, some footsteps from the back of the churchyard and, hand in pocket, Lilith held onto the small working knife she always carried with her. It was less than three inches in length but was sharp as hell. Anyone tried anything with her tonight, they'd get a slashed face.

Her hand released the blade when she recognised Cindy emerging from the shadows.

'Were you following me?' Cindy snapped, bypassing any greeting. Lilith crossed her arms.

'Of course I was,' she replied coldly. 'You've been acting suspicious all week. And now I find you're with *him?*'

'Are you shocked?' Cindy smiled but it was humourless. 'Probably as shocked as I was when I saw you with *her.*'

There was a long moment of silence in the graveyard.

'She said you wouldn't know her,' Lilith replied.

'Well she was a bloody idiot for thinking that,' Cindy folded her arms. 'I've seen the photos. She's not difficult to recognise, even with the—' she made a waving motion to her hair.

'So we have secrets,' Lilith stated. 'We both lied to Rupert.'

She looked at the pyramid.

'Why do we meet here, anyway?' she asked. 'Bloody place gives me the creeps.'

'Because Rupert liked it. And we always did what he asked,' Cindy said, as if it was the most obvious thing in the world.

'Including bodysnatching,' Lilith said, watching Cindy for a reaction. There wasn't one.

'We need to come clean,' she continued. 'They'll work out it was us. We should turn ourselves in, tell them the truth.'

'Sure,' Cindy looked at her watch. 'Which truth would you like to tell them?'

'That we'd made a pact with him and agreed to place him there for his last night,' Lilith replied. Cindy nodded.

'And how do we explain the hand?'

'That's not our fault!' Lilith exclaimed. 'All we did was transport! That's all we need to tell them!'

'We both did more than transport, and you know it.'

Lilith froze, scared of what Cindy was saying. 'I don't know what you mean.'

'I mean, we both guided him to where he ended,' Cindy nodded. 'Whether or not we meant him to die.'

And then, without even a goodbye, Cindy turned and walked out of the graveyard, leaving Lilith alone once more.

They'd never really been friends, she thought to herself. *They'd only met through Rupert. And now he was gone, there was no point in continuing to pretend there was anything there. And Cindy, your taste in men is terrible—*

'I see she's still a cold bitch,' a female voice spoke from the other side of the pyramid, as Lucy emerged from the shadows.

'How long have you been there?' Lilith asked, surprised at the revelation.

'Long enough to hear you compare stories,' Lucy nodded. 'Good plan, coming clean before they find you. Makes you look innocent.'

'We *are* innocent,' Lilith snapped back. Lucy raised an eyebrow, visible in the moonlight.

'I'm really impressed that you can say that with a straight face,' she replied. Because we both know that you sure as hell aren't blameless here.'

Lilith went to angrily reply, but then stopped and nodded.

'So what's the plan?' she asked. 'I take it you still have the hand?'

'If I answered that, you'd be an accessory,' Lucy smiled.

'To *what?*' Lilith half-shouted into the night. 'It's over! He's dead!'

Lucy looked across the graveyard now, choosing her words. 'He started a chain of events that I have to stop,' she said. 'We made his legacy and now I have to end it, especially as we didn't know that *he* would be there too.'

'And what does that mean?' Lilith sighed. 'Always bloody riddles! You're as bad as he was!'

'It'll all become clear soon, Auntie,' Lucy leaned against the pyramid, finally relaxing as the cold stone cooled her.

'I'll ensure that everyone learns their place in the narrative.'

———

THE TALK HAD CONTINUED FOR OVER AN HOUR, WITH ALMOST everyone in the room adding to the list of stories about Rupert Wilson. Even De'Geer gave a story about Rupert Wilson during one of his classes, and for the first time Declan realised how personal this case was to him, something he should have really worked out when the PC appeared on his front doorstep on a Sunday lunchtime.

As everyone rose, a couple of older drinkers thanking Declan for trying to *help* Lucy, Declan nodded to Simon, silently showing that he should come over to their table before they both came over to him.

Reluctantly, Simon rose from his own table and walked over.

'Want to tell me what happened outside?' Declan asked.

'I was late,' Simon said, his voice low and conspiratorial. 'I saw Lucy outside the pub, talking to some blokes, smoking. I assumed she was cadging a fag from them, but as I approached, she was already off. I said hello but she replied she couldn't talk as *the man was coming*. I asked what man, and then bumped into you.'

'You know her well?'

Simon shook his head. 'Only in passing. I'm...' he looked around, blushing.

'I'm dating her aunt,' he mumbled.

'I've got a problem here,' Declan shook his head, pursing his lips. 'You claim not to know Rupert Wilson, but here you are at his memorial, telling me you're dating Marie Wilson's aunt, which makes him, as her father the brother of the person you're seeing? Brother-in-law? You see why I'd suspect your testimony earlier, especially after you were in the same spot where he was laid to rest?'

Simon paled, raising his hands.

'No, no,' he protested quickly. 'Lucy ain't Rupert's daughter. She's Miriam's daughter. It's complicated.'

'So un-complicate it.'

'She thought Rupert was her dad for most of her life, even if her mum forbade her to meet with him,' Simon explained. 'She took the surname in her teens just to piss her mum off. When Miriam knew she was dying, she came clean, said dad was someone else.'

'And that someone else was?'

Simon looked uncomfortable. 'Alés Capioca.'

'And the aunt?'

'Alexandra Capioca. Although she started calling herself Lilith recently.'

Declan looked at De'Geer, who shrugged, unfamiliar with either name. Declan noted the names down and looked back to Simon.

'And you're here completely by chance?'

'No, I was sent here,' Simon pointed around the room. 'The *Ghost Bros* YouTube channel's risen in likes and subscribes, yeah? We went viral after the news came out. And Alfie genuinely believes that doing some kind of tribute to Rupert Wilson might gain some serious numbers, some-thing to keep things ticking along until the police--' he made some kind of motion with his hands, as if indicating to Declan for the purposes of this story, Declan and De'Geer were playing the part of all police, '—allowed us to use the footage.'

Declan looked around the room, seeing that several people were sitting at tables watching them, as if waiting for Simon to finish and speak to them instead.

'These are interviews?' Declan indicated them. Simon nodded.

'Swear to god, mate, I didn't know Lucy would be here. I forgot she's still calling herself Wilson in public.'

'And why is that?' De'Geer asked. Simon shrugged.

'Buggered if I know,' he said. 'And the Greenwich thing? Just a coincidence, I promise. I already said, we had a fall through, venue wise, and I remembered Greenwich as an option. Look, can I go now? I need to get these filmed quickly as I have an early start tomorrow.'

Declan nodded and Simon rose from the table, walking

over to another and sitting down, already with his phone out and filming the interviewee sitting opposite him.

'You think he's telling the truth?' De'Geer asked. 'About Greenwich?'

'I think we need to check into it,' Declan replied. 'It's way too convenient and I'm too old to believe in tooth fairies and coincidences.'

Declan was about to continue, but found Michael, the organiser now took the chair that Tolley had vacated.

'Thanks for coming,' he said to De'Geer. 'Sorry for outing you both.' He looked at Declan, offering his hand. 'Michael Bao. I run this place for my sins.'

Declan took the offered hand. 'DI Declan Walsh,' he replied. 'Sorry for spilling people's drinks.'

'You gave them something to talk about,' Michael smiled. 'And one thing pagans and esoteric love, is to talk about things. Now, I'm guessing you came because of Rupert?'

Declan nodded. 'We can't work out why the hand was cut off,' he replied. 'We have theories, like hands of glory and revenge attacks, but there seems to be more here that we're not hearing.'

Michael nodded. 'That's because there is,' he replied. 'Mystics are a secretive bunch. And we're also fantastic at holding grudges.'

He looked out of the door.

'Sven will hold his for years,' he smiled.

'We think it's connected to some lost library,' De'Geer continued. 'And Rupert—Professor Wilson had hinted he had some big reveal about Greenwich Park in his talk. Did you know what it was?'

'I know that was the grudge Rupert held,' Michael nodded. 'He spent years fighting Greenwich Park, mainly for access into the Naval College and for a comprehensive seismic study of the north of the park.'

'Why would someone do that?' Declan asked.

'They'd do it if they were hunting for treasure,' Michael tapped the side of his nose.

'But I thought he found the treasure?' Declan frowned. 'Are you saying that he didn't?'

'I'm not saying *they* didn't at all, just that perhaps *Rupert* didn't,' Michael smiled. 'Rupert never played well with others unless they were idolising him.'

'Pardon my language but everything I hear about Rupert Wilson makes me think he was a bit of a tosser,' Declan commented.

'Oh, of the highest order,' Michael nodded. 'But then so was Wheatley, Gardner, Crowley... And of course, at the end he seemed to bear strong connections there.'

'Connections?'

Michael nodded. 'He believed Crowley was talking to him from beyond the veil,' he replied.

'The Great Beast on speed dial,' De'Geer muttered.

'Sorry, the Great Beast?'

'A nickname for Aleister Crowley,' Michael smiled. 'Man loved his PR.'

Declan thought back to Lucy's last words.

'He wasn't my dad, I pushed him too far and what he truly was came out. The Great Beast.'

Michael was still talking.

'I suppose all of us have our 'tosser' sides, as you so accurately put it.'

Michael leaned in, ensuring he wasn't being watched.

'Look, I'm not one to play sides,' he said softly, 'but I was around in the nineties. And back then, Rupert was shouting from the rooftops about how bloody clever he was and how everything had been stolen from him, Julie-Anna was shagging anything that moved because of her newfound notoriety, and John was working out who he could sell anything to, claiming it was 'lost treasure'.'

'You missed Miriam.'

Michael shook his head. 'Ah, she wasn't the same as them. She kept her head down, never said a thing, and over the years the rumours spread, rumours that Miriam was the one that found the treasure, not the others. And if that was the case, what were the other three doing? And then a year after the bloody disaster of a press conference where someone died, and the Royal Park threatened court proceedings, they all clam up, cut their hands and bind themselves together. Who does that?'

'Who died?'

'Student of Rupert's,' Michael replied. 'Alex someone I think, I can't remember.'

Declan wrote the name down. 'So who's the best person to ask?' he said. Michael looked at the two men that faced him and shrugged.

'John,' he replied. 'He's the only one left.'

'Julie-Anna still lives,' Declan contested.

'That woman's been dead for a year,' Michael shook his head.

'That can't be right,' Declan argued. 'We have a website, an address for her.'

'I'm sure you do,' Michael rose from the table. 'But I stick to my words. Julie-Anna Watson died a year ago and I have no idea what the hell *that* woman is.'

Yossi Shavit rubbed a hand over his shaven head, letting it stop at the back of his neck as he rotated it, pushing into the tightness at the base of his skull. He was stressed; he knew the signs. Once this was over, he'd find a back cracker and get his back aligned.

Once this was over, he'd be able to do whatever he wanted.

Yossi chuckled at the thought. He was overweight, the years of solid muscle slowly melting into viscous fat around his midsection, and his once-bushy beard was gone, partly for disguise reasons, but mainly because of vanity. He was in his fifties now and the jet black of his hair was more white than black. Shaven, he looked a good ten years younger. He knew if he went back to the gym and picked up some weights again, he might even knock another five off.

The one thing he was grateful for was that his eyesight was still perfect, as he placed down the scalpel and picked up a pair of tweezers, placing them deep into the dead skin and twisting, trying to find purchase on the item within. With a small smile of success, Yossi pulled at the item he now held in the grip of the tweezers, feeling it slide out of its hidden position, now visible in the air as Yossi raised it up to the light. A small, thin tube, millimetres wide and smaller than a max strength flu tablet, the small microchip inside glinted in the light as he examined it.

Just as I remember, he thought to himself as he wiped it clean with an antibacterial wipe.

There was a faint sound in the distance, a car door closing. Glancing out of the window, Yossi saw a delivery driver walking towards his house, a bag filled with takeaway in his hand.

He smiled as he looked back at his table.

He could finish this later.

Wrapping the small pill-shaped tube in some kitchen roll, he took one last look at the severed hand on his desk before picking it up and tossing it into the wastepaper bin beside the desk.

He didn't need it anymore, and it was smelling.

The doorbell brought Yossi back to the present, and without a backward glance he left his study, leaving the small metal tube on the table.

He could always find the lock it worked on tomorrow.

10

THE NAME I'M KNOWN AS

'MEET MARIE WILSON,' MONROE STOOD IN FRONT OF THE team in the briefing room. Behind him, on the plasma screen, was the University ID of Rupert Wilson's assistant, her black and red hair visible in the photo. 'Or, as DS Kapoor and DI Walsh know her, Lucy Shrimpton.'

Anjli glared at the image on the plasma screen; Declan had explained to her the previous night about the eventful meeting in Holborn; in return, Anjli had explained how she would have caught Marie Wilson, and also the exact ways that she would gain revenge.

In *graphic* detail.

'I want the right to bring her in,' Anjli muttered to Monroe. 'And I want the right to use handcuffs that are just a little too tight.'

'I get why you're angry about this, we all are,' Monroe continued, looking to the room which this morning comprised Anjli, Declan, Billy, Davey, Doctor Marcos and De'Geer. 'What do we have on this woman so far?'

'Well, Guv, we know she spoke to DS Kapoor and DI

Walsh in the identity of 'Lucy', in which she claimed to only know Rupert Wilson in passing,' De'Geer said, reading from a notebook. 'Talked a lot about him, but as a member of the public. Then, half an hour later, she arrives at the University as 'Marie' and literally does a one hundred and eighty, telling you she's Rupert Wilson's daughter and that she's been at his constant side for months.'

'She's playing a game, alright,' Anjli muttered, pulling out her own notebook, filled with scribblings she'd received half an hour earlier on the phone. 'Apparently she changed her name by deed poll when she was sixteen.'

'To Wilson?'

'Aye,' Monroe tapped on the screen, and a birth certificate appeared. 'This is who she was beforehand. Lucinda Marie Shrimpton, better known as Lucy. We're yet to work out why she's changed it back.'

'Billy's great-uncle gave us names of people Rupert used to hang out with twenty, thirty years ago,' Declan read from his notebook. 'One of them was Miriam Shrimpton.' He pointed at the birth certificate on the screen. 'Lucy talked about her last night, said she died a year back. Of course, now we know she was lying from the start, that could all be lies too.'

Billy looked at the screen; on the certificate, it named the mother as Miriam Shrimpton, but the father's name was blank.

'Secret daughter?' Billy suggested.

'Possibly,' Monroe mused. 'Maybe mummy there didn't like the fact that Rupert was involved, and Lucy only changed her name when she was sixteen because she finally could?'

'Maybe she did it to spite her mum,' Anjli suggested, 'I was a right royal bitch when I was sixteen. All girls are.'

'Jess isn't that bad,' Declan protested. Anjli smiled.

'Still two weeks before she hits,' she replied. 'It'll happen. And you won't be ready.'

'He wasn't her father,' De'Geer looked up from his notes. 'DI Walsh and I spoke to Simon Tolley, who was also there. He claimed that Lucy's biological father was an Alés Capioca, and that she was only told this when her dying mother came clean.'

'And Tolley knows this how?' Doctor Marcos asked.

'He's apparently dating Alés Capioca's sister, an Alexandra Capioca,' Declan replied. 'I'm guessing she told him.'

'And he didn't tell you this earlier because?'

'We didn't know about Lucy then,' Declan admitted. 'We were only asking him about that night.'

He thought for a moment, remembering the night.

'When I chased after Lucy, she said she needed to fix everything before she was taken in, that he wasn't her dad and that she pushed him too far. She never named Rupert though, just called him the Great Beast instead,' he said.

Monroe nodded. 'Anything else said by her? Perhaps when she was whispering sweet nothings in your ear?'

Declan glanced at Anjli, now reddening. She was the only person who could have mentioned this to Monroe.

'It wasn't sweet nothings,' Declan explained reluctantly. 'It was... Well, it was weird. Anjli was checking the fountain, and Lucy started talking about the spirit of a *dark-haired woman,* with me, and taken from me too soon.'

'Kendis Taylor,' Monroe nodded. 'She cold-read you. Anyone whose read the papers in the last three months saw the whole thing play out. She knew you had a connection, she knew she died...'

'I'm not sure,' Declan shook his head. 'There was more, little things...'

'She said that she misses you, that you don't visit her anymore. She says that you should, that he's moved on now and they won't tell him. Do you understand?'

Declan didn't want to explain this; it was a moment in his life that nobody apart from Peter knew. And this was why he was thrown. *How did she know about this?*

'Well, either way, she left you staring at the trees for a good minute before Anjli woke you,' Monroe chuckled. 'Try to stay on the page for the rest of the case, aye laddie?'

'One more thing,' Declan tried to get the conversation back on track. 'When talking to the organiser later, he mentioned that Rupert Wilson believed Crowley was talking to him from beyond, well, the veil.'

'Wilson was hearing voices?' Davey looked at Doctor Marcos. 'That's new.'

'Billy, see if you can find any other occurrences of him hearing things,' Monroe nodded. 'In the meantime, we need to concentrate on Marie or Lucy or whatever her bloody name is.'

'So, we're picking her up?' Anjli asked.

'We will be, but rather than use uniforms, I thought we'd do it ourselves and do it properly,' Monroe nodded. 'This woman could be the person who killed Rupert Wilson, or even sat in the park at night and methodically sawed the hand off his dead body. That's not a wilting flower, or someone who's likely to come quietly.'

He scratched at his beard.

'And there's the fact that I want a peek at that office of his. Might even find his phone.'

Declan rose. 'I'm good to go now, Guv,' he said.

Monroe smiled.

'Look, I'm sure you want to get your own back here, but how about we wait first and let the University tell us when she comes in? We've got someone watching her house, but she didn't go home last night. You spooked her off when you chased after her.'

Monroe rubbed his beard.

'I think we might also need to have another look at Mister Tolley and see whether he knew more than he was letting on?'

'Oh, he definitely did, sir,' Billy looked up from his screen. 'After Declan mentioned seeing him, I've been having a check through the *Ghost Bros* wiki.'

'*Ghost Bros* has a wikipedia page?' Declan almost laughed.

'It's created by them,' Billy flashed a smile. 'But they talk about special guests on the show. You know, mediums, paranormal device builders, that sort of thing. Last year, they had a medium named Julie-Anna Watson, on a ghost walk in Wanstead.'

'Well, that's intriguing,' Monroe nodded. 'They know one *Musketeer*, are on speaking terms with the not-daughter of another, and were in the same location when his body was dumped?' he looked at Declan.

'I'm guessing Simon Tolley will be at work right now,' he said. 'Be a dear and bring the laddie here while we wait for Miss Shrimpton to appear.'

'One thing about Miss Watson,' Declan added. 'The guy who ran the event, he wasn't a fan of her. Said that she died a year ago, and whatever...'

He looked to De'Geer.

'How do I explain this?'

De'Geer read from his notes.

'He said that Julie-Anna Watson died a year ago, and he has no idea what the hell *that* woman is.'

'What or who?' Anjli asked.

'Definitely what,' Declan replied.

Monroe sighed.

'Why can't we have a nice simple case with gangsters or politicians,' he moaned. 'Does anyone else yearn for the good old days of gangsters or politicians?'

He rapped his knuckles on the desk.

'Where is his postal round?'

'North London, Guv. Tottenham.'

'Good. That's Declan's old stomping ground. Go in, pick him up, bring him here.' Monroe looked at Billy. 'And you can find me John Gale and Julie-Anna Watson, see if we can connect them to any of this.'

'I have Gale working as a features writer for *The Mail on Sunday,* if that helps,' Billy read from his screen. 'Arts section.'

He looked at Declan and Anjli.

'Well, what are you waiting for, a *full moon?*' he shouted. '*Get me a bloody postman!*'

SIMON TOLLEY HADN'T WANTED TO GO TO WORK TODAY. HE'D woken up with a feeling in the pit of his stomach that something *bad* was due to happen, a feeling he'd had since the Wilson memorial the previous night.

He hadn't wanted to go, but Alfie, bloody Alfie, had suggested that with the rising numbers this might be good press, and might even help them get the Greenwich footage back from the police.

Simon didn't think the police would *ever* give them back

the footage. And besides, *YouTube* wouldn't allow them to show a dead body on a vlog. There was that American YouTuber who had tons of hassle a few years back when they filmed a suicide found in a forest. Simon didn't want that kind of exposure at all. And neither did anyone else as Alfie had gone to his go-to *medium*, Jules, explaining that he wanted to do a seance episode in Greenwich, maybe even try to contact Rupert, and Simon's ears were still burning with the expletives she shouted at them before Alfie almost threw the phone at Simon and ran off. Jules had then turned her ire on him; they'd had a chat while on a break during the Wanstead episode a few months back, and he'd briefly introduced her to his girlfriend as she was leaving, but after that Jules seemed to go a complete one-eighty personality wise, refusing to continue and even going so far to demand that Simon deleted everything that wasn't relevant to the mediumship, including tales she'd told about her time as a semi-famous treasure hunter. She even threatened Simon, saying that if he told *anyone* the stories that she'd told him in private she'd *sue* him. Now, on the phone, she was like a woman possessed, once again telling Simon that if he *hadn't* deleted the videos, or if he *had* mentioned anything, especially to the police or that girl he introduced her to, she knew powerful men who could break his legs, and *how many postal workers could work with broken legs?*

At this last threat Simon had finally had enough, told the mad old bitch to do her worst and slammed the phone down.

Some people just weren't ready for prime time.

He'd gone to the event, and he'd spoken to the police.

But he hadn't talked about Julie-Anna Watson. He couldn't risk her being correct in her threats.

Simon had gone to bed that night concerned, but after

waking up had shaken the worry out of his head and, after showering, shaving and dressing, he left his flat and went to work. The advantage of being a postal delivery officer meant he could talk on the phone while doing his rounds; if the mad witch called again, he'd be able to speak to her instantly, and tell her she was overreacting.

As he turned onto the last road on his rounds, changing the podcast playing on his AirPods he looked down the street to see a blue Ford Mondeo at the end. Simon frowned, walking faster as he continued his rounds, seeing that the car was matching his speed, following him.

Stalking him.

He'd seen the car earlier on the rounds, but because of the route, he walked in a large triangle, and even if the driver was lost, there was no reason for it to be here now. He hadn't really seen the driver when he first saw the car; they had been nothing more than a shape. Someone bald, with what looked like a scar on their head.

The car, unaware of Simon's thought process, continued towards him down the street. Looking around, Simon decided he needed some help here, maybe a few witnesses to see that he wasn't imagining this. And, as he considered this, as if hearing his silent plea, salvation arrived in the form of a grey Audi, pulling up at a T-Junction on the other side of the road as two people, a man and a woman emerged from it. The woman, Indian with mid-length black hair was unknown to Simon, but the man was familiar, the Detective Inspector that he'd seen twice the previous day. He knew they were here for him, and that yet again he'd be stuck in a cell and questioned, but compared to the crazy person in the car following him, a cell was a far safer option.

The two detectives were watching him now, waiting for

him to approach, and the car was still getting closer. Simon knew he could try to run, to escape down some side roads and lose his stalker in Tottenham's rat-runs, but he wouldn't get far. He was pretty fit for a postie, but he didn't have stamina.

No, best to choose the lesser of two evils.

Waving to them, hoping the driver was too far away to see the detectives, Simon crossed the road.

He should have turned his AirPods off.

———

DECLAN AND ANJLI HAD BEEN GIVEN SIMON TOLLEY'S ROUTE from his manager; it was a simple one that involved three long streets that fed back onto each other off Turnpike Lane, which was handy as it could have been a labyrinth through an estate, or worse. They'd actually driven down two of the three roads already, finding Simon almost at the end of his route.

'Let me do the talking when we grab him,' Declan suggested. Anjli grinned.

'Yes, because you *always* give off *Good Cop* vibes,' she said as she climbed out of the car.

'I do too,' Declan protested as he joined her, parked at a T-Junction across from Simon, now visible as he continued to deliver letters. 'I'm a definite people person.'

'And how were those people last night when you hammered through them all, chasing Lucy?' Anjli grinned. 'De'Geer said that when you got back you had to pay for about a dozen spilt drinks.'

'It was only three, I was enthusiastic, and I apologised,' Declan waved across the road at Simon, catching his eye. 'I saw Monroe has a new suit on this morning, I hope that Doctor Marcos—'

He stopped as, in front of them a Ford Mondeo in metallic blue struck Simon Tolley full force on the side with a sickening crunch of bone.

As the body crashed to the ground, the car already driving off and turning a corner, Declan ran to the fallen Simon, ignoring the scattered letters as he dialled 999.

'This is DI Walsh!' he shouted into the phone, kneeling beside Simon, seeing that he was still alive, if only just. 'We need an ambulance at the junction of Westbury Ave and Mark Road, N22, immediately! Hit and run victim, probable internal bleeding and broken bones!'

As Declan gave the location again for confirmation, Anjli knelt beside Simon, now wide eyed, scared and with blood bubbling out of his mouth.

'Stay with me,' she commanded. 'You hear me? Stay with me, Simon. We're gonna get you through this.'

'Camera...' Simon wheezed. 'Wanstead... Driver...'

Anjli looked at Declan, shaking her head.

'If the ambulance isn't here soon, he's dead,' she whispered.

Declan looked at Simon, his eyes now closed, and his wheezing stopped.

'I think we might have passed that point already,' he replied, moving Anjli to the side as he started performing CPR on the lifeless body of Simon Tolley. 'Come on, Simon, don't do this to us, mate!'

I am not losing another, he thought as he rhythmically pushed onto the chest, using timed compressions to massage the heart. In the background, he could hear the siren of an ambulance. North Middlesex University Hospital was only a mile or so to the north east, and hopefully there was a local ambulance responding quickly.

'Come on you bastard!' he cried out. 'Not now!'

As if answering the call, Simon's eyes opened, and with a feeble groan, he coughed blood all over Declan's jacket. As Declan fell back, the ambulance pulling up with a screech and paramedics pushing him out of the way, Declan turned to Anjli, now looking down the road, on the phone herself.

'Metallic blue Ford Mondeo travelling south down West-bury Avenue. 2015 plate, driver was bald, possibly Caucasian, possibly male,' she announced, listening. 'Keep me in the loop.'

She disconnected the phone, finally glancing down at Declan.

'Christ,' she muttered. 'That's gonna be a bugger to dry clean.'

Declan couldn't help it. Covered in blood and with chaos all around him, he started to laugh.

11
————

IT COMPELS THEE

'You'll be happy to know that Simon Tolley is stable,' Monroe announced from his office door. 'He's still in a coma though, so if wishes were horses and all that.'

Declan sighed, leaning back in his chair. He was wearing a pair of regulation black trousers and a white shirt, stolen from the desk officer's back-up uniform while he waited for a quick turnaround dry clean. 'So what next?'

'Next?' Monroe stroked his beard. 'Next you stop waiting for a dry cleaner to call and go do your bloody job, laddie! Go find Julie-Anna whatshername or John thingie! Find these two mystery women we're still looking for! This case involves more than one duplicitous lassie with a name fetish!'

Monroe stormed back into his office as Declan glanced at Billy.

'Something I said?' he asked, shaking his head. 'What's got his goat?'

'Monroe hates being on the back foot,' Billy replied, still working as he spoke, staring up at the screens. 'And he's taking his frustrations out on himself, but using you as the proxy.'

'Oh, well then, I feel way better now,' Declan replied, rising from the desk. 'I'm going to speak to Alfie Wasley again, see if he knows anything.'

'Can I come?' Billy looked back from his station. Declan frowned.

'I thought you didn't like field work?'

'Yeah, but I've been watching the *Ghost Bro* videos, and I've really started to enjoy them,' Billy said. 'It's given me a new context to the characters, since we talked yesterday.'

'Christ, you've become a fan,' Declan sighed. Billy smiled.

'At least I got into them *after* we found a body in their possession,' he quipped. 'I hadn't been a fan for years before-hand or anything.'

Declan winced at the shot. He knew Billy was mocking his fandom of the *Magpies* series of books, a fandom that blinded him to the possibility that Tessa Martinez could have been a killer.

'Never fall for your heroes,' he stated. 'Now, find me—'

He stopped as Monroe leaned out of the door once more.

'University just called,' he said triumphantly. 'Marie Wilson clocked in just after four-thirty pm, so ten minutes ago.'

'This could be her going back to pick up things she needs. We might not have long,' Billy replied.

'Well then, grab your things and get over there,' Monroe smiled. 'All hands to the tiller right now. If we work hard and succeed in our jobs, we could have that little mare of a lassie back here by six.'

DECLAN HADN'T BEEN BACK TO QUEEN MARY UNIVERSITY SINCE
the Bernard Lau case; it wasn't because of the issues stem-
ming from his time with DCI Ford, in particular the fact that
she brought him onto her team to act as a scapegoat, it
wasn't even because it was just south of where Jackie and
Johnny Lucas held court in Globe Town. It was because he
never felt comfortable there, always feeling as if he was
being watched, a *walking over your grave* feeling that
unnerved him. Anjli had told him a tale once, around a
month after he joined the *Last Chance Saloon*, explaining that
Queen Mary was the only university to have a *graveyard* on
campus, as they'd built up around the Novo Jewish cemetery,
built in the 1700's, eventually building over three quarters of
it. Which meant that even with a lot of the bones now moved
to Essex, he was walking on the dead. And, with this
mystical Dee Line hitting the same place, Declan just felt
squirmy.

The quicker they could get this sorted, the better.

It felt like a Temple Inn day out, as Monroe had called in
all resources. Even Billy and Bullman were there, the latter
outside, in case anything bad happened. Anjli, Declan and
De'Geer were on point, while Doctor Marcos and DC Davey
were backup. It seemed overkill to Declan, but he understood
that this woman had already made fools of the unit three
times now, and Monroe was taking it personally.

The administrator they spoke to, a middle-aged woman
named Margaret Donaldson was apparently the same one
that Monroe had seen earlier that week, but now she was the
model of helpfulness once a warrant appeared, taking them
personally through the University building to the offices
where Rupert and Marie Wilson worked.

'I was told last night that Rupert Wilson was suspended,'

Declan commented as they walked. Margaret Donaldson nodded.

'We're very embarrassed by it,' she replied. 'We take grooming of students very seriously.'

'But surely they're of legal age?' Declan continued, unsure what Rupert had actually done, but remembering Sven's comments the previous night. In response, Margaret stopped and looked at him.

'There was a video,' she whispered, as if scared the other students in the building would hear. 'Someone sent it to us. Rupert, naked, with other women.'

'A sex video?'

Margaret paused, almost afraid to answer. 'He was performing a ritual, speaking a strange language. And the walls were, well, they were recognisably...'

She shuddered.

'You don't do naked rituals with your students on *university grounds*, and then, well, do the *other* things they did,' she stated, her tone neutral. 'There are rules.'

As they continued down the corridor, Declan tried to take the image of naked rituals out of his mind by looking around the environment as he walked. He hadn't been in this part of the university before; during the Bernard Lau murder, he'd mainly found himself in the piazza and the university library area, whereas this was a maze of corridors and wings, each one taking them lower and lower into the belly of the building.

'Did he have offices in the basement?' Monroe asked, amused at this. Margaret shrugged a little.

'To be honest, a lecturer of Professor Wilson's calibre—well, his calibre back then would have been offered far better locations but I recall that he actively chose this location. It was part of the deal he made with the University Governance Board to bring him here at the start of the university year.'

'Aye, he did, did he?' Monroe glanced at Declan. 'Must be something pretty special about the office.'

'Yes, well, maybe he just felt more comfortable under-ground,' Margaret attempted a smile, and Declan couldn't work out if she was serious, or simply being polite. 'Because down here, it's a nightmare. People claim to see ghosts at night.'

She leaned towards Declan, as if feeling that he was the person most likely to believe her.

'These are corridors built where the dead once lived,' she conspiratorially whispered. Declan nodded, as if believing her. He knew the cemetery was to the east, actually closer to where Bernard Lau's body had been found, but he supposed that a good story was hard to kill. That said, he wasn't sure *where* the bodies really were.

'What I can't understand is why would he take this?' Monroe was speaking to himself. 'The man had offers to lecture at Cambridge, at Oxford. Why choose Mile End? That's like a player turning down a Premier League team to sign for Sheffield Wednesday.'

'Hey,' Declan retorted. 'Dad supported Sheffield Wednesday.'

Monroe grinned.

'I know.'

The office itself was small and square, about twenty feet in each direction. Because they were in the basement, there were no windows, but up-lighters with 'daylight' bulbs in gave the impression of a well-lit area. One wall was filled with bookcases, a second with filing cabinets, while the other walls were where two desks, with monitors and keyboards were positioned, both PC based, old versions of Windows on each. There were no pictures on the walls; in fact, there seemed to be no personalisation in the room.

There was also no Lucy.

'I thought you said that she was here today?' Monroe exploded angrily. Margaret nodded, as surprised as he was.

'She should be,' she replied. 'She said that she would oversee his packing today.'

'Packing?'

'So his next of kin can have his personal items,' Margaret continued. 'She might have gone to the canteen I suppose but we passed through that on the way here and she wasn't in there.'

Declan thought back to his meetings with Lucy, trying to recall every detail.

'Where do the smokers go?' he asked, turning to Monroe as he continued. 'She lit up when we spoke. Makes sense that she might have gone for a cigarette.'

'We would have passed her,' the administrator thought. 'Unless she went up to the roof. A lot of the research assistants go there, as there's a magnificent view of London on a sunny day.'

'Right then,' Monroe was already looking around the room as he spoke. 'Someone call Bullman, tell her to keep her eyes peeled. Billy, Declan? Check the roof. Anjli, De'Geer? Look around the back, see if there are other areas she might have gone. The rest of us will have a quick look around here.'

Nodding, Declan and Billy were already half-running down the basement corridor to the main staircase, taking the steps two at a time as they raced to the upper level. Declan wanted to get this done as quickly as possible; there was a bad feeling in his stomach, like the sky was about to fall on his head. Billy could tell that something was off too, and kept his thoughts to himself as they made their way up to the top floor.

'There's a staircase to the roof there,' Declan pointed to a door marked ROOF ACCESS. 'Stay here, in case she gets past me—' He stopped as, down the corridor, he saw a black-haired woman stop in her tracks the moment she spied Declan and Billy.

'There!' Declan exclaimed, already chasing after her. 'Go the other way! We'll pincer her!'

As Billy ran off in the other direction, Declan turned the corner of the corridor to find it empty, with rows of class-rooms along either side. Luckily, one door was still closing; *Lucy's plan to hide had failed.* Running to it, he opened it, entering the room carefully, in case she was waiting at the side, some kind of weapon in her hand.

As it was, Lucy was standing beside a lecturer's table, a whiteboard behind her. She didn't seem to try to escape, and simply smiled at Declan.

'I hoped it'd be you,' she said, shifting the messenger bag on her shoulder. 'Although I thought I'd have more time.'

'Shouldn't have run last night,' Declan pulled his hand-cuffs out as he moved closer. 'All I wanted to do was speak to you, to learn why you play two identities.'

'It's all I've ever done,' Lucy shrugged. 'And I'm too close, Detective Inspector. I can't let you stop me.'

'Stop you what?' Declan was inching closer, trying to keep her talking as he carefully reached for his extendable baton. He didn't think she'd be a violent detainee, but he wasn't sure. 'Find the treasure?'

Lucy smiled for the first time.

'There's no treasure, detective,' she said. 'There never was. I learned that from mum. But there are secrets.'

'Like Rupert was supposed to reveal last night?'

Lucy shook her head. 'His revelations were for personal glory,' she sighed. 'But at the same time, he only had half the story. He thought he'd be the Edward Snowden for Greenwich, when all he was—'

She stopped.

'What was the name of the man they found in the suitcase? Never mind, he was him.'

'You said last night you were trying to fix things,' Declan added. 'What are you trying to fix? Come in and we can help you.'

'Rupert started a domino effect and I need to stop it before everything collapses, and people die,' Lucy was shaking her head now.

'People are already dead,' Declan added.

'I didn't kill him,' Lucy replied, adjusting her messenger bag as she spoke. 'But you can't stop what he started. Only I can.'

'Is this about your father?' Declan moved closer still. Lucy paused.

'What do you know about him?'

'I know he wasn't Rupert,' Declan continued. 'Was it Alés?'

'I never knew my father,' Lucy shrugged the question off. 'But what I do, I do in his name. For what Rupert did to him.'

Declan stopped as Lucy said this. 'What do you intend to do?'

'Many things,' she sighed, opening her messenger bag and reaching in. Declan flinched, thinking she was about to pull a weapon, but he couldn't have expected the item that she actually withdrew.

Rupert Wilson's severed hand.

He recognised the tattoo on the palm and noted that this too had a small moon-shaped brand by the thumb. It almost didn't look real, as if it was some kind of movie prop as she held it up for Declan to see. It was shrivelled, more than he would have expected for the time it had been removed, and the fingers were now curled in, the middle finger dipped into and covered with wax, a small wick twirling up out of it.

'I didn't kill him,' she said, as if this was all that was needed. 'But I'm not sad that he's dead. He's killed enough to deserve his place in Hell.'

'Killed who?' Declan thought back to her most recent words. 'Did he kill your father?'

Lucy's smile faded.

'We only meant to guide him, to bring out his more baser tendencies. We didn't realise how rotten the man really was, of the things he'd done and who would be dragged in.'

'So tell me.'

Lucy shook her head. 'You're delaying me and I need to get going,' she said, looking at the hand and pulling out a lighter. 'I need to stop a terrible man's legacy.'

She looked up at Declan as she lit the wick on the end of the middle finger. Declan moved quickly now, pulling the baton out, clicking it open as he crossed the room—

'*The hand of glory compels thee,*' Lucy whispered the words, but with conviction, and suddenly every muscle in Declan's body convulsed, stopping him in his tracks.

He was paralysed, unable to even shout, to cry out for help.

Only his eyes, wide and terrified, could move, as Lucy

blew out the finger-candle and placed the hand away, walking over to him, staring sadly at him as she spoke.

'I'm making amends and sealing things back together, I promise,' she explained carefully. 'You'll understand, when everything's fixed.'

And, this said, Marie Wilson, otherwise known as Lucy Shrimpton, walked past Declan, out through the door and into the corridor.

At least that was what Declan assumed she'd done, as he couldn't even turn to look. In fact, he was stuck like this for at least a minute, sixty long, painful seconds, held in place until Billy entered the classroom, seeing Declan and running over.

'Are you okay?' he asked, touching Declan, to see if he was conscious. 'Guys! Quick! There's a problem with Declan!'

Declan could hear movement in the corridor; Anjli and De'Geer entered, facing him as, slowly, movement in his body returned and he slumped down onto the floor of the classroom.

'What the hell happened?' Anjli asked, the concern in her voice obvious. Declan shook his head.

'Hand of glory...' he whispered. 'She held it up... I couldn't move... it's *real*.'

Anjli looked at Billy, who shook his head.

'She didn't pass me,' he replied. 'She's in the wind.'

'Great,' Anjli muttered. 'Monroe's gonna have a field day when he hears about this. Can you move?'

Declan tried to stand; slowly, and warily, he managed it. And, with the help of De'Geer and Billy, he was half carried out of the classroom.

Lucy had stopped him with six words and a severed hand. And Declan Walsh's world had been altered *forever*.

12

HOMECOMING

As Anjli had expected, Monroe wasn't impressed with Declan's plight. In fact, he'd been downright furious when he found Declan in the front lobby, sitting on a bench, drinking a takeaway cup of hot, sweet coffee.

'Christ almighty,' he snapped as he approached. 'You comfortable, laddie? You need a wee blankie to keep you warm?'

'Give him a break, Guv,' Anjli moved to intercept him. 'He's having a bad day.'

'I'll say he is,' Monroe glared at Declan. 'What the hell happened?'

'I don't know, Guv,' Declan bemoaned, looking up at Monroe as he spoke. 'I swear, it was like something grabbed hold of me and wouldn't let me go.'

'I'll bloody grab hold of you...' Monroe muttered, half to himself. 'Did you at least see which way she went?'

Declan shook his head. 'All I could see was the whiteboard,' he admitted. 'She held up Rupert's hand, said *the hand of glory compels thee* and bam! I was frozen in place.'

'Did you get anything of worth out of it?' Monroe asked. 'Please tell me you got something, that we didn't do all this for nothing.'

Declan nodded. 'Actually, yes,' he replied. 'Two things. First, Rupert Wilson's hand had the same crescent moon scar on it. I assume this must be some kind of membership symbol, like a masonic ring. Also, when I spoke to her, before she put the *whammy* on me, she let slip that he'd apparently killed people, but she didn't kill him.'

'What did she say? Word for word?'

'She said *he's killed enough to deserve his place in Hell,*' Declan started. 'That there was no treasure, that her late mother had told her before she died. Also that he'd started a domino effect and she needed to stop it before everything collapses, and people died.'

'That sounds ominous,' Anjli muttered.

'She also said what she was doing was in her dad's name,' Declan was trying to remember everything, but found it was foggy, like a dream. 'She said we only meant to guide him, to bring out his more based tendencies. We didn't realise how rotten the man really was, of the things he'd done.'

'We,' Anjli commented. 'She wasn't working alone.'

'Sounds like you had a nice wee chat,' Monroe muttered.

'I was trying to gain her trust,' Declan snapped back.

'And then you let her leave,' Monroe was still angry. 'Christ almighty. Go home. Get some sleep. Come back to this tomorrow with a clear head.'

'You're benching me?' Declan rose now, his face reddening in anger. 'This wasn't my fault! If I could have done something—'

'Christ's sake, laddie, you let a suspect walk right past

you!' Monroe shouted. 'You're no good to me like this! What if she does it again? Go home, sort your head out and come back when you're feeling better!'

He looked at Anjli and De'Geer.

'Take him home,' he said. 'All we're doing is checking the office, and we don't need all of you there. Get some rest and we'll come back at this from a new angle.'

Reluctantly, Declan allowed De'Geer to lead him out of the university building, ignoring the look that he saw Billy give him, one of confusion and disappointment.

Declan understood the look.

He probably had the same look on his own face right now.

ANJLI DROVE THE AUDI BACK TO HURLEY; DECLAN ASSUMED IT was because she had a fear of him freezing on the M4 and ramming the car into the back of a truck.

To be brutally honest, he didn't blame her. He was worried about doing the same thing.

'It could have happened to anyone,' De'Geer suggested from the back seat, in a misguided attempt to break the silence. Declan, in the passenger seat turned to face him.

'You been possessed by any severed hands recently?' he asked conversationally. 'Because if so, I'm all ears on hearing how you got out of it.'

De'Geer shut his mouth, nodding. Declan sighed.

'Sorry,' he muttered. 'I'm not accepting this well. I don't believe in mumbo jumbo about possession hands, even when I face one.'

He leaned back in the seat.

'I just want someone to explain what happened to me,' he muttered.

As they pulled up outside the house, Declan saw the front door open. He was about to snap at Anjli, berate her for already giving keys to people, when a familiar, black-haired young woman emerged, awaiting at the door.

'Did you know Jess was coming today?' Anjli asked suspiciously. She knew the issues that Declan currently had with his ex-wife Lizzie, ones that came from recent visits with his daughter. Silently, Declan shook his head before exiting the car and walking towards his daughter.

'What in God's name are you doing here?' he asked. 'Does your mum know you're here?'

'Course not,' Jess smiled as she ran to her dad, embracing him. 'I took a leaf out of your book and decided that apologising would be better than asking forgiveness.'

'She's not wrong there,' Anjli said as she walked past with De'Geer, entering the house. Jess straightened as they passed her.

'Um, hi, Morten,' she said to De'Geer, who wisely simply nodded and carried on. Declan smiled for the first time since leaving London. Jess had crushed hard on the Viking police officer since they first met, although *he* found it more of an inconvenience than she did. Declan, however, found it mildly funny.

'You okay?' Jess finally realised that something wasn't right here. Declan faked another smile.

'Just working out how to explain to your mum that you're here,' he replied. Anjli, still in the doorway, glanced back at him.

'Oh, for Christ's sake just tell her,' she snapped. 'She's going to find out anyway, so you might as well come clean.'

'After I speak to her mum, and drive her back to the station,' Declan replied. 'No, scratch that. I'll drive her home. God knows what trouble she could get up to in a train station.'

'Can't I at least stay for dinner?' Jess begged. 'Come on dad, I've not seen you for two months!'

'You're fifteen years old, Jess, and your mum—'

'I'm sixteen in two weeks!' Jess exclaimed in frustration. 'Mum won't be able to do anything then, so she can let me stay here for pizza now!'

'How did you know it was pizza?' Anjli looked up from a pizza menu she was going through with De'Geer.

'You all have your work faces on,' Jess explained. 'Something's happened and you need to work it out. And when you do this, you always get pizza.'

She grinned.

'I'd like vegetarian if possible.'

Declan sighed and closed the door behind him, walking into the kitchen as Jess and Anjli sat down on the sofa, De'Geer looking a little uncomfortable by the door. Declan had planned to reach into the cupboard and make himself a whisky, a ritual of his father's that he'd done since inheriting the house, but it didn't feel right to do so while Jess was around.

'*The hand of glory compels thee.*'

Declan spun in place, convinced that he'd heard the words spoken from the back door, but there was nobody there. Tutting at his own stupidity, he pulled out his phone, reluctantly dialling his ex-wife.

'You okay?' she asked when she answered. Not *hello*, but instantly expecting that something was wrong.

'I just got home to find Jess here,' he said, expecting an explosion down the phone. Instead, there was silence, so he continued. 'I'll drive her home after we've had some dinner. Is that okay?'

'Of course,' Liz sounded friendly, casual here; but it sounded *too* friendly, as if someone had told her to relax, to let this happen. 'She's your daughter. You should spend time with her.'

'Are *you* okay?' Declan now turned the conversation around. 'Because for eight weeks now you've barely allowed me to text her.'

'To be honest, I could do with the break,' Liz sounded tired. 'Jess is in her last weeks of GCSEs, and everyone else's the villain whenever she's wrong about something. And Tessa said that I should—'

'You're still talking to *Tessa Martinez?*' Declan almost exploded. 'What the hell are you doing that for? She's a murderer!'

'I know, but she had her reasons.'

Declan couldn't believe that Liz was actively defending Theresa Martinez, ex-DI in the Manchester police, and arrested a month earlier for her part in the murder of Reginald Troughton, Julia Clarke, Michael Chadwick and Rory Simpson. She'd also offered to assist Declan in explaining to Liz how it felt to be a *teenager fighting violent crime,* but Declan hadn't realised this was an outreach program that progressed past the actual moment of arrest.

'She speaks highly of you,' Liz continued. 'You really should visit her.'

Declan went to reply but bit it back at the last moment. *Maybe he should, as obviously he owed her for calming Liz down.*

'I'll consider it,' he replied. 'And I'll have Jess back in an hour or two.'

'Make it closer to three,' Liz said, and Declan could almost hear the relief in her voice. 'I'm going to have a bath now she's not home tonight.'

And without saying farewell, Liz disconnected.

Declan stared at the phone in abject confusion.

'While you're in there, could you turn the kettle on?' Anjli's voice echoed in from the living room. Declan did so, mainly as he wanted a cup of tea himself, and then walked back out of the kitchen, looking at Jess as he did so.

'You knew she'd be okay with this, didn't you?' he said. Jess grinned widely now.

'I hoped,' she replied. 'And, as I said, it's easier to apologise.'

'She's so like you,' Anjli muttered. 'You need to stop her following you on your destructive path.'

'It's too late, I'm damned already,' Jess said, rising to her feet and holding her hands out like a zombie. 'The hand of glory compels me!'

'Oh, good,' Declan replied humourlessly. 'You've told her.'

Jess slumped back onto the sofa with a smile.

'Don't sweat it, dad,' she replied. 'I already told Anjli and Morten what it was.'

'And she makes a good point,' Anjli added. 'Tell him.'

'Derren Brown,' Jess replied, as if this was the answer to everything.

'Derren Brown?' Declan repeated. 'As in the magician?'

'More the stage hypnotist part,' Jess continued, leaning

forward on the sofa. 'There's a ton of them out there. All fantastic at taking a subject and instantly triggering them.'

'So what, like making me think I'm a chicken?'

'Or, making you believe that someone waving a severed hand and quoting a particular line would force you to freeze in place like you're playing a game of statues,' Anjli added. As if to emphasise this, Jess pulled a leather glove out of her pocket, holding it up.

'The hand of glory compels thee,' she said once more. 'Anything happen?'

'No,' Declan waggled his fingers. 'So what, it has to be the severed hand of Rupert Wilson to work?'

'That's probably what you were told,' Jess replied. 'We saw a guy do it at school, as part of the end-of-year show. He could place someone under in a matter of seconds, and then get them to do things without them even remembering, but they had to be specific, and nothing that the subject wouldn't do, so he couldn't say 'hit a teacher' or something like that.'

She thought for a moment.

'Well, unless that student really wanted to hit a teacher, I suppose.'

'So how do I stop this?' Declan asked. 'Going on the basis that this is slightly more believable than a magic curse being thrown on me.'

'Joanne Davey did clinical hypnosis as part of her degree,' De'Geer suggested. 'She might be able to work out what Lucy did to you.'

'I'll chat to her tomorrow then,' Declan nodded. 'I mean, what's the worst that can happen?'

'She turns you into a chicken,' Anjli suggested. 'And that I'd pay to see.'

Lucy leaned against the outer wall of Bart's Hospital and cried. All she wanted to do was stop, to throw everything away, to start afresh, but she couldn't do that. Not until she stopped the *Consortium* and laid the ghosts of both her father and Rupert Wilson to rest.

The curse had to be severed.

Lucy shook her head as she considered this. The bloody curse was a millstone around her neck. The curse hadn't existed because the treasure hadn't existed. Her mum had created one though, with the pact that they'd all made, the blood pact that had linked them all together.

Yeah, you hadn't thought that through, had you, mum?

The problem with setting some kind of blood ritual, especially one created in some dodgy forgotten book by Aleister Crowley, is that the pact was only as good as those taking it. Virtuous people would use it to build themselves. The rest would try to get out of the Faustian pact they'd made. One that not only affected themselves, but their families, too.

Lucy rubbed at the moon-shaped scar on her hand. She'd done it so many years ago, she'd even forgotten about it until the detective had mentioned it the previous day.

I should never have started the training with her. Mum was right.

Lucy chuckled at the thought; that Miriam Shrimpton could have been right about anything was amusing. She'd spent her life being second place to her mum's work, and that was fine but when she found her mum had slipped, was practising again, she'd felt betrayed. And then, to meet Rupert, the man mum had banned Lucy from seeing her whole life, who she'd only met face to face when she was fifteen—

No. Stop with the lies.

Lucy shook her head. Julie-Anna was the first to realise the truth but held it from her until Miriam died. Alexandra had offered to help Lucy in whatever was needed when they finally connected, and Lucy felt terrible for bringing her in. But someone needed to watch Rupert when Lucy wasn't there, because by this point he was already on the path he'd chosen. He was already working with Yossi Shavit, and the things Yossi wanted, Rupert simply couldn't give.

Idly, Lucy wondered if Julie-Anna had managed to hit them both; Yossi's response to the Watchtower line was proof that he'd been brought under at some point, at least. Lucy felt a pang of regret at this, she hadn't wanted to use it on the detective, but there was nothing she could do. She needed to leave.

You set it up just in case. You planned for the situation. Don't fool yourself.

As she'd said, the detective and his partner were connected to the Dee Line. He was always going to be involved in this. All she was doing was ensuring her self defence.

Something she needed to continue doing.

Picking up her phone, she looked at the evening sky, trying to work out the best way to do this. She could contact her aunt, but she'd made her do enough. It wasn't fair to continue that relationship until this was over. Then she'd return to being a Shrimpton officially, walk away from this whole bloody thing.

You're fooling yourself if you think you're getting out alive. The curse doesn't care who it hits.

Lucy cried again.

'I had so much I wanted to do,' she whispered to nobody. Maybe she could run, start a new life, go abroad—

But the police were still looking for her.

Her course planned and plotted, she stopped crying as a text message appeared from Cindy.

We need to meet. You and me. Tonight, Rupert's place.

Sighing, she closed the phone, taking a deep breath before rising from the wall, climbing onto her bike and cycling off.

13

LONDON CRAWLING

THE PIZZA HAD TAKEN HALF AN HOUR TO ARRIVE, AND IN THAT time De'Geer had made his excuses and left, claiming he had a prior engagement he couldn't get out of, and it made Declan realise that apart from his heritage, that he rode a Triumph motorcycle and lived near Maidenhead, his role in the police force and his ability to crush a man's entire head in his hands (he assumed the last of these, based on De'Geer's size), he had no idea of anything else to do with him. It had even come as a shock to Declan the previous night that other people in the Princess Louise knew De'Geer better than his workmates did, and by *workmates* he meant himself. He made a mental note to rectify this as, the pizza now eaten, he told Jess to pack her things and, wrestling the Audi keys from a reluctant Anjli, he took his daughter back to London.

'You think mum might let me visit more?' Jess said as they travelled down the M4 towards London. Declan shrugged.

'I'd like to think so,' he replied. 'Although let's come back to that after the GCSEs are over, yeah? Maybe during your summer break?'

Jess nodded.

'The case sounds interesting,' she continued. Declan smiled. He knew she was trying to find a *way* into the investigation, but he'd made a promise to Liz to keep his daughter out of these things.

'After the GCSEs.'

'Morten looked cute today. I wonder if I could—'

'After the GCSEs—' Declan stopped as he realised what Jess was saying. 'No. Never. Nu-uh. Walk away from that idea.'

Jess chuckled. 'You're such a *dad*, dad.'

Declan didn't know whether this was a compliment or an insult, and so he kept quiet the rest of the journey, eventually pulling up outside the house he'd once lived in with his family. It felt like a lifetime ago.

'You want to come in?' Jess asked. 'Say hi to mum?'

Declan shook his head. 'Best if I give her space,' he replied. 'So instead, why don't you tell me what's really going on?'

Jess paused before leaving the car, as if working out what she could say to this.

'Mum broke up with Rob,' she said. 'No idea why, came out of the blue. They seemed happy and then bam, it was all over.'

Declan nodded. 'Sometimes these things happen,' he replied. 'And trust me, kiddo, currently, I'm likely the worst person to speak to her about this right now.'

He ruffled Jess's hair.

'Keep me updated on how she is,' he continued. 'If she gets worse, then I'll step in. How's that?'

Jess smiled and, with a last hug from Declan, opened the car door and left the Audi, bounding towards her front door. Glancing down at his phone, Declan saw he had a missed call from Bullman. Dialling the number, he placed the call onto the car speaker as he started the engine back up.

'You called, Ma'am?' he asked when Bullman answered.

'Just checking up on you,' Bullman's voice echoed around the car. 'Monroe explained to me how you froze like a little bitch.'

'I'm good, thanks for asking,' Declan replied, ignoring the obvious jibe. *This was Bullman's broken way of showing concern.* 'Actually, we now think that it could have been stage hypnotism.'

'Are you still driving?' Bullman's tone was now one of concern. 'I thought you'd have been home hours ago?'

'I was, I just dropped Jess back at her mum's. She was waiting for me at the house.'

There was a pause.

''So you're in London?' Bullman eventually asked. 'Are you near the offices?'

'I can be,' Declan indicated right, looking for a side road to turn the car around. 'Any reason why?'

'We just had a walk-in,' Bullman replied. 'The two women with the wheelchair just arrived and gave themselves up. I thought you might want to interview them with me?'

'I'll be there in ten,' Declan smiled as Bullman, with her usual hatred of saying goodbye, simply disconnected the call. As Declan started back towards the City of London, he considered this new piece of news. The two women caught on the CCTV, the ones who wheeled the dead body of Rupert Wilson to the *Motherstone* in Greenwich Park, laid him out and left him there were now surrendering to the police on their own accord.

The question, as ever, was *why?*

DECLAN PULLED UP AT TEMPLE INN AROUND TEN MINUTES after the call, but by then he'd received another text from Bullman saying to take his time, and that they wouldn't be starting for another half an hour as Chief Superintendent Bradley had demanded a report on the day's proceedings from her ASAP, and that took priority. Declan had intended to sit at his desk and wait, but as he walked through the lower level of the Command Unit, he saw a light on in the forensics department. It was past nine pm now, and this meant that either Doctor Marcos or DC Davey were working a late shift. Taking a deep breath, and realising there was a very strong chance that he was about to make a fool of himself, Declan tapped on the door, opening it and leaning in.

DC Joanne Davey looked up from her iPad, where she was working on some kind of DNA helix document.

'Need something, Guv?' she asked. Entering the room, Declan nodded.

'Heard you know a bit about hypnotism,' he said. 'Hoping you might be able to help.'

Davey went to reply to this, but paused, her mouth half open as realisation struck her.

'You think she hypnotised you,' she replied, nodding as she spoke. 'If she had the opportunity, that could have happened in Greenwich. Good call. You come up with it?'

'Jess.'

Davey nodded. 'Clever kid.'

'Is there a way to check, to remove this?' Declan leaned against a high table. 'I really don't want to play statues every time I face Lucy Shrimpton, or Marie Wilson, or whatever.'

Davey shifted in her seat, turning to face Declan.

'I could put you under, see if there's anything there,' she said. 'That is, if you're okay with that?'

Declan shrugged. 'What do I have to do?'

'Lay down on that,' Davey pointed at the table that usually held bodies. 'Yeah, sorry, it's the only thing in here that could work.'

Reluctantly, Declan sat on the edge of the table.

'I still don't get how she managed it,' he replied. "I was speaking to her for literally a minute.'

'It all depends on how they trigger you,' Davey rose from the chair, picking up her phone. 'Some find a personal trigger, some use force, so literally shunt their victim into a trance. They all differ. What was she talking about before you lost time again?'

'Kendis,' Declan spun on the table, now stretching out along the surface. 'This is cold.'

'Usually the dead don't worry,' Davey smiled. 'Kendis is loss, guilt, strong immediate memories, that could easily place you into a suggestible state. So relax, breathe in, out, slow deep breaths...' She placed the phone back down on the side table as Declan relaxed, closing his eyes as he breathed in and out slowly.

'Okay,' Davey intoned softly, her voice quiet and monotone. 'We're going to fall into a deep sleep now, in three... two... one—'

Declan opened his eye, looking at Davey.

'Was something supposed to happen?' he asked.

Davey reached for the phone, turning off the voice recorder app that she'd had running on it, showing the screen to Declan.

'You've been under for two-and-a-half minutes,' she said.

Declan sat up at this. 'Really? Wow,' he said as he stretched his shoulders. 'Did you find anything?'

Davey played the voice app, forwarding along with the audio recording.

'Not for the first minute,' she replied. 'But then we got to this.'

She stopped forwarding and let the audio recording play.

'*Okay, now where are you?*' Davey's voice.

'*I'm in the park,*' Declan's now. Soft, dreamlike, as if half asleep. Which, in a way, he was. '*I'm talking to Lucy.*'

'*And what is she saying?*'

'*She's talking about Kendis.*'

'*Declan, when I ask what she's saying, I want you to repeat exactly what she says, word for word. Do you understand?*'

'*Yes.*'

'*What is she saying?*'

'*She says that she forgives you,*' Declan's voice changed on the audio recording as he repeated the words verbatim. His tone was now soft and calm, emotionless; he was mimicking Lucy. '*She says that she misses you, that you don't visit her anymore. She says that you should, that he's moved on now and they won't tell him. Do you understand?*'

'*That's good,*' now Davey was heard. '*And then what does she do?*'

'*She's leaning closer.*'

'*And what is she saying?*'

'*You have to let her go,*' Declan repeated softly. '*Listen to what your heart—*' his voice changed in tone mid sentence, now more commanding. '*—listen to my voice, listen to my words. You're falling into a trance, only my words are heard. Do you understand? Nod for yes. Good.*'

Declan stared at Davey as the recording continued, and was about to comment on this, but she held a finger up.

'Wait,' she hissed. 'This is the good part.'

On the audio, the tranced Declan continued to repeat Lucy's words.

If we meet again, and I pull out a severed hand and light the middle finger, while saying the words the hand of glory compels thee, you will find that your muscles have turned to stone, and you cannot move. Do you understand?'

His voice changed, now talking as Declan. *'Yes.'*

Back to Lucy. *'What are the words?'*

Declan. *'The hand of glory compels thee.'*

Lucy. *'And what must I be doing?'*

Declan. *'Holding up the hand and lighting the middle finger.'*

Davey looked at Declan. 'I'm glad you're good at voices because this shit is confusing,' she muttered as on the audio, Declan continued as Lucy.

'And what will you do when I say this?'

Declan once more. *'Stop still, like a statue.'*

Lucy. *'Good man. Another thing. When I ask you where is the watchtower, you must answer on the cliff. Where is the watchtower?'*

'On the cliff.'

On the audio, there was a pause before Davey's voice was heard. *'What's happening now?'*

'She's riding off on her bike,' Declan replied.

'Okay,' Davey was fainter, likely meaning closer to Declan and, in the process, leaning further from the phone. *'You have two new tasks. First, forget this last order. You must not turn to stone. In fact, if this happens again, you will feel nothing. Do you understand?'*

'Yes.'

'*Good. Second, if anyone asks you where the watchtower is, you will not respond, okay?*' Davey's voice was determined. '*Good. And relax back into your body, as we'll be coming back out of trance in three... two... one...*'

Declan's voice. '*Was something supposed to happen—*'

The sound stopped as Davey turned off the recording.

'There,' she said. 'You were right. She put the whammy on you. But she won't be able to use that again.'

'Good,' Declan rose, sliding off the table now. 'Can you do me a favour?'

'Delete the audio file?' Davey smiled. 'Of course.'

Declan stared at the wall for a long moment. 'Was she lying?' he asked. 'When she spoke of Kendis?'

'That's not a hypnotism question,' Davey replied. 'That's more of an *existentialism* one.'

'Okay then, as a forensic scientist,' Declan rubbed at his head. 'You see dead bodies all the time, working on them as pieces of meat. Do you think we have souls?'

'I hope we do,' Davey replied, 'my family are all Methodists, and I know they believe a lot. But personally? I don't know.'

'What was that about a watchtower?' Declan asked. Davey looked at the phone, as if expecting it to reply.

'It's a trigger question, to see if you're still under someone's control,' she replied. 'Where's the watchtower?'

Declan shrugged, so Davey continued. 'Where *is* the watchtower?'

'Am I supposed to say on the cliff?' he asked.

'If you were under her control still, that'd be the first thing that you'd reply,' Davey said. 'You wouldn't even realise what you were doing.'

'But I'm okay?'

'I think so,' Davey was already typing on the iPad. 'I know a couple of people I'm going to contact, if that's okay? The watchtower line struck a memory. It's not a usual trigger, so if we find who uses it, as in what type of hypnotism relies on the watchtower trigger, we might find who taught Lucy, although it was probably her mother.'

Declan was about to reply to this, when Bullman peeked her head around the door.

'Ready to speak to some Goths?' she asked. Declan nodded thanks to Davey and followed Bullman up the stairs.

'So they just came in out of the cold?' he asked as they continued up to the interview rooms. 'They weren't given up, or spotted, or anything like that?'

Bullman shook her head. 'Billy was doing well with CCTV and traffic cams, but we weren't going to find them quickly,' she replied as they walked into the corridor that led to the interview room. 'I'm guessing that their consciences got to them, and they turned up just before nine.'

'Have you seen them?' Declan asked. Bullman smiled.

'Yeah, and I don't think they killed anyone,' she replied. 'If I did, I'd get Monroe in to do this, rather than screw around on my own time.'

'So why do this then?'

'Honestly? Boredom and curiosity,' Bullman grinned as she opened the door to the Interview Room. 'Let's have some fun.'

14

THE LADIES OF AVALON

IN THE INTERVIEW ROOM WERE TWO WOMEN, ONE IN HER MID-forties, the other a few years younger, so possibly late thirties. They were both dressed in black, one with long, dark red hair, the shorter, older one with an asymmetrical peroxide blonde cut. Declan assumed that, like the *Ghost Bros,* this was going to be a more informal interview, as usually only one would be in the room at a time, and Bullman seemed more relaxed than usual as she sat in one chair facing them.

'Detective Superintendent Bullman and Detective Inspector Walsh interviewing Cindy Mitchell and—' she looked at her notes, '—and Lilith Babylon. Is that correct?'

The two women nodded. Bullman glanced at Declan before turning her attention to the taller of the two women.

'Sorry,' she continued. 'I have to ask. Lilith Babylon is your real name?'

'Legally changed it a year ago,' Lilith replied.

'What were you beforehand?' Declan asked. Lilith turned her gaze on him, and Declan noted her green eyes were coloured contacts. Like her name and her hair, this woman was doing her best to change her identity.

'My *name* was Alexandra Capioca,' she muttered. Declan recognised it.

'Your brother is Alés Capioca?'

Lilith stared at him. '*Was*. He died a long time ago.'

'I'm sorry to hear that, Miss...?' at a nod, '*Miss* Babylon.'

He wanted to continue this line of enquiry, especially now he knew this was the girlfriend of Simon Tolley but didn't feel that much would come out of it right now.

'Now, which of you wants to explain why you were wheeling a dead body into Greenwich Park and leaving him beside a megalithic stone?'

'We'd promised him we would do it,' Cindy replied. 'It was his dying request. We're his *Ladies of Avalon*.'

'His what now?' Bullman leaned back in her chair. Declan could see from her expression that this was exactly the distraction that she was hoping for. 'Like King Arthur?'

'Exactly like that,' Lilith continued. 'His Ladies took him from the battlefield at Badon Hill and sailed with him to Avalon.'

'So what, you're hired to take his body to Greenwich? Not quite the same.'

'Depends on what you think of Greenwich,' Cindy sat back in her chair and folded her arms. 'To some, it's a spiritual home.'

Declan nodded, conceding the point. 'But to be clear, your job was to steal his body after death and place it beside the *Motherstone*. Why?'

'Because his family are fundamentalist Christians,' Lilith replied. 'Rupert knew that even though he was the eldest, they'd contest his wishes and eventually he'd be buried to theirs, so he wanted at least one last night of rest beside a stone of power.'

'Minus his hand,' Bullman commented.

'No, we had nothing to do with that,' Lilith protested. 'He had both hands when we prepared him.'

'Is Marie Wilson, or rather Lucy Shrimpton part of your little club?' Bullman asked. 'Because currently she seems to be the one that has it.'

At this minor revelation, the two women glanced nervously at each other.

'She used to be, but she ghosted us,' Cindy said.

'You mean some kind of astral attack?' Declan asked. Lilith looked back at him, her voice dripping with scorn.

'No, you idiot,' she snapped. 'I mean *ghosted*. Disappearing from our lives without so much as a call, email, or text. Wouldn't even see me when I went to the university to have a go at her.'

Declan watched Lilith look away after speaking. She was calm, irritated even, but Declan had a feeling that she was lying.

'Did you know her before she changed her surname?'

Cindy nodded. 'I didn't know her, but had connections with people who knew her back in the day,' she replied. 'Her mother, Miriam was a true believer until she left the scene. Third gen occultist too, her grandfather worked curses with Crowley in the thirties.'

'Why did she leave 'the scene'?'

'I think she wanted Lucy to grow up away from the life.'

'And do you think Professor Wilson was Lucy Shrimpton's real father?'

Declan noticed Lilith stiffened slightly at that.

'Problem?' he asked.

'No,' Lilith replied, her tone clipped and emotionless. 'It's just... well, Miriam was with my brother for a while.'

She looked at the wall.

'He never recovered after she—well, I was only about eleven back then, too young to really understand at the time, but there was some drama with her, some third party and him, and he...'

She stopped.

'He never recovered,' she repeated.

'An affair?'

'I thought so, but now I think it was something polyamorous, but a decade or two too early.'

'Sounds like a piece of work,' Bullman muttered. 'We've heard stories that your brother was Lucy Shrimpton's father. Care to comment?'

Lilith chose not to reply, glowering at Bullman. Declan assumed that this meant that the possibility was definitely there.

'Was Professor Wilson with either of you?' Declan asked, and the awkward silence that both women gave him once more was answer enough. Neither of them really fitted the image that Declan had been given of 'young Goth girls', and he assumed that the two women in front of him had a serious case of unrequited love.

'No,' they eventually both replied.

He went to ask a follow up question, but stopped as he spied Cindy's hand.

'That brand,' he said, pointing at the crescent-shaped mark between her thumb and index finger. 'What does it mean?'

Cindy looked at it for a moment.

'It's symbolising the Moon Goddess,' she started. 'And also to honour Holda, the Ice Queen and Winter Solstice—'

'Bloody hell, Cindy, give it a rest!' Lilith snapped, showing the back of her hand, where a similar brand could be seen. 'Miriam had one before she died, and so we did it to honour her.'

'And Professor Wilson?'

'No,' Lilith replied. 'He did it because Marie—I mean Lucy had one.'

Bullman audibly cracked her neck as she rolled it around her shoulders, tiring of this. 'Where did you get the wheelchair from?'

'Cindy's Nana.'

'And how did you know he was dead?' Declan asked.

'He contacted us,' Lilith replied. 'And no, I don't mean magically, before you ask. He sent us a WhatsApp.'

'Do you have it to show?' Bullman asked. Lilith nodded, pulling out her phone. After a few taps on the screen, she showed it to Bullman.

Rupert - 16.46 I'm sorry ladies but I can't go on. I will be found in my Sanctum. Bring a knife to cut me down. Blessed Be.

'It's a group chat,' she explained. 'Me, Cindy and Rupert. There were more, but they dropped off over the years.'

'Like who?' Bullman showed the screen to Declan.

'A couple of mad Americans, a weird German woman, a bloke from Overton in Surrey who didn't understand what we were... also Julie-Anna, but she was never a Lady of A, and I think Rupert just spoke to her on it there because there were witnesses to the chat.'

'He didn't want to talk to her alone?' Declan looked up from the phone.

'She always claimed he was a fraud,' Lilith sniffed. 'That Miriam was the one who did the legwork, and that all he wanted to do was to gain the glory for it. She was angry every time he played at giving a hint and lost her mind with rage when he tattooed his fingers.'

'And a year ago she went mad,' Cindy added.

'That's unfair,' Lilith replied. 'She had a brush with mortality. It can change someone.'

'Changed her into a bloody mental person. We all saw what she became.'

'Became?' Declan looked up.

'She was a little passionate about their shared history,' Lilith explained cryptically.

'Hence the angriness and the claims of fraud,' Declan continued. The two women nodded.

'Can you explain what you mean by brush with mortality?' Declan asked.

'She was struck by lightning,' Lilith replied.

'We were told that Miriam was struck.'

'That's right,' Cindy nodded.

'They were *both* struck?'

Lilith nodded. 'Same bolt.'

'Jesus,' Declan muttered.

'You'd like that, wouldn't you?' Cindy snapped. 'God smiting the deviant women with a lightning bolt—'

'No, it was just an expression,' Declan back-pedalled, now watching Cindy warily. Bullman was typing a message into her own phone as she continued.

'So you get this message, you fear the worst and you go to his apartment, right?'

'Not at first,' Lilith admitted as Declan scrolled down through the replies.

Cindy - 16.47 Is this a joke? Rupert, don't do this to us.

SexyHexy - 16.50 R Cindy just called you answer your phone

'I'm guessing SexyHexy is you?' he asked Lilith, who nodded.

'Nobody answered his phone, so Cindy and I went to the flat,' she explained. 'We took Cindy's Nana's car, as it was big enough to put a wheelchair in and a blue badge for parking.'

'She was okay with this?'

'She's on holiday for the weekend, climbing Scafell Pike.'

'I thought she was wheelchair bound?' Declan asked.

'So what, someone in a wheelchair can't wheel up a mountain? Real progressive of you,' Cindy snapped.

Declan went to reply to this but thought better. He wasn't making friends in this interview at all. 'And you both went to the apartment?'

'No,' Cindy interjected. 'I had to make sure we weren't clamped, so Lilith took the wheelchair upstairs. A few minutes later she returned with... with Rupert.'

'How did you cut him down?'

'Cindy's white handled ritual knife,' Lilith replied. 'It's an ivory handled Swiss Army one. She passed it to me before I went up the stairs.'

'And where was he in the apartment?'

'There was a chin-up bar screwed into the wall, by the door to the kitchen. I heard he used it for rope work and bondage sessions with his...' Lilith struggled for a word. 'Well, with *others*. It was real high up, and a noose had been looped over it. He was hanging on one end and the other was tied to a door handle.'

'How did he get up there?' Bullman asked.

'There was a stool at the side, I assumed he stood on that.'

'Any signs of a struggle?' Declan asked. Lilith shook her head.

'No, he was peaceful. Well, as peaceful as he could be.'

'And you had no idea he'd do this?' Bullman asked. 'Even with his suspension?'

Lilith didn't reply, but Cindy leaned closer.

'He told us the video was fake, and it'd been made by someone who wanted to discredit him.'

'And why would someone want to discredit him?' Declan looked up from his notepad.

Neither woman answered.

'Had you been in the apartment before?' Bullman continued.

Lilith shook her head. 'I'd only heard about it.'

'And you?' Declan asked Cindy, who glanced at Lilith before replying.

'I was there a couple of days back.'

'You *what?*' Lilith seemed furious at this. 'You said you were in guided meditation!'

'I didn't say who I was guiding!' Cindy was unapologetic. 'Rupert was being attacked, psychically and needed guidance.'

'You could have done that by *FaceTime*,' Lilith folded her arms and glared at her companion. 'It's not like Rupert didn't know how to do a virtual sabbat.'

Declan was about to reply, but a beep on Bullman's phone distracted him.

'So this is what, six pm by now?' she asked as she looked down at it.

'Six forty,' Cindy replied sullenly. 'And the roads were a nightmare, so it took about an hour to get into Greenwich. We ended up parking on a double yellow and getting in with about twenty minutes to spare.'

'We wheeled him to the stone, and laid him out,' Lilith continued. 'We knew he'd be found, and that his family would get their wish, but for the first night this was his time.'

'Did you tell anyone about this?'

'Of course not.'

Declan looked at Lilith. 'Not even your boyfriend, Simon Tolley?' he asked. 'Who turned up at the same time to stand guard over it for the next three hours?'

Lilith shook her head. 'I didn't tell him anything,' she replied. 'I broke off a meeting that night, nothing more.'

Declan nodded. 'Spoken to Simon today?'

'No,' Lilith replied. 'We don't talk every day.'

Declan considered telling Lilith about the accident, but decided against it for the moment. For all he knew, she could have been the one who arranged the driver.

'Do you know anyone whom could have wished Mister Wilson harm, or even death?' Bullman looked up from the message that she'd received.

Lilith remained quietly sulking at this. Cindy, noticing this, looked back at Bullman.

'He was a visionary,' she replied. 'Of course he had enemies.'

'He made a lot more in his final year,' Lilith added. 'He was a little 'out there.'

'You were only around in his final year,' Cindy snapped at her sister of Avalon. 'Don't pretend you knew him better.'

'Good, then I'd like a list of them,' Bullman forced a smile as she interrupted yet another argument, but there was no warmth to it. 'As well as where you were in the hours that led up to the message.'

'You think someone did this to him?' Lilith's voice was faint now. Nervous, even.

'Oh, I *know* someone did,' Bullman replied, placing the phone on the table. 'I just dropped a message to one of our forensics team who's still in the building, asking for Rupert Wilson's time of death. It's not precise, but she just replied saying it was around ten or eleven in the morning.'

She leaned in.

'I don't know who else knew about your little Ladies of Avalon group, but currently, I'd suggest the two of you get comfortable, because you're not going anywhere for a while. We don't have Professor Wilson's phone yet, and we can't confirm where it was between four and five pm on the afternoon of his death, but considering it sent this message a good five to six hours after Professor Wilson died, we might need to revisit the ideas of either life after death, and Professor Wilson's ghost reaching out from the afterlife to send it, or his killer contacting your group using Professor Wilson's ID, effectively convincing you to remove the body.'

She leaned back.

'Which now makes you accessories to *murder*, and I *will have my names*.'

DIGGER HATED BEING IN THE CHURCHYARD. THE *BODIES* WOULD get him.

But if he stayed on the streets, then the *bullies* would

come out, and Digger was more scared of them than the bodies.

Bodies were underground. Bodies were dead.

He liked St Anne's church though. It felt welcoming. And he could climb over the railings and run off down the Commercial Road if anything got too scary.

He was alone.

He sat in the north-west corner of the churchyard, leaning against the northern wall, the metal tines of the wrought-iron fence concreted into the three foot high brickwork as he opened his bag and pulled out dinner—a Tesco extra-large sausage roll. He'd been looking after Minty's greyhound earlier that evening, and a young woman had given him a two-pound coin and the sausage roll for the dog. And, when Minty arrived back, he already had dog food with him, so Digger kept quiet about the sausage roll. However, although he had food, he didn't have enough money for a bed in a hostel for the night. Which was fine, as it was almost May, and the nights were getting warmer. He hated staying in the graveyards at this time of night, but at the same time it was like he was camping alone.

But he *wasn't* alone. He could see a figure standing beside the pyramid in the yard. He hadn't seen them enter the churchyard though, and this scared him. But they must have cycled in when he was rummaging through his bag, because they'd placed what looked like a bike beside a tree before walking over to the pyramid.

It wasn't locked, but who expected a bike to be stolen at night in a graveyard.

Maybe the bodies would come up to ride it.

He could hear talking, but couldn't see who was doing it. Maybe the ghosts were loud tonight. He finished his sausage roll and gathered his items together. *The ghosts might see him and do something to him.*

There was a yell, a violent male scream of pain; Digger knew that sound well, and a man's voice followed it, echoing through the yard.

'You bitch! You deliberately sent it to her! She's killing me because of what you did! I lost everything!'

Digger rose at this. He wasn't strong, but this sounded like a woman was in trouble, and people should always help women in trouble—

There was a bloodcurdling scream, terrifyingly loud, that gurgled off into nothing and then a man appeared, staggering back, at a distance and in shadow, but with an obvious knife in his hand as he looked around.

Digger pushed against the brick wall, hoping that the shadows would hide him. And they seemed to work as the man, after looking around the churchyard, moved back behind the pyramid, as if continuing the job he'd started. And, now alone again, Digger grabbed his bag and climbed up onto the brick wall, almost throwing himself over the metal fencing and running for his life towards Cable Street before stopping.

Almost.

He looked back into the graveyard. The bullies might be vicious, but tonight the bodies in the graveyards had *knives.* He knew that he should leave. *After* he took the bike by the tree.

After all, the bodies wouldn't be using it. And it looked like it'd been just left there.

Quickly, Digger ran to the tree, grabbed the small black bike and wheeled it quietly out of the graveyard as behind him, he could hear a rasping noise, as if something was sawing through wood.

He didn't know what to do with the bike, but he knew that selling it would make him enough for a few nights in a hostel.

As long as someone else didn't steal it from him first.

15

<hr>

TO MEET AND PART AGAIN

PC Morten De'Geer had felt bad about ducking out of the evening pizza session, but he hadn't lied when he said that he had something else to go to; what he hadn't mentioned was whether it was actively related to the case in hand.

It was a cold evening in Henley-on-Thames as De'Geer climbed out of a cab outside the *Three Tuns* pub on Market Place. He was annoyed at this inconvenience; cabs in the area were always expensive, but he'd left his motorbike in London, and unfortunately this was the only way to make it to the pub.

The building itself was a bit of an enigma, and a focus point for people with a more esoteric belief in nature; unlike the other pubs in the town, all claiming their various 'oldest pub' heritage with stories of coaching inns and breweries, the *Three Tuns* wasn't an old pub; it had actually been a mortuary before being converted into the pub that De'Geer now stood in front of, and rather than traditional stories of unquiet spirits, the pub boasted a mysterious, locked door in the cellar, one that was believed to link to a selection of old tunnels and passageways that criss-crossed under Henley's Old Square.

It was the perfect pub to meet in.

Entering the bar, De'Geer looked around for the person he was meeting. The front bar was square and medium-sized, with the ceiling rafters giving the pub an old, Tudor building feel, even though the green and white paint scheme and the hardwood flooring made it feel a little more modern. There, at a corner of the bar, sitting behind a small, square two-person table, was his dinner companion.

'I wasn't expecting this,' she said as De'Geer walked over and kissed her on the cheek. 'You've been so busy with work recently.'

'I know, mum,' De'Geer sat down, forcing a smile. Freya De'Geer was as unlike her son as she could be; petite and with dark brown wispy hair, she was in her late forties, dressed in jeans, a chunky jumper and with an olive-coloured *Barbour* coat hung on a hook behind her.

'I wasn't sure what you were drinking, so I didn't bother ordering,' she said, sipping at her own glass of Malbec. 'While you're up there, grab a bag of pork scratchings.'

'I thought you were still vegetarian?' De'Geer rose, walking to the bar and waving for service. Freya shrugged.

'It gets boring,' she smiled. De'Geer tossed over a packet of scratchings and, sitting back down with a pint of craft ale, he clasped her hand in his for a moment before letting go.

'So, what's the problem?' his mother observed him as she spoke. 'You've not asked for counsel for a while now.'

De'Geer took a deep mouthful of his ale before speaking.

'I think I might be in trouble,' he replied. 'I don't know yet, I thought I was doing the right thing, but it might backfire on me.'

'Go on.'

De'Geer chose his words carefully. 'I had a lecturer,' he started. 'Rupert Wilson.'

'I know,' Freya replied. 'Man off the telly. Saw he was dead.'

De'Geer nodded. 'I thought it was wrong that nobody was properly investigating his death, so I pushed to have my new department investigate it.'

'That doesn't seem too bad.'

De'Geer shook his head. 'That's not the problem,' he said. 'There're complications involved. Professor Wilson might have been murdered as part of some weird occult ritual, and it might be because of lost treasure.'

'Still don't get where we're going with this,' Freya De'Geer sighed. 'I thought you were going to tell me you'd met a girl or something.'

'I have, but that's irrelevant,' De'Geer replied, grabbing his mother's wrist, holding it onto the table as he did so. 'Something came up, a clue, and it led to something I need to know about.'

He slowly turned the hand over, palm down, on the table, looking into his mother's eyes as he spoke.

'Tell me about the moon shaped scar, mum.'

Freya looked at her son for a long moment before replying. 'Are you sure you want to know?'

'I need to,' De'Geer nodded. 'Professor Wilson had the same. And his daughter had it too. Mum, I know you hung out in London in the nineties, but were you part of any cult connected to him? The scar is almost identical, and I know that you've always had a fixation with Ragnarok, and the cleansing flame of *Surtr*.'

Freya laughed.

'Is this what the police have done to you?' she chuckled. 'Made you see suspects everywhere?'

De'Geer shrugged.

'You acted like you'd only seen Professor Wilson on TV,' he replied. 'But I know that's not true. I know you used to go to a lot of the same conferences he did back in the nineties. It's not a leap of logic to think that you two might have... You know...'

'*Morten De'Geer!*' Freya half rose angrily. 'I will not have you say such slanderous things about me! *I am your mother!*'

De'Geer backtracked quickly.

'I'm being a detective,' he muttered.

'Well, how about being a son instead?' Freya leaned back in her seat, taking a large mouthful of Malbec. 'The moon isn't some kind of brand, it's just a scar. I had a body modification in there about twenty years back, and I removed it. That's all.'

'What kind of—'

'It was a *magnet*, Morten,' Freya snapped. 'It gave a tingling sensation when you went near metal. And the metal tingled too, so if you were doing something... personal...'

Morten De'Geer paled at his mother's words.

'I don't think we need to go any further,' he replied. Freya shook her head.

'Oh no, you wanted to know, and know you shall,' she replied with malice. 'I enjoyed it very much, especially the party tricks you could do with someone who had a metal Prince Albert piercing through their... well, their whatnots.'

'Did dad—'

'Oh yes. For several years. Jingled when he ran for the train.'

There was a silence in the bar as De'Geer processed this. Feeling a little sorry for him, Freya changed direction.

'But in the end I had to take it out, because I'd keep setting off shop security scanners as I entered and exited stores.'

De'Geer looked at the mark. 'So, it's just an implant scar?'

'I'm afraid so. Sometimes not everything has to be a secret symbol or a clever clue. Sometimes a scar is just a scar. Sorry for not being something worse,' Freya De'Geer sighed. 'Now, if you're done treating me like a suspect, why don't you order us some dinner and tell me about the woman you like, the one you're scared to talk about?'

AT THE SAME TIME THAT MORTEN DE'GEER WAS LEARNING things about his late father that he probably didn't want to know, Billy Fitzwarren was having his own family meeting, although this one was in a far posher location. Which was impressive considering how posh Henley-on-Thames was these days.

'I'm surprised you agreed to meet for dinner,' Chivalry said as he cut into his steak, currently sitting at a window seat in *The Ivy* restaurant. Billy considered this.

'I don't know why,' he replied. 'You're the one who should turn my requests down, not the other way around.'

Chivalry ferociously chewed at his meat as he pondered the statement.

'True, but you've been in the cold long enough,' he replied after swallowing. 'It's time for the family to unite and welcome their lost sheep back into the fold.'

Billy paused, his fork halfway to his mouth, the asparagus tipping off it, falling back onto his plate.

'No,' he replied. 'This seems a little too easy, a little too convenient.'

'How?' Chivalry waved his own fork like a conductor. 'You're the one who emailed me, asking to meet. How am *I* being the suspicious one?'

'Because you're making it too easy for me,' Billy replied, digging back into his dinner. 'There's no negotiation. Your son, uncle Bryan is in prison because of me, and you're treating it like it never happened.'

Chivalry's eyes clouded as his face darkened.

'Oh, it happened,' he hissed and finally, the true personality of Steven 'Chivalry' Fitzwarren was revealed. 'And I'm very much aware of how much *you* had to do with it.'

'Then why are you being so nice?' Billy, exasperated, replied. Chivalry shrugged.

'Professional curiosity,' he stated. 'You called to meet, so I wanted to see what you were offering. I mean, I'm guessing you're offering me something, or we wouldn't be here.'

Billy found he didn't have an answer for this.

'I miss my mother,' he said eventually. 'When I put away Bryan, it was because he was hurting people. Doing underhanded things. I thought I was doing the right thing, that my family would understand.'

'And instead they threw you under a bus,' Chivalry grinned, steak juice running down his chin as he mopped at it with his napkin. 'That must have really hurt. Forgive me if I don't seem to express any concern.'

'You made a comment back in the pub,' Billy continued. 'That there was a chance that I could return.'

'That's a tough one,' Chivalry leaned back. 'We gave you

an opportunity to return, when Rufus Harrington offered you a stupidly well-paying job to leave the force. And for a moment, we thought you'd take it, too.'

'I thought so as well,' Billy nodded. 'I quit and everything. But then I realised something. I saw I made a genuine difference here. We've taken down some real vicious bastards in the time I've been here, and we're helping people. Good people.'

'People who aren't your family,' Chivalry muttered.

Billy shook his head.

'Don't give me that,' he replied. 'You've not given two shits about the family for years, either. You and my dad barely talk, and great-grandfather disowned you because of your hobbies.'

'No, it was actually because I was spending too much on them,' Chivalry corrected. 'My father was as much an occultist as I was. He was just a miserly one.'

He placed his cutlery on the side of the plate, not finished but deciding instead to get this conversation out of the way before he continued.

'You can be a black sheep of the family, you can be a loyal drone, or you can be out of the family, constantly trying to beg your way back in. Currently, you've been both two and three on that list. If I was to back you, they'd listen. They might not forgive you but you'd be back for Christmas brunch, and that's something.'

'I just want to look at my mother again and not see disappointment,' Billy replied.

Chivalry snorted.

'My boy, you'll never get that, even if you're welcomed back into the bosom of the matriarchy,' he said. 'Fitzwarren women are harsh by necessity.'

'Okay, so what do you need from me?' Billy asked.

Chivalry leaned closer.

'When you were a kid, you loved playing with my trinkets,' he said carefully. 'You understood the cost, the importance of these items. And now I want your help in gaining new ones.'

'The Humphrey Library.'

Chivalry nodded. 'The chances are that it's fake,' he replied. 'That they found nothing. Hell, a week after they claimed to have found it, they then said they'd made it up, regardless of the four items they found—and there were rumours of a fifth man called Marcus dying because of the curse, but nobody ever saw him, and nobody knows what to believe.'

'So if it's fake, why hunt it?'

'Because it might *not* be,' Chivalry continued. 'And if you meet a group called the *Consortium*, let me know immediately. Night or day.'

'Is this who you were talking about at lunch?' Billy noted the name down on a napkin, although this was mainly for show. 'The ones who had painted targets on peoples backs?'

Chivalry looked around before replying.

'Big item seller,' he explained. 'And they don't care how they get things. If they think someone can find them an item, they'll use that person until they don't need them anymore. I've had my run-ins with them, lost myself a beautiful silver scrying mirror to them two years back. Shame, as it was once conjured through by Aleister Crowley.'

'And you think the *Consortium* will lead you to the library?'

Chivalry started on his food again, eating with relish, and speaking in half filled mouthfuls.

'I don't care about the library. I'd like it to exist, I'd like the books to be real. But what I want to do is steal it from right under the *Consortium's* nose.'

He finished his mouthful and, with a downward slicing motion, speared the remnants of his steak with his knife.

'You get me *them*, and I'll get you your family back,' he said.

Billy took a few moments before nodding.

'I'd like that, great-uncle,' he replied.

'I'd like that very much.'

'Good,' Chivalry pulled out a notepad, placing it on the table beside the napkin. 'So let's work out some Enochian together, and find a secret library.'

16

TO THE UNDERWORLD

AFTER THEY'D FINISHED WITH THE LADIES OF AVALON, Bullman asked Declan to arrange for an overnight stay elsewhere; even though the Temple Inn offices had cells on the upper level, they were mainly for placing people in who were imminently about to be questioned, rather than kept in holding for long periods of time, especially overnight. To be honest, this wasn't an unusual situation either; although the City of London's 'square mile' had almost half a million commuters and tourists entering it every day, the actual resident population was only around nine thousand people, which meant that out of the four City of London Command Units, *Temple Inn, Guildhall, Wood Street* and *Bishopsgate*, only the last of these had a custody suite built into it, with around fifteen available cells inside.

Thirteen cells now, as both Cindy and Lilith had been taken to Bishopsgate to spend the night.

From there he'd driven back to Hurley, and an irate Anjli who, having learned he'd wrangled some kind of interview scenario with Bullman after simply dropping off his daughter, demanded all the details. Which was fine, to be honest, as Declan found that discussing the case with a fellow officer, even if it was one that now lived in his house, helped work out in his head *what the hell was actually going on.*

The following morning, De'Geer woke Declan by knocking on his front door. Sheepishly, the officer explained that because of bringing Declan directly back from the university the previous evening, he hadn't brought his motor-bike home, and therefore needed a lift into the office. Which meant, after a breakfast consisting mainly of cold pizza and terrible coffee, they had an almost full car back into London.

An almost full car that was diverted back to Queen Mary University when Declan received a cryptic message from Monroe as they pulled off the A501 near Euston Station.

You'll want to see this. QMU now

'What do you think it is?' De'Geer asked. 'Do you think they've found something in Rupert Wilson's office?'

'I'd be very surprised if they hadn't,' Declan replied as he now made his way towards Mile End. 'Either that or Monroe wants a lift into the office too.'

As it turned out, Monroe hadn't discovered anything. It'd been Charlie Williams, one of the crime scene photographers who'd caught the lead. And, as Declan, Anjli and De'Geer entered the basement office to see Monroe waiting for them, it was Charlie who started talking.

'My SD card was corrupted,' he explained as an introduc-tion. 'I took all these pictures while everyone was around earlier, and every one of them was gone. Spooky, to be honest. Never happened before. But, as I knew nothing was going to be done until today, I popped in early this morning to take them again with a fresh card, because I knew nothing had been moved in between.'

'So, is this about the photos, or the fact that you did it today?' Declan asked.

Charlie grinned. 'Well. I'm in here alone. Not like yesterday with every bugger and their dog wandering about, clattering around the bloody place. I take some photos, and then I stop as I hear a beep.'

'A beep.'

'Yes, a beep,' Charlie nodded. 'One that carried on while I was working, every ninety seconds.'

He held up his wrist, showing his watch.

'I timed it.'

'Shh,' Monroe said, looking at his own watch. Everyone stopped as they looked at him. He held a finger in the air, and in the distance there was a faint yet audible *beep*.

'Ninety seconds to the dot.'

'Smoke detector?' Anjli suggested.

'Not in this room,' Monroe pointed at a filing cabinet. 'When I arrived, Charlie told me to check out that wall cabinet. Said the beep is coming from behind it.'

'So it's next door.'

'That's the fun part, laddie,' Monroe grinned at Declan. 'There is no next door. That there? It's the *external* wall. According to the layout map, the other side should be solid concrete.'

Everyone stared at the cabinet as, in the distance, they could hear another faint beep.

'So we move the cabinet,' De'Geer suggested. Monroe nodded.

'Why do you think I called you here?' he replied. 'There's no way just two of us could have done this. We need a team effort. It's bloody heavy, but Thor there could do it himself.'

Sighing, Declan took off his jacket and, with De'Geer, Monroe and Anjli taking corners of the cabinet, they shifted it out of the way, moving it off the wall and revealing a small, handmade hole in the brickwork behind it, large enough for someone to clamber through.

'Bloody secret rooms,' Declan muttered. 'Did Wilson know my dad?'

Anjli chuckled as she leaned into the hole, shining a torch around. 'It looks like a crawlspace,' she said, listening for a moment. 'The beep is coming from the left. Someone else can go down there first.'

Declan allowed Anjli to step back before pulling himself into the hole, his own torch in his hand. Now in the crawl-space, he realised it was about two feet in width, so a narrow but easily moveable path. The floor was dusty, but he could make footprints out in the dust, heading left from the entrance.

'Someone's definitely been this way recently. I'll have a quick look,' he said, inching his way along the corridor. The air was stale, musty even, and about five feet along it he found a similar sized hole in the opposite wall.

'There's another room here,' he exclaimed, clambering into it.

The space was small, around the same size as Rupert Wilson's office; there was a metal door across the room with what looked like a card scanner lock on it, and beside this was an old computer, turned off. In the room's corner was what looked to be a small GoPro camera on a tripod, as if standing guard over the empty room. There was a light switch by the door, and Declan clicked it on, jumping back as he looked at the room in the light.

In the centre of the room, on the floor, was a pentagram painted in something red; it was likely paint, but Declan couldn't help but wonder if it was *blood*. At each of the points of the star was a chunky black candle, most of which had obviously been used recently because of the melted wax on the floor, and around the circumference of the pentagram were strange, yet familiar symbols.

Enochian.

The tiny screen of the camera in the corner lit up briefly, but after a solitary *beep* it turned off.

'There was a second door here, but it's been bricked up,' Anjli, who had somehow entered the room without Declan noticing was shining her torch on another wall, where the brickwork, although painted to match the rest of the room, was slightly different. 'I'm guessing we now know why Professor Wilson wanted to teach at Queen Mary, and why he wanted that particular office.'

Declan shuddered. *What the hell was this place?*

'We need to get out of here,' he was already walking back to the hole. 'Touch nothing. Doctor Marcos can work out what this is before we do anything else.'

Making his way out of the room, down the crawlspace and climbing back into the office, Declan looked at Monroe.

'I don't know how this links to what we know about the case so far, Guv,' he breathed. 'But that's some seriously screwed up stuff. It looks like he had made a ritual area, and was filming it.'

'Need some air?' Monroe asked, a little too patronisingly. 'Go upstairs and call Billy. He's trying to contact us and there's no signal here.'

'Or I could use the office phone,' Declan smiled as he walked to Wilson's desk and picked up the receiver, dialling nine for an outside line. After dialling Billy's extension, he waited for his colleague to pick up.

'It's me,' he eventually said as Billy answered. 'Monroe said you were trying to contact him.'

'*I might have something for you,*' Billy replied down the phone.

'Good, because we've definitely got something here for you,' Declan looked back to the hole in the wall. 'You need to get your arse here pronto before someone else looks at the ritual circle we just found in a secret room—'

Declan smiled. Billy had already disconnected the phone, and right now was probably pulling on his jacket while running out of the Command Unit. Taking a moment to call Doctor Marcos, informing her of what they had found, Declan looked back to Monroe.

'That's not a hand built room,' he said, 'that's a room that was built when the underground floor we're on was, but it's been removed from all the University wall maps. We need to speak to someone about this, find out what it was, and where the other door leads.'

'Already ahead of you,' Monroe nodded to Anjli as he walked to the door. 'Both of you come with me, PC De'Geer can keep Charlie company while we wait for forensics. Let's go chat with the administrator.'

MARGARET DONALDSON WAS JUST AS CONFUSED AT THE mention of a secret, underground room.

'Maybe it's not part of the university?' she asked. 'Like

some criminals enter bank vaults by tunnelling in from the shop next door?'

'We considered that,' Monroe nodded. 'Unfortunately, judging from the location, it seems to be directly under us. And I can't believe that nobody knew about this, especially as it has power, an old computer and a locked door.'

Margaret was already searching through old maps as she tried to work out what it could have been.

Declan stared out of the window, trying to think of anything that could help. There was something, he was sure of it—

'Throw a stone in London and hit a nuclear reactor. No, better still, hit two.'

'Where was the reactor?' he asked suddenly. 'The nuclear one?'

'Oh no, that wasn't here,' Margaret looked at a colleague, a tall, thin, balding man who'd appeared out of nowhere. 'That was the Marshgate site, where the Olympic Village is. And that was decommissioned back in the early eighties.'

'Well, it *was* there,' the tall man nodded, 'but before that, it was on the Mile End site. They moved it.'

'But that wasn't *here*, was it?' Margaret, realising she'd made an error, was now backtracking.

They were interrupted by Billy coming through the main entrance in a run.

'Am I too late?' he asked breathlessly.

'We're discussing secret rooms and nuclear reactors,' Declan explained. 'What did you have to say?'

Billy pulled out his notepad as he sidled Declan, Anjli and Monroe away from the administrator and her colleague, now arguing over the map.

'My great-uncle, he and I—that is we—we talked last

night,' he stuttered, his voice low. 'He thinks he knows what the pictures on Rupert Wilson's wall meant.'

'We know what they meant,' Monroe replied. 'The secrets on a tomb near a Devil's Temple. Look at someone historical and work out what they're known for.'

'Yes, that's the translation,' Billy smiled. 'But I think we worked out the meanings.'

Declan noted the use of *we* here; Billy had obviously been talking to his great-uncle more than he was letting on.

'There was an architect named Hawksmoor,' Billy explained. 'We've already heard his name a couple of times. He was nicknamed the *Devil's architect*, because five of his London churches were believed to form a pentagram, he was a Freemason and sacred geometry fascinated him.'

'Okay, so what's the temple?'

'St Anne's Church Limehouse,' Billy opened his phone, showing the map location. 'It's on the Dee Line we keep hearing about, it was the first church that he built and designed fully on his own, and it has the added mystery of having an eight foot high stone pyramid, designed by Hawksmoor, placed on the grounds to the west, inscribed with the words *the wisdom of Solomon*. People believe it was supposed to be his own tomb, but it never happened.'

'Secrets on a tribute tomb, to the west of the Devil's temple,' Declan muttered. 'Could be right.'

'If Billy and his mad uncle think it's true, then others could as well,' Monroe mused. 'We have to go on the belief that whoever killed Wilson also gained this information.'

He looked at Declan.

'Take DS Kapoor and go check it out. See if any familiar faces have been around there recently. I think we'll be here a while.'

'We're on treasure hunt duty?' Declan was surprised.

'Currently laddie, we're on *find any bloody clue we can because we're scrabbling in the dark* duty,' Monroe smiled. 'Or did you miss the wee clues in my tone?'

Declan nodded, and with Anjli matching step, they left the university, heading for his car. It was a mile and a half southwards to the church, and a ten-minute drive in the morning traffic.

Declan intended to make it there in five.

As they drove down Aston Street, en route to the A13, Anjli looked at Declan, concern on her face.

'You think it's healthy?' she asked. 'That Billy's talking to his family again?'

'Maybe,' Declan replied. 'I know it hurt him to be cut off.'

'Yeah, but how far will he go to be let back in?' Anjli questioned. 'Maybe letting his family gain a magical occult library?'

'That only happens if the library even exists,' Declan shrugged as they pulled out onto the Commercial Road. Across the street and on the right, they could see the spire of St Anne's Church. However, it was what was around the church that surprised him.

The blue flashing lights of three police squad cars.

'That's not good,' he said as they turned into Threecolt Street, flashing their own lights to allow a police officer to raise a hastily placed crime scene tape to let them pass through, effectively closing off the road.

Pulling over onto the pavement, Declan and Anjli exited the car, walking into the churchyard from the south-east corner. A police sergeant ran over to them, nodding as they flashed their warrants.

'Bloody hell, you're fast!' she exclaimed. 'We only just called it in!'

'Called what in?' Anjli asked. 'I think you might find we're here for something different.'

'Well then, your timing is impeccable, Guv,' the sergeant said as she led them around the north of the church, and towards a stone pyramid, eight feet in height, currently cordoned off from the public. 'We haven't even had forensics arrive yet.'

'What happened?' Declan asked as they approached the pyramid. Behind the cordon, just out of sight, was a pair of legs.

'Dead body,' the sergeant explained. 'Dog walker found her first thing this morning. Just resting against the pyramid like she's waiting for someone, her throat slashed open, and left to bleed out. We're waiting for someone to help us identify her—'

'No need,' Declan replied, staring down at the lifeless face. 'We know who she is.'

'Excellent news,' the sergeant beamed with relief. 'That'll make the paperwork easier. Although, can you also explain why someone cut off her right hand?'

Declan stared at the handless body, noting that above her, wiped onto the stone in what must have been her own blood, a bloody handprint at the end, was a line of words.

3 BLINDE MICE

'Cut off their tails with a carving knife,' Anjli mused. 'Are the tails the hands? And if so, does this mean there's one more to go?'

'Let's hope not,' Declan sighed, turning away from the body. For all that she did to him, Declan hadn't wanted this ending for Lucy Shrimpton.

The question was, *who did?*

17

PARK POLICE

IT WAS CLOSE TO LUNCHTIME BEFORE THE FORENSICS HAD finished at St Anne's Church. Declan and Anjli had stayed until Doctor Marcos arrived, annoyed that she had to check over a murder scene instead of some conspiratorial secret bunker, but her professionalism shone through as she started bringing a semblance of order to the scene, the first of which was to tell Declan and Anjli to go away, and that she'd contact them when she had anything. By then Billy had texted to say he was heading back to the Command Unit, so Declan assumed whatever secrets Queen Mary University's secret room held had already been found.

They were getting into the Audi when Bullman phoned.

'I'd suggest you get back here,' she said through the car speakers as Declan started the engine. 'We've got people trying to take your case from you.'

'Shouldn't you be stopping them, Ma'am?'

'What do you think I'm doing?' Bullman snapped before disconnecting.

Arriving at Temple Inn, Declan stopped at the reception;

the officer on duty, PC Mastakin nodded to him as he entered.

'You been told we have guests, sir?' he asked.

'Something to that end,' Declan stopped at the counter. 'Who is it?'

'Inspector Saeed from the *Royal Parks Operational Command Unit*,' Mastakin replied. 'Apparently they hold jurisdiction for Greenwich Park and only heard about your case last night.'

'They didn't know they had a dead body in their park all weekend?' Anjli chuckled. 'That bodes well for them.'

'Yeah, and that's the problem, Sarge,' PC Mastakin leaned closer, as if scared he'd be overheard. 'They're on the back foot and they're defensive. Came in twenty minutes back with a face of fire.'

'So they're here for a fight,' Declan sighed. 'They can't be seen to have missed this, so they'll claim we took it from them.'

Nodding to the desk officer, they walked through the doors, making their way up the stairs towards the main office.

'Why weren't they told?' Anjli asked as they climbed the stairs. 'I mean, seriously, Deptford should have worked with them from the start. And didn't Park police find the *Ghost Bros* in the first place?'

'Park police are overlooked for a lot of things, like the transport police,' Declan shrugged. 'I reckon we're going to find out more about this very soon.'

Entering the upstairs floor, Declan immediately saw that Inspector Saeed was in Bullman's office; that was, a short, overly large man in a police uniform stood irritably stroking at his greying beard, a scar running down his left temple, cutting through his greying eyebrow while Bullman ignored him. A police Inspector was the same rank as Declan, and so while he would have to treat Saeed as an equal, Bullman, being two ranks higher had no such concerns. Looking up, she nodded at Declan, as if telling Saeed to *go speak to him.* Saeed, seeing Declan and Anjli, left the office without a word, stomping over to Declan with a face like thunder.

'Inspector Saeed,' Declan held out a hand. 'I'm Detective Inspector Walsh, this is Detective Sergeant Kapoor.'

Saeed took the hand. 'Finally, someone who plays well with others,' he said as he glared back at Bullman's office. 'How do you work with that woman?'

'She's an acquired taste,' Anjli smiled. 'What seems to be the problem?'

'The fact that a man died in our park, and none of my people have been kept in the loop, Saeed replied sullenly. 'We—'

'I'm going to interrupt you there,' Declan raised a hand. 'Saving time for all of us. First, Professor Wilson wasn't killed in your park, they left him there. Second, your own officers would have driven past him while checking for stragglers before closing but didn't notice him. And third, unless I'm mistaken, you have no CID or forensics available in Greenwich Park, hence the need for Deptford being called in. And, as they *were* called in, I'm assuming you had no issues with them running the case, and you only have one now because *we're* involved.'

'This is a Met police affair,' Saeed replied, the smile now gone. 'Not a City police matter.'

'The victim was believed to have been murdered within the City walls,' Anjli replied. 'Where the body was dumped is irrelevant.'

'But you didn't know that until you took the case.'

'And you didn't know that Wilson didn't die in the park until just now,' Declan snapped. 'So why don't we drop the ranks, take off the IDs and discuss what's really going on here?'

It was as if all the air suddenly escaped out of Inspector Saeed; his shoulders slumped, and his puffed out chest retreated as he leaned against the table.

'I'd like to be kept involved,' he said, softer now. 'It's a personal matter.'

'The last police who asked if they could be involved, turned out to be a killer,' Anjli replied. 'So forgive us if we need a little more, sir.'

Saeed looked around. 'You got a coffee place nearby?' he asked. 'Off site?'

'That can be arranged,' Declan smiled. 'Come on, let's see if City coffee's better than Met coffee.'

INSPECTOR SAEED LEANED BACK ON THE COUCH AND SIPPED gingerly at his chai tea latte. They'd moved to a small coffee shop on Fleet Street, a chain branch with one long bench seat along the wall with tiny tables spread along it, and smaller, more comfortable chairs surrounding small coffee tables by the window. It was at one of these that Anjli, Declan, and Saeed now sat.

'I'll let that cool down,' he muttered as he placed the glass cup back on the table.

'So,' Declan said, as if hoping to lead Saeed into conversation. When nothing happened, he continued. 'I see police riding horses in a lot of the Royal Parks. Do you have a horse?'

Saeed stared at him for a moment.

'Do I look like I ride a bloody horse?' he asked. Declan shrugged.

'Sorry,' he said. 'Don't know much about park police.'

Saeed nodded at this. 'Fair enough,' he said. 'It's the same as normal police, except for the times it's not.'

Anjli leaned in, blowing on her coffee. 'Like how?'

'Well, policing open spaces like a park differs from what you guys do, because you haven't got a resident population,' Saeed started. 'In a park, people come to enjoy themselves, to see family, walk the dog, have picnics, all that sort of thing and the conflicts often arise when one person's enjoyment is another's annoyance.'

He sighed, as if tired of the whole thing.

'One of the first jobs I got sent to was a vicious stabbing attack in Regent's Park,' he finished. 'People thought it was a gangland thing, but in the end it turned out to be an argument because of a bloody Cocker Spaniel.'

'So what, a dead body is more interesting?'

Saeed shrugged. 'Which would you prefer?' he smiled faintly. 'But as I said, this was more of a personal matter. I knew Rupert Wilson.'

Declan glanced at Anjli. 'Do you mind telling us the nature of your relationship?'

'We had similar interests,' Saeed replied. 'We were part of the same lodge, for a start.'

'Rupert Wilson was a Freemason?'

'You make it sound so secretive,' Saeed laughed. 'We have our share of academics, too. But I met Rupert way before that. During the park protests in the nineties.'

Anjli looked confused at this, and it was Declan who replied. 'You mean the ones about the concrete steps?'

'Among others,' Saeed nodded. 'I was a starting off, wet-behind-the-ears copper in the park service back then. Mainly crowd control, walking about with an oversized helmet on my head rather than a peaked cap. We didn't even have stab vests back then. And to be honest, in the parks we never really needed them.'

He tried his tea again, wincing at the heat.

'Rupert was a good man,' he said. 'The problem with park policing is that we're in the moment, we never take on long running cases. So, when they found the body, they called in CID, which was Deptford. Which meant that I didn't hear about this until today.'

His face darkened.

'I want to catch the person who did this,' he hissed, the emotion drained from his voice. 'Do you have a suspect?'

Declan frowned, pulling out his phone as he spoke.

'Now, this is the interesting part of the conversation,' he said, tapping a message on the phone. 'Because currently, we don't have a clue. We thought it was to do with Marie, his alleged daughter, but she's just been found in Limehouse. We'd just got back from there when you arrived, and I'm just checking for an update right now.'

He leaned in.

'So why don't you tell us who *you* think killed Rupert? And for that matter, Marie Wilson?'

Saeed stared in shock at Declan.

'Lucy's dead?' he whispered.

Declan glanced at Anjli, who looked just as confused at Saeed's response as he was.

'Found about an hour ago,' he continued. 'Forensics is on the scene now. I assumed you'd heard.' He now re-considered about how to progress the conversation.

'What was her connection to you?'

Saeed looked away from the two detectives.

'I knew her mother,' he said. 'She was a genius, you know. Super high intellect, worked for GCHQ, had an amazing career. Far more than the others.'

'You think one of the others could have killed Rupert?' Declan asked. Saeed paused before answering.

'I think one or two of them were probably involved, yes,' he nodded. 'It's no secret they all hated each other in the end. But I don't know if any of them would have killed Lucy too.'

Declan noted down that Saeed was comfortable saying *Lucy*, even though she was announced as *Marie*.

Saeed slumped back in his seat.

'I realise now how being a simple park copper hasn't really trained me for this sort of thing,' he admitted. 'But if there's anything I can do to help you, please let me know.'

'Of course,' Declan replied, smiling. 'And if you can think of anything that could explain all this, then please let me know.'

There was a moment of silence in the coffee shop before Saeed spoke again.

'Do you think I could visit his apartment?' he asked softly. 'Of course, I'd expect one of you to chaperone me. It's just that Rupert spoke so fondly of it over the years, and I'd love to see it before it, well before whatever happens to it. And I know there are police still around, so I wouldn't want to hassle them.'

Anjli was nodding, but something about the request, or more likely how it was phrased, sent a warning down Declan's spine.

There was something not right here.

'Of course,' he said, joining Anjli in nodding. 'We can get

someone to go with you today. Although you won't really see it as it was.'

'What do you mean?' Saeed was confused, but not as confused as Anjli, who glanced at Declan, keeping her thoughts to herself for the moment.

'Well, the forensics team went a little gung-ho,' Declan continued. 'Took all the paintings down off the west wall and piled them in a corner.'

He shrugged apologetically.

'If I'd known you wanted to see them, I could have asked Detective Superintendent Bullman to sort you a pass through the cordon, but to be honest they're taking the art prints to Scotland Yard tomorrow morning, and by the time we'd get the pass sorted, it'd be empty.'

Declan smiled.

'Still want to go look at the apartment after they're gone, Inspector Saeed?'

There was a long moment of silence as Saeed stared at Declan.

'I wouldn't want to put you out,' he replied.

'Well, that's mighty courteous of you, but it's really no trouble. We can see if we can get you in later,' Declan nodded. 'Do you have a number we can contact you on?'

'Of course,' Saeed fake-smiled as he pulled out a business card, but it was a forced, nervous one as he passed it across.

INSPECTOR KHALED SAEED
ROYAL PARKS OPERATIONAL COMMAND UNIT

Underneath it was an email address and a mobile phone number.

Declan immediately pulled out his phone, tapping the number and holding it to his ear.

'Uh-oh,' he frowned. 'Looks like your service has gone down.'

Saeed shrugged.

'Oh, it might be my old number,' he suggested. 'We upgraded recently.'

'Excellent,' Declan held out his hand. 'Pass me your phone and I'll just dial myself. That way you'll have mine too.' His own phone buzzed, and he glanced at the message before looking back at Saeed, now looking at his watch.

'Maybe we can do this another time,' Saeed replied, rising. 'I need—'

'You need to *sit back down*,' Declan snapped, grabbing Saeed's arm. 'And then you need to give me your phone before I have my Detective Sergeant here *arrest* you.'

'Now listen here—'

'*Phone.*'

Reluctantly, as if not wanting to cause a scene, Saeed pulled out a phone, passing it to Declan who, with some quick taps on the keypad, called his own number. As his own phone beeped, he smiled back at Saeed.

'There you go,' he said as he tapped once more on Saeed's phone. 'All friends here. And look, I'm even putting myself into your contacts list, in case you forget whose number it is.'

He passed the phone back at the now angry Saeed.

'One last thing, have you ever heard of the *Consortium*?'

'No.' The answer was brisk and unfriendly now.

'Even when talking to Rupert?'

'No.'

'And would you care to explain how you know Marie Wilson under her older name, Lucy?'

'I'm sorry, but I'm feeling decidedly *got at,* here. Good day, detectives,' Saeed took his phone, briefly checking it as if checking that it was the correct one, rising once more from his seat, and walking out of the coffee shop without continuing the conversation.

Declan breathed out a sigh.

'Was that wise, Guv?' Anjli asked. 'He's the same rank as you. He could make things hard for us if he raises a police complaint.'

'You have to be *police* to raise a police complaint,' Declan mused. 'And I think if we look for Inspector Saeed, we'll find either a confused stranger or a blank file. All he wanted was to gain a look around the apartment. And we can guess why.'

'The treasure clues,' Anjli shook her head. 'Either to find the answers, or maybe even destroy them. But how can you be sure?'

Declan showed his phone to Anjli. On it were two messages.

'Because I checked with De'Geer,' he said.

Ask your friend in Deptford how they were told about Rupert in Greenwich

He said the park coppers called them in after they caught the ghost bros trying to climb the gates

'The Royal Parks police knew about it, and told Deptford,' Declan explained. 'And if that's the case, then there's no way that our Inspector Saeed there wouldn't have known.'

'And you just let him go?'

'Don't worry, we've got him on tracking,' Declan smiled.

'Billy gave me a small, cloud-based tracker address to put in a phone in case someone captured me again.'

'Again?'

'Well, it's not like he doesn't have a point,' Declan smiled. 'I just put it into Saeed's phone browser, while placing my contact details in.'

He finished his flat white, wiping his mouth and rising from his chair.

'It won't last long and I'm sure he'll find it soon, but for now, wherever our mysterious man goes? We'll be right behind him.'

18

INTERVIEW WITH A VAMPIRE

RETURNING TO TEMPLE INN, DECLAN HAD LEARNED THERE WAS unlikely to be any forensics movement on Lucy's murder until late afternoon, and with the Ladies of Avalon not due to return to the interview rooms from Bishopsgate until around an hour before then, Bullman sent Declan and Anjli off to interview the two remaining *Musketeers*, John Gale and Julie-Anna Watson. Anjli had offered to take the latter, as Watson was advertised as a psychic, and the last thing Anjli wanted was Declan being mind controlled again, but Declan replied that thanks to DC Davey, he had mind control resistance wards better than *Batman*, and so he took Watson to interview. Which was fine by Anjli, because John Gale sounded a little more interesting.

In fact, Anjli couldn't have predicted how interesting John Gale would be. *The Mail on Sunday's* receptionist had claimed not to know where he was when she called, however had aimed her towards a website listing guided walks around London, where his name was down for a walk that day. The receptionist had explained *this was his new job*, before disconnecting before Anjli could ask why he needed one.

Slim, tall and in his late sixties, his grey hair slicked back into a ponytail, John Gale was standing at the junction of Ava Maria and Paternoster Lane, to the west of St Paul's Cathedral, dressed like Count Dracula.

'It's not what it looks like,' he smiled as Anjli introduced herself. 'I'm a blue badge tour guide, and I'm doing a walk in ten minutes, showing the *dark side of London*,' he pointed across the road at Amen Corner. '*You follow that around, and you walk beside one of the few remaining walls of Newgate Prison*, that sort of thing.'

'And you're dressed like that because...'

'I talk a lot about Bram Stoker later,' John explained. 'We eventually end up at the Lyceum Theatre, where he wrote *Dracula* while working as Henry Irving's business manager.'

He leaned in, speaking in a stage whisper.

'I'm not really a Vampire,' he smiled, showing two pretty convincing fake fangs.

Anjli pointed at his cheek, where a long plaster currently resided. 'Nasty cut?'

'I have cats,' John smiled. 'Sometimes they like to show me love, other times...' he shrugged.

'Another cat attack?' Anjli pointed at a red mark on his neck.

'Burn scar, actually,' John replied casually. 'Runs from under my ear to my shoulder. Accident at a scout camp fire when I was about nine. Not major, but it pops out to say hello every now and then.'

Anjli looked around and saw, around twenty feet away, a small group of Japanese tourists taking selfies beside a tall, metallic statue, the sign stating that it was "Angel's Wings" by *Thomas Heatherwick*. 'Busy walk?'

John shrugged.

'Mid week, lunchtime walk. Always slow, but they're often the better ones. More personable. Would you like to join it? Free for City Police. Or, I'm doing a Ripper walk tonight, starts at Tower Hill station at seven-thirty.'

'Not a good time.'

'Well, I do those every day of the week,' John gave a winning smile. 'I'm one of the most popular Ripperologists in London, and you're always welcome.'

Anjli looked through her notes. 'I thought you were working for *The Mail on Sunday?*' she asked. 'Surely doing this eats into your time?'

A shadow crossed John's face. 'We've parted ways.'

'Oh? Was it—'

'Is this why you've come to speak to me, Detective Sergeant?' John replied irritably. 'My exit from a Sunday paper?'

'Actually, if you have a couple of minutes before you start, I was hoping to talk about Rupert Wilson,' Anjli coldly stated, refusing to rise to his anger. John's face showed no emotion at this.

'Yeah, I heard he killed himself,' he muttered. 'Sorry, we weren't really talking at the end.'

'Falling out?'

'People move on.'

'Can you tell me where you were on Friday, same sort of time as now?' Anjli had pulled out her notebook. John made an attempt of remembering.

'I had a lunchtime walk, Noses of Soho,' he replied. 'Started on Essex Street. Am I a suspect?'

'Looking at all angles here,' Anjli was noncommittal in her answer. 'How did you meet Rupert?'

John chuckled, an unnerving sight considering his attire.

'He joined us robbing graves,' he said.

DECLAN DIDN'T KNOW WHAT TO EXPECT FROM JULIE-ANNA Watson, but the one thing he didn't expect was to find her in the lobby of a corporate headquarters, smack bang in the middle of Canary Wharf, sitting on a sofa beside the window, thirty feet from the security and reception desk. She was elderly, probably mid seventies, dressed in a long, flowing blue dress, her grey hair in what looked like a perm, her oversized glasses nestled within the curls. As Declan approached her, she smiled, almost apologetically.

'Sorry love, I only do employees and clients,' she said. Declan looked around the lobby.

'How do you know that I'm not either of those?' he asked. Julie-Anna shrugged.

'Years of practice,' she smiled. 'And your aura isn't the same as the others.'

This surprised Declan. 'My aura?' he asked, looking at his reflection in the window, as if expecting to see it. At this, Julie-Anna laughed.

'Oh, sit down, officer,' she said, through wheezing breaths. 'I saw you show your warrant card to the doorman. No magic there. My Angels didn't tell me anything.'

Declan sat down, a little relieved at this. 'I'm guessing you're Miss Watson?'

Julie-Anna's smile dropped as she nodded confirmation.

'I'm guessing this is about Rupert? Poor man.' She looked

over at one of the security guards at the reception desk, currently watching them. 'I'm taking five, Richie, okay?'

The security guard nodded as Julie-Anna looked back at Declan. 'I do this twice a week. Company thinks it makes them stand out, you know? While waiting for a meeting, have a quick tarot reading, or a mediumship session. Does well for them, and of course pays the bills for me.'

'So you're a medium?' Declan asked, settling into his chair.

'It's one term I use,' Julie-Anna replied. 'I also use Christian psychic.'

'Isn't that a contradiction?'

'How so?' Julie-Anna asked. 'They get visions, just like everyone else. Look at Joan of Arc.'

Declan was opening his notebook. 'You said *they*.'

'Well, yes,' Julie-Anna nodded. 'I mean, my guides are Angels, and I believe very much in the theology of Christ, but I'm aware of *more* out there, you know? I feel that I'm more a follower of all traditions.'

'But you're still the outsider,' Declan stated, more a comment than a question. Julie-Anna shrugged.

'I don't perform rituals or howl at the moon, if that's what you mean,' she said. 'So what's the problem? I saw about poor Rupert. And they took his hand? That's barbaric.'

'Where were you on Friday, Mrs Watson?' Declan ignored the question.

'Please, call me Jules,' Julie-Anna waved around the lobby. 'And I was here all day.'

Declan nodded. 'And how did you meet Professor Wilson?'

Julie-Anna thought about the question. 'I met him at a *Talking Stick*,' she said. 'It was an esoteric meeting group that met every two weeks in central London. I think we'd see each other there now and then, you know, enough to nod *hello* at. And then John brought him into the group.'

'Group?'

'We were dowsing in Greenwich,' Julie-Anna continued. 'Me, John, poor Miriam. She was younger than us, and when Rupert arrived, it was like a rock star appeared.'

'What's dowsing?' Declan was writing the word down.

'It's a type of divination,' Julie-Anna explained. 'You take a Y-shaped twig or rod, or more often two L-shaped ones, and you use them to locate things; underground water, buried metals or gemstones, gravesites, Ley Lines, all sorts of things. Also, we'd use them to gain readings on the *Motherstone*.'

'Readings?'

Julie-Anna smiled.

'All items have power. We're all part of the same cosmic stardust. And if an item is removed, the area it possessed beforehand could still keep the power within.'

'So what, you could take the stones out of Stonehenge, but you can't take Stonehenge out of the stones?'

Julie-Anna laughed. 'I like that. I'm going to steal it, as it's very good.'

'And this energy, it would be good or bad?'

Julie-Anna considered the question.

'The thoughts of an innocent,' she eventually said. 'Oh, how I love those. Let's give you an example.'

She rubbed her hands together.

'A swimming pool. Sunny day, Jack is playing in the water. He's jumping in, splashing his friends, having a great time. However, as he walks back to the changing rooms, he passes Jill. Now Jill hates water. She can't swim, and she fears it. Jack, playing a joke, pushes her into the water as he passes. She falls in and drowns.'

'Not the version I know of Jack and Jill,' Declan muttered.

'The point is this, Inspector,' Julie-Anna continued. 'The water killed Jill. Is the water evil?'

'No, it's just water.'

'Exactly. Jack had a great time in it. Water is water. However, it was *his* action that killed Jill. What if it was *malice* that caused him to do it?'

'Then he's the evil one.'

'Yes,' Julie-Anna clapped her hands. 'The water was simply the tool. And it's the same with energy. It's just energy, and it's only what you do with it that matters.'

'What would *you* do with the energy?' Declan attempted to change the subject. Julie-Anna smiled.

'Oh, so many things.'

'What if it was lightning?'

Julie-Anna smiled wider. 'I'd welcome it,' she said. 'Lightning is no enemy to me.'

'So I've heard. Could you tell me more about this dowsing you did?'

'We'd go in blind, not researching the area, and then with John's dowsing and my psychic readings, we'd try to find certain things.'

'Would these things be the lost library of Duke Humphrey?' Declan asked.

Julie-Anna stopped smiling.

———

'I MEAN, DON'T GET ME WRONG, WE WEREN'T *BURKE AND HARE*,' John Gale continued, 'but we knew there were things in

Greenwich that hadn't been uncovered. The place had count-less battles there over centuries, and the *Motherstone* was an enigma. We were ambitious, all three of us. And we were seeing others making serious coin over similar bollocks.'

'How do you mean?' Anjli frowned. John swished his cloak as he tried to express himself. All it did was make him look more like Dracula.

'The late eighties and early nineties were filled with trea-sure hunter books,' he explained. '*The Holy Blood and the Holy Grail* came out, claiming it knew about secret treasure connected to Jesus Christ and started a whole ton of copycats. We had books on lost Templar treasures, Grail locations, the Pyramids, King Arthur, everything.'

'And you found your own?' Anjli enquired, half mock-ingly. If John noted this, he didn't comment.

'They were talking about renovating Greenwich Park,' he replied. 'We thought that if we could gain an interest in it, we could get more names on the petition to stop it destroying the various lines of energy flowing through it.'

'Are there lines of energy?'

John shrugged, 'I believed so at the time. But to be honest, we weren't that worried about the building works. We were more worried it'd cave in on Duke Humphrey's lost library.'

'The one you found, apparently,' Anjli smiled. 'At least, that's what everyone seems to think.'

John looked at his watch, checking how long they had left before he started the walk.

'We thought we'd be famous, like Lord Carnarvon when he found Tutankhamun's tomb.'

'Didn't he have a curse attached to it?' Anjli asked.

'Everyone who steals from the dead to the extent that he did finds a curse,' John started waving to the group of tourists, reminding them that the tour was about to start. 'Even us. But then Greenwich Park stated that everything we found was technically theirs, and so we had a choice of telling them the location or saying that it was all a lie to stop us from being sued.'

'Did you?' Anjli asked. 'Say it was a lie?'

'Look at me,' John replied, half snapping at her. 'Do I look like I have money to burn? Would I be dressing like Dracula and talking about ghosts if that were the case? Would I have spent ten years writing about bloody flower shows for *The Mail on Sunday*? Of course we bloody rescinded. But even when you say you were joking, there are people who still believe you.'

'You were protesting too much.'

'Yeah. People knew the authorities were clamping down on us. We didn't have to say anything. Just a cheeky wink, and everyone was hunting for the bloody library again.'

'That's when you started having issues with Rupert,' Anjli hinted, and John nodded.

'Bloody fool got that tattoo on his hand. Thought it was a game, that he'd hint where the library was, gain some kind of cult following. Nobody realised, though, that he was following bloody Miriam's lead. That caused a ruckus where she worked, I'll tell you.'

'How come?'

'Because on the day Miriam Shrimpton stupidly tattooed wardings onto her hand, she was one of the senior analysts at the *Ministry of Defence*.'

Declan looked up at Julie-Anna as she leaned back in the chair, smiling.

'Never?' he asked. Julie-Anna shook her head.

'God no,' she replied. 'I didn't lust after Rupert Wilson. Don't mistake the look I have here, this is all for show. Wig and fake glasses, all for the 'medium' trope people expect. Identity is power, and it's more than just names. Back then we were all over each other; I was with John, Miriam was with Rupert, then Alés, the bloody woman couldn't decide— although I probably didn't help there.'

'What did you do?'

Julie-Anna looked uncomfortable.

'Showed her what her life was likely to look like,' she replied.

'What about Marcus?' Declan chanced. 'Did anyone have flings with him?'

Julie-Anna laughed.

'Marcus was around for a heartbeat in the scheme of things,' she explained. 'He died the day of the press conference. Bus hit him on the way there.'

She thought about this.

'Sure, he probably fancied Miriam, they all did. But Alés, poor doomed Alés was Lucy's father, no matter what Rupert thought.'

'Rupert was wrong?'

'Rupert was unaware,' Julie-Anna replied. 'Miriam never told him anything. And the dates never matched up. When Lucy was a teenager, Miriam told her it was Rupert, and Lucy managed to meet him when she was sixteen. Rupert promised to legitimise this but before he could, the silly mare changed her name to Wilson as a rebellious action, which right royally pissed Miriam off and buggered up the plans, I can tell you. Instead of becoming 'dad', Rupert disappeared on a dig in Israel for three years, and Lucy found the truth years later when her mum died.'

'So why not tell the truth before then?' Declan asked. Julie-Anna shrugged.

'Who knows?' she said. 'Maybe she liked the idea of her daughter having the infamy of being a Wilson. The Shrimptons may have had links to Aleister Crowley back in the day, but pretty much every occultist and his dog back then had some connection to either Crowley or Gerald Gardner.'

There was a moment of quiet as Julie-Anna stopped, keeping the gaze with Declan, as if reaching for something.

'She's dead, isn't she?' she said softly. 'Oh, that poor girl.'

Declan felt a shiver go down his spine. *The name of the St Anne's Church victim hadn't been given out yet.*

'Did you speak to Miriam before her death?' Declan refused to be thrown off track.

'We talked twice before she died,' she continued. 'They weren't pleasant talks, though. Miriam had learned I'd been seeing Lucy and was unhappy about it.'

'Seeing?'

'She was like a surrogate daughter to me,' Julie-Anna explained. 'I was around from the day she was born. But after she left the scene, Miriam wouldn't let her talk to us.'

'Us?'

'Any of us,' she looked out of the window, remembering. 'However, that didn't stop Lucy learning her own path, and she secretly reached out to me while starting her 'A' Levels, after she changed her name and had been abandoned by Rupert. Later, while she was at University I'd secretly visit her on weekends.'

She sniffed.

'It wasn't like her mum gave a shit. She had a vicious back hand shot she'd give whenever Lucy was out of time, which was apparently often.'

'So going back to the library, what happened next?'

'Rupert tried to become a rock star,' Julie-Anna sniffed, returning to her smiling self. 'Started to main-event conferences like *Wildwood* at Conway Hall or the *Pagan Fed regional* at Fairfield. John claimed Rupert even tried to take the stage at a *Broomstick Rally* near Lewes one year, halfway through a *Damh The Bard* gig. Completely went to his head.'

'I'm guessing the *Four Musketeers* ended around then?'

Julie-Anna chuckled. 'That's the problem with that name,' she said. 'In the books there were *three* Musketeers. And then the *outsider*, D'Artagnan arrives and screws everything up. Same happened here.'

'Had you seen Rupert recently?' Declan asked. Julie-Anna shook her head.

'Not since he started branding himself with moons and holding weird naked sabbats in dark rooms over the internet. It was like he was having some kind of midlife crisis, even though he was almost bloody seventy,' she said.

JOHN GALE NODDED TO THE GROUP OF TOURISTS, NOW WAITING irritably by the statue.

'Look, I have to start soon or they'll demand their money back,' he said. 'Rupert was a self-gratifying glory hound prick at the best of times and I wish I'd never met him. But I didn't kill him, I'm not hunting for a lost library and I sure as hell didn't bundle his body into the back of a Rover hatchback and drive it to Greenwich.'

He held out his hand to shake and, after glancing at his palm for a moment, Anjli shook it.

'Now, if we're done?'

'One last thing,' Anjli looked back through her notes as she broke off the handshake. 'You talked about the press conference, and how Rupert tried to take credit for the find, but you never stated for the record whether or not you actually discovered the lost library.'

'I thought I had,' John replied cautiously.

'No,' Anjli looked up. 'It's almost as if the group took the credit for something only one of them found.'

John stared silently at Anjli and then, with a dramatic swish of his cape and a *mu ha ha* laugh, he turned to his audience in full performance mode, leaving Anjli alone in the street, the question unanswered as they walked away.

Anjli reviewed her notes before pulling out her phone and dialling it. After a couple of rings, Billy answered.

'Quick question,' she started. 'What car does Cindy Mitchell drive?'

There was a tapping of keys on the other end of the line.

'A 2005 Rover 75,' Billy replied. 'Why?'

'Just checking. Back in a bit.' Anjli looked at her notes once more as she disconnected, recalling John Gale's last words.

'I sure as hell didn't bundle his body into the back of a Rover hatchback and drive it to Greenwich.'

Anjli never said it was Cindy who'd taken the body. And she'd sure as hell not mentioned it was a Rover she'd done it in.

So how had John Gale known?

19

THREE BLINDE MICE

IT WAS ALMOST TWO IN THE AFTERNOON WHEN BOTH DECLAN and Anjli arrived back at the Command Unit, each with their own tale to tell, combining their separate interviews into one historical narrative. Neither of the surviving *Musketeers* had spoken well of Rupert Wilson, and to be brutally honest, Declan was thinking there could be a whole new collection of reasons why someone wanted him dead.

Monroe was back from Queen Mary University and Declan had seen Doctor Marcos in the morgue, so assumed she'd found all that she could at Limehouse. As Declan and Anjli stood around Billy's monitor station, Monroe emerged from his office and called everyone to the briefing room.

'Things are moving faster than we can keep up,' he muttered as Declan sat down at his usual spot. Doctor Marcos was standing beside Monroe; DC Davey was either downstairs or still at one of the locations. There was no De'Geer either. Instead, Billy, Anjli and Bullman had arrived, Bullman taking a chair rather than standing by the door.

'What?' she asked as Declan looked inquisitively at her. 'I pulled my back. That a crime?'

Monroe waited for the conversations to cease before continuing.

'This could be an occult treasure hunt, or it could be far more. We've got another body and a cryptic message, and to be honest I'm thinking that De'Geer was passed this one as a punishment from Deptford for God knows what.'

He looked at Declan and Anjli.

'Okay, let's go from the start. What do you have, chronologically?'

Anjli glanced at Declan, who nodded for her to start.

'So the earliest we go is around 1994,' she began. 'Rupert Wilson meets Miriam Shrimpton, John Gale and Julie-Anna Watson at a variety of esoteric conferences. They're dowsing in Greenwich Park, looking for Duke Humphrey's lost library—'

'Duke Humphrey,' Billy replied, reading from his laptop. 'Inherited Greenwich in 1426. Two years later, he marries his mistress, Eleanor Cobham, and builds Greenwich Park, building a palace, *Bella Court*, by the Thames.'

'And this is relevant why?'

'When his wife Eleanor was accused of Witchcraft against the King, the belief was that she'd used Humphrey's occult library to find the spells. And when she was convicted, Margaret of Anjou, the King's wife, took over Humphrey's estate, renaming it the *Palace of Placentia*. It's said that Humphrey then hid the occult library somewhere on his grounds so she could never use it.'

'Okay, and this is the treasure that they were hunting?'

'Yes.'

Monroe nodded to Anjli. 'Go on,' he smiled. 'I think *History with Billy* has ended.'

'So we're in the nineties, and John and his *Musketeers* are looking for the library,' Anjli continued. 'Enter Rupert, who's lived in Greenwich all his life and loves the park. Also, who seems to have a crush on Miriam, who at this point is about fifteen years younger than him. Although it could be because she has some kind of family connection to Aleister Crowley, and we know Wilson had a thing for him.'

'This is around the time the Park planned to quietly push through plans to build a massive concrete staircase by the Observatory, and these four want to build awareness, to stop it going through,' Declan spoke now. 'The *Musketeers* claim they find the library, showing four items they took from it. However, they refuse to reveal where it is, and are eventually forced to 'admit' that the library doesn't exist before they're taken to court by the Royal Parks, as this is technically on park land. Their fifteen minutes of fame are over.'

'Okay,' Monroe nodded.

'Also, there's some fifth member called Marcus, no surname yet,' Declan added. 'Can't find anything on him, and he wasn't at the press conference, as apparently he was hit by a bus the same day and died.'

'Is this where the curse started?' Monroe questioned. Declan shrugged, unable to answer as Anjli continued.

'But Rupert doesn't want it to end. Over two decades he tattoos magical wardings and Enochian letters on his hand, all part of this mysterious new image, while apparently ensuring that he was invisible to curses. And, over the years, he sells into it, building his entire reputation as a new *Aleister Crowley*, a *Dark Magus* for the millennial age on this. During that time, Miriam also tattoos her own hand with anti-curse wardings, just like Rupert—'

'Or possibly before Rupert,' Declan interjected. 'Witness reports are contradictory here.'

'And has a daughter, Lucy, allegedly with Alés Capioca,' Anjli continued. 'The brother of Lilith Babylon —'

'Who is?' Monroe shook his head. 'And can we get some kind of character list for this?'

'Lilith Babylon is one of the two women who took Rupert Wilson's body to the park,' Bullman added from her chair. 'While she was a kid, her older brother Alés dated Miriam and had a child with her.'

'It's a shame Alés is dead,' Monroe muttered. 'I'd have loved to see what he knew.'

Anjli nodded. 'Anyway, a year or two after this, the group falls apart. Mainly, it seems, because everyone thought Rupert was a massive bell end.'

'Life goes on for a couple of decades,' Declan read from his notes. 'Ten years ago, Lucy changes her name when she turns sixteen to Wilson, after learning, incorrectly, that Rupert was her father.'

'Which means what, for sixteen years she didn't know?'

'Possibly. Then a year ago Miriam dies. Cause of death on the certificate is terminal bone cancer, possibly gained from her classified work, although the coroner's report states she died on the way to hospital in Lewes after being struck by lightning at some kind of Spring camp. This was also the same lightning bolt that strikes Julie-Anna Watson, who was touching Miriam at the moment of impact.'

'We're guessing here,' Declan added, 'but it's a pretty good chance that at the funeral, Lucy, now in her mid-twenties, meets John for the first time, although that's doubtful.'

'Julie-Anna?'

'Most likely still recovering from the lightning,' Billy answered, bringing an image of a piece of legal paper up onto the screen. 'A week later, Marie Wilson changes her surname back to Shrimpton—'

'Wait,' Monroe looked at the screen. 'Is this official?'

'*I, Marie Lucinda Wilson, have given up my name, Marie Lucinda Wilson and have adopted for all purposes the name Marie Lucinda Shrimpton,*' Billy read from the screen. 'It's signed by a solicitor, and as long as she's over sixteen, it's technically legal. It's not an enrolled deed poll change, as that goes through the courts, and technically, she can still use her old name until this is registered—'

'So why do it?' Anjli asked.

'The timing,' Doctor Marcos suggested. 'She's learned that Rupert isn't truly her father and has changed it back. What makes it interesting is that she didn't do it publicly. This was more of a symbolic gesture.'

'It *was* put into the courts,' Billy was checking a spreadsheet now as he spoke. 'Again, the joys of having a building in the Inns of Courts gives me leeway with the data. She officially registered this, starting the process of legally becoming Lucy Shrimpton again—' he looked up in surprise.

'She filed it Friday morning,' he said in surprise. 'An hour before Rupert Wilson died.'

'Well, that's convenient,' Monroe mused. 'Shame we can't question her on that now. What do we know about her before that?'

'Ordinary childhood,' Anjli replied. 'Although Miriam would have been occult magician royalty thanks to her granddad, she'd moved out of the scene by this point and was a senior analyst at GCHQ, working at Cheltenham in the 2000s.'

'There's one thing,' Declan added. 'Rupert met Lucy when she turned sixteen, and while she was in university Julie-Anna trained her in witchcraft.'

'Anything on the moon scars?'

'Apparently Miriam had one from the start, Lucy got one when she was sixteen, no idea of Rupert.'

He looked at his notes.

'Oh, and Julie-Anna claims she didn't know Rupert was holding weird naked sabbats in dark rooms with his students over the internet until after he was suspended.'

'Please don't have photos,' Billy muttered.

'There aren't any photos but there is video,' Declan replied. 'It was sent anymously to the university's board and that's why he was suspended. But before this, Rupert started his tenure at Queen Mary's University last year, demanding a particular basement room from the University Governance Board, which according to the maps is pretty much under the *School of Engineering and Materials Science* building. Where, sixty years ago, the University had a working nuclear reactor with a core the size of a bucket.'

'One moved to Marshgate Lane in Stratford in 1964,' Billy added, 'before being decommissioned in 1982.'

'Any connection to the room we have?' Monroe asked.

Declan shrugged.

'No smoke without nuclear fire,' he said. 'Even if there's nothing there anymore, that's a room that had once had energy, on some kind of magic line that also has energy.'

'You seem to be an expert suddenly,' Monroe was amused.

'I had lots of explanations about kids in swimming pools and water being evil,' Declan explained. 'Please don't make me repeat it. Suffice to say Julie-Anna and apparently Rupert believed that when an item is removed, the area it possessed beforehand could still keep the power within, and be used.'

'So the nuclear reactor's *memory* powers the ritual?' Monroe shook his head. 'I give up.'

'The important bit, going back to what Billy said on Monday, is that Rupert *believed* it did,' Declan replied. 'What we have to do now is work out what he believed his ritual would do.'

Now, at a curt nod from Monroe, Doctor Marcos stepped forward.

'Late Friday morning, Rupert Wilson was hanged,' she said. 'On examination of the body, we found both oblique and partial ligature marks situated above the thyroid carti-lage, and that the cervical vertebra was still intact. Added to this, we found petechial haemorrhages in the conjunctiva of the eyes and eyelids.'

She looked up from her notes.

'Interestingly, the rope that we found matched fibres from around the throat, but not *all* of them. As if someone had also hanged Professor Wilson with a different rope at a separate time. With the lack of any scuff marks in the apartment, I'm wondering whether they brought Professor Wilson to the apartment *post*-murder, and set it up to look like the same cause of death, but at a more explainable location.'

'So they moved him?'

'Either that or he was hanged there, but the rope was changed,' Doctor Marcos said. 'Obviously it's speculation, but currently this leans us strongly to the fact that he was murdered.'

'We then know Tweedledum and Tweedledee arrived, stuck him in a wheelchair and removed him from the apartment, taking him to Greenwich Park,' Monroe chimed in. 'However, what we don't know is at what time Lucy arrived and cut off the hand, or even if she did it. All we know is that by Tuesday evening, it was in her possession when she used her magic wizz-wozz powers to turn Declan to stone.'

Declan flushed at this.

'She caught me off guard,' he muttered.

'Aye, laddie, and then someone did the same to her,' Monroe mused. 'What we need to know was whether this was connected to her plans for the future, or revenge for Rupert Wilson doing, well, whatever.'

'What do we have on the murder scene?' Bullman asked.

'Well, apart from the fact it matched the location given to Billy by his great-uncle, the location that would lead questers to the next part of the hunt for this mysterious and probably bollocks bloody library, not much,' Doctor Marcos replied. 'The body wasn't moved, as blood spatter on the pyramid showed Lucy was standing next to it when her throat was cut left to right, severing the carotid artery. She slumped down onto the sloped pyramid as she died, thus explaining the marks on the wall behind her. At this point the killer used a small saw to cut through the wrist, taking it with them when they left, but not before writing a note on the pyramid.'

She nodded to Billy, who pulled up a photo, placing it on the plasma screen. On it, the body of Lucy was clearly visible under a message, wiped onto the pyramid in her own blood.

3 BLINDE MICE

'I take it she couldn't have written this herself?' Anjli enquired.

'Once the carotid artery was severed, she'd have been

dead in under ten seconds,' Doctor Marcos considered the answer. 'From the severity of the wound, I'd say closer to five. At least it was quick.'

'And they took the hand after death?'

'I'd bloody hope so,' Monroe mused from the front of the room. 'Time of death?'

'Still waiting for a conclusive time, but I think it was late evening, maybe nine, ten pm. It was dark, so people probably weren't walking through the graveyard around then.'

'Only a few hours after she ran from us?' Anjli shook her head. 'She should have come in.'

'So, what does the line mean?' Monroe asked. 'Three blind mice, cut off the tails with a carving knife?'

'The tails could be hands,' Anjli suggested. 'Two down, one to go?'

'Why the spelling?' Declan asked. 'Blinde with an e?'

'I'll look into it,' Billy replied, already typing.

'And so we now move onto our Mister Saeed,' Monroe said, tapping a finger on the screen, changing it to a tall, thin Indian man with a thick head of black hair. 'Glaswegian Inspector of the Park police for over twenty years—'

'That's not the man we saw,' Anjli interrupted.

'—And transferred to Edinburgh three years ago,' Monroe finished, tapping the plasma screen again. Now an image, a CCTV picture from outside the Fleet Street coffee shop appeared on it, with the Saeed that Declan and Anjli had seen walking out. 'Not this man, who is as yet unknown, but believed to be part of a shady organisation known as the *Consortium*.'

'My great-uncle claims these guys are collectors of occult items in a big way, and don't take no for an answer,' Billy added. 'Makes sense that if there's a mysterious occult library up for grabs, they'd be looking.'

'And they're sure of themselves,' Bullman added. 'He stood in my office for a good ten minutes before Walsh and Kapoor arrived. Didn't waver for a moment.'

Declan looked up. 'Ten?'

'Around that,' Bullman replied. 'Why?'

'Because the officer on the desk said that he'd arrived twenty minutes before we did,' Anjli looked at Declan. 'Which gives us ten minutes unaccounted for.'

'Find out what he wanted,' Bullman was furious. 'And then find the bugger. If he wanted to look at Wilson's apartment, he could have found a dozen other ways. To walk in here, that took balls. Or, he needed to be in here for something bigger.'

'Could he be connected to the mysterious room at the university?' Anjli asked. 'Maybe there's something more about it we don't know?'

'Look into it, see if any park police have been sniffing around the room.'

'About the room,' Billy added. 'The camera in the corner was a full spectrum night vision camera and branded *GhostPro*,' he smiled. 'You know, like a spooky *GoPro*.'

'So, Rupert has a night vision camera in the corner of his room, recording, or was it placed there without his knowledge,' Bullman surmised. 'Can we check the serial?'

'Already done,' Billy looked up. 'It's registered to Alfie Wasley.'

'Shock twist,' Anjli said. 'Maybe we should chat with him.'

'Maybe he's more involved than *Ghost Bro* Simon,' Monroe replied. 'He's still in intensive care, but he was dating

Lilith Babylon, and was the one who suggested a last-minute venue change, something that might have had someone try to kill him.'

'They found the blue Mondeo half a mile up the road,' Doctor Marcos continued. 'Forensics have gone over it, but there are no fingerprints or traces of DNA.'

'Whoever drove it knew what they were doing,' Anjli added. 'We should—' she stopped, looking at the door, as a man in jeans and a leather bomber jacket leaned against it.

'Someone call the *Ghostbusters*,' Monroe spat. 'We seem to have a *spook* problem.'

'Hello, uncle,' Tom Marlowe smiled at Monroe as he nodded to the briefing room. 'Sorry to bother you, but I understand you've found a little room that's covered by the Official Secrets Act.'

'How did you even get in here?' Monroe asked. Tom flashed a smile.

'I'm a spook,' he replied. 'I just floated through the walls.'

'So are you going to give us all a small sampling of your amazing wit and intellect, and explain what the bloody bunker is for then, laddie?' Monroe asked.

Tom nodded his head, staring at the image on the plasma screen, currently showing the fake Inspector Saeed on it.

'Absolutely,' he replied, mesmerised by the image. 'As soon as you explain why you have a photo of a dead ex-*Mossad* agent on your wall.'

20

CONGESTING CHARGES

'WE NEED TO FIRE THE DESK SERGEANT,' BULLMAN MUTTERED as Tom Marlowe lounged against the door frame. 'First there was the fake Saeed, now MI5–'

'Please, don't insult me,' Tom smiled. 'MI5 *wish* I was still with them.'

Declan almost joined Tom in smiling at this; Tom was a member of *Section D*, a covert Westminster organisation that was overseen by Prime Minister-in-waiting Charles Baker and Emilia Wintergreen, Monroe's estranged ex-wife. Which also explained why Temple Inn was the only City of London unit to have a government level spy on call.

'Go on then,' Monroe replied. 'Amaze us with your insights and tell us who this bugger is. And then explain why you're really here.'

'Nice to see you too, uncle Alex,' Tom walked to the screen. Although not biological, Declan knew that Tom had grown up around both Alex Monroe and Declan's father, Patrick Walsh. More reasons why the *Last Chance Saloon* had his help.

'This is Yossi Shavit,' Tom explained. 'Well, that is, this was Yossi, until a bomb in Tel Aviv killed him four years ago.'

'So he faked his death?'

'Or used a near miss to his advantage,' Tom was examining the image. 'Mossad were pissed at him for selling Israeli antiquities on the black market and were about to pull him in, or maybe put a hit on him. He's put on weight but it's definitely him, although he doesn't usually have that much hair, preferring to be clean shaven. There's a scar over his eye, though that's a dead giveaway.'

'This guy had a scar on his eyebrow,' Anjli admitted.

'That's him then. How's he involved?'

'We think he's a buyer of high-end occult items,' Declan replied. 'Working for an organisation called the *Consortium*.'

Tom laughed.

'If he is, then he doesn't work for them, he *is* them,' he said.

'A minute ago you thought he was dead,' Bullman leaned back in her chair, watching Tom. 'How can you be so sure of this?'

'Because we've heard chatter about the *Consortium*,' Tom replied calmly. 'We knew it was a solo organisation, just not what their identity was. So, thanks for that.'

'What do you know of him?' Declan asked. Tom shrugged.

'As you said, high-end antiquities,' he said. 'Illegally picked up for the highest prices from archaeological digs around the world. It fits Yossi's MO too, as he has prior form of getting others to do his grunt work.'

'We have him under surveillance,' Billy added from the laptop. 'DI Walsh linked the browser on his phone to a website that picked up the IMEI code, so we can triangulate on carrier signals where he is.'

'That won't last long,' Tom shook his head. 'If Yossi hasn't already dumped it, he'll do it soon. Where do you have him now?'

Billy tapped on the keyboard, and his face fell.

'The phone's turned off,' he replied, crestfallen. 'Looks like it happened twenty minutes ago.'

'Where was he when he turned it off?' Declan asked. 'Maybe we can get something on CCTV?'

Billy was already typing. 'Central London, off the Strand,' he replied. 'Aldwych end.'

'Maybe we can get something,' Bullman suggested. Anjli, however, sat straighter in her chair at this.

'Any chance of zooming in on the tracker's last location?' she asked. 'Can we see if it was around the Lyceum Theatre?'

'It's not that specific, but we're within a hundred feet or so,' Billy replied. 'Why?'

'Because that's where John Gale was ending his Blue Badge walk today,' Anjli checked her notes. 'And based on the walk he was doing, I'd have expected him to be there around now.'

'So Mister Shavit was either meeting him there, or waiting for him,' Monroe nodded. 'See if the theatre has any cameras and check the local area. If we can pick up a meeting, that'd be good.'

'If you find him, I'd appreciate being kept in the loop,' Tom offered. 'Although he's a master of disguise.'

Monroe snorted.

'So, what, you want us to keep you updated, so you can pick him up and dump him in a hole?' he replied. 'We'll tell you after we've got what we needed.'

He sniffed, folding his arms as he faced his almost-nephew.

'Talking of which, why don't you tell us what we need from you? About the secret room?'

'That's covered by the Official Secrets Act,' Tom stated. 'And unless you've signed it—'

'We all have,' Doctor Marcos interrupted. 'When we proved Declan wasn't a terrorist, and that Malcolm Gladwell was using *Rattlestone* for his own needs.'

Tom faltered for a moment, obviously not knowing this. Declan glanced around, ensuring that De'Geer wasn't in the room; he was the only member not around at the time.

He wasn't.

'Oh,' Tom's face fell as he deflated a little.

'So just tell us what we need to know, laddie,' Monroe grinned. 'And then you can bugger off back to the Bitch-Queen.'

'We're guessing that nobody visits this room anymore because someone would have noted the bloody great big hole in the wall and the pentagram,' Doctor Marcos said. 'And because of the location, we're guessing this is connected to the nuclear reactor. How close are we, and do we win a prize?'

Tom thought for a moment. 'You're scarily close,' he replied. 'They took the reactor offline in 1982, and everything moved to the JASON reactor in Greenwich.'

'The other reactor?' Declan asked.

'The Argonaut series 10 kW research reactor, created by the Ministry of Defence wasn't decommissioned until the mid-nineties,' Billy chimed in.

'When the *Musketeers* were telling the world they'd found a secret library,' Anjli noted.

Tom ignored Anjli's comment, focusing on Billy as he continued.

'There was pressure from Europe to close it down in the nineties, especially as the cladding had gradually become irradiated and needed some sort of controlled removal and disposal. They eventually removed it in 1999.'

Tom looked a little uncomfortable here.

'That is, the Ministry *told* everyone that it was.'

'Christ,' Monroe muttered, leaning against a table. 'So, there's still a nuclear reactor in Greenwich?'

Tom shook his head. 'Now we're moving past even the Official Secrets Act levels of knowledge,' he replied. 'The Navy is very close lipped about whether it's still there. And the analysts give nothing away. You'd have to gain confirmation from someone in a Naval uniform.'

Declan wrote this down. 'Are there any analysts we can speak to?'

'I'm not sure,' Tom admitted truthfully. 'They always called them Analyst A, or Analyst B, to ensure nobody could get to them. They didn't even have ID cards.'

'So how did they swipe in?' Anjli asked. 'Like magic?'

'In a way, yes,' Tom nodded. 'They had RFID chips inserted into their hands that worked with the doors. They would have worked with the one in Mile End, too.'

He looked at his watch.

'And that's all I can tell you,' he finished. 'Just try not to get yourselves arrested for treason, yeah? And I'd appreciate anything on Yossi.'

'That's all you came here for?' Monroe was amused. 'You really are bored over there.'

'I have more to say, but I'm on a deadline, and think I'm being tracked,' Tom nodded to Declan before leaving the doorway, visible through the glass wall as he left the offices. 'I'll call later.'

'Anything he's told us, let's get some conclusive confirmation on it, yeah?' Monroe snapped. 'I don't want us beholden to any bloody spies. Especially my ex-wife.'

He paced around the briefing room.

'This whole bloody case is annoying me now,' he muttered. 'Remind me to thank PC De'Geer personally for dumping it on my lap.'

As if appearing on cue, De'Geer entered the office, walking over to the briefing room.

'My cup brimmeth over,' Monroe was speaking to himself now. 'Any news?'

'We might have fingerprints from the blood message,' De'Geer replied. 'DC Davey is waiting for confirmation right now.'

He walked to the back, but stopped at his usual chair, as if unsure whether to sit.

'Something the matter?' Monroe picked up on this. De'Geer turned to face the others.

'I had dinner with my mother last night,' he said.

'And this is what you wanted to share with the class?' Monroe shook his head.

'No, it was—you see, she has a scar on her hand, right here,' De'Geer pointed at the webbing between his thumb and index finger. 'A moon shaped one. She's had it a while.'

'And you thought she was part of Rupert Wilson's little sex cult?' Doctor Marcos raised an eyebrow. 'My my, De'Geer. There's more to you than meets the eye.'

'No, it wasn't like that,' De'Geer protested. 'Well, actually it came out a little worse. She explained that she'd once had body modification, a magnet placed in there.'

'Why would you do that?' Anjli asked. De'Geer visibly shuddered.

'I asked the same thing,' he explained. 'I then learned a lot about the magnetic vibrations of Prince Albert piercings.'

There was a long and awkward moment of silence, marred only by the scratching noise of Bullman writing something down in her notebook.

'That better not be the end of the story,' Monroe growled. De'Geer shook his head.

'No, sir,' he blurted. 'It made me wonder that if my mother could place a magnet in her hand and get that scar, what else could be inserted?' he looked around the room. 'Maybe this *isn't* some kind of ritual thing?'

'I think you're onto something there,' Monroe nodded. 'Especially with what we just learned about RFID chips in hands—'

'You think Miriam was the analyst in charge of this nuclear computer?' Declan worked it through as he replied. 'She was definitely intelligent enough, according to everyone, and we know she worked for the Ministry of Defence. Maybe she was working on this back then, before she met the others?'

'Miriam must have told Lucy about the reactor before she died,' Anjli thought aloud. 'Guv, you okay? You've gone pale.'

Monroe nodded unhappily. 'I think we might need to exhume a body,' he replied. 'We need to see what was in her hand.'

'I'll get onto it,' Doctor Marcos started tapping on her phone. 'I have a gravedigger who owes me a favour.'

Declan decided not to ask about that. And even if he wanted to, before he could speak, Billy spoke up.

'Got something interesting,' he said, tapping on his

screen. 'Anjli called me earlier, asking about Cindy Mitchell's car.'

Bullman looked at Anjli, who shrugged.

'John Gale knew that Cindy Mitchell's car had been used, when we hadn't said anything about it,' she explained. 'Thought it felt suss.'

Billy pulled up an image of a 2005 Rover 75.

'This is Cindy's Nana's car,' he said. 'Not the actual one, but you get the idea. This is the vehicle that Cindy and Lilith drove into Chancery Lane to get Rupert Wilson.'

Click. The image on the screen now showed CCTV traffic footage of a similar car, but in a different, darker colour.

'Here's Cindy's Nana's car on a City of London traffic camera, six-thirty on Friday evening, heading towards Rupert Wilson's house.'

Click. Now the image was a CCTV of the building that Rupert's apartment was in, although it was distant, taken from a camera just too far away to get a good image. The front entrance could still be seen.

'This is where the main entrance is, and no car appears there. In fact, we only see a brief flash of it as it drives down Southampton Buildings, on the *other* side of the apartment block.'

Click. They could see the rear part of a car driving into a car park entrance beside a security gate.

'There's an underground car park that covers the whole place,' Billy explained. 'They most likely drove in, parked up and brought him out this way.'

'Okay,' Declan wrote the address down, wondering if it was worth visiting. 'I get that this is good, but I'm not getting the *interesting* part.'

'Congestion Charge,' Billy grinned, leaning back in his

chair smugly. 'We all pay it—well, *we* don't as the *police* pay ours, but anyone who drives into London now has to pay the charge once they enter a certain area, seven days a week. You can pay it beforehand, after you do it, or even the next day, but if you forget, you receive a hefty fine.'

'Okay,' Anjli nodded. 'Did Cindy not pay the charge?'

'No, and that's it,' Billy was excited now. 'She did pay it. At around ten in the morning, hours before she knew she'd be driving into London.'

'Did she drive in often?'

'No,' Declan replied. 'She said it was her *Nana's* car. Not hers. She didn't know until late afternoon that it'd be need-ed.' He tapped more on the keys.

'And what I've saved until last, the car on the CCTV is registered to a *Verity Myles,* ninety-two and in a Putney nursing home, who has one surviving family member.' Billy paused for dramatic intent.

'Her son, John Gale.'

'Nana is John's mum?' Doctor Marcos smiled in delight. 'Cindy has a very loose approximation of what the term means.'

'So we have a suspect who not only took Rupert's body but also who might have had advance knowledge that she might soon need a car,' Bullman rubbed at her chin. 'Can you check the cameras for the rest of the day, see if the ANPR cameras pick her up anywhere? Maybe there's another reason she comes into London.'

'It'll take time, but it's doable,' Billy nodded, already tapping on the keys as he logged into the network. 'I'll contact Bishopsgate and get them to bring her over now, and we can ask her ourselves—' he stopped.

'Problem?' Declan asked.

'They're not in the system anymore,' Billy looked up from his laptop. 'According to this, they were released around one this afternoon.'

'On whose orders?' Monroe was only just keeping his anger in check. Billy read the release form, eventually throwing it up onto the plasma screen.

'Apparently you did,' he replied, zooming in on the document. On it, the name DCI ALEXANDER MONROE was visible.

'According to the documents, a DC Davey called Bishopsgate from here, saying that they were to be released on your orders, and that an Inspector Saeed would pick them up.'

'Now we know what he was doing for those ten minutes,' Declan muttered. 'With Davey and Doctor Marcos out of the office, it meant that he could spend time in the morgue undetected. Probably called from there and used Davey's email to send the requisition form.'

'He risked a lot to get them out,' Bullman was also angry now. 'Or was it just one of them he needed?'

'Bishopsgate are sending over CCTV now,' Billy replied. 'Maybe we'll get something from it.'

At a beep, Doctor Marcos looked down at her phone, frowning.

'Well, that's not all we have to get irritated about,' she moaned. 'Joanne put the partial prints through the system, hoping that something would pop up.'

'We have a match?' Monroe asked.

'We have a match, but it's a bloody annoying one,' Doctor Marcos shook her head, still reading. 'The prints came from GCHQ. Which isn't what we expected. High-level analyst, deceased.'

Declan almost dropped his pen, which, considering it was

a window-breaking tactical one might have done some damage.

'You're kidding,' he said, already knowing the name. Doctor Marcos, in response, shook her head.

'Apparently not,' she replied. 'The fingerprints in the blood stained message over Marie Wilson aka Lucy Shrimpton's body are those of her dead mother, *Miriam Shrimpton*.'

21

THREE BLINDE CLUES

<small>After the revelation about Miriam Shrimpton and</small> losing their two witnesses, it was decided that Declan and Anjli should check out Lucy's apartment, while Billy hunted through the Bishopsgate CCTV footage for anything that showed not only where Yossi Shavit had taken them but also *why* he'd done so.

Lucy lived in Greenwich, to the east of the park in a shared room within a Victorian five-bedroomed house. This made sense, as Declan had originally met Lucy driving in from Maze Hill. The house itself was a terraced red brick building on Ulundi Road, a five-minute walk from the park, in a quiet street where the windows all had ornate white frames and the doors matched.

'Nice place to live,' Declan muttered. 'If you can afford it.'

'Yeah,' Anjli replied, looking around. 'Pretty much every house here is a million and a half, starters.'

'We're definitely in the wrong profession,' Declan muttered. Anjli chuckled.

'What?' he looked back at her.

'You are aware how much your house is worth, right?' she asked. When Declan didn't reply, she continued. 'I did a check up for you, back when you were thinking of selling it.'

'And?' Declan almost didn't want to know.

'You're looking at just shy of a million,' Anjli walked up to the door, knocking on it. 'So let's have a little less of the 'how the other half live', Mister Millionaire.'

The door opened and a woman with frizzy brown hair and a *Foo Fighters* tee shirt stared out at them. Anjli showed her warrant card.

'DS Kapoor and DI Walsh,' she said. 'We're here to see Marie Wilson's room,' then, at a blank expression, 'maybe known as Lucy?'

The woman nodded, backing away as she did so to allow them in.

'You live here?' Declan asked as he entered.

'Upstairs, on the first floor,' the woman explained, holding out a hand. 'I'm Laura.'

'How many people live here?' Anjli started down the corridor, looking into the first room on the right, which seemed to be a living room.

'Five, over two floors,' Laura replied, eager to please. Declan stopped as he mentally counted.

'How many floors does this have?' he asked. Laura shrugged.

'Four, technically,' she said. 'There's the basement, where we have a utility room and a storeroom, this floor which has a dining room and kitchen to the right, and straight ahead there's a reception room—oh, and a music room that leads out into the garden.'

'A music room,' Anjli repeated, as if this was the most normal thing.

'Then upstairs there's three rooms,' Laura continued. 'I have the smallest, Michelle has the one with the en suite and Heather the middle. And then up from there on the top floor we have Mandy and Lucy.'

She thought for a moment.

'Lucy has the biggest room, but she has to come downstairs to use the bathroom because there aren't any on that floor.'

'Can we look?' Declan asked. Laura nodded, waving upstairs.

'Go wild,' she said as she walked into the reception room at the end of the corridor. 'Everyone's out except for me, and I'm teaching violin on a video call in ten minutes.'

Declan looked at Anjli.

'She seems very concerned for her friend,' he whispered.

'She doesn't know Lucy's dead,' Anjli shrugged, already starting up the stairs. 'Also, these shared houses aren't like the TV sitcom *Friends*. Half the time they barely speak to each other.'

She stopped on the fourth step.

'I've changed my mind,' she said. 'I don't want to live with you. I want to live here, with a music room that leads out into the garden.'

On the top floor, they found two doors facing them as they reached the top of the stairs. One to the left was ajar, unlocked, as if the inhabitant was in the house and wasn't worried about visitors. The one directly in front was closed, the door firmly locked by a small padlock as Declan tested it, pulling out his *Gerber* tactical pen as he did so.

'What's the rules about breaking into dead people's rooms again?' he asked as he grabbed the flimsy padlock on Lucinda's door in his hand.

'Declan,' Anjli started, and Declan knew this was likely to be a cautionary comment on breaking rules, especially as she'd used his first name, so Declan placed the tactical pen in the gap between padlock and base and twisted, using the door frame for leverage. With a crack, the padlock gave way, no match for the heavy-duty machined metal of the pen, and as Declan removed the now unlocked padlock, the door opened inward.

'Was like that when we arrived,' Declan smiled, pushing the door fully open. He stopped, though, as he entered the room.

It was empty of all furniture and boxes were scattered across the floor. It looked like someone was about to move out, or had just moved in.

'How long was she living here?' Declan asked. Anjli looked at her notes.

'Records say ten months.'

'So, she's looking to go somewhere, and fast,' Declan looked around. 'We'll need to go through these, see if we can find out why—'

'There's more in the basement,' a voice said beside them. A young black woman was standing there, about to enter her own door.

'Are you Mandy?' Declan asked. Mandy nodded.

'She was supposed to stay until the end of June, but then on the weekend, she packed everything up. She's been up and down the stairs for days, leaving the boxes in the storeroom.'

Declan nodded. 'When was the last time you saw her?'

'Saw her? Yesterday morning. Heard her? Last night, when she was moving more boxes.'

'What time last night?' Anjli asked. Mandy shrugged.

'Dunno,' she said. 'But it had to be after eleven because I was shouting out that some of us had work in the morning. I've been on a five am shift this week. Is she alright?'

Declan looked at Anjli.

There was a no way that Lucy could have been moving boxes that late, as she was slumped against a pyramid, her throat slashed by that time.

'Where's the storeroom again?' he asked.

———

THE STOREROOM WAS AT THE VERY BOTTOM OF THE HOUSE, behind a door barred with a number-pad lock.

'It's because it's easier for us to remember a number than carry a key we're barely going to use,' Mandy explained, rubbing at her eyes. 'I think Lucy's the only person who's used this since I moved in. Are we done here? I'm exhausted.'

'If you could open the door, that'd be great,' Anjli replied. 'And I'm really sorry, but you might have some police asking you questions later, so don't start sleeping too deeply.'

Mandy took Declan's notepad, writing **9467** on it.

'And you're telling me this why?' she asked. Declan shook his head.

'I'm sorry, but I can't—'

'She's *dead*, isn't she?' Mandy interrupted. 'Lucy. They're always dead on the TV shows when the police turn up poking around.'

'I still can't tell you,' Declan replied. Mandy nodded.

'Well then thanks for the warning,' she said sarcastically as she left, her footsteps echoing around the basement as she climbed the steps. Declan tapped in the number and opened the door.

There was a small pile of moving boxes in the storeroom, piled in the middle, but they'd been disturbed; some had been opened and there were discarded papers all over the place, as if someone had been going through them, looking for something.

But none of these mattered to Declan, as he stared at the item on the rug in the middle of the floor.

It had been stood up to face the detectives as they entered, the tattooed palm facing away, the middle finger rising as the others were clenched, the wax of the candle that the finger had become having dripped down the side.

Declan took a deep breath, calming himself. The last time he'd seen this was when Lucy had held it up to him.

And now, in the storeroom of Lucy's house, it almost looked as if the wrinkled and severed tattooed hand of Rupert Wilson was flipping them the finger.

BILLY WAS WORKING AT HIS STATION, STARING UP AT HIS BANK OF monitors as Monroe angrily paced around his office. Although he was a good thirty to forty feet away and on the carpet, even with the door closed, Billy could hear him pacing.

Billy tried to put the sound out of his mind; he was checking CCTV footage for images of Cindy Mitchell's—well, John Gale's Rover, while following up on three other leads.

Billy smiled. *At this computer, he was God, able to follow multiple options simultaneously.* As much as he enjoyed proper police work, it was *so slow.* This was quicker. This was the future.

This was bringing up something very interesting.

'Guv?' he called out. Monroe leaned out of his office and seeing Billy's expression walked over.

'Tell me you have something super exciting that can break this case wide open,' he replied. Billy grinned widely.

'I think I have three things,' he replied, pointing at a monitor screen, where a scan of a front page news report from 1998 was visible. 'I thought you might be interested in this.'

MAN DIES DURING CAVE COLLAPSE IN GREENWICH

The image was low-quality newsprint, but showed a young man in his early twenties, an eleven-year-old girl next to him. He was brunette and smiling; a man with his whole life ahead of him.

'This is Alés Capioca,' Billy explained. 'In 1998, he was exploring under Greenwich Park, or rather Maiden Hill when the cavern he was in collapsed. He died on the way to hospital.'

Monroe was examining the photo. 'And the girl there is Alexandra Capioca, I'm guessing? Now Lilith Babylon?'

Billy nodded as he pulled up another scan. 'Exactly. Alés was a student at King's University, working on a Master's in Folk History, and his lecturer back then was...'

'Rupert Wilson,' Monroe stroked at his beard as he thought to himself. 'What's the chances that Alés here learned about a magical treasure from Professor Wilson? Maybe even died because of this?'

'I'd say quite high, sir,' Billy replied. 'But way higher than the chances of his sister, distraught, becoming the biggest acolyte of the same man, and bringing his body to his last resting place.'

'So Alexandra changes her name twenty years later and unites with Lucy,' Monroe nodded. 'To gain revenge?'

'Hanging and dismemberment are good ways to gain revenge,' Billy suggested. 'But that's not all.'

He swiped his fingers across his track pad and a new screen appeared on a monitor, this time showing a poem.

> *Three Blinde Mice,*
> *Three Blinde Mice,*
> *Dame Iulian,*
> *Dame Iulian,*
> *the Miller and his merry olde Wife,*
> *shee scrapte her tripe licke thou the knife.*

'What in God's name is this?' Monroe asked. Billy looked up at him.

'When we saw the title in blood, I wondered why it was *Blinde* Mice with an 'e', so I checked into it,' he explained. 'This is the first version of the song, recorded on paper in 1609 by Thomas Ravencroft in his book *Deuteromelia or The Seconde part of Musicks melodie.*'

'Catchy name. I don't see any tails being cut off.'

'No, and in fact, it seems to be a rather boisterous story about a lecherous Miller and his wife. The *scraping of the tripe and licking the knife* were euphemisms for—'

'I get what they mean,' Monroe grimaced. 'What excites you on this? Other than sexy words?'

'These two lines here,' Billy pointed up at the screen. '*Dame Iulian.*'

The screen swiped again. Now Monroe saw a wood carving of what looked to be a female Saint.

'Dame Iulian is also Dame Julian,' Billy explained. 'Better known as Julian of Norwich who lived in the 14th Century. But not, as you'd think, a bloke named Julian.'

Billy was moving around in his chair now, excited.

'Dame Julian was also called Dame *Juliana*, and she was a Christian Mystic who spoke to Angels. Maybe the killer placed this message as a warning to our *own* Christian Mystic, Julie-Anna Watson.'

Monroe nodded. 'But why?'

'When Declan talked to Julie-Anna, she hinted she had gotten involved with Alés and Miriam,' Billy replied. 'The impression I got was although their bed hopping was gossip at the time, with Miriam, Lucy and Alés now dead, only two people would really know about this.'

Monroe looked at him, a faint smile on his face.

'Julie-Anna and her then partner, John Gale,' he continued. 'Who we know had issues with Rupert, and whose nursing home-bound mother had an incredibly convenient car.'

He thought for a moment, staring at the screen.

'Still not enough,' he muttered. 'To do this, there needs to be something more personal here. You don't kill someone over an affair three decades ago. You said you had three things?'

'Yes,' Billy tapped on the screen one last time, and a CCTV image, grey and blurry, appeared on the third monitor. It was of a theatre, with pale pillars in front of it.

'This is the Lyceum Theatre,' Billy started scrolling through the video. 'It's where Anjli suggested we check, and this is exactly when Yossi Shavit turned off his phone.'

On the screen, an overweight, bald man could be seen throwing something small, possibly a phone of some kind into a bin.

'I thought our man was bearded?'

'Tom mentioned he was usually clean shaven, so I ignored anyone who had facial hair. This one stood out.'

Monroe leaned closer to the screen.

'I can't get a great view of him, but he stands here another fifteen minutes, so he's obviously waiting for someone,' Billy carried on, enjoying this. 'And then he has a visitor.'

'If the image is this grainy, can we even tell who it is?' Monroe asked.

'Oh,' Billy grinned again. 'I think it's pretty obvious when you see them.'

On the screen the now clean-shaven Yossi turned away from the theatre, speaking actively, his arms waving as he angrily gestured at someone off the screen. Eventually, a figure walked into view, holding his cape in one hand.

'Count Dracula,' Monroe nodded. 'Anjli was right. John Gale and Yossi Shavit know each other.'

He leaned against the table behind him as he considered this.

'Yossi's an ex-Mossad agent, now occult treasure hunter,' he said slowly, working through the facts. 'Makes sense that he'd attempt to turn John into an asset. Maybe John and Yossi worked together?'

Billy's computer dinged as an email came through. Reading it on a side monitor, he pulled it across to the main screen.

'I think we might have something more,' he said. 'Says here that John Gale's wife, Susan Turner-Gale filed for divorce the same day that Professor Wilson was suspended.'

'Coincidence?' Monroe mused. Billy shrugged, typing.

'Maybe, if she hadn't been one of Queen Mary University's Governance Board members,' he replied, pointing at an image on a hastily pulled up web page. 'But she is, and she would have been one of the people who received the video and suspended Wilson.'

'And the same day divorces John Gale,' Monroe nodded. 'That's not a bloody coincidence. We have a woman whose brother had died possibly because of Rupert Wilson's actions, a man on a screen who wants Rupert Wilson's secrets and who freed our first suspect from Bishopsgate, another who's possibly being divorced because of something connected to Wilson and a mystic who's linked to a four hundred-year-old song, written in blood over a dead body connected to all of them.'

Monroe took a deep breath, releasing all of his pent up tension.

'We need another chat with Mister Gale right now,' he nodded. 'Get everyone in.'

22

FLINT STONES

Lilith Babylon hadn't expected to be released; after spending over twelve hours in the cell, she assumed that the police would have realised by now who her brother was and decided Rupert's death was a pre-meditated revenge on him. Yet the man waiting outside the Bishopsgate police station when they arrived, claiming to be an Inspector Saeed, seemed to know Cindy too well, to the point that after nodding to Lilith, he hailed a cab, bundled Cindy in and drove off before Lilith could ask what the hell was going on. But there was a thought, something itching at the back of her mind, that she'd seen this man before.

But he wasn't a police officer, then.

She'd felt that something was wrong after Rupert's death. She hadn't wanted it to go so far; he was only supposed to be ruined, not murdered. Things were moving too fast; she wondered if this was Lucy somehow trying to bring things back under control. She needed to—

That was where she'd seen the man.

Pausing, she rummaged through her bag, pulling out a pack of half-sized *Rider Waite* Tarot cards. Shuffling them in her hands, she cut the deck, placed the bottom half on top, and flipped over the top card.

A blond man in a flowery top, a little white dog jumping up beside him, was upside down.

The Fool reversed.

Lilith tried to recall what the reversed Fool meant as a reading, but all she could remember was that it meant she was literally acting like a fool by disregarding the repercussions of her actions, and like the young man facing her in the card, she hadn't seen how dangerous a position she was in.

Well, she knew now.

Putting the cards away, Lilith felt a tightness in her chest; *a panic attack was on its way.* She was about to lean against a wall and gather her breath when a woman in her fifties, short, spiky peroxide-white hair almost glowing in the sun walked over to her, grabbing her by the arm and moving her along.

'Well then, Alexandra,' Julie-Anna Watson said, almost conversationally. 'You've right-royally buggered everything up, haven't you?'

'WELL, IT'S DEFINITELY MIRIAM SHRIMPTON'S HAND,' MONROE said as he sat behind his desk, Declan and Anjli standing in front of him. 'The fingerprints match her GCHQ clearance, and the wax residue and prints match those we found on the pyramid above Lucy's body in Limehouse. So, going on the fact that a day earlier Mister Walsh here was spooked into paralysis by Lucy waving a severed hand around, one that was as shrivelled up as this was, we can pretty much concur that *this* is the hand she used two nights ago, and has probably had since her mum died. The killer then took it from her and wrote the message—'

'And then left it in Lucy's house?' Anjli frowned. 'I don't get it.'

'Maybe it was a different message?' Declan suggested. 'It looked like someone had been searching for something in the boxes. Perhaps the leaving of the hand was on purpose?'

'In the middle of the floor and with the middle finger raised?' Monroe smiled. 'Aye, I reckon we can both assume this was a message.'

He leaned back.

'Doctor Marcos has a few things she's already found and she's on her way up,' he continued, looking at Anjli. 'Get what you can from her, and then find me some bloody killers. And this Mossad guy. I really want this Mossad guy.'

'Before Marlowe gets him?'

'Definitely.' Monroe looked out of the window to his office, seeing Doctor Marcos approaching with what looked to be a coolbox in her hand.

'What about John Gale?'

'Declan should go have a wee chat with him,' Monroe replied, checking his watch. 'What time did you say he did his little Ripper walk?'

'Seven pm at Tower Hill,' Anjli replied. Monroe nodded.

'Then you've just got enough time to get there and ruin his day. Chop chop,' he said to Declan as he rose and, with both detectives in front of him, stepped out into the main office. Doctor Marcos had stopped however beside Billy's workstation and was opening the coolbox on Declan's desk.

'Hey!' Declan cried out. 'Not on *my* desk, please!'

'Don't be such a girl,' Doctor Marcos pulled out the severed hand of Miriam Shrimpton. 'It's not as if it's going to leak or anything. This thing's been a husk for years.'

'Still don't want it on my desk,' Declan muttered, half to himself.

'What do we have?' asked Bullman, leaning out of her office, as if happy to keep her distance.

'I can see why DI Walsh confused it for Rupert's hand,' Doctor Marcos was turning it in her own hands, showing all the angles in a gruesome show and tell. 'The wardings are almost identical, the lack of Enochian words on the fingers would have been hidden, and it has a scar on the back.'

'You said almost?' Anjli asked. Doctor Marcos nodded, showing the palm of the hand as she pointed at the Monas symbol.

'As you can see, it's identical except for these four symbols, found here and here,' she showed the two sets of Enochian on either side of the Monas image. They were smaller than the others but still visible. 'I understand they mean *Affa*, which—'

'Which means *Empty*, or *Nothing*,' Billy finished, looking back from his screen smugly. 'I might know *some* words.'

'Is the ink the same age as the rest, or was this added later?' Anjli was leaning in to examine the hand.

'We're still checking but they look the same.'

'So Miriam Shrimpton had the same warding tattoo as Rupert Wilson, but adding *nothing*, or *empty?*' Monroe scratched at his bearded chin. 'Did she mean the curse they believed in was empty, or that the library was? Lucy had to know this.'

He nodded at the scar.

'Is that what we think it is?' he asked. Doctor Marcos nodded.

'There was a small RFID chip in there. Looks to be mid nineties in design but long dead,' she replied. 'I've already sent it off with some black-suited men from the Naval College who promise to let us know if anything comes up. I thought it was better to keep them on our side this time. Another interesting thing is that the tattoo covers a faint scar across the palm. An old one, likely twenty years old by the time she passed away.'

'John Gale had a faint scar on his palm, too,' Anjli added. 'I saw it when we shook hands.'

'I never held hands with Julie-Anna, so I don't know if she did,' Declan shrugged. 'That said, she's very strong on identity, so I don't even know if I even saw the *true* Julie-Anna Watson there.'

'Why would they all have scars?' Doctor Marcos thought aloud. 'Going on the basis that both Rupert and Julie-Anna also had them...'

'Blood brothers,' Declan reached for his notebook, pulling it out. 'Michael, the guy at the talk said something about this.'

He read from the notes, remembering the line spoken.

'*And then a year after the bloody disaster of a press conference, where someone dies, and the park threatens court proceedings, they all clam up, cut their hands and bind themselves together. Who does that?*'

Billy thought for a moment.

'Blood magic is powerful,' he continued. 'All the books make a thing about that. There's a strong chance they did this to make some kind of unbreakable pact. And if they believed it...'

'Could they believe in it enough to kill?' Declan asked. Billy shrugged.

'I've seen worse done for less, so most likely. This could even be the curse that my great-uncle hinted at.'

He looked back at his screen as a window suddenly flashed up.

'Oh, that's interesting,' he said as he started typing, pulling up more files. 'That administrator, Margaret Donaldson? She's sent me the video that got Rupert suspended.'

He pointed at a file called *Rupert Wilson ritual.mp4.*

'Shall we?' he asked.

Monroe nodded. Billy pressed play—

'Dear Christ,' Monroe said, looking away. 'My eyes.'

Billy paused the video as Declan shook his head.

'Well we know now what they were doing in the other room,' he replied. On the screen, frozen, was an image taken from a camera, set up in the secret room. Around the painted ritual circle, on each pentagram point were masked ritualists, with Rupert Wilson and another, slim masked man standing on the final two. The other three were obviously females while masked because they were naked, and left nothing to the imagination. And Rupert, although masked and naked also, bore the familiar tattoos on his hand and skin, revealing his identity.

'What the hell are they doing?' Bullman was walking over now, seeing the expressions on her team's faces.

'It's a ritual,' Billy replied for the team.

'Why are they naked?'

'It's called being *sky clad*,' Billy continued. 'It's believed that by being naked, the energy they raise from the ground can enter them easier.'

'You're telling me that energy that's brought up god knows how many feet from the depths of the earth can't manage a millimetre or two of *cotton?*' Monroe shook his head. 'It looks more to me like Rupert there wanted to get his rocks off with some naked lassies.'

'It's not just Rupert,' Anjli pointed at the other masked man. Even through the night vision, the burn mark running from neck to shoulder was prominent. 'That's John Gale. He said he had a burn mark there.'

'He was with Wilson? I thought they weren't friends?'

'Seems John was a little lax with the truth,' Billy smiled.

'Are any of them his Ladies of Avalon, or even Lucy?' Anjli asked, peering closer. Billy shrugged.

'It's not that great footage, and they're shadowed,' he admitted. 'But possibly. This was definitely enough to have him suspended, though.'

'And John's wife to divorce him,' Monroe nodded. 'That must have been an unpleasant shock. Getting a video of one of your Professors, and seeing hubby waving his whatnots on the screen during it.'

'What's the text at the bottom?' Declan leaned over, pointed at some numbers on the screen.

'Timing numbers for a live feed,' Billy peered closer. 'This was being recorded off site.'

'*Not since he started branding himself with moons and holding weird naked sabbats in dark rooms over the internet. It was like he was having some kind of midlife crisis, even though he was almost bloody seventy.*'

'Julie-Anna knew about this,' he stated. 'And Lilith also talked about virtual sabbats.'

'Maybe Lilith told Julie-Anna,' Billy suggested.

'And a sabbat is?' Monroe asked.

'It's a name given by Wiccans for the eight fire festivals in the year,' Billy replied. 'Solstices, equinoxes, New Year, that sort of thing.'

He checked the file info.

'They recorded this on March the 20th, so the Spring Equinox.'

'Why's it tinted green?' Anjli asked.

'It's night vision,' Billy answered. 'The room was probably too dark to film normally. You get that on a lot of ghost shows —' he stopped.

'They filmed this on Alfie Wasley's *GhostPro* camera. The one we found in there.'

'Keep checking the SD cards Simon had in his bag,' Monroe muttered, still averting his eyes. 'And get me Alfie right now. Maybe we can get some behind the scenes. *Clothed* behind the scenes.'

'You said eight festivals,' Declan said. 'When's the next one?'

'Beltaine,' Billy looked a little worried now. 'On Friday.'

'Two days from now?' Monroe nodded. 'Aye, that could explain why things are getting a little insane. So what next?'

'Can we hear what they're saying?' Bullman asked.

'That would involve watching it,' Billy replied. 'Although I can probably place something over the video.'

'Do it, see what's being said,' Bullman turned away. 'Maybe we'll get something from it.'

'Try to split the audio from the footage,' Monroe suggested. 'Maybe your great-uncle can help us again.'

Billy nodded, and Declan noted that this time he didn't seem to have a problem with this idea. It could mean he was finally healing rifts in the family, or it could mean he was working against the needs of the Unit.

Declan hoped it was the former of the two.

'What's the issue with Beltaine?' Declan asked softly, leaning closer to Billy. 'You looked a little queasy when you realised the date.'

'Pagans believe that Beltaine, or May Day celebrates the union of the Goddess and the Green Man, the coming together of both male and female energies to create new life,' Billy replied. 'The name originates from the Celtic God 'Bel', meaning 'the bright one', and the Gaelic word 'teine', meaning fire.'

He shuddered.

'It's believed to be the most powerful of the festivals, and charges the land itself. And whether I believe or not, I don't like the idea of a festival linked to fire and energy empowering a Ley Line that's running through a nuclear reactor.'

'But it's done every year,' Declan questioned. 'Why would this year be different?'

'Because we don't usually have rogue Mossad agents involved?' Billy forced a smile. It looked sickly. 'I mean, if Shavit's talking to Gale, and Gale's hanging around naked in unused rooms with Wilson, this can't be unconnected.'

Declan patted him on the back.

'We'll sort it out,' he replied. 'We always do. And what's the worst that can happen? Surely a bucket sized reactor can't do that much?'

Billy nodded. 'I'll isolate the sound,' he replied.

Declan started across the office back towards his desk—

'She's with you. The dark-haired woman. She was taken from you too soon.'

'Where is the watchtower?'

Declan spun, looking to see who'd spoken the words.

Across the office, Anjli looked up from her desk.

'You okay?' she asked. Declan nodded.

'I'm off to see a Ripperologist,' he fake-smiled as he left the office, walking down the stairs. He *was* going to meet with John Gale but first, he needed some different answers. So, outside the morgue, he cleared his throat, straightened his tie and entered the room.

'Can I help you with something?' Doctor Marcos asked, looking up from the severed hand, of which she was prodding with what looked like a pair of pliers. Declan glanced around, seeing that Doctor Marcos was alone.

'No, sorry, I'm off to speak with John Gale,' he said, backing out of the room.

'Joanne will be back in half an hour,' Doctor Marcos smiled. 'I guess you were hoping to chat to her about hypnosis?'

Declan stopped.

'She told me she'd delete the file,' he muttered.

'And she did,' Doctor Marcos smiled. 'But she still told me what happened, mainly in case it happened again when she wasn't around. You shouldn't be ashamed of being tricked. It happens to us all. Think how many times we've had people turn out not to be who we thought they were? Nine times out of ten, we've given them the benefit of the doubt. Christ, you were the one that worked out Trix was a plant, who found Monroe when he'd been kidnapped, even worked out that your childhood mechanic was a serial killer.'

The smile widened.

'Of course, you took your time with that one.'

'I keep hearing her,' Declan leaned against the morgue

table. 'Lucy. Things she said to me. But not in my head, they're like—'

'Auditory verbal hallucinations?' Doctor Marcos finished. 'They can manifest because of intense stress, sleep deprivation, drug use, loads of things. Any of those sound familiar?'

At Declan's nod, Doctor Marcos continued.

'She got into your head, Declan. Into your brain. And your brain is trying to fix itself. You need to accept them for what they are and ignore them. Find something new to focus on.'

She looked at a sheaf of papers beside her, picking one up and passing it over.

'Have a look at that.'

Declan examined the paper; the coroner's report for Marie Lucinda Wilson.

'Is this a joke, or some kind of therapy session?' he asked.

'Bit of the latter, definitely not the former,' Doctor Marcos replied. 'Look at the cause of death.'

'Throat slashed open from left to right,' Declan read out. 'I know this, we saw—'

He stopped as he continued on.

'Stone flecks?'

'That's right,' Doctor Marcos smiled, taking the sheet of paper back. 'They found small flecks of razor sharp obsidian in the wound, which to me means a blade made of obsidian made the cut.'

Declan nodded. 'An obsidian blade,' he whispered, knowing that he'd heard the term before.

'I just remember John and his bloody dagger. Made of obsidian, it was, and he slashed it around like he was a bloody Musketeer in more than name.'

'Billy's great-uncle,' he replied, rising and already walking for the door. 'He told us that John Gale took an obsidian blade from the library.'

'You carry on seeing Gale, I'll let the others know,' Doctor Marcos nodded. 'Just be careful when you meet him. He might play a Ripper on that walk, but he's likely to have a sharper blade hidden.'

23

THE RIPPER CALLS

NOW WITH A CLEAR AUDIO FILE OF THE RITUAL, BILLY GRABBED his jacket and, with PC De'Geer, recently returned from Bishopsgate, currently out of uniform and caught by Billy before leaving, they headed out of the North Entrance to Temple Inn.

Usually, Billy would have passed the information he had to Anjli, so she could go out into the field with it, but this was still a personal situation and so instead, Billy and De'Geer made their way quickly up Drury Lane, past Covent Garden and heading towards Museum Street. Billy knew that since the journey was less than a mile, it would take as much time to get there by foot as it would by car or bike on a busy London evening. So it was by foot that they arrived at the blue-fronted *Atlantis Bookshop*, and an irritated Chivalry Fitzwarren who waited for them in the doorway.

'As happy as I am to see you, you're eating into my day,' Chivalry muttered, nodding to De'Geer. 'I still have to get to *Watkins* on Cecil Court and they close at eight.'

'I need you to translate a ritual,' Billy passed a pair of

earphones to his great-uncle, who reluctantly put them in. As Billy scrolled to the audio file on his phone, De'Geer pulled out his notebook.

'This had better be a bloody good ritual...' Chivalry said, stopping as Billy adjusted the sound and pressed play. '...Oh,' he listened, before waving to Billy. 'Is there any way to put this on speaker?' he asked. 'I'm going to need you to keep rewinding bits.'

'Sure, but it's a little noisy out here, and I'd rather not scare the public,' Billy looked around the street as he spoke. Chivalry smiled.

'Then we'll go downstairs,' he said.

'NOT MANY HERE FOR YOUR TALK, ARE THERE?' DECLAN SMILED, walking over to John Gale and showing his warrant card. 'DI Walsh. You met my partner while you were dressed as Dracula.'

Even though they'd never met, Declan knew that this was Gale by the simple fact that, amongst the many tourists that were around the station, only John Gale was wearing a top hat and cape. The same cape, it seemed, that he'd worn as Dracula.

John, standing beside a chalk sandwich board that read RIPPER TOUR - 7:30PM - NINETY MINUTES OF FEAR!!! shrugged. He was outside Tower Hill Underground Station, where steps up from the ticket office emerged onto a patio area, one that led down steps to the right of him to Tower Hill Road, led behind him to one of the last remaining pieces of the original Roman London Wall, or up steps to the right that led to Coopers Row and Trinity Square, with Fenchurch Street Station to the north.

'There's football on tonight,' John replied testily. 'Also, it's a pleasant night and people rarely come out in the spring or summer for a Ripper talk. They come out in winter for those.'

'So why do them?' Declan asked. John smiled.

'Because sometimes you get good ones,' he admitted. 'I mean, I'd do a walk for twenty quid, as it's more about spreading the story, telling the history, but the bigger groups are better. Yesterday, for example, there were fifteen German tourists here for another Ripper tour, but he hadn't turned up. So I offered to do it instead, gave them a ten percent discount.'

'Was he angry?' Declan raised his eyebrows at this, but John chuckled.

'Bloody furious,' he replied. 'But he shouldn't have been late. That's how it works here. So, how can I help you?'

'Need to have a little chat,' Declan forced a smile. 'Few discrepancies in our investigation, and they seem to fall around you.'

'You arresting me?' John looked around. 'I don't mind, as long as you're happy for me to stay in the character of 'Saucy Jack' as you take me off. Get some people filming, make me viral, I could make a mint out of it when I return to do walks later in the week.'

'That depends on whether you answer my questions,' Declan replied. 'Where were you last night, around nine-thirty?'

John thought for a moment. 'Henriques Street, in Whitechapel,' he eventually said. 'Outside Harry Gosling Primary School. That's where I end my talk. Every night.'

'Interesting choice.'

'It wasn't always a school,' John replied. 'It used to be called Berner Street, and it was where Elizabeth Stride, the third victim of Jack the Ripper was murdered. It's also a ten-minute walk from here, so they can loop back to get home.'

Declan nodded as he wrote this in his notebook. 'We'll be able to check with the school's security cameras for that.'

'Sure,' John smiled, tapping on his top hat. 'It's not like you won't recognise me.'

'Oh, we know,' Declan continued to smile back, although his smile was faker than John's and that was saying something. 'We have you at the Lyceum yesterday, dressed like Dracula. The costumes really help, you know?'

John froze and Declan knew that the man in the top hat was now remembering who he'd met with.

'So, how about we chat about your conversation with the *Consortium?*' he asked.

John looked at his watch.

'I'm sorry, but it's gone seven-thirty and nobody's here,' he said. 'I think I'll call it a night. Unless you want to arrest me?'

Declan reached into his jacket pocket and John flinched, expecting handcuffs. However, Declan pulled out his wallet, passing John a twenty-pound note.

'I'd like to do your tour,' he said calmly. 'You said you'd do it for twenty? Here's twenty. We could chat on the way.'

'What sort of chat?' John knew he was cornered. Declan shrugged.

'Dodgy occult item sellers, cheating girlfriends, nude rituals, divorces and hidden treasures for a start,' he said. 'Anything I missed?'

DOWNSTAIRS AT THE *ATLANTIS BOOKSHOP* WAS MORE OF A lecture area, and Billy knew, over the decades, many famous occultists had held talks down here. The druidic order *The Order of the Hidden Masters* had held meetings in the basement, with occultists including both Gerald Gardner and Aleister Crowley attending, and Gerald Gardner had even started his first coven in this room but currently it was a half-lit, quiet space that was filled with unsold stock where Chivalry listened to the ritual's audio.

'Okay, the first part is a call to prayer,' Chivalry said as he listened. 'Lots of *Highest God our God, the Highest God is One, the Highest God is love* type stuff. Then we have a blessing of the space—is this Rupert? It sounds like Rupert. He could never pronounce the vowels correctly.'

He listened some more.

'God, now they're trying to obtain knowledge and conversation of the Holy Guardian Angel,' he muttered, grabbing the phone and scrolling back a little to listen to some of the Enochian again. 'As if that'll work. Wait, that's interesting. Now they're asking the Angels for power over the Earth. For what? Ley lines, perhaps? They want the area where they are, charged with—'

He looked at Billy.

'Where was the ritual held?' he asked. Billy looked at De'Geer, shaking his head.

'I can't tell you,' he said.

'You have to if you want a proper reading,' Chivalry replied. 'This is location specific.'

'Near his office, at Queen Mary University,' De'Geer answered, keeping as close to the truth as he could give.

'The Dee Line!' Chivalry nodded excitedly. 'Runs up past

the university. Makes sense. They're charging it up. Or, at least, they believe they are.'

'What else are they doing?' Billy asked as Chivalry started the audio again.

'They're reconciling themselves with the energy of the sign of Taurus,' Chivalry continued. 'That's in power right now, so this could be a precursor to Beltaine but they're talking about this being in the future. This is an Equinox ritual. March? That would lead to Taurus in April. Now they're asking for protection against the elements? Energy? I can't quite get that. Why would they...'

He stopped, looking at Billy.

'Most Enochian rituals are for help or assistance,' he said. 'Angels are good beings and all that. This isn't. This is a ritual to power up the Dee Line over Beltaine and protect them from what's going to happen. So, William, what's going to happen on Friday?'

'Nothing,' Billy replied. 'You know how rituals are usually just talk.'

'This isn't the pomp and ceremony of a ritual,' Chivalry protested. 'This is the sound of a zealot.'

He shook his head.

'Rupert knows a basic amount of Enochian, but this is being spoken phonetically,' he paused the recording again. 'Remember how I said he has issues with his vowels? He's speaking the words correctly, but there are pauses, as if he's reciting the words as learned. Someone else wrote this.'

'Who else is this good?'

'There's a long list, but people involved with these lunatics, I'd say probably John Gale. He was an expert in all languages. Maybe Julie-Anna too,' Chivalry was back to listening to the recording. 'They're trying to raise energy to power something, but they can't work out the term to use,' he said. 'It's the problem with the twenty-first century. There's no God or Goddess for IT assistance, so you phrase the issue to fit an established archetype. They're trying to overload something? Is that making sense?'

Billy turned off the recording, nodding.

'Yes, that does,' he said. 'Thank you.'

'But you're not going to tell me what it is?'

'No,' Billy looked at De'Geer. 'I think we have what we need.'

Chivalry leaned closer.

'You might not,' he replied. 'You see, I was speaking with the owners of this shop, and might have mentioned that I was helping you with your enquiries.'

'And you did that why?'

'For a discount, of course,' Chivalry replied, as if it was the most obvious answer in the world. 'They told me there was a talk here, with Rupert in this very room a year back on *Hereward the Wake* that had some footage filmed. And in the background were Miriam Shrimpton and Julie-Anna Watson, having a right old barney, about a week before the weekend rally where they both *died*.'

Chivalry smiled.

'You have no idea what you've walked into,' he said. 'So, how about you stop all this cloak and dagger bullshit and tell me what I want to know?'

Anjli was at her desk when Billy's desk phone rang. Walking over, she picked it up.

'Billy's not here, Declan,' she said. The voice, however, was not her partner.

'I guessed that,' Trix's voice returned.

'Trix,' Anjli's tone took on a colder, more official turn. She knew Trix had helped Declan save his career, and she knew she'd also helped the *Last Chance Saloon* catch a German serial killer, but there was still the fact that before all of this, she was a *Pearce Associates* mole that actively worked against the team. 'How nice to hear from you.'

'Yeah, whatever,' Trix was amused at this. 'Tell Billy we sent him the most up-to-date photo we have on any asset Yossi Shavit currently has in the field, and it's on his desktop. Don't ask how I managed it.'

'Thanks,' Anjli was already leaning over the station, phone to her ear as she used the mouse to bring up the image. 'Any idea of why ex-Mossad agents are buying occult items?'

'Actually, yeah,' Trix replied down the line. 'Before he blew up, Yossi was doing a side hustle in selling Israeli antiquities, in particular those on the En Esur dig in the 2010s.'

'I know that date,' Anjli said, looking back at her own desk. 'How do I...'

She stopped.

'Rupert Wilson ran some of those digs,' she said.

'Bingo, give the girl a toy,' Trix replied. 'Wilson and Shavit worked well together for about five years. And then he faked his death in a bombing before Mossad could bring him in. Word on the street though is that he's resurfaced, trying to broker an amnesty and return to Mossad.'

'Rupert's gone, so his golden goose is over,' Anjli nodded. 'But what sort of deal do you have to make to get that much red wiped off your ledger?'

'A lot,' Trix continued. 'Like proof that there's a nuclear reactor still under Greenwich levels of deal.'

'Christ,' Anjli exclaimed. 'But how did he...'

Her words died in her throat.

The image of Cindy Mitchell, forgotten in the conversation, was now on the screen.

'Oh God,' Anjli whispered, disconnecting the call and looking in horror towards Monroe's office.

'Guv!' she shouted. 'We've got a problem!'

'WELL, I HAVE TO SAY, I WASN'T EXPECTING THE FIRST STOP TO be a car park at the back of a hotel,' Declan smiled.

They were currently standing at the back of the *Royal Leonardo Hotel*, at the junction of Cooper's Hill and Trinity Square, staring up at a twenty-foot high slab of ancient brickwork.

'Talk's not just about the Ripper, you know,' John replied. 'We have until we hit Mitre Square before we start truly on that. First, I have to explain how the Met and City police came to, well, both royally bugger up the case.'

Declan grinned darkly. He knew John was trying to get a rise out of him, so he conceded the point.

'So, as we have a walk ahead of us, how about we talk about your own 'buggering up', in particular the loss of the library?'

To his credit, John was unfazed by this. 'I've already told your partner, the Indian girl, everything,' he replied as they emerged back onto the street, turning right.

'That 'Indian girl' is a detective sergeant,' Declan snapped. John shrugged.

'I'm in my late sixties,' he replied. 'Every woman under fifty is a girl to me.'

'So let's talk about something you didn't speak to DS Kapoor about,' Declan changed tack. 'How do you know Yossi Shavit?'

'He was nothing more than a broker,' John looked both ways before crossing the road, not even trying to deny the question. 'I'm getting divorced, and it was suggested I sell some occult antiquities on the quiet, so my ex-wife doesn't get them.'

'Ah, yes. Let's talk about the divorce,' Declan replied. 'Mutual, was it? Amicable?'

'It was until recently,' John admitted. 'We were moving in different directions, it wasn't working out.'

'I bet the video coming out last week didn't help though,' Declan smiled. John's face darkened.

'Rituals are supposed to be private, not filmed,' he whispered. 'She sent it to my wife. She sent it to my *paper.*'

'Who did?' Declan asked, noting the *she.* John stopped speaking however, as if realising he'd said too much.

'Okay, let's go back to Shavit,' Declan changed direction, realising there was nothing more coming from that line of enquiry. 'Who arranged the introduction to him?'

John shrugged.

'Rupert put me in contact with them, and then Cindy was the liaison,' he explained. 'Because of her connection to Rupert, you know, as one of his Ladies and all that, he felt safer with her doing the grunt work.'

'When was this?'

'A few months back.'

'So you were friendly with Rupert then?'

'He was a tool, nothing more,' John rubbed at his cheek nervously.

'Did your wife give you that?' Declan asked, indicating the plaster on John's face.

'Girlfriend's cat,' John replied, a little too quickly.

'That'll be Cindy Mitchell, right?' Declan said conversationally. 'You don't know where she is, do you?'

'I thought you had her.'

'We did until lunchtime. Then your Mister Shavit got her out.'

John chuckled.

'Maybe he is more than a broker,' he replied.

'Something like that, walking into a police station and faking a release is a big thing,' Declan continued. 'That's a big owe. What were you selling him?'

'Firstly, I have nothing to do with that, and secondly, what I look to sell is nothing to do with *you*.'

'It does when you're selling a library you don't have yet, and the bodies are piling up around you,' Declan snapped.

John stopped in the street, staring away from Declan.

'I'm not the only one who could have gotten it,' he snarled. 'Speak to Julie-Anna.'

'Yes, Julie-Anna,' Declan nodded. 'Don't worry, she's on the list, too. Tell me, though, what was it that broke the two of you up back then? Was it the fact that you couldn't get the library out, that you were a laughing stock in the academic community, or that your girlfriend at the time, Julie-Anna, was having an affair with Alés Capioca and Miriam Shrimpton?'

By now they were walking up Fenchurch Street, crossing the road into Mitre Street. John, back in tour guide mode, pointed at a church, built with brown and cream bricks, a tall, square spire rising to view down at them, about another hundred yards down the road.

'That's Saint Botolph Without Aldgate,' he said as they crossed. 'Otherwise known as Aldgate Church. Also known as the prostitutes' church, because the ladies would walk around it in order to attract clients.'

'Sounds tiring,' Declan glanced around, unable to shake the impression that he was being followed.

'It was against the law to stand in one place and solicit,' John explained. 'Doing a loop meant they couldn't be arrested. Catherine Eddowes, one of the victims, was seen drunk there the night of her murder.'

He pointed up Mitre Street where, halfway along, was a clearing to the right.

'Over there in Mitre Square,' he explained as they walked along the street, emerging into a small open area built between a tall, black steel and glass office block and an older, red-brick school building. The ground was paved, and there were two large raised grass ovals with benches built into the walls.

'Right here,' John stood beside a set of iron gates, a sign on which proclaimed NO PARKING - FIRE BRIGADE ACCESS. 'There used to be a bench here with a plaque, but that's gone now. Back in the day, though, this was a great place to kill someone.'

'Is this the speed you usually walk?' Declan asked, finally tiring of the game they'd been playing. 'I was promised *ninety minutes of fear.*'

At John's expression, he continued.

''Your sign at the station said that,' Declan reached into his pocket and pulled out his handcuffs, noting John's expression as he did so. 'An hour and a half from seven-thirty.'

'So?' John turned to face Declan full on, as if about to confront him.

'Well, I've worked in London and the East End for a while now, and I know that walking from Whitechapel to St Anne's Church in Limehouse? It's about a twenty-minute walk,' Declan explained. 'Your ninety minutes takes you to nine pm, twenty minutes away from where Lucy Shrimpton was murdered, around half an hour later—'

There was a noise behind him and Declan spun around to confront whoever was approaching, trying to keep John in his peripheral vision.

He'd expected to find Cindy behind him; he'd known that someone else had been following, thanks to that niggling sensation on the back of the neck.

What he hadn't expected was to find Yossi Shavit, gun in his hand, facing him from Mitre Street.

'Leave, John,' Yossi smiled. 'I'll sort out the Detective Inspector. Permanently.'

24

THE WATCHTOWER

JOHN DIDN'T NEED TO BE TOLD TWICE and quickly made his excuses, exiting the square through the north entrance. Yossi moved closer, gun still aimed at Declan.

'Beretta 70?' Declan asked, looking at it. Yossi smiled.

'It's a 71, actually. You have a good eye.'

'Ex-military police. I've seen a few,' Declan shrugged. 'It's the go-to for a lot of Mossad agents. But you're not one anymore, are you, Yossi?'

If Yossi Shavit was surprised at Declan's knowledge of his name, he didn't comment. Instead he looked around quickly, ensuring they were alone before aiming.

'Lot of witnesses in these buildings,' Declan commented.

'Not really,' Yossi shook his head. 'Eight pm on a weekday in the city? It's dead. And the school closed hours ago.'

Declan saw the finger tighten on the trigger and knew there was nothing he could do to get out of this. Even throwing himself to the side would just end with Yossi firing a second time.

He didn't know why the idea popped into his head; it was a Hail Mary idea, but he tried it anyway—

'Where's the watchtower?' he asked.

Immediately, Yossi's arm dropped as his eyes glazed over.

'On the cliff—arrghhh!!' The scream wasn't because of Declan, as Yossi staggered back, clutching his head, shaking away an intense pain as he tried to focus on Declan once more—

Who by this point was already moving in, extendable baton out as he slammed it down on Yossi's wrist, sending the gun clattering across the Square. If Yossi was in pain from this, he didn't show it as he blocked Declan's second strike, palm striking Declan hard, sending him staggering backwards, his nose exploding in a spray of blood. Yossi moved in now, quickly striking Declan hard again on the bridge of his nose, sending bright lights and pain into his eyes as he stumbled to a knee—

"Where's the watchtower?' he shouted, half in desperation. Yossi screamed once more as he grabbed at his skull.

'Where's the watchtower?' Declan rose, shouting the words now, moving in.

'Uh-on the cliff—' Declan brought his knee up hard, slamming it into Yossi's own nose as he spoke the words, sending him tumbling onto the floor. Unfortunately, he landed near his gun, and with a look of fear, he grabbed at it—

'Where's the watchtower?' Declan ran in now, kicking the gun away as Yossi froze in place, the pain once more slamming through his skull. Before Yossi could give his reply Declan kicked out hard, his foot connecting with Yossi's jaw, snapping it back as the ex-Mossad agent, unconscious, fell to the floor.

His own nose still streaming with blood, Declan turned Yossi over, now face down as he handcuffed his wrists behind his back. Then, grabbing the gun and emptying it of bullets, he tossed it to the side and pulled his phone out.

'It's me,' he said, as he called Anjli. 'Send squad cars to Mitre Square ASAP. I've got a present.'

Before Anjli could reply, Declan disconnected the call. The last thing he needed was to be fussed over. Slowly, he rose to his feet. John Gale couldn't have gotten far—

Who are you kidding? John could be anywhere by now.

Sighing, Declan walked over to the unconscious Yossi, checking his pockets and pulling out a burner phone. Using a handcuffed fingerprint to open it, he swiped through to the texts on it, ignoring them until he found JOHN GALE.

You promised me library.

Hand will be there all night get it yourself

Declan didn't scroll up; he could do that later at the Command Unit. Instead, he typed and sent a single word.

Done.

It was best to have John not realise that the *Consortium* was now arrested. With luck, he might make a mistake.

There was a groan beside him as Yossi Shavit opened his eyes.

'How?' he asked, simply. Declan knelt down and shrugged.

'I knew your weakness,' he said. 'I knew you'd been hypnotised.'

'I can't be hypnotised,' Yossi muttered, shifting up, so that he was sitting now. 'Mossad has training—'

'Well, your training sucks,' Declan replied. 'I'll prove it. Where's the—'

'No, no, I believe you,' Yossi interrupted. 'Please don't say it again.'

As Declan relaxed, Yossi chuckled.

'I knew you were different when we met,' he said. 'You remind me more of the old days.'

'Look, Yossi,' Declan continued. 'I don't know what your situation is here, or even why you're involved. All I'm doing is solving a murder. Two, actually.'

'I'm not the villain here,' Yossi spoke softly. 'I'm saving the world.'

'How are you doing that?'

'By telling it about a secret your government has kept hidden for decades.'

'Whistleblowing about a nuclear reactor the size of a bucket, when pretty much everyone seems to know isn't really a secret.'

'That's not the secret,' Yossi said, and as Declan glanced at his captive, he saw a fire in the eyes.

'So what is?' Declan asked.

'It's not the reactor, it's what it's powered by,' Yossi continued. 'A line of energy and items of occult power, all charging the reactor up!'

Declan couldn't help himself and started to laugh.

'You can't be serious,' he replied. Yossi shook his head.

'In the Second World War, Adolf Hitler collected many occult items, and was hunting high and low for the *Spear of Destiny*,' Yossi started. 'He knew that with these occult items, ones powered by dark magic, he could overthrow the world.

He was stopped by Aleister Crowley, who worked with the Royal Navy to place a nuclear bunker on the Greenwich Line.'

'Yossi, Aleister Crowley died years before then,' Declan started. 'The reactor at Greenwich didn't open until the sixties.'

Yossi shook his head. 'He told me how it worked,' he replied. 'Her mother had a chip in her hand. One that he was going to utilise.'

'Wait, you're talking about Lucy?' Declan now turned to face Yossi. 'You were working with her?'

No, wait. He's saying he, not she.

'You were working with Rupert,' Declan realised.

'A mutual decision,' Yossi replied, confirming this. 'He wanted the library. I wanted the proof. We were going to use a chip in his hand, one that had been powered by ritual.'

'What did the chip do?'

'Miriam had one that opened the door,' Yossi explained. 'The ritual was to link a new one, in Rupert's hand, one that would do the same.'

'And you believe this?' Declan asked. 'Cloning chips by magic?'

'Of course not. I thought if I could get her one I could reverse engineer it. But to do that meant playing his stupid game. He was going to give me the map but there were always excuses. And his requests, his demands became stranger and more deviant in nature, as if he was starting to really enjoy causing the pain that he did.'

'What did he do?'

'Anything he could get away with,' Yossi muttered. 'Even though Lucy said she was his daughter, we knew she wasn't. He was intending to drug her, have his way with—'

'Okay, you can stop now before I ask about watchtowers again,' Declan felt sick.

Yossi shrugged.

'It never happened, because then he died. I gained the chip that he believed had been charged in his ritual,' Yossi was wild-eyed now. 'I tried to pressure Lucy to honour his bargain, to give me the location of the door in the Naval College where the chip was used. But then last night she died too.'

Declan remembered how shocked Yossi, when playing Inspector Saeed had been when hearing that she was murdered.

'I shouldn't have gone elsewhere,' Yossi continued. 'I should have trusted Lucy, she—they—I don't know...'

'You were working with John Gale, too.'

'Yes,' Yossi admitted. 'He wanted to sell me the library, which I knew from Rupert was to be found through the same door. I knew he could give me the location, and then with the chip to open the door, I wouldn't need Lucy or Julie-Anna.'

'You worked with Julie-Anna?'

'I had her help John translate the ritual,' Yossi laughed. 'He couldn't do it himself. But that was when she worked out what I was doing.'

He sighed.

'That was when she tried to hypnotise me. But it didn't work.'

'You sure?'

'I don't think sending sparks of pain into my brain was what she intended,' Yossi smiled.

'Why release Cindy and Lilith?'

'I needed Cindy. She works for me.'

'Doing what?'

Yossi shrugged. 'Whatever I need,' he said.

There was a moment of silence. Declan went to reply, but this was the moment where five SCO 19 officers in full tactical gear, tipped off about *the crazy people with a gun* outside the Mitre Street *WeWork* office came into the Square, assault rifles aimed at Declan and Yossi, screaming at them to *get on the floor*.

Declan felt it was best to comply in this situation.

LILITH BABYLON STARED ACROSS THE BAR TABLE AT JULIE-ANNA Watson.

'They said it was a car accident, not that he was hit by one,' she muttered.

Julie-Anna sighed.

'All I heard was that a bald man in a Mondeo took him out while he was walking to the police.'

Lilith nodded. 'The guy Lucy spoke to was bald,' she said. 'I remember bumping into him once.'

'I saw him talking to John Gale, too,' Julie-Anna nodded as she sipped from a small bottle of orange juice. 'And he was the one that freed you too. He's called Yossi Shavit, also known as the *Consortium*.'

'How do you know he spoke to John?'

'Because *I* spoke to John,' Julie-Anna sipped at her drink. 'By phone, of course, he's not stupid enough to let me meet him in person. We've been talking for a while. I helped with a translation or two.'

'But this doesn't explain why this Shavit guy would hurt Simon?'

Julie-Anna frowned.

'I thought you'd know that part,' she said. 'Yossi saw him at Greenwich Park that night and assumed Simon was there for the same reason as he was. He was convinced you had set him up.'

Lilith paused, realising what this little chat in the back room of a London City pub truly was.

'You think *I* told him,' she muttered. 'You think I did this? I didn't even know this was going on until the afternoon!'

'What was Lucy's plan?' Julie-Anna was calm, rational. Lilith waved her arms around the room in frustration.

'It didn't involve people bloody dying!' she exclaimed. 'I just wanted Rupert to get what he was owed! For what he did to my brother!'

Julie-Anna stayed silent at this, and Lilith stopped.

'What, no pithy comment about how he deserved it?' she asked.

'I'm just as guilty as Rupert about what happened to Alés,' she whispered. 'I was the one that broke him and Miriam up.'

'With the threesome?' Lilith shook her head. 'Don't fool yourself. You were a distraction. Miriam and my brother were doomed way before you turned up. She was mad, even then.'

'How do you know this?'

'Lucy told me,' Lilith replied. 'She explained Miriam was an analyst in some Naval bunker, never allowed to see daylight, and unable to tell people what she knew. Like the women in Bletchley Park during the war. And it weighed on her. And when she found out she had cancer, she sat Lucy down and told her the truth.'

'You know nothing of the truth,' Julie-Anna snapped in reply. 'And Miriam wasn't mad.'

'She might not have been, but Rupert certainly was,'

Lilith leaned back in her chair, almost chuckling now. 'In the end, he convinced himself that he could use the energy to do something big at the Naval College. He kept saying how the Naval College was a lie, how Marcus was a lie and how he was going to reveal everything.'

She shook her head.

'And then Lucy got him to put that bloody chip in his hand.'

Julie-Anna watched Lilith for a moment and then chuckled.

'Oh you poor woman,' she eventually said. 'You haven't got a bloody clue, have you? Lucy didn't make Rupert do anything. Rupert was planning this all along. You may have wanted to discredit him, but he was already on that journey. *He* was the one working with Yossi Shavit, *he* was the one that was trying to power a chip and *he* was the one that wanted to reveal that Greenwich Park still had a nuclear reactor underneath it. To hurt them for what they did to his reputation decades ago.'

Lilith shook her head.

'Lucy's dead, Rupert's dead, why do I feel that it's still not over?' she asked.

Julie-Anna shrugged.

'Because it isn't,' she said. 'I still have to finish things with John, and you're going to help me.'

'STOP GETTING BLOOD ON YOUR JACKET,' MONROE FORCED A smile as he sat in front of Declan. 'You're going to end up running out of spares.'

Declan nodded; he knew Monroe was trying to make light of the situation, but currently he didn't want to make light of anything. He wanted to know what the hell was going on.

'And you need to stop being punched in the face,' Monroe finished. 'It looks bad enough as it is. You keep making it worse, it'll stay like that.'

Declan was currently sitting in the back of a police car, his jacket on his lap, as Doctor Marcos checked his broken nose. Monroe had been the first to arrive, standing down the armed police as they released Declan from their custody, getting some Temple Inn officers to take Yossi back to the Interview Room at Temple Inn before any government agency could come and take him.

They hadn't managed it, because by the time Yossi was standing, suited men arrived in black SUVs, taking Yossi away before Monroe could even build a reason to keep him.

MI5 didn't care about an academic's murder.

'Bloody Tom, he grassed us to them, I bet you,' he muttered to himself.

'He won't need stitches but it'll need to be reset,' Doctor Marcos muttered, looking at Monroe. 'More's the pity. Bloody idiot, going off after him on your own.'

'Did Gale say anything?' Monroe asked. 'Before he left?'

'Only that Yossi is his broker,' Declan replied. 'I'm guessing that if she works for Yossi, then Cindy connected with John to soften him up for the deal. Maybe even caused the marriage issues, filmed and then sent that video in to his wife, forcing John to need to make a deal as he watched his whole life crumble around him.'

'Harsh.'

'I've met a few agents from my time in the SIS,' Declan shrugged, wincing again as Doctor Marcos wiped antiseptic on the wound now. 'None of them were exactly people person material. Cindy was probably brought in to be Rupert's principal contact as well, hence her joining his little gang, but John wouldn't have known this.'

'We need to find them all,' Doctor Marcos muttered. 'We need to find them all now and stop this.'

She leaned back, smiled at Declan and then, with a *crack* reset his nose.

'That's the plan,' Monroe stretched his arms as he rose. 'Get home and try to get some sleep, laddie. DS Kapoor, you're his babysitter for the next twelve hours. Any problems, call me.'

Anjli nodded, motioning for Declan to follow her. Reluctantly, taking one last look around the Square, he walked to the Audi, settling into the passenger seat.

'You ready to go?'

'Not really,' Declan muttered. 'But I'd rather be anywhere else in the world, in case Doctor Marcos wants to work on my nose again.'

'Do you have anything you need to pick up at the Unit?'

Declan shook his head. 'Nothing that can't—'

'I said, *do you have anything that you need to pick up at the Unit?*' Anjli was more insistent now.

'I suppose I might have left something on the desk?' Declan was unsure what was going on. Anjli started the car.

'Well, we ought to go pick those up first,' she said, before continuing. 'Look, Guv. I think I know you by now well enough to see that if I took you home, all we'd end up doing is going over the case repeatedly in your—I mean, *our* living room. So we might as well do that at the Command Unit.'

'Monroe won't be happy.'

'I'll tell him you pulled rank,' Anjli smiled. 'Threatened to evict me. And, you're not technically out in the field, so I think it'll be okay.'

And with this act of mutiny decided, Anjli drove out of Mitre Square, and back towards Temple Inn.

25

THE DEAD WALK

DECLAN HAD SHUT HIS EYES, TRYING TO LET HIS THROBBING head wound slowly fade into a kind of background hum as they drove through the City. When he opened them, they were parking up outside Temple Inn.

'You were snoring,' Anjli almost laughed as they got out of the car.

'I don't snore.'

'You don't usually have a broken nose. You were snoring.'

Declan wisely ignored her.

'Simon Tolley. Did we ever look at the SD cards in his camera bag? The one he mentioned?' he asked.

'I think Billy was still going through them by date,' Anjli nodded to the desk sergeant as they entered the building who, obviously having heard what had happened, nodded to Declan rather than making a quip, buzzing them both in. Entering the main office, Declan was surprised to see Billy rise from his station, walking over and stopping short, as if wanting to give Declan a hug but settling for a friendly fist bump on Declan's shoulder.

'Glad you're not dead, Guv,' he said.

'I've had worse,' Declan smiled, before realising that the dried blood from his nose probably made this look ghoulish.

'Monroe said you were going home,' Billy was already returning to his bank of computer monitors. Declan shrugged.

'He told me that too, but what exactly is home?' he asked. 'Home is where the heart is, and currently my heart is in solving this case. Got anything new?'

'Actually, yes,' Billy started typing on the screen. 'De'Geer and I went to see my great-uncle again. The Enochian that Rupert speaks back in March in the horrifyingly naked ritual is basically some kind of charging chant, looking to power up either the Ley Line or the RFID chip, depending on which random conspiracy you believe this week.'

Declan nodded. 'Sounds like the craziness Yossi was spouting. What else did I miss?'

'After you told me what Simon Tolley said to you after a car hit him, I'm trawling through the unused footage on his SD cards,' Billy added. 'It's taking a lot of time because he has dozens in there, but aside from him, I have some extra footage for you.'

He swiped with his mouse and an image appeared on a screen. It was a video, taken at some talk. Declan didn't recognise the person on the screen but Billy wasn't bothered about her, zooming into the side.

'This is a talk at the Atlantis Bookshop, taken last spring. *Hereward The Wake*, by Rupert Wilson. This was a small interview for the webpage, taken directly after the talk.'

'Why do I know that name?' Declan asked.

'Because Simon Tolley told us it was the only time he ever met Rupert Wilson,' Billy replied. 'Look at this.'

He pointed at the two women in the background, their body language obviously confrontational.

'One of them, the painfully thin one, is Miriam Shrimpton, about two weeks before she died.'

Declan examined the image. 'She was terminal, right?'

'Hold that thought,' Billy pointed at the other woman, with curly greying hair and a pair of black-rimmed glasses. 'This is Julie-Anna Watson.'

'That's not Watson,' Declan peered closer. 'Her hair is different, and—'

'Again, hold that thought,' Billy smiled. 'We can't really work out what's being said, as the mic is focused on the person being interviewed, but I'm pulling the background audio out and converting it. So far, all I can work out is that Miriam, at one point says *she knows the truth,* and then maybe *I've told him too.*'

'And then a few days later she was dead.'

'Actually, a few days later they were *both* dead,' Billy tapped on his keyboard. 'Two weekends after this, both Miriam and Julie-Anna were at a pagan rally down south. It was, by all accounts, a terrible one as it found itself in the middle of a storm on the Saturday night, one that tore down the main marquee.'

'God being unimpressed?'

'Or the Gods were having a party,' Billy shrugged. 'Either way, in the middle of this storm, Miriam and Julie-Anna decided to have it out once and for all.'

'This is when they were hit by lightning?' Declan asked. 'We know she was touching Miriam when it struck.'

'Touching is a little understated, apparently,' Billy replied, looking at his notes as he spoke. 'According to witness reports, in the middle of an argument, Miriam slapped Julie-

Anna and called her a whore, said that *she couldn't just leave everything alone.* Julie-Anna then strangles Miriam, screaming that *she's going to kill her.* A second later, before anyone can intervene, a bolt of lightning hit them both.'

'You're kidding,' Anjli exclaimed. Billy shook his head.

'Nope, and that's the kicker. Lightning storm, you're having a massive row beside a tree, chances are good that you could be hit by lightning, everyone knows this, but most people ignore it. Anyway, there were a couple of doctors there, off-duty but able to keep the two women alive until the ambulances came. Both were burned badly, and Julie-Anna had lost most of her hair, completely burned off. On the way to the hospital, both women died, but the paramedics brought Julie-Anna back. Miriam, because of her weakened condition passed away.'

'Surely we would have heard about this,' Anjli was still stunned. 'I mean, the newspapers—'

'Reported on it, but simply as two women hit by lightning bolt,' Billy explained. 'I found the piece. The event organisers didn't want it out that two pagans were hit by lightning at their event, as it'd sound very much like *divine judgement.* So they played it down, and the names were never given.'

'And Julie-Anna died and came back to life,' Declan mused.

'Did you get anything on the walk?' Billy asked. 'Apart from almost being killed?'

'I worked out that John Gale could have gotten to St Anne's Churchyard in time to kill Lucy,' Declan replied. 'And that Julie-Anna tried to hypnotise Yossi, but it wasn't properly taking.'

'Maybe it was Lucy that scratched John's face? That's how he got the scar under the plaster?' Anjli suggested.

'We would have found DNA evidence under the nails,' Billy said before his eyes widened.

'Unless John cut the hand off that scratched him.'

'We're so busy trying to work out why all three hands had been removed, we're not thinking of the obvious answers,' Declan slammed his fist on the table. 'I am sick of being on the back foot here.'

'I have a hospital report for Julie-Anna,' Billy said, reading the screen. 'They kept her in for a month while she recovered, with burn grafts over eighty percent of her head.'

He looked back at the screen.

'I think I was coming up to something that could match this.'

Declan thought back to the meeting again.

'She told me her act was for show, wigs and glasses,' he replied. 'I assumed she just meant for the punters, not for everyone.'

'Wait,' Anjli looked up. 'She was bald, then? What if it was *her* that struck Simon Tolley?'

'Maybe she'd seen his show,' Monroe said as he entered the office, looking at Declan. 'Taking it easy, laddie?'

Busted.

'Come on Guv, you must have known I wouldn't go home,' Declan smiled as Billy pulled on his headphones and returned to the screens, choosing to not be a part of this conversation and hunting the video he'd just thought of.

'I know,' Monroe glared at Anjli. 'That's why I told the grown up in the room to take you.'

'He pulled rank on me,' Anjli said.

'I pulled rank on her,' Declan said.

'Guys, I have something,' Billy pulled off the headphones, pausing a video, one of the many *Ghost Bro* hours of footage that had been playing on the screen. 'This is six months back, in Wanstead. They bring Julie-Anna along as a medium, to sense the spirits or something, back before they changed their style to more tech based investigations. I'd only just got to these, and this is when they're having a break.'

He pressed play, ensuring the sound now went to speakers.

'*It was terrifying,*' Julie-Anna was saying on the screen. '*I believed I was going to die. And then I didn't, and I realised the curse didn't want me to die. That in being reborn, I was the curse.*'

'She's right,' Monroe muttered. 'That is terrifying.'

Declan stared at the peroxide-blonde spiky hair. 'That's not the wig she was wearing for the corporations,' he said. Billy opened up a screen on another monitor, and on it was Julie-Anna again, with curly permed hair and glasses.

'That's from the show,' he explained. 'There was a bit earlier on here where she swapped wigs off camera, stating that the other one made her head sweat. She's done here, they're wrapping up with her before they continue.'

'So curly hair and glasses Julie-Anna is on brand,' Declan nodded as, on the screen, the camera moved away as Simon carried on setting up the next segment. However, in the background, she could still be heard.

'*I've found that spirit works better with me since I visited them,*' she was saying. '*And I know I'll find something far better next time.*'

'*Well, we'd love to have you back,*' now Alfie was speaking, but it was getting fainter. Simon was still filming as a car arrived and a woman got out.

'*I didn't think you were coming,*' Simon could be heard saying, as the camera aimed at some trees.

'I'll keep out of the way, but wanted to wish you luck,' a woman's voice.

'That's Lilith,' Declan said.

'Who's that?' Again, Lilith's voice.

'That's our medium,' Simon aimed the camera at Julie-Anna. *'Jules, can I introduce you to my girlfriend?'*

On the screen, Julie-Anna looked up, squinting.

'Hold on,' she said, walking towards the camera. *'Is that—it is!'* The camera spun around though as the sound of a car door being slammed was audible and, as Simon looked back to the car, it was already reversing out of the car park.

'Was that Alexandra?' Julie-Anna, off camera, spoke.

'No, Lilith—' Simon stopped as Julie-Anna's voice cut through, furious.

'I want to know where the hell you—'

The footage ended.

'Is that all?' Declan asked. Billy shook his head.

'No,' he replied. 'There's another video, one he tried to delete. And with what you've just been telling me, I think it explains who tried to kill him yesterday.'

PC DE'GEER HADN'T INTENDED TO GO TO ST ANN'S HOSPITAL in South Tottenham after he'd travelled with Billy into London, but after talking to Chivalry at the *Atlantis Bookshop* and seeing the video of the *Hereward The Wake* talk, DC Fitzwarren had quietly suggested to De'Geer he follow his great-uncle afterwards to see what he did next, because of a hereditary distrust of his own family that seemed to go back for generations.

As it was, Chivalry did what he'd said, and went to

Watkins Books on Cecil Court, near Leicester Square Station, where he bought some more leather bound first editions before heading north in a cab to the hotel he was staying at in St Pancras, De'Geer following in another. And, having heard about Declan's attack and Yossi's arrest when calling in, De'Geer was about to return, claiming that *all the fun stuff seemed to happen when he was away* when he saw Lilith Babylon waiting at a bus stop to the side of King's Cross Station. Knowing that she was on warrant to be taken in, De'Geer considered calling up the local transport police, as the sight of a tall, Viking-looking man in motorcycle leathers grabbing a young woman might not be immediately construed as an *arrest*, Instead he stopped.

What if she was going somewhere that helped with the case?

And so De'Geer had followed her onto a bus, passing north through Stoke Newington and up the Seven Sisters Road, giving her time to leave the bus before he followed.

And, entering St Ann's Hospital, De'Geer didn't need to follow her to know where she was going; he knew only one patient who was relevant.

Simon Tolley, currently in the Intensive Care unit.

Walking into the unit, having allowed Lilith time to find her own way there, De'Geer had texted Anjli to let her know what was happening. Then, showing his police warrant card (the only thing he'd remembered to bring with him when leaving with DC Fitzwarren earlier) to the nurse on duty, he walked to the door of Simon Tolley's ward room.

'You idiot,' Lilith said softly to the still unconscious Simon, still wired up to a variety of machines, and with both an arm and a leg in traction. 'You never watch where—'

She stopped, looking around at De'Geer in the doorway.

'Do I know you?' she asked. De'Geer showed his warrant card again.

'I might not look it, but I work for the Command Unit working on the Rupert Wilson case,' he replied. At this, Lilith stiffened.

'Are you here to arrest me?' she asked. De'Geer smiled. He'd been told that he had a warm and friendly one, and he was putting on all the charm he could muster to get her to trust him.

'No,' he replied. 'But you look like someone who needs a friend and some coffee. I can't be the first, but I can definitely help with the latter.'

He pointed down the corridor.

'There's a small cafe down there,' he finished. 'Why don't I buy you a drink?'

BILLY POINTED AT A FADED LINE OF CODE ON THE SCREEN.

'That's a corrupted file,' he explained. 'Tolley tried to delete it, but as anyone in computers knows, nothing is ever truly deleted. He should have formatted the card, but he probably needed to keep the other video files, so did it by hand.'

With a swipe of his track pad and a few taps of the keys, Billy brought up a new video file.

'I pieced it together earlier,' he said while typing. 'The problem is that it's still corrupted, so not complete. However, it's complete enough.'

As the video started, Declan saw it was the same green tint that the ritual video had been.

'It's on night vision,' Billy nodded, as if reading Declan's mind. 'I think he'd placed it on right before the conversation. It's a static camera, possibly even the one we found in the secret room, so not being held by Simon.'

On the screen, the curly haired Julie-Anna Watson was rummaging in her bag, pulling out the spiky-haired wig. Then, pulling the curly wig off, she stood there, bald-headed.

'That's who drove the Mondeo at Simon Tolley,' Anjli nodded.

On the screen, Julie-Anna picked up a phone, dialing a number.

'*It's me,*' she said. '*I need you to speak to your Ladies of Avalon. No, I know you—now listen to me—*'

'Sounds like the call isn't going well.'

'*Where's the watchtower?*' she suddenly snapped, listening. '*You're damn right it's on the cliff. Now, I'm going to give you a—*' she stopped as more noises could be heard, pulling on the new wig quickly and disconnecting the call.

'*Sorry, forgot to change batteries on the camera,*' Simon, off screen spoke as Julie-Anna stared directly at the screen.

'*You've been filming me?*'

'*Well, not deliberately.*'

'*Delete it.*'

'*I'm sure you—*'

'*I said delete it now,*' Julie-Anna was furious, staring off screen at Simon. '*Do it or I never come back—*'

The video stopped.

'That's where he turns it off,' Billy said. 'We never hear who she spoke to, but we know who has Ladies of Avalon.'

Declan leaned back, considering this. 'When Lucy did this to me, the response was the same. And I used it on Yossi to stop him firing his gun.'

'But Lucy definitely hypnotised you,' Anjli replied. Declan nodded at this.

'What if Julie-Anna was the one who taught her?' he asked, thinking back to the accident, and the last words Simon Tolley had spoken to him.

'*Camera... Wanstead... Driver...*'

He looked back at the image. 'We assumed that the driver of the blue Mondeo was Yossi, because he was bald. But I think Anjli's right. It was Julie-Anna, probably making sure he was removed, maybe as a loose end, or maybe because she too believed Lilith had told him to go to Greenwich on Friday.'

Monroe tapped Declan on the shoulder.

'Do you have the sheets we found in Rupert's room?' he asked. Declan walked to his desk, picking up A4 scans of the pages.

'What do you need?' he asked.

'The map with Chislehurst Caves on,' Monroe replied as Declan picked out one page and passed it over. It was the same page that Monroe had seen in the apartment the first time they had arrived, a map of Greenwich with the Dee Line on it. But along the side were hand-written notes.

IT'S ON THE CLIFF IT'S ON THE CLIFF IT'S ON THE CLIFF

'Christ, she definitely had Rupert Wilson then,' Anjli muttered. 'From the damn start, she's played everyone.'

'But when did she get him?' Declan looked at a smiling Billy. 'What did I miss?'

Billy opened up the Atlantis video again, scrolling through the footage until he nodded and paused the image. It was of a lady talking to the camera, but that wasn't what Billy had seen. In the background, they could see Rupert staring blankly ahead while Julie-Anna whispered into his ear.

'I think she's been controlling him even before Miriam died.'

'But you can only make someone do something that they would naturally feel comfortable doing,' Declan said. 'Are you saying that Rupert Wilson wanted to become a new Great Beast?'

'We need to find Julie-Anna Watson immediately,' Monroe rubbed at his chin.

Anjli's phone beeped. Reading the message, she smiled.

'That might be easier than we thought, Guv,' she said.

———

26

MISSING PERSONS

'I WASN'T LOOKING FOR ANYONE,' LILITH SIPPED AT HER GREEN tea. 'But he just appeared, you know?'

'Your postman.'

Lilith smiled, the first genuine one since they'd sat down. 'I know. Such a cliche.'

Another sip.

'We've dated for about six months. Nothing serious, as I had other things I was supposed to be doing—'

'Avenging your brother?' De'Geer nodded. 'We know he was caught in a collapsed tunnel after Rupert sent him there to find treasure.'

'Rupert sent him there to die,' Lilith snapped. De'Geer sipped at his own coffee, giving her a moment.

'Tell me what happened,' he replied. 'Help us understand the truth.'

'There was no truth,' Lilith laughed. 'The whole damn thing was a lie. All the way from the very beginning. Lucy told me a few months back, explained that her mum, after years of being a grade A bitch had suddenly had her *come to Jesus* moment and confessed everything.'

De'Geer didn't pressure, he simply stayed silent, giving Lilith the time to talk.

'She was in love with Rupert at the start,' Lilith explained. 'No, more of a *hero worship* thing. Her job was so boring, and there was a man who talked about mythical heroes. And when he turned up with some note he'd found, written by Hawksmoor, showing that the entrance to the library was under the college, it was like the Gods had spoken.'

'Why?'

'Because it was where the JASON reactor was,' Lilith replied. 'And only Miriam could get into it. She was finally needed.'

'And she found it?' De'Geer was confused, but Lilith laughed.

'She found bugger all,' she chuckled darkly. 'There was no library, no door. They had rebuilt the basement area again and again over decades. And even if it was there, they'd poured so much concrete around the bloody thing she'd need the drill they built the channel tunnel with to get through.'

'But she had items,' De'Geer watched Lilith intently. 'One for each of them.'

'Her family had rooms of the bloody things,' Lilith shook her head. 'Probably stole them from daddy's cabinet. She told them she had help in finding it, a fifth member named Marcus, but he didn't exist because she never found the library. But when they did the press conference about the renovation protest, she realised she couldn't keep the lie up, so 'killed' Marcus in a freak accident and claimed it was the curse.'

'That's why Rupert had the wardings?'

Lilith shook her head. 'They did some kind of blood pact first. Julie-Anna, Miriam, Rupert, they all had scars on the palms of their hands. Probably John Gale too. They did a blood ritual, a nasty one too. The plan was to swear to never attempt to gain the treasures, or else terrible things would happen to all involved and their families.'

'A powerful, dark spell to counter a lesser, and actually imaginary curse,' De'Geer understood. 'The wardings were to hide the wearer from the pact, not the curse.'

Lilith nodded. 'Miriam did it first, because she knew that as the curse was bollocks, by doing the pact she'd aimed some real nasty stuff to herself, especially as she still had to keep going down there for work. Rupert realised what she'd done and followed her.'

'How did he find out?'

'He recognised the item she gave him,' Lilith explained. 'It was a sword, an old one which could have been in the library, but they had used it in a PR shot of Crowley.'

Lilith smiled faintly.

'Miriam inherited it after her grandfather was given it and forgot how big a fan Rupert was. And in doing so, she showed him that the treasure hadn't truly been found.'

'So why go on with the lie?'

'Because he was gaining something better. Notoriety.'

De'Geer nodded at this. 'So how did your brother get involved?'

Lilith's face fell. 'They met, I don't know where. By then Rupert and Miriam were already breaking up, probably because she realised he knew, and that was why he'd also tattooed himself. Alés and Miriam were great together; I was only a kid then, but I remember them being very happy. And then baby Lucy came along. They were talking about leaving the country altogether.'

'But then Rupert stepped in?'

Lilith shook her head. 'Julie-Anna,' she replied. 'The two of them were like sisters, and Jules was going through her own issues with John by then. I don't know the full story, I was only a kid, but there was a screwed up three-way that happened, with Jules, Alés and Miriam, and it split them apart. Then Rupert told Alés that if he could get the library out, he could gain Miriam back. Gave him a map something he'd found in a book somewhere, showing an entrance that led into an unstable cavern with nothing inside.'

'Rupert deliberately killed Alés?' De'Geer was shocked. Lilith nodded.

'Miriam told Lucy that Rupert had examined all the known caverns and knew which ones were safe and which weren't. There was no way that he didn't know,' she said. 'It's why we destroyed his reputation, by creating the video, ensuring he'd never be given tenure again.'

'So where did Julie-Anna fit into this?' De'Geer was watching the door to the cafe now. Lilith, not noticing this, shrugged.

'She was different, more passionate about the curse,' she explained. 'Miriam had never told her the whole thing wasn't real, as at the time she'd have told John and he was known to be terrible at secrets. And then, years later she'd had her brush with death and had learned that Rupert had been black marketing archaeological finds.'

Lilith looked at the floor.

'She was talking to Lucy at this point, and I tried to keep my distance. But then she saw me at a paranormal lockdown that Simon was doing. It was around then that Lucy started talking to the *Consortium*.'

'I don't think Lucy started that,' Declan said, sitting down beside them, having entered through the door behind Lilith.

Who stiffened, glaring at De'Geer.

'You lied to me!' She pointed a finger at him. 'You said you weren't taking me in!'

'And we're not,' Declan replied calmly. 'We're just talking. I think we have a common enemy.'

He looked around the cafe, as if searching for how to explain.

'Lucy hypnotised me,' he started. 'It was the same style of hypnosis that had been worked on Yossi Shavit, better known as the *Consortium*, and the man who freed you today.'

Lilith nodded. 'I recognised him.'

'We also believe Julie-Anna had hypnotised Rupert Wilson before Miriam died, getting him to want to destroy the library somehow, rather than find it,' Declan continued. 'We have proof that Rupert was at least some way controlled.'

Lilith was about to take a mouthful of tea but the cup just hung in the air in front of her mouth, her hands locked in position.

'So what, all this time we were ruining him, Julie-Anna was playing her own game? I'm going to kill that bitch,' Lilith muttered before remembering that she was sitting in front of two police officers. 'Is what I'd say if I was *really* vicious. Instead, I'll ask how I can screw her over? Did she kill Lucy?'

'No, we think John Gale did that,' Declan said.

'He must have thought that Lucy sent his wife the video,' Lilith shook her head. 'She didn't.'

'Unfortunately, with Lucy, Rupert and Miriam now dead, a lot of our evidence is circumstantial. But we have a plan, and with your help, both with filling in some holes and making a couple of calls, I think we can end this tonight.'

Lilith looked at the door to the cafe, as if staring through the corridors at Simon Tolley.

'And us?' she half-whispered.

Declan smiled.

'Well, considering we have bigger people to aim at, you might just slip out of the net if you help us. So how about we fix some wrongs and create a curse of our own?'

LILITH HAD AGREED, AND HAD RETURNED TO TEMPLE INN WITH Declan and De'Geer, the latter grateful for the lift back. It was almost midnight by now but the Unit was almost full strength, with Billy searching through Yossi Shavit's phone, which Declan had 'forgotten' to pass to the black-suited men while the others sat in the briefing room.

'The problem is, none of this is admissible in court,' Monroe stood in front of the plasma screen now, obviously tired but fighting it with solid Scottish stubbornness.

'But we have a timeline,' Billy replied, pointing at the screen. On it was a screenshot of some text messages, sent on Friday morning, from John to Yossi:

Package destroyed everything

Ignore. Gain destination.

Won't corporate. Lied to me.

Try harder

'Won't corporate?' Anjli asked. 'Does he mean the package isn't from a corporate company? What even is the package?'

'I think he's saying that the package won't *cooperate*,' Declan replied. 'Autocorrect is your friend and all that. And I think the package is Rupert.'

God help me

The package is broken

How

Dead he's ducking dead

'I see autocorrect's working overtime here,' muttered Monroe. 'And the rest, laddie.'

Billy continued to move through the screenshots.

I want the hand

I need the money I need to run lost everything

The money was for library

'I think we can agree here that John Gale was trying to gain some money from the *Consortium* before his wife divorced him,' Anjli said.

Wait C has idea says package had deal to be left in Greenwich park will do it tonight

Hand?

Do your own ducking hand you promised me money

You promised me library.

Hand will be there all night get it yourself

'Did they text anything else?' Declan asked.

Billy tapped on his laptop.

'Not until you replied with one word,' he said.

'So John kills Rupert, arranges to get the body home—Cindy takes it back to the apartment—and then fakes the *WhatsApp* from his phone,' Monroe leaned against the wall.

'Explains why we never found it,' Declan agreed. 'John probably wrote the message while on a walk and then tossed the phone.'

'Then the Ladies of Avalon pick Rupert up, and Shavit intercepts?' Monroe shook his head. 'So why were *Ghost Bros* there?'

'That's my fault,' Lilith admitted. 'I was supposed to go to Pluckton with Simon, but then I got the call. I said I couldn't go, that I was going to Greenwich Park instead. I didn't expect him to cancel and follow.'

'He didn't,' Anjli replied. 'I checked, the place they were visiting did get a better offer and cancel. And your mention of Greenwich probably reminded them of this as a backup. It was literally a coincidence.'

'Yossi follows Lilith and Cindy into the park and waits until dark to cut the hand off,' De'Geer suggested, reddening when everyone looked at him. 'Maybe.'

'Still, none of this is evidence!' Monroe moaned. 'We have

no confessions we can use, apart from Miss Babylon here, and a back-from-the-dead Mossad agent who's already been taken by our government—'

'I've got an idea,' Declan raised a hand.

'You shouldn't even be here!' Monroe snapped, sighing. 'Go on then, tell us your bloody awesome idea.'

'Nobody knows that Yossi Shavit was arrested,' Declan said, rising from his chair and walking to the front of the room, facing the Unit. 'John's with Cindy and is looking for an exit strategy, Lucy is dead and Julie-Anna is in the wind. John needs money. He fought with Rupert, probably believing that he knew some entrance to the library. He's been trying to sell the location to the *Consortium*, and probably tried to force it out of Lucy in St Anne's Church, who he also believed had personally destroyed his life by sending the video. Meanwhile, Julie-Anna believes she's the curse made flesh, that John Gale is the last surviving *Musketeer* and will do anything to stop him getting the treasures.'

'So how does this give us evidence?'

'Stick them all in the same room and let them turn on each other,' Declan was rummaging once more through pages on his desk, the same scans of the pages he'd passed to Monroe earlier. He pulled out two pages; the first was the google map printout of the Dee Line, running through Greenwich Park, and the other was a map of underground caverns. He held them up together to the light, examining them with a smile.

'Or, rather, we have them do this in a cavern, tonight, before they learn the *Consortium* is gone,' he said, showing that the map and cave map almost lined up, showing several unopened areas under Greenwich.

'So what do you need us to do?' Anjli smiled. Declan

looked up at the texts on the plasma screen before grinning at Billy.

'Tell me about your squash matches,' he said.

'I DON'T GET WHY WE'RE HERE,' CINDY COMPLAINED. 'WE should be hiding.'

'He told us to meet him here,' John said, looking around the street nervously. They stood in a small alcove beside the *Plume of Feathers* pub, looking westwards towards the junction of Park Vista and Feather's Place, around a hundred yards from the National Maritime Museum, once part of the *Palace of Placentia* after it was built over *Bella Court*. On the wall opposite them was a small plaque, and some cobbled brickwork leaving the wall at an angle on the pavement; this was the *Prime Meridian Line*, heading north. Behind the buildings, older than the others around it, was the park, the Meridian sun dial, and the boating lake.

John looked back down at his phone; the message from Yossi had been simple and exciting.

Found library. Park Vista opposite Four Feathers. Come now. We share then part.

'Even with half of it, we can live like royalty forever,' he said.

Cindy read the text.

'Sure we can,' she smiled.

ACROSS THE STREET AND UNSEEN AT THIS POINT WAS JULIE-Anna Watson, Lilith Babylon beside her. Julie-Anna wasn't sure about this, but Lilith had contacted her with news of a meeting when at the hospital with a mysterious bald man who claimed to be the *Consortium*, who was checking on Simon's health and who knew where the library was but who wanted Lucy to have it. On hearing this, Julie-Anna had phoned Yossi Shavit and although the signal was terrible, most likely because he was underground, she could still speak to him, asking where the watchtower was, and receiving confirmation that it was still on the cliff. This done, she'd agreed to attend, purely to have her moment with John Gale, curbing his enthusiasm for the treasure with a knife in the throat, moments before he touched it.

Standing at the T-junction, listening to the night and feeling incredibly exposed, she hadn't seen John and Cindy outside the pub. What Julie-Anna saw however was a man, clean shaven and overweight, a hat hiding his bald head emerge from a driveway to the left, almost opposite the pub, look around in the dark and then drop a glow stick, snapped and glowing onto the floor before leaving, returning into the driveway. Julie-Anna was about to move when Lilith pulled at her hand.

'Wait,' she said, pointing at the pub where, having also seen this, John and Cindy had now emerged, crossing the road and entering the driveway.

'No,' Julie-Anna stated, and it was the tone of a woman who'd had enough and was looking to finish something. Determinedly, she followed suit, crossing the road and entering the driveway.

Quietly and with a little nervousness, John and Cindy made their way across the drive beside the building, past what looked like construction equipment, including a couple of wheelbarrows filled with bricks and stones, and into the garage.

At the back, half-lit by the glow stick, was a hole in the wall, roughly hewn out of the brickwork. Looking through it, John saw a narrow stone staircase that led downwards towards the west.

'Bloody hell, he found it,' John marvelled. 'This is heading straight to the library.'

His fears now abated, he led Cindy down the steps, finding himself in an underground chamber twenty feet by ten, with a vaulted roof above them and a series of arched recesses on either side. John scrabbled for his phone, intending to use the flashlight as a torch, but the snapping of more glow sticks suddenly revealed at the end of the chamber a doorway to another, larger one.

'Come on,' he said, pulling the still reluctant Cindy with him, not hearing the steps echoing down from behind as Julie-Anna, Lilith close behind her and a borrowed shovel in her hand as a weapon followed them through the chamber into the second, deeper one.

John, meanwhile, had moved into the larger chamber to see Yossi Shavit, aka the *Consortium,* silhouetted by the glow sticks at the end.

'I can't believe you came through!' John laughed. 'Is it a tunnel? I'm guessing this was some kind of emergency exit back in the—'

He stopped as Julie-Anna entered the chamber.

'What the hell are *you* doing here?' he asked, looking back. 'What the hell is *she* doing here?'

'He invited me!' Julie-Anna snapped, brandishing the shovel like a spear. 'I told you what would happen if you went against the curse!'

'There is no curse!' John angrily shouted back, turning to confront her. 'Only the one in your head, you deranged witch!'

The sound of a shovel hitting the wall of the chamber echoed around the room as Julie-Anna swung at John, and the shadowed figure stepped into the light of the glow sticks, pulling off the hat to reveal Declan Walsh.

'I really wish you hadn't done that,' he said, removing the extra padding around his waist as, at the back of the chamber, they could hear a rumbling. 'This wasn't the sturdiest of rooms.'

As John and Julie-Anna stared at him in shock, there was a louder rumble as behind them the entry into the chambers was suddenly filled with falling brickwork and rubble.

As the smoke from the fallout cleared, Declan leaned against the wall.

'Well, that didn't go as planned, but don't worry,' he smiled. 'You're still all under arrest.'

'We're trapped,' Cindy whispered. 'There's no way to get out.'

In the light of the glow sticks, John pulled out his phone, holding it up.

'No signal,' he muttered, looking at Declan. 'Did you tell anyone you were here?'

Lilith shuddered. 'This is exactly how Alés died. How Rupert killed him.'

Declan raised a hand.

'Before we all turn on each other, I have a little confession to make,' he said. 'There's no treasure here. It was all a lie.'

'What do you mean, it was all a lie?' John Gale exploded. 'You don't think we'd know if it was fake?'

'No, I don't,' Declan waved around. 'This is just a monastery crypt. No secret route to treasure.'

'I didn't come here to find treasure,' Julie-Anna snapped.

'No,' Declan replied, letting his extendable baton slide into his right hand. 'You came to kill John before he broke your blood pact.'

As John went to question Declan's statement Julie-Anna raised the shovel, and with a scream of rage ran at him—only to be struck across the temple by Declan's baton, sending her sprawling to the chamber floor as he kicked the shovel across the ground.

'You brought us here under false pretences,' Cindy realised. 'I'm guessing you had a reason, before your plan went to shit?'

'I wanted to see who'd turn up,' Declan replied honestly. 'And, really, I didn't have it all worked out in my head until now. So, let me tell you a story. It's not like we're going anywhere.'

27

THE WITCHING HOUR

'WE START THE STORY BACK IN THE NINETIES,' DECLAN started. 'When John, Julie-Anna and Miriam are playing detectorists.'

Julie-Anna leaned up on her elbows, furious.

'We never *played* at anything,' she snarled.

'No, but you didn't find anything either,' Declan retorted. 'The three of you were forming quite a bond. And then Rupert turns up.'

John nodded. 'At a London moot,' he replied. 'Claimed he had something that could help us, a note from Nicholas Hawksmoor showing a secret passage, created when building Greenwich Hospital, when he split the building to allow an unobstructed view of the Thames.'

'The Wisdom of Solomon,' Julie-Anna muttered. 'Splitting in two.'

'Exactly,' Declan nodded, looking around the group. 'It looked like Duke Humphrey's Library was under the hospital, which was now a Ministry of Defence Naval College and barred to civilians. But you weren't *all* civilians, were you?'

'No,' Julie-Anna replied. 'Miriam was an analyst at the JASON nuclear reactor. That was deep underground, but still using the old building. We thought if she could get access, she could find an entrance to the library.'

'And she agreed to do this for you?' Declan asked.

'She agreed to do it for Rupert,' Julie-Anna muttered. 'Anyway, she got in, gained access to the room thanks to a co-worker named Marcus and found the secret door.'

'But you couldn't go with her,' Declan looked at John.

'We didn't really have a choice there.'

Declan smiled. 'And you all met Marcus, right?'

There was a silence in the chamber as both John and Julie-Anna stared at each other.

'I thought you did,' John muttered, as Julie-Anna shook her head.

'Either way, the two of them manage it, and she even brings some items back out,' Declan pulled out another glow stick, shaking it alight and tossing it onto the floor, brightening the room again. 'Four old, never seen before items. And you reveal them at a press conference.'

'That's right.'

'But you also agreed to leave the library in peace.'

'Yes.'

'It wasn't because you couldn't get down there without government clearance?'

Again, silence.

'Or was it because Marcus died en route to the press conference, hit by a bus in a freak accident? That's pretty much when the world falls down,' Declan smiled. 'You're talking book deals, lectures, fame and notoriety amongst your peers, then Greenwich Park throws a curveball, claiming that it's their property. To stop yourselves being sued, Miriam being arrested for treason and the library being taken by the wrong people, you state publicly that there wasn't a library, that it was all lies.'

'Miriam stated it,' Julie-Anna was rising to her feet now. 'And once she said it, we had to comply or be seen as speaking against her.'

'Marcus dying started the chain of bad luck,' John added. 'We knew we had a curse on us, like Lord Carnarvon. But we'd only stolen a couple of items, and the curse wasn't that big.'

'So you counteracted it,' Declan nodded. 'I'm guessing this was Miriam again?'

Without confirming or denying this, John looked at the palm of his hand, where a faint scar was still visible.

'We did a blood ritual. A binding one, ensuring it entwined our fates. Miriam had a grimoire, once owned by Crowley.'

'In layperson's terms, you bound yourselves together, right?' Declan asked carefully, trying not to sound skeptical at this. 'If one of you broke the pact, then you'd all suffer?'

'Pretty much,' Julie-Anna nodded. 'Very *one for all and all for one.*'

'So, you hope that this bigger, worse magic will counter the curse,' Declan nodded at Julie-Anna and John. 'Probably didn't help that you two are sleeping with each other, while Miriam's tattooing wardings on her hand and seeing Alés Capioca, a student of Rupert, who fathers a child with her. *Lucy.*'

'Alés wasn't part of this,' Lilith stated. 'Miriam dumped him after Julie-Anna had a threesome with them.'

'Rupert asked me to do it,' Julie-Anna replied, ignoring

John's angry expression at this revelation. 'And I was happy to get rid of him. Miriam barely spoke to me anymore.'

'After Alés and Miriam split, Rupert befriends Alés, and tells him his deepest secret; the location of the library,' Declan continued. 'Rupert explains he can't remove the treasures for himself because of the pact, but Alés could bring them out and win Miriam back. Alés follows the directions to a cavern passage near Maiden Hill.'

'There was no treasure,' Lilith hissed. 'Just a dangerous hole in the ground, and when my brother went in there, it collapsed and killed him. Rupert wanted Alés out of the way, so Miriam couldn't go back to him.'

'But it didn't work the way it was supposed to, did it?'

'No. Miriam took a job with GCHQ in Cheltenham, dropping completely out of the scene.'

Declan thought about this for a moment. 'Well, until about a year ago.'

There was a rumble from above, and he straightened.

'Sounds like the roof's about to cave-in, killing us all,' he said calmly. 'I'd better talk faster. We're getting to the good bit now.'

Declan started pacing around the chamber.

'Air's feeling a little thinner,' he muttered. 'Can you feel it?'

As the others grabbed at their throats in fear, Declan looked at Julie-Anna. 'Want to continue the story?'

'You have nothing,' she spat.

'I have a video that shows Miriam arguing with you a week before her death, at a talk by Rupert in London. Interesting that she turned up, considering she'd been out for twenty years.'

'She was dying. She wanted to make amends. You have nothing.'

'It's the same video in which we see you hypnotising Rupert,' Declan continued. 'Checking where the watchtower was, like you did when you thought I was Yossi on the phone.'

He smiled at Julie-Anna's shocked expression.

'Lucy spent her teens believing Rupert was her father, until Miriam gave a deathbed confession, making amends.'

'She was a bloody drunk,' Julie-Anna snapped back. 'Quick to anger and give a slap after she moved away. Blamed Lucy for destroying her life. Poor little cow was three when they moved. Lucy had no clue what was going on, and for the rest of her life had scattered memories of the time. Of *me*.'

She shifted her position, kicking a fading glow stick across the cavern floor.

'I was always around back then,' she said. 'And then she got that stupid tattoo, and Rupert followed suit and blamed me for sleeping with her. Like he hadn't begged me to! She was trying to break the curse she created, just to go steal more.'

'No, she wasn't,' Declan replied sadly. 'If you'd read it correctly, you'd see it wasn't the same as Rupert's. She had one extra word on hers. *Affa*. It means—'

'*Nothing*,' Julie-Anna chuckled. 'Oh, you silly cow. You should have told me.'

'But she didn't,' Declan continued. 'And so, after this confrontation you visited her at a pagan camp where, in the middle of a storm you took the fight outside and the two of you were struck by the same lightning bolt, one that almost killed you but finished her because of her terminal cancer.'

'It was an accident,' Julie-Anna muttered. 'She'd found out that I was tutoring Lucy in witchcraft and hypnotism at her university. The fight started at the London talk, and then she followed me to the camp. We struggled. And then the lightning hit me, going through us both.'

'Killing Miriam, and freeing Lucy from her drunken mother's clutches,' Declan replied. 'Who now knew the treasure was fake.'

'And how do you know that?' John asked.

'Because she told me, the night she died,' Declan looked at Julie-Anna, now visibly paling in the green glow of the sticks.

'Miriam told Lucy everything,' he explained. 'That the treasure wasn't real, that Marcus wasn't real, even the curse wasn't real.'

'But the blood pact—' John started.

'She needed something strong to bind you, to stop you searching,' Declan replied. 'She created the curse, so she created the cure, remember?' he looked back at Julie-Anna.

'But she never broke the pact.'

Julie-Anna began to cry as John turned to face her.

'You bitch!' he growled. 'I ought to—'

'Shut up,' Declan's tone was commanding. 'You don't get to take the high road here. We haven't gotten to you yet.'

He looked back at Lilith.

'By this point, Lucy searches *Alexandra Capioca* out, finally able to reveal herself as her niece,' he said. 'She explains how Rupert killed Alés, her father, and how Miriam did nothing. You show her how to make a hand of glory from Miriam's severed hand—'

'I never needed to show her anything,' Lilith interrupted, almost proud of this. 'Miriam still had a few of the old family books around. She'd already done it, taking it off right before the funeral. She knew the library was bollocks, but she still had fears about the pact hitting her.'

Declan nodded, looking at the others. 'They both then decide to avenge Alés. Alexandra changes her name to Lilith, and infiltrates Rupert's growing harem of loyal, female acolytes, the Ladies of Avalon. Lucy, meanwhile, meets Rupert at a *Treadwells* event, who takes the poor orphan, and possible daughter, in as his assistant.'

'Miriam can't have lied!' John, almost pleading, now looked around. 'She found items! She brought them out!'

'Yes,' Declan nodded. 'Items that she brought from her family's old collection. We've got photos that show Crowley using the Templar sword she gave Rupert, and the obsidian knife she gave you. The knife you showed Yossi Shavit to prove the existence of the treasure. The knife you slit Lucy's throat with.'

John stared silently, shocked at the statement. Declan carried on.

'As I was saying, Lucy wasn't just told about the treasure, she was told about the nuclear reactor and about the RFID chip Miriam had in her hand that was used to pass through security. Problem was, that by the time she found out, Lucy had taken that hand and turned it into a *hand of glory*, killing it.'

'So that's what the ritual was for?' Cindy asked. 'To power up a bloody chip?'

'In a way,' Declan smiled. 'First, Rupert took a position at Queen Mary University, asking for a particular room. He knew about this thanks to Lucy, who thought she was guiding him towards breaking about a dozen University guidelines and destroying his reputation, not realising someone else already controlled him.'

He looked at John.

'This is where you come in, right?' he asked.

John remained silent as Declan continued.

'This was the point when John here starts a rather brutal and messy divorce, when he was caught shagging, well, Cindy there. John needed money, and so contacted the *Consortium* about finding the library again, using the item Miriam gave him in the nineties as proof. What John didn't know is that Yossi Shavit, the head of the *Consortium,* was actually an ex-Mossad agent who'd faked his death years earlier after being caught selling Israeli artifacts provided by Rupert Wilson, and was looking for a way back into the service. A way that presented itself when John told him that the treasure was behind a secret nuclear reactor that only Lucy's mum, and now likely Lucy herself, could get to.'

'Christ preserve us,' Julie-Anna whispered, apparently giving up on all of her pagan deities. 'You dealt with terrorists?'

'No, he dealt with the man *who dealt* with them,' Declan corrected. 'In fact, you both did. Yossi knew how to build assets from his time in Mossad, and so contacted his old friend Rupert, offering to help him get a working version of the chip Lucy's mother had, military grade RFID chips that Yossi had access to. His plan was to gain access to the reactor while leaving Rupert with the blame.

'And how did he do this?' John snapped. Declan pointed at the now paling Cindy.

'Ask her,' he replied. 'She's been working with Yossi since Rupert sold him items from the En Esur digs in the 2010s. We found her name in the lists of archaeologists.'

John, betrayed, stared at Cindy as she shrugged.

'If it makes you feel better, the sex was okay,' she said, already taking a step away.

'So now Rupert does naked rituals on the Dee Line with his students to power the chip to open the door to it, but he can't work out the wording. Julie-Anna is roped in to help John with the translation, working out later what was really going on. And to ensure it's done correctly, John joins Rupert in the ritual, hoping to find the actual location during it and unaware that it's being recorded by Lilith, using equipment passed to her by her boyfriend, Simon.'

Declan cracked another glow stick.

'Anyway, whatever he planned never happened, because the Friday before Beltaine, the University suspended Rupert because the video of him appeared. John, meanwhile, sees his life turn to shit when both his wife and his employer, *The Mail on Sunday* receive the video too, and he's fired and loses any case for an amicable divorce in the same moment. By now, we're around ten am on the day he died.'

'I thought he'd done it deliberately,' John muttered. 'I needed money, was furious—I didn't know yet that he'd been suspended too. We fought...'

'I grabbed a tow rope from John's garage,' Cindy continued. 'It was the first thing I had to hand. I looped it around his throat, trying to pull him off John. It was self defence.'

'Whatever it was, now you have a dead body,' Declan turned to Cindy. 'You go grab John's mother's Rover and drive back. You put the body in a wheelchair, drive to Chancery Lane and set up the suicide, hanging him with another rope, one he used on his bonding bar.'

'You're fishing,' Cindy snapped back.

'We have your phone pinging a City of London tower,' Declan replied. 'We have you paying the congestion charge six hours before you 'heard' from Rupert. And we have the car captured on a traffic cam, driven by you in London.'

Cindy was silent at this as Declan continued.

'You set up the body, left, and then John used Rupert's phone to send a message hours later, a call you and Lilith then attend. You bundle the body into the car, drive to the park, and fulfil Rupert's last request. But what you don't realise is that John also contacted Yossi during this time, asking for help in covering up the murder. Yossi, who knows Rupert has a stolen, military grade RFID chip in his hand that could, if found, come back to him.'

'He cut the hand off?' Cindy was surprised at this.

'So now it's Saturday and Rupert's found,' Declan continued, watching John as he spoke. 'We take the case on Monday and Lucy tries to find out what we know, thinking that her actions caused his suicide, but in the process leading us right back to her. She escapes from us when we come for her, for some reason goes to St Anne's Church. Finishing a Ripper walk nearby, John heads there and slashes Lucy's throat after a brief confrontation, with the same obsidian knife he gained from her mother.'

'Lies,' John was resolute.

Declan shook his head. 'You believed that she sent the video to your wife, and to your newspaper,' he replied. 'You thought she'd done terrible things to you, and you struck out. What you hadn't realised was the video had only gone to the University Governors—but one of them was your wife, Susan. Who recognised you and, as part of her own lashing out, sent the video to your editor. Neither of which had been deliberately set up by Lucy.'

John stared quietly at Declan as he realised the implications of his actions.

'Lucy scratches your face though, so you cut off the hand to ensure no DNA is found and, finding Miriam's desiccated severed hand in Lucy's bag, uses it to write a message on the Pyramid as a warning, threatening Julie-Anna.'

'And why would I do that?'

'Because you assumed that thanks to her help in translating Rupert's ritual, she was the one who'd told Lucy to do this, perhaps? The murder was a statement, an *I know you did this and you're next* message.'

'Bullshit,' John snapped, recovering. 'No witnesses and hearsay.'

'We have a witness,' Declan shook his head. 'We found a homeless man trying to sell Lucy's very specific Brompton bike. He told us everything he saw that night. How he saw someone cry out in pain, call someone else a bitch and raise a knife.'

Declan stepped back a little, giving John space.

'I'm guessing this is when you went to Lucy's house? We found your fingerprints all over her boxes.'

John sighed, as if realising this was all over.

'I took her keys and went to her room, but there were only boxes,' he explained. 'I went to the basement but couldn't find anything that helped with the treasure's location. I left Miriam's hand there because it would get you chasing your tails and give me more time.'

Declan rubbed at his chin as he pondered this. 'I'm guessing you called Yossi at this point?'

John nodded. 'I told him that if he got Cindy out of Bishopsgate and told me where Julie-Anna was, I'd give him the map.'

'When did you first meet him?' Declan asked Julie-Anna.

'He'd sniffed around before Miriam died,' she said.

'Looking for items she might want to sell. I'd primed him, just to keep him in my pocket.'

'You make mind control sound so pedestrian,' Declan replied. Julie-Anna shrugged.

'There was a problem, though,' Declan continued. 'Yossi was Mossad. They were trained to beat psychological manipulation, but he was in a bombing a few years back which gave him serious concussion, affecting it.'

'Hypnotism shouldn't affect anything,' Julie-Anna contested.

'It does if your broken anti-manipulation training is still sparking away,' Declan replied harshly. 'He has seizures every time you ask where's the watchtower.'

Julie-Anna shook her head.

'You can't prove anything,' she said. 'Miriam was hit by lightning. Yossi is a spy and, as you said, a bit broken. Simon was hit by a car—'

'Yes, about that,' Declan smiled. 'We have witnesses who saw you get out when you abandoned it, and Simon himself saw you when you struck him.'

Julie-Anna glared at Lilith. 'You told me he was dead!'

'I lied, you bitch,' Lilith snapped back, turning away.

'John and Cindy kill Rupert, and John kills Lucy and tells Yossi to kill me. Meanwhile, Julie-Anna tries to kill Miriam and Simon,' Declan stated as the glow sticks around him were fading. 'Basically, you're all guilty, in one way or another. The only person without literal blood on her hands is Lilith, and she's the one who had most reason to want revenge.'

There was a long moment of silence.

'Shame you won't be able to tell anyone,' Cindy said, her face smug.

'I don't know why you're so chipper,' Julie-Anna snapped at her. 'He won't tell anyone because we'll all be dead.'

'Yeah, about that,' Declan smiled, raising his voice. '*We're done in here!*'

There was a third rumbling, and as the others in the small cavern looked around in fear, expecting the roof to collapse, the fallen stones and earth that had supposedly blocked their route out seemed to shift, as the collapsed tunnel rubble rolled into the chamber, revealing a variety of high-powered torch beams, all aimed at the people in the cavern.

'You lied to us!' Cindy moaned. Declan shook his head.

'You wanted a place that didn't exist, a story to believe. I gave you that. I just ensured in advance that the chamber was safe, secure and able to be rigged. You even walked past the wheelbarrows filled with rubble that they upturned down the stairs.'

'Balls to this,' John pulled out the obsidian blade from his jacket pocket. 'I'm not going to prison—'

He hadn't expected the solid right-hander that Lilith Babylon now threw, a vicious haymaker punch that snapped his jaw backwards and sent him stumbling to the floor, the knife falling from his hand.

'That was for my niece, you *wanker*,' Lilith snapped as, amid the torchlights, Anjli and De'Geer moved in, pulling hands behind backs as they cuffed the suspects.

'You alright?' Anjli asked. Declan nodded.

'Nothing can be used as evidence here!' Julie-Anna was claiming now. 'We were confused, convinced we were going to die. It's dark, you couldn't see our faces.'

'About that,' Declan grabbed a torch from Anjli, shining it

into the corners of the cavern. There were a variety of different cameras placed along the walls.

'Thermal cameras, night vision cameras, the lot,' he said as he passed the torch back. 'Alfie Wasley at *Ghost Bros* was thrilled to help us get revenge for his best mate's broken limbs, so lent us loads of cool toys. That camera there? It picks up temperature in a room, and it's so sensitive, it'll even show your face change colour when it's affected by minor temperature changes.'

He grinned.

'Did you know that when we lie, the temperature of the tip of our nose drops up to two degrees Fahrenheit, while the forehead heats up? I'd love to see what yours does.'

EPILOGUE

It was three days later when Simon Tolley woke up out of his coma to find Lilith Babylon, now returned to Alexandra Capioca watching over him. Because they'd both helped with the case, Bullman had promised they would show both leniency when the court case came around; Alexandra, or rather Lilith, had only really pushed for Rupert's true self to be revealed, and Simon hadn't really been involved, apart from minor trespass, and lending a camera to his girlfriend.

Julie-Anna Watson had immediately started claiming that the lightning bolt had affected her mental cognitive functions, looking to get away with the things that she had done with a plea of diminished responsibility. However, the recordings Declan had through the various cameras didn't show Julie-Anna to be diminished in any way, and so her legal team had been politely refused the opportunity to attempt this until a separate team of doctors, never to be left alone with her could examine her.

The obsidian blade that John Gale held was confirmed to

be the one that killed Lucy Shrimpton, and John admitted during his interview that he'd followed her from Queen Mary University, using Cindy's phone to text Lucy, aiming her at St Anne's Church in Limehouse, for no reason more than he knew it was Rupert's favourite place. He never realised that this was in any way a clue to the lost treasure, and his blood-stained message was purely for Julie-Anna, convinced that she had been the one that had destroyed his life, not realising that, if it wasn't for a burn mark on his shoulder, none of this would have happened.

As for Cindy, she was charged with John for the murder of Rupert Wilson, and because of her connection with Yossi Shavit, was taken away by some very irritated men in black suits. Rupert's fundamentalist family had pushed for grave robbing and kidnapping to be added as charges on both Cindy and Alexandra but Bullman had met with them, pointing out that you couldn't both kidnap and grave rob something simultaneously, and that weirdly, that they did this actually gave them the case to solve—if he'd been left hanging in his apartment, nobody would ever have known.

They relented.

Chivalry Fitzwarren placed an offer in with the family the same day to buy the Chancery Lane apartment.

Declan hadn't had any more auditory hallucinations since then either, but, he didn't really want to risk anything, so took it easy. He did visit Kendis Taylor's grave though, daring anyone to tell her widowed husband when he did so. Nobody did, but that could have been because of Anjli, standing by the gate to the high street, glaring at anyone who left, warrant card visible in her hand.

Sometimes it was good to have a housemate.

The university sealed back up the hole in Rupert's room,

and some nice, black-suited men, possibly the same ones that had visited Temple Inn had bricked up the other door, stating that it wasn't connected to the other reactor, because there *was* no reactor, and *everyone was confused*. People seemed happy with this explanation, and the university received a hefty donation the same week, which made them even happier.

And they buried Lucy Shrimpton in St Anne's Church graveyard, in a strangely low key and quite Christian burial, attended by Alexandra, Simon, Michael Bao, Declan and De'Geer. Neither of the last two needed to attend, but De'Geer had gone because he was a nice guy and didn't want Lucy to have an empty service, while Declan felt he owed it to the woman he met in a park and at a bar, who seemed conflicted and lost, and never found happiness, no matter what she'd tried to do.

'People find grief in many forms,' a line she'd spoken to him at the bar echoed through his head. Pulling out a hip flask, he raised it above the grave.

'Skol,' he said, taking a draught before passing it to De'Geer. Alexandra, Simon, and Michael had already left, and the two were alone.

'I wish we'd gotten to know her earlier,' De'Geer said softly. 'Maybe we could have helped her.'

He looked at Declan.

'I know it's not my place, Guv but you should consider paying DI Martinez a visit.'

'Intuition?'

'Jess,' De'Geer replied. 'She got hold of my number and keeps texting me. I'd appreciate it if you could find a way to stop her.'

Declan took his hip flask back, smiling as he placed it away.

'I will,' he replied. 'You on your way home?'

'Taking Anjli to a motorcycle shop,' De'Geer smiled. 'She's trying on some leathers.'

The thought of Anjli in leathers made Declan smile. De'Geer noticed this.

'Guv?' he asked. 'Does the thought of Anjli in leathers put you in your happy place?'

'Now you're moving away from your place,' Declan laughed. 'Go on, sort her leathers. And I'll buy you lunch all week if you can convince her to buy something dayglo and hideous.'

As De'Geer left the churchyard, Declan looked up to the sky.

'You can come out now,' he said.

A young woman, in a long black hoodie and a pair of jeans, a baseball cap covering her brunette hair, emerged from the side of the church.

'How did you know I was there?' Trix asked.

Declan shrugged.

'I knew it'd be you or Tom,' he said. 'You can't seem to keep away from me in graveyards.'

Trix stared down at the grave. 'Tom says thanks for the heads up about Shavit,' she said. 'We were able to get into his house at the same time as forensics, take the more sensitive items. We've also helped deprogram him, so he doesn't wince when you talk about watchtowers. This alone has made him a very cooperative witness.'

'I know,' Declan smiled. 'Billy was there and saw Tom. You know, for a supersecret government thing, you guys are rubbish at hiding.'

Trix nodded. 'Well, we are the screw-ups,' she said.

They stood awkwardly for a moment.

'What aren't you telling me?' Declan asked.

'Tom wanted to know if you'd read the USB he gave you.'

'No, he didn't,' Declan replied. 'Tom knows I haven't, so quit with the small talk.'

Trix nodded, but didn't reply.

'Just tell me, Trix,' Declan sighed. 'It has to be the other thing. There's nothing else. What does he want?'

'We had a call from some friends,' Trix eventually spoke. 'Karl Müller, or rather Karl Schnitter has been asking for you.'

Declan felt a sheet of ice slide down his spine.

'He can ask,' he replied. 'He'll never see me again.'

'That's the problem,' Trix sighed. 'He has some information we need, and this is his fee. To have ten minutes with you, one to one.'

Declan looked around. 'How important is the information?' he asked.

'Could save some lives,' Trix admitted.

'Fine,' Declan nodded. 'Give me the place and date and I'll be there.'

'Unarmed.'

'I'm not walking into any room with Karl Schnitter unarmed,' Declan snapped.

'It's more for him than you,' Trix replied quickly. 'In case you retaliate on what he did to Jess.'

Declan pursed his lips together for a long moment.

'Done,' he said. 'Stay safe, Trixibelle.'

And without another word, Declan turned and walked out of the graveyard.

There were too many *ghosts* in there right now for him.

Billy was waiting outside the St Pancras hotel when Chivalry Fitzwarren checked out. He'd spent a lot of money ensuring that the concierge would give him the nod, and it was money well spent. As his great-uncle walked his bags to a waiting car, with two porters carrying what looked like three suitcase's worth of purchases, Chivalry smiled and waved to his great-nephew.

'Seeing me off?' he exclaimed. 'That's a very Fitzwarren thing to do. But usually it's to ensure we're truly gone.'

'Wanted to thank you for the help you gave us,' Billy showed a small box that he held. 'A little gift.'

'But not from the lost library, eh?' Chivalry grinned. 'I suppose that's a legend that'll stay forgotten for a few more decades. Until someone new comes along. Maybe you?'

'We'll see,' Billy passed the box to his great-uncle. 'In the meantime, there are still treasures that can be found.'

Chivalry tore at the box, pulling open the flaps and reaching into the paper that filled the inside and, with a cry of joy, pulled out a small, silver mirror.

'Aleister Crowley's scrying mirror!' he exclaimed. 'How did you get it?'

'The *Consortium*, or rather the man behind it, is gone,' Billy replied. 'I was there when they went through his house to check for anything connected to our case. I found this and remembered you saying he took it from you.'

Chivalry nodded. 'You're definitely pushing towards a warm welcome back to the family with this,' he smiled. 'A real chip off the Fitzwarren block.'

'No, not yet, but I'm learning,' Billy replied, pulling out a USB stick and tossing it to his great-uncle. 'You see, I didn't go there for that. I went to see what else you'd gotten up to.'

He indicated the drive.

'Seems you were a bit of a rival to the *Consortium*,' he continued. 'No wonder you wanted to see him suffer. Your name—your *true* name is everywhere, constantly arms deep in something dodgy, usually stolen archaeological finds and suchlike.'

'I see,' Chivalry stopped smiling. 'This is where I join my son in Her Majesty's finest?'

Billy shook his head.

'Seems there was some kind of issue on the server, and it was all corrupted,' he said. 'That there? That's everything involving you. Keep it, I have a copy.'

'Which you'll use to your advantage if I don't support you,' Chivalry actually laughed at this. 'Maybe the police haven't been bad for you after all. Seems to me it's given you teeth.'

'It was good seeing you again, great-uncle,' Billy held out a hand to be shaken. 'Enjoy the gift, and thanks for your help. I hope I see you again.'

'Oh, I can be sure of that,' Chivalry took the offered handshake. 'After all, Christmas is never fun without some family drama.'

DECLAN HAD BEEN TO PRISON BEFORE, BUT THERE WAS something about this one that really felt imposing. *HMP Send*, near Woking in Surrey, was a closed women's prison, in a building that had once been a smallpox isolation hospital.

Maybe the ghosts of the smallpox victims are still here, Declan thought to himself as they led him through one cordoned off area into another. *Maybe Ghost Bros could do a stay-over one night.*

After two more full-body pat downs and allowing a hand-held metal detector or two to run over his body, Declan was brought into a small, empty room with two chairs placed in the middle.

'This doesn't look like the visiting room,' he replied. 'There's a damn sight more tables and chairs there.'

'That must be why you're a detective,' one of the female guards mocked as she left the room. The other, an older woman in her fifties, nodded at the other door, on the other side of the room.

'That leads to solitary,' she said, as if this made everything clear.

'Why is she in solitary?'

'Because she was a bent copper,' the guard sniffed. 'Didn't go down well that she was, well, a *gamekeeper turned poacher,* if you get my drift?'

'She was attacked?' Declan was concerned now. The guard smiled.

'Yeah,' she said.

'You don't need to sound so happy about it,' Declan snapped, but the guard just smiled wider.

'Man, you should have seen it,' she said. 'She kicked the shit out of the bitches. We had to put her in solitary for *their* protection.'

Declan was going to reply to this but the door at the other end opened and a woman, in a grey sweater and jogging bottoms entered, led in by another female guard. She was in her mid-forties and Mediterranean in looks; her bobbed black hair was just as frizzy over the sweater as it had been the last time he'd seen her.

She stopped as she saw Declan, as if surprised to see him.

'Bloody hell,' Tessa Martinez said as she watched Declan carefully. 'Never thought I'd see you again.'

She frowned.

'You look tired.'

'Long week,' Declan smiled in return. 'Hello Tessa, it's good to see you.'

DI Walsh and the team of the *Last Chance Saloon* will return in their next thriller

KILLING THE MUSIC

Order Now at Amazon:

http://mybook.to/killingthemusic

And read on for a sneak preview...

PROLOGUE

FROM THE MOMENT THAT HE ARRIVED AT THE VENUE, DAVE Manford knew that this had been a *terrible* mistake.

The venue itself was fine; *Eastcheap Albums,* a corner bar in the heart of the City of London at the junction of Eastcheap and Lovat Lane was a structure amid a strange mish-mash of Gothic style buildings and steel and chrome monstrosities, where international corporations rubbed shoulders with hipster coffee bars and juice lounges.

Eastcheap Albums was part of a chain of music-themed bars that leaned into the aesthetic, with vinyl albums racked up in shelves behind the ornate, golden-lit bar on the left of the room. Here you could sit in luxurious red velvet high chairs and stare up at Prince, David Bowie, the cast of Grease and Bob Marley among others, all immortalised on album covers with even *more* albums, apparently several thousand in total interspersed among the various tables, chairs and loungers in the venue.

To the right of the bar and against the back wall a small stage had been set, so that customers, dining on what looked to be expensive cocktails and stone-baked pizzas, could be entertained by some of the best upcoming acts in the industry, now rocketing up the ladder of fame.

Or, as Dave mused, staring around the bar, *tumbling haphazardly down it.*

It hadn't been his idea to start his comeback tour here. He'd wanted to start at the *O2 Arena* in Greenwich, or more likely, the *Indigo Lounge* there. He'd seen a few other eighties bands re-invent themselves at the Lounge, and they always said good things about it. And, more importantly, it was on the Jubilee Line, so it was easy to get home from.

Or maybe somewhere like the *100 Club* on Oxford Street would have been good, even an intimate gig at the *Roundhouse* off Primrose Hill but no, Lydia had explained slowly to him that *this was a great place;* not only was it swish and trendy, but they could hire it out completely, so that every person there tonight was hand-invited for the return of *Dave Manford's Alternator.*

Dave originally wanted to call the new group *Alternate Tour*, a play on words of the title of the band that he and his brother had started decades ago; *Alternator*, a five-piece indie rock band that hit the charts and even broke America with their second album, *Secrets and Lies* back in 1987. But, after his brother Nick had disappeared right before Christmas 1998, believed to have committed suicide after finally becoming sick of the fame that his band gave him, Dave found himself ousted by his own band.

Apparently this was because of some contractual morality clause he'd broken, although it was more likely that Benny Simpson was a bitter old queen who should have been fired as manager years earlier, The clause he'd allegedly broken by giving his brother means to defend himself, and the items he also needed to function on a day-to-day basis meant he could no longer be part of *Alternator*, couldn't *call* himself part of *Alternator* or even sing any of the *Alternator* songs, as pretty much all of them had been written by Nick and guitarist Andy Mears, who'd continued writing solo for the band after Nick disappeared.

Well, that was bollocks.

He might not have written them, but he'd certainly contributed to them, especially the ones on *Secrets and Lies*. By then Nick was whacked out on coke and painkillers every night and unable to focus, let alone create on a daily basis, and Dave had been the one to hunt him down, clean him up, give him shiny new pills to bring him back to coherence and drag him to the studio every morning. Sure, Andy had done the heavy lifting, the smug little prick, but it'd been Dave that cared for his brother, that kept him coping, no matter what it took, and what rules he had to break in the process.

That *Hollies'* song *'It ain't heavy, he's my brother'* could literally have been written for him.

And so, just over twenty years ago, Dave Manford had found himself without a band. His band.

And, more importantly, was no longer a shareholder in *Secrets and Lies, n*o longer gaining the yearly royalties, while still silenced by the NDAs he'd signed when agreeing the deal.

But that was fine as he had money, he absolutely detested the bag of dicks he laughingly called his old *bandmates*, and he had plenty to do with nothing *Alternator*-related cluttering up his valuable time. He'd always talked about his planned solo work, especially a musical he wanted to write about *Jack The Ripper,* but over the years he'd failed at both; the solo album, although critically acclaimed by several niche magazines had failed to chart when it came out in 2007, resulting in the label dropping him before he could complete his agreed subsequent two albums, and his *Ripper* musical was considered by everyone to be a clever meta joke because of some throwaway line in a rock parody called *This Is Spinal Tap,* where two band members, seeing their band breaking up, decide to write a *Jack The Ripper* musical.

A sketch that haunted Dave at every meeting he tried to pitch it at.

In the end, Dave had gone into record producing; when the band had been big in the early nineties, and with the album royalties he made from *Secrets and Lies,* he'd bought an old church in Shoreditch and renovated it into a recording studio. The acoustics were great, and he'd built in some sound-proofed booths for when the tracks needed to feel more closed in and personal. He'd also built a state-of-the-art production booth with the control room stolen piecemeal from the Islington *Britannia Row studio* when they moved to Fulham. As such, he had the same equipment that had recorded parts of *Pink Floyd's The Wall,* a far better album than anything that *Alternator* had released for years, and over the last two decades he'd enjoyed a healthy income from that side of the business, producing for a varied collection of artists, many of whom didn't even know who *Alternator* were.

Which always made him warm and cosy inside.

A couple of years ago, though, things moved again. For a start, Marna, the bitch of a wife that married Nick a few years before his disappearance had pushed to have him declared legally dead, most likely to gain whatever was left by him she hadn't already stolen. Then Lydia, probably hearing this through Marna had heard news that *Alternator,* still touring the regional theatre routes with *Greatest Hits* shows were planning on recording a new album, their first studio recording for over a decade and the first with singer Peter Suffolk, who'd joined the band around nine years earlier. Digging deeper, and pushing hard on her family connection, Lydia had heard that *Alternator's* back catalogue was gaining interest with some serious hedge fund investors, especially after *Dog Tired,* the biggest selling single from *Secrets and Lies* had charted again after being used in some Marvel superhero movie. Buying back catalogues had become big money of late; Bob Dylan had sold his to Universal for three hundred million dollars, while the rumour mill claimed Stevie Nicks gained about a hundred million for eighty percent of her *Fleetwood Mac* rights.

Lydia was convinced that despite the fact that they hadn't had a hit in years, with the new fans coming in through streaming platforms due to *Dog Tired* being a bona fide hit again, they could be looking at *eight figures* for the rights to the back catalogue.

Money that *Alternator* would get.

Money that Dave should have a legal right for a percentage, kicked out of the band or not.

Money, more importantly, that couldn't be made until Marna controlled Nick's estate, which explained why she was so desperate to have him classed as *deceased,* after decades sponging off his name.

And if they didn't class Nick as dead, then there'd be some lengthy court battles, because even though Smug Andy co-wrote the songs, he wasn't a founding member of *Alternator*. And couldn't do anything.

But Dave could.

So, with the notoriety gained from *Dog Tired* and *Secrets and Lies,* Dave had put together a comeback tour, half his own solo work and half classic *Alternator* songs that he had a hand in creating. He knew they wouldn't come after him; there was every chance that to get the sale through they'd need him, and as such he was currently untouchable.

Which brought him to *Eastcheap Albums* on a Tuesday night, with a session musician band he'd only played with twice before for an audience of City moneymen, the point being to gain an interest in the songs from people who could truly put together a solid counter-deal. People who'd be interested in backing Dave Manford's right to gain money from the band he'd created with his younger brother when they were teenagers.

It was, however, the first live gig he'd played in almost fifteen years. And the stage fright had hit him the moment he'd stepped onto the tiny wooden dais they laughingly called a stage.

He was sweating; he could smell it. But he was wearing a black shirt, so hopefully it wasn't too noticeable. And the session was only forty minutes, so as long as he stayed hydrated, he'd be fine

His main worry was his heart; he'd had a murmur a couple of years back, not a full-blown cardiac issue, but enough to scare the living hell out of him, and he'd worried about overloading himself tonight. Lydia had given him a ring to wear; it felt uncomfortable on his right hand, the cool-ness of the silver plating mixing with the slickness of his sweat. She'd called it *wearable tech,* explaining that it was some kind of heart rate monitor, body temperature gauge and a dozen other things that told her in real time how he was doing physically, all given to her through bluetooth by three small prongs in the base of the band that touched his skin, but all he cared about was that if his heart rate or temperature spiked, she'd call the event off, which could kill everything here.

So deep breaths then, Davey.

Nodding to the other band members—although to call this rag-tag bundle of musicians a 'band' was frankly insulting, he moved to the microphone as the lights turned on, momentarily blinding him.

'Um, hi, everyone,' he said, unable to see anyone now. The middle area of the bar, usually filled with tall tables and chairs, had been emptied to provide a 'gig experience', and around thirty people were standing there, only slightly lower than Dave because of the stage's lack of height.

Not exactly Glastonbury, he thought to himself. At the back of the small crowd there was a familiar face; his nephew, watching silently, expressionless. A sudden, irrational fear came over Dave, that he might be asked tonight to repay a substantial loan he'd borrowed three years back.

To hell with that, he thought bitterly. *The little shit can afford it. Maybe he's here to buy the whole bloody catalogue? Maybe I should try to be nice to him. Maybe I can get another large loan off the gullible fool.*

The audience was still silent, and Dave realised he'd been drifting. Forcing a smile, he glanced at Lydia to the side, beside the bar, giving a thumbs up signal.

Dave had expected a slow start, but he hadn't expected *apathy.* However, he remembered these weren't *Alternator* fans; these were invited city stooges. Leaning back, he grabbed a bottle of water, taking a large mouthful. He hadn't been the lead singer back in the day. That was Nick.

But whatever Nick could do, Dave could do better.

'Well, that was shit,' he said, tossing the bottle aside. 'I said *hello everyone!'*

This time, spurred on by his own enthusiasm, the crowd reacted with a few half-hearted whoops and cheers.

Good enough, Dave smiled to himself.

'I'm Dave Manford, and with my brother Nick I created the rock band *Alternator,'* he said, warming to the moment, feeling the mic stand in his hand, the coldness of his ring resting against it. 'My brother disappeared over twenty years ago, but I'm still going strong.'

A louder cheer now, and Dave was feeling the audience. He was winning them over and he hadn't even sung a single note. Maybe he didn't need to. Maybe those singing lessons Lydia had sorted were for nothing.

No, he had to give them a show.

'So how about we start with the big one, eh?' he asked. 'The one you've all come to hear me sing?'

He paused for dramatic effect.

'How about *Dog Tired!!'* he yelled.

With a song that they actually knew, the audience went wild. Instantly, Dave Manford was transported back to one of their first gigs in London, at the long-gone *Marquee Club* on Wardour Street. They hadn't known who *Alternator* was there either, mainly because for years Nick had been playing the wrong music. But by the end of *that* gig, one that showed the *new* side to the band, one suggested by Dave, they had a three-record deal with EMI, and within a year they recorded *Jester's Childhood.*

By the end of this one, I'll start something that'll ensure that I'm more famous than Nick had ever been.

Nodding to Mickey, the fat, bald drummer who was squeezed tightly into his drum kit at the back of the small stage, Dave looked out into the crowd as Mickey clacked the rhythm on his drumsticks for a count of four before starting the beat of *Dog Tired*. The guitars began gently and the base would kick in before Dave, lead-singing here, would join in around the eighth bar.

However, Dave wasn't counting.

Dave was staring out into the crowd, his mouth half-open as he looked at the figure in the middle of the hand-picked audience; a hoodie up over their head and round, *John Lennon*-style shades over their eyes, nodding in time with the beat, mobile phone in their hand. However, unlike the others, holding up their phones and filming the performance, this one was held loose, with the figure holding a finger over the screen as they stared back at Dave.

'*Dave!*' hissed Mickey, and returning to the moment, Dave realised the band was replaying the first eight bars again, allowing him to recover. He nodded and looked back into the audience.

The figure was still there.

'You shouldn't be here,' he whispered, but the words fed through the microphone and the audience, all invited, wondered what the hell the old guy on stage was talking about, or whether this was a new version of the song they hadn't heard before. 'You're not real.'

The only person who didn't wonder what Dave meant looked up at him with a smile, the light catching a face under the hoodie as, while keeping Dave's gaze, they tapped the screen of their phone, activating some kind of app on it.

It didn't hurt at first; Dave hardly even felt the electricity as it ran from his hand, currently gripping the microphone and up his right arm. In fact, there was a split second where he wondered if this would blow up the bio-ring. Instinctively he grabbed at his wrist, trying to pull it away, but managed to somehow fuse his hands together, with the electricity now flooding up his right arm, through his shoulders and now back down his left arm, only to start the journey again. Dave was sure that he could even see the electric currents moving through his body like a sine wave. It would have been fascinating if the screaming hadn't been so distracting.

No, wait. You're the one screaming.

The screaming stopped as the bar plunged into darkness, the main fuse now shorted and Dave Manford, founder member of *Alternator,* fell backwards into the drum kit, his eyes wide open and glazed over in death. The energy that pulsed through the microphone stand had terribly burned his hands, and around him was a sickly barbecue smell.

The audience stood confused for a moment, unsure whether this was part of the show, whether Dave Manford was trying to be a new *Alice Cooper* or something, but as the lights came back on, they saw the hideous truth of Dave Manford's tragic end.

In fact, the only person who *didn't* see was the stranger in the hoodie who, using the darkness and lack of power to their advantage had left *Eastcheap Albums* the moment the shock to Dave had started, heading south down Lovat Lane at a leisurely pace, their phone now back in their pocket.

Dave Manford would get none of the hedge fund *Alternator* money. But he had been correct about one thing.

Dave Manford was about to become more famous than his brother *ever* was.

KILLING THE MUSIC

Order Now at Amazon:

http://mybook.to/killingthemusic

ACKNOWLEDGEMENTS

When you write a series of books, you find that there are a ton of people out there who help you, sometimes without even realising, and so I wanted to do a little acknowledgement to some of them.

There are people I need to thank, and they know who they are. People like Andy Briggs, who started me on this path over a coffee during a pandemic to people like Barry Hutchinson, who patiently zoom-called and gave advice back in 2020, the people on various Facebook groups who encouraged me when I didn't know if I could even do this, the designers who gave advice on cover design and on book formatting all the way to my friends and family, who saw what I was doing not as mad folly, but as something good.

Also, I couldn't have done this without my growing army of ARC readers who not only show me where I falter, but also raise awareness of me in the social media world, ensuring that other people learn of my books, and editors and problem catchers like Maureen Webb, Chris Lee, Edwina Townsend, Maryam Paulsen and Jacqueline Beard MBE, the latter of whom has copyedited all seven books so far (including the prequel), line by line for me, and deserves *way more* than our agreed fee.

But mainly, I tip my hat and thank you. *The reader.* Who, five books ago took a chance on an unknown author in a pile of

Kindle books, and thought you'd give them a go, and who has carried on this far with them.

I write Declan Walsh for you. He (and his team) solves crimes for you. And with luck, he'll keep on solving them for a very long time.

Jack Gatland / Tony Lee,
London, July 2021

ABOUT THE AUTHOR

Jack Gatland is the pen name of *#1 New York Times Bestselling Author* Tony Lee, who has been writing in all media for over thirty years, including comics, graphic novels, middle grade books, audio drama, TV and film for *DC Comics, Marvel, BBC, ITV, Random House, Penguin USA, Hachette* and a ton of other publishers and broadcasters.

These have included licenses such as *Doctor Who, Spider Man, X-Men, Star Trek, Battlestar Galactica, MacGyver,* BBC's *Doctors, Wallace and Gromit* and *Shrek*, as well as work created with musicians such as *Ozzy Osbourne, Joe Satriani* and *Megadeth.*

As Tony, he's toured the world talking to reluctant readers with his 'Change The Channel' school tours, and lectures on screenwriting and comic scripting for *Raindance* in London.

An introvert West Londoner by heart, he lives with his wife Tracy and dog Fosco, just outside London.

Locations In The Book

The locations that I use in my books are real, if altered slightly for dramatic intent. Here's some more information about a few of them...

Greenwich Park is a real park, and one I've spent over half my life visiting. It's also my spaniel Fosco's favourite place in the world, especially for changing squirrels. I was lucky enough to learn about the hidden side in the early 90s by South East London historian Jack Gale (who's been a little character-assassinated in this book as he's genuinely one of the nicest guys in the world), and more recently from Stephen Saleh when we plotted our graphic novel *Dark Lines of London*, which takes a lot from the Dee Line, and the two nuclear reactors. Talking of which—

The Motherstone is real, the location where Rupert Wilson's body is found at the very start, and is an actual location.

It's a former drinking fountain, and was thought to have been constructed between 1855 and 1863, mainly to replace a wooden hut nearby that sold refreshments until it was demolished in 1855. However, the Motherstone was first mentioned in print in 1863, which gives an eight year window for its construction. The water bowl originally drew water from a nearby spring, which you could drink from thanks to two metal cups chained to the bowl. However, the spring was capped in the mid 1950s after concerns over the water quality, especially due to lead in the pipes, and the Motherstone's function as a fountain has been redundant ever since.

Although the Motherstone was of Victorian construction, the stones appeared to have had a far older origin and it is now believed that they originated from the Bluebell Hill area of Kent.

The Royal Naval College's Nuclear Reactor was also real, and around until the late nineties. I kept it there to current date for story purposes, but to my knowledge the JASON reactor is long gone.

Atlantis Bookshop does exist, and did indeed hold the events I mention in this book. I met the one-time owner, Caroline Wise many times over the years, as her husband Steve Wilson was the 'voice' / MC of the (also existing) *Talking Stick* esoteric meeting venue, which in its life moved from the *Black Horse* on Rathbone Place (now a gourmet burger place) up the road to the *Bricklayers Arms* and then to the *Princess Louise* pub in Holborn, before splintering into about a dozen separate events.

Mitre Square was indeed where Catherine Eddowes, the third victim of Jack the Ripper was murdered in the 'night of the double murder'. The square occupies the site of the cloister of *Holy Trinity Priory, Aldgate* which was demolished under Henry VIII at the time of the Dissolution of the Monasteries.

Eddowes' murder on the site of the old monastery is ascribed to an ancient curse in a contemporary penny dreadful entitled *The Curse Upon Mitre Square A.D. 1530–1888* by J.F. Brewer, and the Roman wall remains are a staple of nearly all the *Jack the Ripper* walks that start at Tower Hill, of which there are many.

67-69 Chancery Lane was where the then 24-year-old Aleister Crowley once lived, and is just within the remit of the City of London Police. He lived there with fellow magician and member of the *Golden Dawn,* Alan Bennett, and during the Spring of 1899 was under his tutelage. In the apartment, Crowley installed two temples dedicated to dark gods and goddesses. It was reputed he kept a skeleton in one corner, which he fed on small songbirds and cups of blood.

By November 1899 however he'd allegedly fallen out with various members of the *Golden Dawn,* in particular the writer W.B Yeats, and Arthur Edward Waite (who co-created the *Rider-Waite* tarot deck, the most famous of all tarot decks), and had moved to a mansion on the banks of Loch Ness, his Summer in London long forgotten.

The building itself was demolished in 2005, replaced by the apartments and shops we have now, but during this workmen allegedly found a human skull and a pentagram in the building...

Queen Mary University of London, previously Queen Mary College, was first connected to Declan in the prequel, *Liquidate The Profits*, but having used it in other books as well, I wanted to return. Its history dates back to 1785 and beyond, with each of its four founding institutions established to provide "hope and opportunity" to under-represented members of society.

From 1964 until 1982 QMC maintained a nuclear reactor, the first to be built for a UK university. A reactor was commissioned on the Mile End site beneath Mile End Road and operated from around 1964 to 1966 at around 1 kW energy. In 1966 it was decommissioned and a new 100 kW Argonaut class reactor was built at the new QMC Nucleonics Laboratory in Marshgate Lane, Stratford. This was upgraded in 1968, and decommissioned in 1982, with the site licence surrendered in November 1983, with the Marshgate Lane site becoming part of the Olympic Park from 2006.

St Anne's Church, Limehouse was one of Nicholas Hawksmoor's *Twelve Churches,* built to serve the needs of the rapidly expanding population of London in the 18th century. Completed in 1727 and consecrated in 1730, the church is best known because of a strange, eight-foot high Pyramid in the churchyard bearing the inscription "The wisdom of Solomon" on it, one that, after the churchyard closed to burials in the 19th Century and was converted to public gardens by landscape gardener Fanny Wilkinson, she decided to leave it where it was in the churchyard, designing around it.

It does seem likely that the pyramid was made for Hawksmoor to use as an architectural feature, but he then had second thoughts, and with nowhere else to put it, it ended up in the churchyard.

The final cavern at Park Vista also existed at one point—although not owned by a friend of Billy's, and without an entrance down there now.

There was a newspaper piece written however, an antiquarian cutting describing an undercroft discovered in Park Vista, probably dating to about 1700 entitled *Discoveries at Greenwich - Underground Chambers - Overseas Teacher's Visit* that explained "*the occupant of a house in the heart of Greenwich—a house scarcely more than 40 years old—was curious to learn the secret of a bricked-up arch of the inner wall of his cellar. Removing the bricks he was astonished to discover stone steps leading to an underground chamber with vaulted roof measuring 20ft. long by 10ft. broad. He informed Mr J.W. Kirby, the secretary of the Greenwich and Lewisham Antiquarian Society, and, as an expert having examined the chambers, it was concluded that they were cellars of an old house that stood on the spot in 1695.*"

For more information on this visit https://subgreenwich. wordpress.com/2021/04/13/an-undercroft-in-park-vista/

Finally, **The Novo Jewish Cemetery** I mentioned also existed, and is still seen within the University grounds. England's first Jewish cemetery, called the *Velho* Cemetery, was built on a small plot of land in Mile End in 1657. As the nearby Jewish community grew in size, and the Velho began to fill up. By 1726, it was nearly full, so land for a second, larger Sephardi cemetery, the *Novo* Cemetery, was leased, with the first burials taking place in 1733. By 1895 however the cemetery was almost full, and it was closed for burials for adults in 1905, and for children in 1918. The area visible today is a small percentage of the 'newer' graves. The 'older' section was carefully cleared with around 7,000 graves moved to Brentwood in Essex.

If you're interested in seeing what the *real* locations look like, I post 'behind the scenes' location images on my Instagram feed. This will continue through all the books, and I suggest you follow it.

In fact, feel free to follow me on all my social media by clicking on the links below. They're new, but over time it can be a place where we can engage, discuss Declan and put the world to rights.

www.jackgatland.com

Subscribe to my Readers List: **www.subscribepage.com/ jackgatland**

www.facebook.com/jackgatlandbooks
www.twitter.com/jackgatlandbook
ww.instagram.com/jackgatland

Want more books by Jack Gatland? Turn the page...

THE THEFT OF A **PRICELESS** PAINTING...
A GANGSTER WITH A **CRIPPLING DEBT**...
A **BODY COUNT** RISING BY THE HOUR...

AND ELLIE RECKLESS IS CAUGHT IN THE MIDDLE.

JACK GATLAND

PAINT
— THE —
DEAD

A 'COP FOR CRIMINALS' ELLIE RECKLESS NOVEL

A NEW PROCEDURAL CRIME SERIES WITH
A TWIST - FROM THE CREATOR OF THE
BESTSELLING 'DI DECLAN WALSH' SERIES

AVAILABLE ON AMAZON / KINDLE UNLIMITED

THEY TRIED TO KILL HIM...
NOW HE'S OUT FOR **REVENGE.**

NEW YORK TIMES #1 BESTSELLER **TONY LEE** WRITING AS

JACK GATLAND

THE MURDER OF AN **MI5 AGENT**...
A BURNED SPY **ON THE RUN** FROM HIS OWN PEOPLE...
AN ENEMY OUT TO **STOP HIM** AT ANY COST...
AND A **PRESIDENT** ABOUT TO BE **ASSASSINATED**...

SLEEPING
SOLDIERS

A **TOM MARLOWE** THRILLER

BOOK 1 IN A NEW SERIES OF THRILLERS IN THE STYLE OF
JASON BOURNE, JOHN MILTON OR **BURN NOTICE,** AND
SPINNING OUT OF THE **DECLAN WALSH** SERIES OF BOOKS

AVAILABLE ON AMAZON / KINDLE UNLIMITED

JACK GATLAND

THE LIONHEART CURSE

HUNT THE GREATEST TREASURES
PAY THE GREATEST PRICE

BOOK 1 IN A NEW SERIES OF ADVENTURES
IN THE STYLE OF 'THE DA VINCI CODE'
FROM THE CREATOR OF DECLAN WALSH

AVAILABLE ON AMAZON / KINDLEUNLIMITED

Printed in Great Britain
by Amazon